In My Girls I Trust

In My Girls I Trust

Brandi Johnson

www.urbanbooks.net

Urban Books, LLC
78 East Industry Court
Deer Park, NY 11729

In My Girls I Trust Copyright © 2010 Brandi Johnson

ISBN 13: 978-1-60162-355-3
ISBN 10: 1-60162-355-0

First Mass Market Printing July 2012
First Trade Printing June 2010
Printed in the United States of America

10 9 8 7 6 5 4 3

*This is a work of fiction. Any references or similarities to
actual events, real people, living, or dead, or to real locales
are intended to give the novel a sense of reality. Any simi-
larity in other names, characters, places, and incidents is
entirely coincidental.*

Distributed by Kensington Publishing Corp.
Submit Wholesale Orders to:
Kensington Publishing Corp.
C/O Penguin Group (USA) Inc.
Attention: Order Processing
405 Murray Hill Parkway
East Rutherford, NJ 07073-2316
Phone: 1-800-526-0275
Fax: 1-800-227-9604

Dedication

In loving memory of
Aunt Mary, Aunt Elanda, and Poppa

Acknowledgments

Here I go once again, and this just means that God's blessings never stop.

First and foremost, I must give all praise to God for His continuous love and blessings that He has bestowed upon me, allowing all my dreams to come true.

Nikki Ajian, thanks once again for all the hard work you put down. I don't know what I would do without you in my corner. Thanks for sticking by me, through my attitudes and all. I truly appreciate everything you have done for me in and out of my literary journey, even when it seemed like I didn't care. Trust me, I did.

Joylynn Jossel, you have not only been my agent, but my friend. Thank you for taking me under your wing, and may God bless you in all that you do.

Montias, Brei'yonte, and Amir'aki, my three sons. You guys are my purpose for living. Thank y'all for all y'all unconditional love and support.

Mommy love y'all, and just think, we're one step closer to Disneyworld.

Mommy and Daddy, your baby girl has done it again. Thank you, Mommy, for being my walking billboard. You were the one who told half of Columbus about *Spoiled Rotten*. I can't thank you enough. I am so proud to be your daughter. You have supported me through everything.

Special thanks to my King; you came along at just the right time. I don't know if you know it or not, but you have been the ray of sunshine that I've been searching for for so long. Loving you has truly changed my life. Thanks for always having my back, but most of all, thanks for allowing me to be your Queen.

To all my brothers and sisters (it's too many to name), thanks for always having my back . . . I love y'all.

I would like to thank Tysha (*The Boss: Story of a Female Hustler*) and M. Raye Turner (*Pretty Monster*)—thanks for all the advice and friendship that you two have shared. Keep up the good work, ladies, and I wish y'all much success.

I gotta give a shout out to all my *Spoiled Rotten* fans: thank you for all your love and support, and I hope and pray that I continue to give y'all what y'all looking for with each piece I put out. Holla atcha girl: www.BrandiAJohnson.com.

Chapter One

"India, can you please come get me?" Alexis cried into the phone receiver.

India pushed Martell off her. "Where you at? Are you okay?"

"I'm at the hospital. I had a little accident," Alexis said quietly.

India sighed. "Did Ronald jump on you again?"

"Somethin' like that." Alexis had shame all throughout her tone.

India stood up and slipped on a pair of jogging pants and one of Martell's Fubu T-shirts. "Where the kids at?"

"At home with Ronald."

India became angry. "What the fuck you mean? You left the kids at home with *Ike Turner* while you sittin' up at the damn hospital?"

"They were in bed asleep so I didn't wanna wake 'em up," Alexis snapped back.

India was disgusted. "Alexis, you will never learn."

"India," Alexis whined. "All I got is a black eye."

"What you mean 'all I got'? Be standing at the front door, I'm on my way." India hung up the phone and kissed Martell on his forehead. "I'll be right back." Martell pulled her back on top of him. "Martell, please, not now, sweetie, Alexis needs me."

"What about me? I need you too. I've been gone on business for five days, and this is the first we have been able to spend some time together since I've been home. I'm sick and tired of every time those hood-rat friends of yours call, you go running." Martell was fed up.

"Martell, baby, I'll be right back," India whined. She knew Martell hated for his woman to whine.

"Well, I won't be here when you get back!" Martell jumped out of India's California king sized bed and started putting on his clothes.

"Martell, don't go," India begged.

"You know one of these days you gon' be without me if you don't get your shit together," he barked while buttoning his Armani dress pants.

Nigga, please, you know yo' ass ain't going nowhere. You say the same shit every time, India thought as she tied up her Nike Air sneakers. India knew she had Martell wrapped around her clit. She also knew that when she got back from dealing with her best friend's drama, he would be laying in her bed waiting for her. *What man would leave after having had the pleasure of being with India Ariel Davenport*? She grabbed her purse and was on her way out, but not before checking herself out in the mirror real quick.

India had a strong resemblance to Kenya Moore; she was just a few shades lighter. India would sometimes use Kenya's name to get her and her girls into a club and it always worked. They would walk in with their heads high, and the guy at the door would escort them straight to the VIP section where they would rub elbows with some big-time ballers.

India always knew she would amount to something. She looked too good not to. India's mother being Hispanic and her father being an African American blessed her with long, silky, black hair that came just a little past her shoulders. Her caramel complexion was flawless; she had dark, almond-shaped eyes, and the body of a goddess, thanks to being in the gym three to four times a week. India's parents always wanted her to become a model, and she was on her way until she hooked up with her two best friends, Alexis and Keaundra.

Keaundra was the dominant one of the three, while Alexis was the wild one—open to almost anything. In any group of friends you always have a follower and that's where India came in at. She was so sheltered growing up, that once she got a taste of freedom, it was on and poppin'! Her parents couldn't tell her anything. Hanging out late, skipping school and getting high with Keaundra and Alexis took precedence over everything, including modeling.

Davenport was a high-class name in Mansfield, Ohio. Her father, Richard Davenport, had pull and lots of it. Richard Davenport was the mayor's right hand man, and one of the most bourgeois, prominent judges around. He had the reputation of sending all the big-time drug dealers up the river, and you could bet your mom's best Sunday outfit that they were doing Buck Rogers time! Mr. Davenport hated drug dealers just as much as he hated his mother-in-law.

India climbed in her truck, and in spite of her best friend's drama that awaited her, she thought back six years to some drama of her own.

"One of the biggest drug raids," Mr. Davenport read aloud from the front page of the newspaper as he sat at his oak dining room table eating his breakfast. *"I can't wait to prosecute those bastards. They'll be doing forever and a day."*

"Oh my goodness. Richard, come quick, it's Indy on television," Mrs. Davenport yelled to her husband from the living room.

India chuckled remembering her mother's dramatics as she had replayed their reactions to her arrest. Mr. Davenport jumped up from the table and stood in front of the sixty-two-inch plasma television next to his wife. His eyes bulged out of his head as he watched his only child being escorted out of one of the largest dope houses in the area in cuffs.

"Here we are reporting from WBAJ News Center twelve," a news anchor came across the TV screen and said. "This has to be one of the biggest drug busts in a long time. The Metrich unit seized fifteen pounds of marijuana, three guns, one hundred and sixty grams of cocaine, and over fifty thousand in cash. The Feds have been watching this house for two years. While searching the house they looked in an upstairs closet and found a young lady hiding. The young lady has been identified as Judge Richard Davenport's daughter. India Davenport has been arrested and is being held on a million-dollar bond, back to you Curtis."

Mrs. Davenport screamed at the top of her lungs as their phone rang off the hook.

While her parents were frantically trying to get her out of jail, India knew once she did make bail, the shit was gon' hit the fan.

"Davenport, you made bail," the officer yelled.

India got up slowly as the officer unlocked the holding cell. India glanced in the plastic mirror before leaving. She looked a hot mess. Her mascara was running down her face from all the tears she had shed, her hair was standing all over her head because they had made her take all the bobby pins out of her freshly done French roll, and her breath needed a date with some Listerine. "Who's out there?" India asked the officer, hoping that it would be her mother instead of her father. She knew she could shed a few tears and get sympathy from her mother, but her father couldn't care less about tears.

"Does it matter who's out there? You just made a million-dollar bond. I wouldn't care if a gang of midgets were out there, you're free, pretty lady." The officer smiled.

That compliment went straight to India's head. India smiled at the rather large officer before exiting the cell. Her smile soon faded as she spotted her father talking to the chief of police.

"Indy, baby, are you okay?" Mrs. Davenport pushed through the media and over to her baby girl and asked in her heavy Spanish accent.

"I'm fine, Mommy." India attempted to smooth her frizzy hair down as cameras flashed and microphones were being stuck in her face.

"India, what were you doing in that drug house?" someone yelled from the crowd.

India rolled her eyes, pushed the mic out of her face, and continued fighting through the crowd of people. Police officers barricaded the media so India and her family could make it safely out of the building.

"Did anyone hurt you or try to molest you?" Mrs. Davenport asked.

India became agitated. "No, Mom, they didn't!"

"Enough small talk. What in the world was my seventeen-year-old daughter doing in a drug house? I'm so embarrassed. As of today I disown you as my daughter, and I want my million dollars back!" Mr. Davenport said before storming out of the county building.

India was shocked and hurt by that remark.

"Don't worry honey your father didn't mean that," Mrs. Davenport said as she rubbed the side of India's face.

India didn't know what to say. How was she going to pay her father back a million dollars when she only got fifty dollars a week for allowance? India laid her head on her mother's shoulder and cried.

Mrs. Davenport watched as her husband stormed back into the county building, walking toward her and her daughter. "Oh, yeah, all of your expenses are cut off, and if you don't have

my million dollars paid by the time I die, then
you will be cut out of my will, understand me?"

India knew her father meant every word.
When they got home, Mr. Davenport confis-
cated her brand new Trailblazer, took her cell
phone, and unplugged the phone in her room.
He then asked for all six of her credit cards and
cut them up in her face. That hurt worse then
being hit in the head with a hammer.

"Richard, don't you think you're being a
little harsh on our little Indy?" Mrs. Davenport
pleaded.

"Helen, your little Indy has to get money the
best way that she can. Hell, she's been labeled as
a drug kingpin, so let her go out and sell drugs
to get what she needs!"

"Richard!"

Mr. Davenport was disgusted with his daughter. "Helen, can't you see that people don't give a
damn about all the drugs and guns they found?
Only thing they cared about was that it was
Richard Davenport's daughter in the house.
They didn't even bother mentioning the fact that
her friends were in the closet with her. Their parents' names meant nothing in this town, so their
bonds were nowhere near as high and they're
not making examples of these girls, just India!

She put a mark on my damn name and my reputation, and I will not forgive her for that."

India began crying. "I'm sorry, Mommy."

"Don't worry, Mommy's little Indy, your father will get over the embarrassment sooner or
later. It's just going to take some time," she assured her daughter.

India waited until her mother and father
went to bed before sneaking down to the kitchen
to use the telephone.

"Hello?" Alexis answered on the first ring.

"Hey, Lexy," India whispered.

"Hey, girl! You know you're the talk of the
town, don't you?" Alexis said, cracking up laughing. "You're all over the news."

"Yeah, thanks to you and your bright ideas.
'Let's skip school and go over to Meeko's house',"
India said, repeating the words Alexis had said
to her earlier that day. "And now look, me, you,
and Keaundra are known as drug dealers."

"No, actually, you're the one known as a
drug dealer, Mr. Davenport's daughter," Alexis
chuckled.

"That shit ain't funny, Alexis. My million dollar bond is non-refundable. I'm on probation
for a year and I have to do community service,

which is manual labor. I have to attend drug classes, not to mention my father took every-thing away from me. I don't have nothin' in my room but a bed, and he said he's only giving me shit that the state requires me to have."

"Dang, where's your truck?"

"Gone."

"Your big-screen TV?"

"Gone."

"Your stereo, your hundred and fifty CDs, your computer?"

"Gone, gone, and gone," India replied.

"Dang, that's deep. Your dad must really be mad. He took ya truck from you."

"Yeah, and it's all your fault."

"Didn't nobody put a gun to yo' head and make you skip school, India."

"If yo' ass wasn't fiendin' for a blunt we would not have even been up in that dope spot. Of all the days we go to Meeko's the door gets kicked the fuck in! Now, how ironic is it for Meeko to have to run to the store to get a loaf of bread at seven in the morning? If you ask me, I think the nigga probably set us up to take the fall," India said.

"I wouldn't put it past his shiesty ass. I know one thing: he ain't got to worry about me buying no more bud from his ass." Alexis changed the subject. "Are you goin' to the Summer Jammy-Jam on Friday?"

"You know I'm on punishment. I would have to sneak out, and plus, I don't got nothin' to wear. I don't get any more money, and my dad cut up all my credit cards, remember?"

"Oh, yeah, that's right. Well, wear somethin' you already got," Alexis recommended.

"Bitch, please! India Ariel Davenport wear somethin' old to the biggest party of the year? I don't think so."

"I got an idea, since you don't wanna wear nothin' old to the Summer Jammy-Jam," Alexis smirked.

"I hope it's not somethin' that's gon' land me in jail again."

"Trust me, it won't."

"Davenport, you made bail," the officer said. "Nice to see you again." The chubby officer smiled at India. "You must like coming to jail."

India rolled her eyes as she walked out of the cell and into her mother's arms.

"Indy, how dare you shoplift!" Mrs. Davenport shouted.

"Mommy, I needed somethin' to wear to the Summer Jammy-Jam and I didn't have any money," India whined, as the fake tears fell from her eyes.

"Why didn't you just come to me for the money?"

India shrugged. "I don't know, I thought maybe you felt the same way about me as Daddy," she lied.

"I could never feel that way about you, Indy. I'm so glad your father is out of town or he would disown the both of us. The judge not only extended your probation but now you have to report. Now, promise me that you will stay out of trouble," Mrs. Davenport said as she and her daughter walked to the car.

"I promise, Mommy," India said in a child-like voice.

India shook the old memories from her head as she pulled into the hospital parking lot.

"About time," Alexis said, jumping into India's fully loaded, brand new Infiniti QX56.

"Anyway, what did Ronald kick yo' ass for this time?" India asked sarcastically.

"He thinks I'm messin' around with David."

India turned out of the hospital parking lot and looked over at Alexis. "I know you ain't talkin' about David that works at the barber shop over on Park Avenue."

Alexis rubbed her temples before speaking. "No, I'm talkin' about David that *owns* the barber shop on Park Avenue."

"What would make him think a thing like that?" India asked as she drove.

"Because somebody told him they saw me and David talkin'."

"Just 'cause he heard you was talkin' to the nigga doesn't mean you fuckin' him. Ronald needs to grow the fuck up, and your stupid ass needs to leave his abusive ass alone."

"I know. All me and David was talkin' about was the latest CDs. I love Ronald but I know he ain't no good for me or the kids."

"You the type of bitch who thinks if a nigga is beating that ass on a regular basis, he loves you. You got the game twisted!" India shook her head, disgusted by the entire situation.

Alexis sighed heavily. "I'm gon' leave him."

India became angry. "When?"

"I don't know when. I don't have a man who owns his own cell phone company and every time I tell the nigga to jump, he ask how high. I'm sorry we all can't be like India Ariel Davenport. I wish you would get the fuck off my back and leave me the fuck alone about my man. Now, I said I was gon' leave his ass alone, I just don't know when. Damn!"

India felt kind of sorry for her best friend. She knew Alexis wasn't happy. But she kept trying to tell her to just pack Ronald's shit, set it by the door, and when he came home, tell his black ass to get to steppin'! India and Alexis sat quietly for the next fifteen minutes while India drove. Once India pulled up in Alexis's apartment complex, she put the truck in park, and sat there. The only noise that was coming from the radio was R. Kelly singing about being trapped in somebody's closet.

Alexis put her hand on the door handle and smiled. "This song brings back a lot of memories, doesn't it?"

"Yeah, being trapped in Meeko's closet," India laughed.

"Thanks, India, for picking me up from the hospital."

"Anytime. And, hey, *are* you fuckin' David?" India inquired.

Alexis smiled before opening the truck door. "Naw, but I would love to."

"You nasty, hefah!" India laughed.

Alexis waved her friend off and walked into her apartment. When she went in Ronald was lying on the sofa asleep with their son, R.J., lying beside him, and their daughter, Ro'nisha, lying on top of his chest. Alexis grabbed a cover out of the linen closet and covered all three of them up before walking into the bathroom to run herself some bath water. She took off her bloodstained Fetish T-shirt, slid out of her tight Fetish jeans, and gave herself a complete look-over in the mirror. *Damn-girl, you look too good to be fuckin' with a no-good, jealous-ass nigga like Ronald*, she thought as she turned around and made her ass clap like she used to when she was a stripper. Alexis looked closely at her black eyes and busted lip as she stood in the mirror. *I can't hide this time.*

Alexis was high yellow with light brown eyes. She kept the top of her hair cut really short while the back hung almost to the middle of her back. She bore a striking resemblance to Laila Ali but with a much better body. Alexis used to be a stripper at Club Bo-Bo's. She stripped for extra money while she was going to college, but gave up stripping after she got pregnant with her firstborn. That's where she had met Ronald. He was a frequent customer and would come in with a bunch of his friends every Friday night just in time to see Alexis, a.k.a. Lady Dynamite, perform. He kept Lady Dynamite's G-string filled with fifties and hundreds while he threw the other girls a dollar or two. That made Lady Dynamite feel like she was that thang, like she was special. Now she wondered what she had done that made her not so special anymore.

India walked into her condo after dropping Alexis off at home, threw her see-through Coach bag on the sofa, and walked into the bedroom. *I told you your ass wasn't going anywhere. I can't blame you for not wanting to leave all of this.* India slid out of her sweatpants and T-shirt. She walked over to the bed, where Martell lay sleeping like a newborn baby. Martell had fallen asleep with his Armani dress pants unbuttoned and his left hand resting on his manhood. India smiled at her man. She picked up the remote that was laying on the marble nightstand and turned the television off. She climbed into bed, trying not to wake her knight in shining armor, and kissed his lips before straddling his well-built body. His eyes opened up as she rested her head on his chest. Martell wrapped his strong arms around his woman and they both fell soundly to sleep.

Chapter Two

India called Keaundra as she brewed her daily pot of coffee. "Girl, let me tell you about Alexis," she started as soon as Keaundra answered. "You know I had to pick her ass up from the hospital last night."

"What the fuck happened to her? Don't tell me, Ronald kicked that ass again, didn't he?" Keaundra said, shaking her head.

"You guessed it!" India said as she poured coffee into her cup.

"I don't know what her problem is. Ain't no way I'm gon' stay wit' a nigga who whoops my ass like I'm his child. Alexis is twenty-three years old; she is too old to be gettin' her ass kicked," Keaundra said as she got dressed for work.

"I tried to tell her that," India added.

"Well, while the bitch goin' around perpin' like she Laila Ali, she need to start actin' like her and kick off in Ronald's black ass." Keaundra slid into her black Coach boots and checked her image in the full-length mirror that hung on her bedroom wall.

"Hush truth," India laughed.

"I'm for real. She done been with this nigga for four years and he's been kickin' her ass the entire time," Keaundra ranted.

"I know," India agreed as she stuffed her college English book into her book bag.

"I just don't get it, do you?"

"No, but maybe she'll wake up one day." India grabbed her car keys and headed out the door.

"I hope so."

"Well, Keaundra, I'll talk to you when I get outta class," India said as she climbed into her truck and slammed the door.

Keaundra sighed heavily. "Okay, talk to you later." Keaundra hung up the phone and sat back. She tried her best to come up with a plan to get Alexis away from Ronald, before she ended up in the same predicament as her own mother.

Keaundra walked into the Richland Bank where she was the head loan officer, and went straight to her office. She took off her coat and shook the snow from it before hanging it up on the coat rack. She then picked up her message notepad and briefly roamed over her messages. She went through the list and the only name she recognized was Alexis

8

Tucker. She picked up her phone and quickly dialed Alexis's telephone number.

"Hello?" the male voice answered.

Keaundra closed her eyes and counted to five.

"Hello?" he said again.

"Is Alexis home?" she asked Ronald.

"Naw, she's at work, where yo' ass need to be," he said before hanging up the phone.

"Bitch!" Keaundra dialed the number to the dentist office where Alexis worked as a dental hygienist.

"Dr. Gavenstein's office, may I help you?" the pleasant voice said on the other end of the line.

"Yes. May I please speak with Alexis Tucker?"

"Her patient is just leaving; if you can hang on for a brief moment I'll call her to the phone," the lady said in a professional tone.

"Is this Kay-Kay?" Keaundra asked.

"Yes, it is. May I ask whom I'm speaking with?" she asked, sounding like a white woman.

"Bitch, this is yo' cousin, Keaundra. You sound just like a white girl on the phone, tryin' to sound all professional and shit," Keaundra laughed.

"Damn, you know I gotta answer these phones like that. All these white people I work around," she whispered. "I really wish I could be like, this is the muthafuckin' office of this white, racist, dickhead doctor Gavenstein," Kay-Kay laughed too.

"You silly."

"I'm for real. If I didn't need the money, I would answer the phone just like that, 'cause some muth-afuckas be talkin' all disrespectful and shit. No matter how pleasant you are to them, there's always one asshole that has to get all smart and shit."

"Like Gran used to tell us: kill your enemies with kindness."

"Fuck that, I be wantin' to kill some of 'em with a thirty-eight special," Kay-Kay stated.

"You crazy, girl. Is Alexis almost done talkin'?"

"Yep. Girl, you know I'm not the type to be gettin' in anybody's business, but what's up wit' yo' girl and them dark-ass sunglasses she sportin' up in here? You know this ain't the first time she done wore sunglasses all day."

"I don't know, girl." Keaundra replied, not wanting to put her best friend's business out there.

"Here she is, and I'll see you at Gran's house on Sunday," Kay-Kay said before handing Alexis the phone.

"Alexis here," she said into the phone receiver.

"What's up? I saw on my message pad that you called. Is everything all right?"

"Yeah, I called, but I can't talk right now. The phone is off the hook." She meant that somebody was all in her mouth.

"Look, Alexis, I know you can't talk right now, so just listen to me. I already know about Ronald kickin' yo' ass last night."

"Dang, India got a big-ass mouth."

"Never mind that. We are sisters and we're very concerned about you and them babies. You really need to leave Ronald's ass alone before he end up killin' you," Keaundra suggested.

"I know," Alexis said sadly.

"This nigga got you walkin' around your job with sunglasses on. You a damn dental hygienist. How in the hell can you see in people's mouths?"

Alexis shot Kay-Kay a dirty look. "Look, my next patient just walked in the door, I'll talk to you when I get off work," Alexis said, not wanting to hear any more of Keaundra's nagging.

"We're meeting over India's house tonight for dinner, okay?"

"Okay, I'll be over there as soon as I pick up the kids from daycare."

Keaundra became angry. "Alexis, you mean to tell me that those babies are still in daycare, when Ronald's ass don't even have a job? What part of the game is that?"

"Bye, Ke-Ke." Alexis hung up the phone before her best friend could say anything else.

Keaundra flipped open her cell and dialed India's number. She didn't want to use the company's phone just in case someone was on the line listening to her conversation.

"What do you want, girl? You know I'm in my report writing class," India whispered when she answered.

"This is an emergency!" Keaundra snapped.

"Hang on." India raised her hand and pointed toward the door to let the professor know that she was going to the bathroom. India stood and walked out of the class. "Okay, I'm back. What's the emergency?" she asked once she reached the bathroom.

"Girl, did you know that Alexis was still sending R.J. and Ro'nisha to the daycare?"

India was furious. "No way! Ronald's punk ass ain't workin', how come he can't keep his kids?"

"I don't know. She all up in that damn dentist office wearing sunglasses and tryin' to work."

"Hell, naw. How you know?"

"I called her ass today, you know my cousin Kay-Kay is the receptionist there and she told me," Keaundra stated in a matter-of-fact tone.

"We gon' have to beat some sense into her." India pulled up her skirt with one hand and held on to her cell phone with the other.

"Is that pee I hear in the background?"

"I couldn't help it, I had to go," India laughed.

"Anyway, I told her to meet me over your house later on for dinner."

"And who's cooking?"

"I'll stop at Red Lobster and pick up a couple of shrimp platters for us," Keaundra said as her secretary, Debbie, stuck her head in the door. "Hang on. Yes, Debbie?"

"You have someone out here waiting to see you."

"Don't you see me on the phone? Tell them to wait some more!" Keaundra snapped. Debbie held her head down and closed Keaundra's office door.

"Damn, who was you talkin' to like that?"

"Debbie's dumb ass. She seen me on the phone when she stuck her big-ass head through my office door!" Keaundra snapped.

"Fuck that, you wouldn't be talkin' to me like that. If I was Debbie I would tell yo' smart-ass mouth to meet me in the parking lot after work," India laughed as she checked her makeup in the mirror.

Keaundra became serious. "Let the bitch try it and I'ma beat that ass."

"Oh, well, some of us do have a job to do, so I'll see you around five-thirty."

"Okay, and don't forget the shrimp sauce this time."

"I won't." Keaundra hung up the phone and continued to work.

***

Alexis sat around the office looking through her charts. There were no more patients scheduled, so she decided to pick her kids up early from daycare and take R.J. to the barbershop to get a haircut.

"Kay-Kay, I'm leaving early, so if anybody calls me tell them I'm with a patient," Alexis said as she put on her coat.

"Will do," Kay-Kay replied as she turned up the radio and bobbed her head to Bobby Valentino's "Slow Down."

Alexis smiled and shook her head while walking out the door.

"Why you leavin' so early?" Ronald asked as Alexis got into her car, nearly giving her a heart attack.

"What the fuck you doing sittin' in my car, Ronald?" Alexis grimaced.

"You sho' done got funny acting with yo' shit. Ever since I got laid off from that punk-ass factory, everything is yours!" Ronald snapped.

Alexis rolled her eyes. "Ronald, I'm not in the mood to argue."

"Where the fuck you on your way to?"

"I'm goin' to get Kay-Kay and me some ice cream if you don't mind," Alexis lied.

"Ice cream in December? I bet' not find out you lyin' or I'ma kick yo' ass." Ronald looked at Alexis and smiled. "I'll take you to the Dairy Queen and drop you back off 'cause I need to use the car."

"For what, Ronald?"

"Oh, I can't use yo' ride? You know mine is broke down."

Feeling that she was in a no-win situation, Alexis agreed to let Ronald use her car. She closed her eyes for a brief second and took a deep breath before driving to the Dairy Queen. She went in an ordered herself something, a banana split for Kay-Kay, and nothing for Ronald. She walked back to the car, noticing that Ronald had moved into the driver's seat. She rolled her eyes, went around to the passenger's side, and got in.

"Where my ice cream at?" Ronald asked.

"I didn't know you wanted any."

"Did you ask if I wanted any?" Ronald snapped.

"I never had to ask before." Alexis rolled her eyes so hard she nearly passed out.

"Don't get smart with me, bitch," Ronald said as he pulled out of the Dairy Queen's parking lot. Alexis was hotter than a firecracker as Ronald drove her back to work. When Ronald pulled up into the dentist's parking lot, he looked over at Alexis. "I'll be back to get you at five-thirty."

"I get off at five, Ronald."

"Daddy loves you," he said mockingly.

Alexis looked at Ronald with disgust, got out of the car, and slammed the door behind her. She walked into the office and handed Kay-Kay the banana split she had bought for her.

"Thanks!" Kay-Kay said, taking the ice cream from her hand. "I thought you were done for the day?"

"There's been a change in plans." Alexis walked into her office and closed the door. She sat behind her desk in her big, comfortable chair, put her head down, and cried like a baby as her ice cream melted before her.

Chapter Three

"I told yo' ass not to forget the shrimp sauce," India said, looking through her refrigerator for some ketchup.

"I said I'm sorry, damn," Keaundra replied.

Alexis sat at the table quietly picking over her shrimp.

"You can take the sunglasses off, up in here. We ya girls, not yo' coworkers," Keaundra said to Alexis.

"I forgot I had 'em on." Alexis removed the glasses and laid them on the table.

"Damn! Both of your eyes are black." Keaundra was shoc-ked.

India walked over to her friend and examined her face. "Last night it looked like only one of your eyes was black."

"It's nothin'." Alexis put the sunglasses back on to hide the two black circles that hugged both of her eyes.

"It's nothin'? Bitch, I'm gon' kill Ronald myself if he ever put his hands on you again and I'm not playin'!" Keaundra had tears in her eyes.

"Calm down, Ke-Ke," Alexis pleaded.

"Calm down? I'ma tell you this, the next time that nigga puts his hands on you, you better not let me know. You bet' not even let India know 'cause you know she gon' tell me and I'm gon' fuck Ronald up!" Keaundra was fed up.

India was at a loss for words. "Alexis, you gotta leave that nigga alone or he's gon' fuck around and kill you."

"We see that shit all the time on Lifetime. That is some for real-ass shit," Keaundra said.

"I know. I'm gon' leave him."

"When?" Keaundra and India asked simultaneously.

"I don't know yet."

"This bitch is fucked up just like Ronald. Y'all deserve one another!" Keaundra snapped.

"That's enough, Ke-Ke," India warned. "It's her life, let her live it."

"You right." Keaundra brushed her hands as if she was done with it.

"Hold up. Y'all sittin' here talkin' about me like I ain't even here," Alexis shouted.

"For real, you're not. Alexis is somewhere else and a sorry-ass broad is sittin' here takin' her place!"

"Look, I'm not about to sit around here and let y'all keep doggin' me." Alexis stood up and grabbed her jacket off the back of the chair.

"Sit yo' five-dollar ass down before I make change," Keaundra said, sounding like Nino Brown did on *New Jack City*.

Alexis reluctantly sat back down because she knew Keaundra meant business. Alexis crossed her arms and poked her lip out.

"Quit poutin'. That shit don't work with me. Now, I'm tired of that nigga puttin' his damn hands on you. I'm about to ask you a question and you better be truthful." Keaundra had a dead serious look on her face.

Alexis grabbed a piece of her hair and began twisting it between her fingers just like she always did before she told a lie.

"You 'bout to tell a lie," India said.

"How you know I was about to lie and you ain't even asked me nothin' yet?" Alexis asked.

"You act like I just met yo' high yellow ass, now tell the damn truth," Keaundra said.

Tears welled up in Alexis's eyes. "No, I don't fight him back if that's what you was gonna ask."

"What?" Keaundra and India yelled in amazement.

"Y'all heard me. I don't fight him back."

"Why not?" India asked before taking a bite of her shrimp and throwing the tail back onto her plate. "I bet if you gave his ass a couple of lumps upside his head he'd think twice before putting his hands on you."

"Yeah, why don't you fight back? I gotta hear this." Keaundra folded her arms and waited impatiently for Alexis to reply.

"I'm afraid," she said sullenly.

"Of what?" India asked.

Alexis held her head down and whispered, "He said if I hit him back, he would kill me."

"Bitch, you sound like a fool." Keaundra grimaced.

"Not if you kill him first," India suggested. India wiped the corners of her mouth with her napkin and stood up from the oak kitchen table.

"Yeah, kill his ass first. Me and India will keep yo' books fat so you can go to the commissary seventy-five strong every week."

India leaned up against the counter and took a sip from her water bottle before speaking. "That nigga ain't worth doing a day in jail for, let alone twenty-five to life."

"You right about that," Keaundra agreed. "Plus, Alexis is too pretty to be goin' to jail. Those bitches up in there would be at her ass as soon as she gets off the bus."

"Shit, I'll be up in that bitch fighting every day," Alexis said as she threw punches at the air.

"Bitch, please, you won't even fight Ronald, and I know it's some big bitches up in Marysville who would work Ronald's ass over with no problem. Yo' scary ass wouldn't stand a chance," India laughed.

"You right. But I bet you this, my yellow ass would stay in protective custody," Alexis laughed, too.

"Scary bitch." Keaundra laughed so hard that tears fell down her caramel cheeks.

"Hey, this is my song," India yelled as the music poured out of the speakers from the living room.

"'This is how we do/ We make a move and act a fool while we up in the club/This is how we do/ Nobody do it like we do it so show us some love.' Turn that shit up, that's my cut," Keaundra yelled and threw her hands up in the air and waved them from side to side. "I haven't heard this song in a long-ass time."

Keaundra, Alexis, and India walked into the living room. India grabbed the remote to her stereo and turned the volume up as loud as it would go. They all danced around like they were at a club as The Game rapped his ass off.

Alexis started dancing just like she used to do when she worked at Club Bo-Bo's.

"Go Lexy, it's yo' birthday, we gon' party like it's yo' birthday," Keaundra and India sang.

"'Whoooa, that felt good. I haven't danced in a long time." Alexis smiled, falling back onto the Brandon chenille and leather sofa with the wooden arm panels and base.

"I can tell, 'cause yo' ass is outta breath," Keaundra laughed and plopped down in the coordinated oversized chair, placing her feet up on the leather ottoman.

"Anyone up for a shot of Tres Agaves tequila?" India asked.

"Count me in," Keaundra said as she got comfortable.

"Me too," Alexis added.

India walked into the kitchen and came back out with three shot glasses and the tequila on a platter, and set them on the coffee table. She filled all three glasses to the top. "Let's make a toast."

"To friendship," they said in unison.

"May we always have each other's backs through thick and thin," India said.

Alexis added her two cents. "May we always love one another like sisters."

A huge smile spread across Keaundra's face. "And may Ronald's bitch ass be takin' a bath with the radio sittin' at the edge of the tub and a bee come in through the bathroom window, he swats at it, and accidentally knock the radio in the water."

India laughed and shook her head.

"Wishful thinking." Alexis laughed too.

***

Keaundra walked through her front door after leaving India's house and turned on her radio. Kelly Price was singing "It Will Rain." Keaundra closed her eyes as Kelly crooned through the speakers.

"It will rain for you too, Alexis," she said aloud. She sorted through her mail before tossing it on top of the coffee table. "Come here, Peaches," she said to her black cat.

Peaches jumped up on the back of the sofa and buried her head into Keaundra's stomach. Keaundra stroked her fat, black cat, kissed her on the forehead, and walked into her bedroom. "This place is a mess," she said aloud, as she looked around at the pile of dirty clothes in one corner and the pizza box lying on top of her bed. She looked into her open closet door at the shoes and clothes that were scattered everywhere.

Keaundra peeled off her khaki Calvin Klein dress slacks and tossed them on the pile of dirty clothes. She lifted up her white Calvin Klein button-down shirt and looked at her round backside in the full-length mirror that hung from her bedroom wall. "It still looks good."

Keaundra smiled as she lay across her bed and looked up at the mirrors that hung at the top of her wooden canopy. She rolled over to her nightstand and opened the drawer. She then pulled her Silver Bullet out. *Good ol' Peter*, she thought as she turned him on to make sure the batteries were still strong.

After doing so, she slid her lacy fuchsia Victoria's Secret panties off with one hand and found the speed she wanted on her vibrator with the other. "I think I'll use you in fifth gear today." She spread her legs wide open and played with her clit to make herself wet. Once Peter took a dive in her waterfall, she didn't want anything getting in his way of taking her to complete ecstasy. She rested Peter right at the tip of her clit. She held her head back and let out little moans as Peter did his thing. Right before she was about to explode, the phone rang.

"Ah hell naw," she said as her eyes popped open. Keaundra turned Peter off and reached for the phone that sat on the nightstand. "Hello," she screamed into the receiver without checking the caller ID.

"Ke-Ke, this is Gran, what ya yellin' for, sweetie?"

"Oh, hi, Gran. I didn't mean to yell. I knocked my water over when I reached for the phone," Keaundra lied.

"Well, baby, that ain't no reason to be yellin' into the phone."

Keaundra rolled her eyes. "I'm sorry, Gran."

"You tryin'a bust my eardrum? You know Gran already hard of hearin'."

You must be,'cause I already said I was sorry. "Did you need somethin', Gran, 'cause I'm kinda in the middle of somethin'?"

"I was just callin' to remind you about Sunday dinner."

"Gran, don't we have dinner at your house every Sunday?"

"Yeah, but I just thought I would call to remind you."

"Okay, Gran, I'll see you on Sunday."

"Bye, baby."

"Bye, Gran." Keaundra hung up the phone, rolled back over on her back, and put Peter back in his favorite spot. He had just started working his magic when the phone rang again. "I'll be damned," she shouted as she rolled over and reached for the phone. "Hello?" she snapped, frustrated.

"Damn, what's the matter with you?" The sexy masculine voice asked.

"Oh, hey Kenneth, what's up?"

"I should be askin' you that question," he chuckled. "I ain't keepin' you from doing anything important, am I?"

Keaundra smiled. "Naw, boy. What's up?"

"I was just callin' to see if you were goin' to Gran's house for Sunday dinner?"

"Nigga, don't I be there every Sunday? You startin' to act like Gran," Keaundra said to her twin brother.

"I was just askin'. You know you don't come around that much anymore since you moved out on your own," Kenneth responded.

Tears began to fill Keaundra's eyes. "I know. It's just that being in Gran's house brings back a lot of memories."

"I know. But we still can't let Momma's death tear the family apart; I'm still your older brother."

"Nigga, you only two minutes older than me," Keaundra laughed.

"All right, sis, I'll see you Sunday," Kenneth said laughing.

"Okay." She smiled.

"Hey, Ke-Ke?" Kenneth said before hanging up.

"Yes, Ken-Ken?"

"I love you."

"I love you too," she said before hanging up the phone. She looked down at her vibrator. "Well, Peter, that's enough of you for the day." Keaundra rolled over, put Peter back in his safe haven, and climbed out of bed.

She walked into the bathroom and turned on the shower. Keaundra looked at herself in the mirror and instantly turned away. *Damn, I look just like Mommy.* Keaundra was light brown, with short, naturally curly hair. When other girls were at the beauty shop getting Jheri Curls, all she had to do was put some grease in her hair and wet it. The easy blend concoction would make her hair curl up just like everybody else's.

Keaundra stepped her five foot six-inch, one hundred and forty-pound frame into the hot water and let it run down her body. Her mother kept popping up in her thoughts as the hot water stung her body. The horrible memories of their father's murder-suicide would not fade; in fact, it was still fresh in her mind as if it had happened only yesterday. Although it had been sixteen years, Keaundra still could not get over the pain and suffering of their mother's death.

Tears fell from Keaundra's eyes, rolling down her already wet body, as she attempted to shake the horrible memories out of her head. She wiped the tears away with the back of her hand and continued to shower. She climbed out the shower and wiped the steam off the bathroom mirror. "Mommy, I'm gon' get Alexis away from Ronald if it's the last thing I do. I cannot watch another person I love lose their life because of a jealous man. I'm so sorry, Mommy, that I couldn't do anything to help you. I was just a child." Keaundra fell to the floor, balled up into a fetal position, and cried.

Chapter Four

Martell stuck his key in the door and entered India's condo. He threw his keys on the coffee table before heading to her bedroom. He smiled once he spotted her relaxing on her bed. "Hey, baby," he said, bending down, kissing her on the cheek.

"Oh, all I get is a kiss on the cheek?" she replied.

"I was saving the good stuff for later on." He smiled, looking just like Taye Diggs did in *Brown Sugar*.

"You so nasty," India laughed. India looked down at Martell's feet. "I know you're not walking on my white carpet with those wet boots on, Martell?"

"My bad, Daddy's sorry." Martell removed his boots and carried them into the living room, setting them on the rug by the front door to dry.

"You gon' get my rug cleaned," India stated as she looked around for any signs of dirt.

Martell walked back into India's bedroom and walked over to the Louvre hand-painted Bombe dresser and pulled out a pair of sweats. "You got that coming. Baby, when are you gon' quit playin' games and let a brotha move in?"

"Martell, you know my parents are paying my mortgage and if they found out a man lived here with me without us being married, they would die," she said, sitting up.

"Oh, so I'm just a man, now?" Martell asked as he removed his Tommy Hilfiger slacks, throwing them on the white leather chaise.

"You know what I mean, boo," India replied before standing up from the bed.

"Well, let me pay the mortgage for you and there wouldn't be anything your parents could say." Martell put on the sweats, walked over to India, and picked her up. She wrapped her legs around his waist and kissed him on his lips.

"Baby, we're not married yet," she said, hoping to steer their conversation into a different direction while rubbing on his chest.

"Oh, we can fuck while we're not married, but we can't live together?"

"Put me down, Martell," India spat. Martell put India down. She walked over to her closet, opened it up, pulled out a pink velour sweat suit, and grabbed her white Baby Phat Sublime Sporty boots.

"Where you 'bout to go?" Martell asked.

"I'm going over to Keaundra's house for dinner," she replied as she walked over to her dresser and pulled out a brand new, crisp white T-shirt.

"It's always about them damn hood-rats," Martell yelled.

"Those were the same girls I was with the day I met yo' ass at the bank. So if you think they are hood-rats, then you think I'm a hood-rat too." India was fed up with this entire conversation. She wished Martell would go to his own house and stay until she needed some good loving.

India loved Martell and hoped to one day become his wife, but lately he was suffocating her. Every time she turned around, he was over at her condo complaining about them not spending enough time together. She loved her best friends more than any man, other than her father. In her opinion, men came like the RCT bus, every thirty minutes, but good, wholesome friends came once in a lifetime.

"No, I don't think you're a hood-rat. But yes, I do think Keaundra and Alexis are. Take Keaundra for instance; she doesn't even have a man but she's always up in somebody else's relationship acting like Dr. Ruth. And we ain't even get on Tina Turner, I mean, Alexis."

India shot Martell an I-wish-you-would look and he quickly got the picture.

"Look, all I'm saying is that we never spend time together anymore. It's always about school or your friends," Martell said as he removed his tie and hung it up in India's closet.

That's how it starts, they leave one thing over your house and next thing you know, you look up and the muthafuckas done moved in on you, India thought. "We do spend time together, Martell. You're always going on your little business trips, so you say." India hoped her comment would start an argument so Martell would get mad and be quiet and give her the silent treatment, or better yet leave and go to his own place.

"Those little business trips I go on keep your high-class ass dressed in Louis Vuitton, Georgina Goodman, Kate Spade, and the rest of them names that I've never heard of before," Martell said as he removed his shirt, throwing it on top of his pants. Martell lay across India's bed and picked up the remote to the forty-two-inch LCD television that was stationed at the foot of her bed.

"I'm serious, India, one day you are gon' be without me," Martell warned.

"Whatever." India rolled her eyes and walked out of her bedroom into the adjoining bathroom so she could soak in the tub.

"You'll see," Martell said before turning the channel to watch the stock market.

"Where the fuck you think you goin'?" Ronald snapped as Alexis walked out of her bedroom dressed in a pair of tight Jordache Vintage jeans, with a white Dolce & Gabbana sweater, and a pair of silver Christian Louboutin pumps that she had bought after she and Sex-C did that show together.

"I'm going over to Keaundra's house for our weekly dinner," Alexis said.

"Well, where the kids at?" Ronald asked, scratching his nuts.

"They in the room playin'."

"Well, you better get 'em dressed 'cause I'm 'bout to go." Ronald stood up and slipped on his pants.

Yo' bitch ass wasn't going nowhere until I decided to leave, Alexis thought, but didn't have enough nerve to say because she didn't feel like getting her ass kicked. She had other plans and didn't want Ronald to fuck up her night. "R.J., get you and your sister's jackets on, we 'bout to go," she yelled.

"I don't wanna go, Mommy. I wanna play with my Power Ranger," R.J. whined as he came into the living room.

"Bring it with you 'cause Daddy is about to go," Alexis said.

"Can I go with you then, Daddy?" R.J. asked his father.

Ronald picked up his son and kissed him on the cheek. "Not this time, big man. Daddy's 'bout to go handle some business with Tyrone."

Not this time or no other time either. That bitch-ass nigga ain't got no time for y'all, she thought. Alexis gathered the rest of their things before walking out the door.

"Hey, I need you to be back here in a couple hours, 'cause I'm gon' need to use the car," Ronald yelled out the door.

"Yeah, okay," Alexis said sarcastically.

"I'm for real," Ronald yelled as Alexis buckled the kids into their seatbelts.

"I heard you," she said uncaringly.

"Don't make me come lookin' for you. If I do, I'ma kick yo' ass."

Alexis shook her head and got into the car. She knew Ronald would come looking for her, but tonight she had something in store for him, so she could not have cared less if he came looking for her. She started up the car, backed out of her assigned parking space with a huge smile on her face, and drove to her destination.

***

"Dang, bitch, what took you so long to get here? The food is all cold and shit," Keaundra said as Alexis walked through the door.

"Yeah!" India added.

"The roads are slippery, and plus, I had to take the kids over to my mother's house, 'cause Ronald wouldn't watch'em," she said, walking into the kitchen with Keaundra and India behind her.

"Why not?" India asked, while grabbing three plates out the cabinet.

"He talkin' 'bout he had somethin' to do."

Keaundra rolled her eyes. "That nigga ain't got nothin' to do, but sit on his ass."

"I know it, girl," Alexis said as she washed her hands in the kitchen sink.

India admired Alexis's outfit. "My, don't we look all cute today."

"Thank you and so do you."

"Yo' ass got a date or somethin'?" Keaundra asked.

"No, not really. But I am supposed to be meeting David over here." Alexis took a seat at the kitchen table and smiled at her two friends.

"Did I just hear you say that you were meeting David over here?" India asked.

"The same David you got both of your eyes blacken for?" Keaundra asked.

Alexis and India shot Keaundra a dirty look.

"What? Well, she did."

India set a plate of chicken breast, steamed mixed vegetables, and sauerkraut in front of her two friends and walked back over to the counter to fix herself a plate. "Do you need to use the guest room?" India smiled wickedly.

"Naw. It ain't even like that between us. We're just friends. He's coming to get me and we're going over to his house so he can make me a few CDs," Alexis said before placing a forkful of sauerkraut into her mouth.

India smiled at her friend. "What if Ronald comes over here?"

"If he does, tell him I left with Keaundra."

Alexis, India, and Keaundra sat at the table and talked about all the hottest movies, books and CDs that were out. Alexis's ringing cell phone interrupted their conversation.

"Hello?" Alexis said, flipping open her cell phone and answering it. "Okay, I'm on my way out." Alexis smiled at her two friends and grabbed her coat. "I shall return."

"Be careful. You know how Ronald's psychotic ass will pop up at any time," India said.

"I will." Alexis hugged both of her friends before rushing out the door and jumping into the car with David.

Keaundra and India lay around the condo watching television until they both fell asleep.

They jumped up when someone began pounding on the front door like the police.

"Who is it?" India asked. Her heart was racing.

"It's Ronald, tell Alexis to come on up outta there," he yelled.

"She ain't here," India yelled back.

"Where she at? Her car is parked out here."

"She left with Keaundra," India said, walking toward the front door.

Keaundra ran into the bathroom to hide as India opened up the door. Ronald walked in and looked around.

"Where they go?" he asked, snottily.

"I don't know. I'm not Alexis or Keaundra's keeper."

"I see you still got a smart mouth."

India rolled her eyes. "Whatever; when Alexis and Keaundra get back I'll tell her that her daddy came over here lookin' for her," India said sarcastically.

"You bitches kill me; I'm tired of y'all always gettin' in me and Alexis's business. I'm gon' make sure she don't fuck with y'all hood-rats no more."

Oh, no he didn't, Keaundra said to herself as she listened with her ear against the door. It took everything in her soul not to walk into the living room and beat the shit outta his ass.

"I'm far from a hood-rat," India snapped.

"I forgot; you don't live in the hood, so you a suburb-rat," Ronald laughed on his way back out the door.

"Fuck you!" India yelled at his back and slammed the door behind him.

Keaundra rushed out the bathroom. "That nigga got a lot of damn nerves."

"Fuck Ronald. He's just miserable." India picked up her cordless phone and dialed Alexis's cell phone, but the call went straight to her voice mail.

India left a message after the greeting. "Alexis, this is India. Ronald just came over here lookin' for you. So yo' ass better get David's dick out yo' mouth and get back here." India hung up after leaving the message.

Ten minutes later Alexis was calling back. "Oh, I see you took the dick out ya mouth long enough to call me back," India replied.

"Girl, I'm on my way over there to get my car."

"Okay, well, call me when you get home," India said.

"I sure will," Alexis said before hanging up the phone.

Once Alexis made it home, she called India to let her know she made it safely. After hanging up from a brief conversation, Alexis got ready for bed. Just as soon as she got into a deep sleep, all hell broke loose.

"Bitch, you knew I wanted to use the car," Ronald yelled as he walked into the bedroom.

Alexis woke up from a deep sleep.

"Instead you out runnin' around with Keaundra's lonely ass."

"Ronald, I am not in the mood for yo' shit tonight," Alexis mustered up enough nerve to say.

Ronald began taking off his leather belt. "Bitch, you don't tell me what you not in the mood for. You gon' start listening to me, ain't you?" he asked, striking Alexis across the face with the belt.

"Ronald, stop!" she screamed.

Ronald swung his leather belt with force. "You gon' start listening to me, bitch, ain't you?" Ronald asked again as he swung the belt over and over, beating Alexis like she was a child.

"Ronald, stop it!" Alexis screamed at the top of her lungs.

"Oh, yo' ass ain't gon' answer me?" he continued to ask.

Alexis jumped up from the bed. "Ronald, get the fuck outta my house before I call the police!"

"Call 'em, bitch!"

"Please, just leave, Ronald," Alexis begged.

"Give me the keys then!" Ronald yelled loudly.

"I ain't giving you the keys to my car. I gotta go to work in the morning,"Alexis cried.

"Call one of ya girls to come take you to work," Ronald said uncaringly.

"Why should I have to when I got my own car?" she shouted.

"Bitch, call a cab then!" Ronald snapped as he grabbed the keys off the dresser and walked out the door.

"Stupid muthafucka', I hate you!" Alexis scream-ed as tears rolled down her burning cheek. Alexis climbed out of bed and walked into the bathroom to see what her face looked like this time. She shook her head from side to side as she ran her face towel under some cold water and lay it on her face before crying herself to sleep.

The next morning, Alexis picked up the phone and dialed India's number. She let the phone ring two times before hanging up. She knew she couldn't tell India what happened because she would end up telling Keaundra, and then she would never hear the end of it.

"Girl, why you hang up?" India asked when she looked at the caller ID and called Alexis's number back.

"Oh, my bad, I dialed the wrong number. I meant to call my auntie," Alexis lied.

"Have you been crying, Alexis?"

"No, why you ask that?" Alexis tried to hide the fact that she had been.

"You just sound funny."

"I think I'm catching a cold," Alexis lied again.

"You think?"

"Yeah, I think. I woke up feeling a little clogged up this morning."

"Um-huh? Where's Ronald punk ass at?" India inquired.

"He's asleep."

"That's funny, 'cause I just got off the phone with Martell and he told me that he saw Ronald on his way to work and he was driving your car. Do he got a twin now, or is there somethin' you wanna tell me?"

Tears fell down Alexis's cheeks as she told her friend what went down between her and Ronald.

"Get the fuck outta here! You mean to tell me that nigga whooped you with his belt? Alexis, if you stay with that nigga after this, I don't know what to tell you."

"I told him to get out," Alexis whined.

"You always tell him to get out, but he never does. Alexis, you need to show Ronald that you're serious."

"He knows I'm serious," Alexis continued to whine.

"Bitch, please! That nigga know yo' ass is soft as Charmin. Ain't no way I'm gon' tell a nigga to get outta my damn house and he look at me like I ain't said nothin'. You see, you done let this shit go on for too long. Everytime you put his broke ass out, he always sucka' his way right back into your queen-sized bed."

"I'm dead serious this time, India."

"Yeah, okay. You were dead serious the last ten times, too. Alexis, I love you, and I can't sit up here and tell you to leave Ronald alone, 'cause you grown. All I can do is give some good advice to you. You really need to sit back and weigh your options."

"What options do I have?"

"What good is Ronald doing you? He don't work. He tried to sell weed, but his dumb ass ended up smokin' up all of Jarrod's shit. You were the one paying Jarrod back so that he wouldn't put a bullet in Ronald." India rolled her eyes.

"I know," Alexis stated.

"Well, act like you know. You need to stop acting like some love-sick high school girl! Bitch, we're grown now. Ronald whooped you like you was his child!" India yelled loudly.

"Stop yelling at me," Alexis whined. "You startin' to sound like Ke-Ke."

"Look, you better be glad I don't click over and call Ke-Ke. You know what she said 'bout what she was gon' do the next time that ho-ass nigga put his hands on you."

"I know." Alexis thought back to Keaundra's threats that she knew her friend would make good on. "You ain't gon' tell her, are you?"

"Hell naw, I ain't gon' tell her. 'Cause Ke-Ke was not playing. Besides, Ronald ain't worth her going to jail. Get it together, girl."

"I am."

"Now, I gotta get ready for school, but call me if you need me."

"I will," Alexis promised.

India hung up the phone, shook her head, and continued getting dressed, wishing that for just once she could have one drama-free day. But that would have been too much like right.

Chapter Five

Alexis paced back and forth, contemplating whether to call Keaundra for a ride. She had left all her money in the console of her car, so she couldn't catch a cab to work. She argued with herself for about twenty minutes before picking up the phone to call her friend.

"Hello?"

"Ke-Ke, can I get a ride to work?" Alexis closed her eyes and prepared herself for a long, drawn-out lecture.

"Sure, I'll be there in about ten minutes." Keaundra hung up the phone and hurried out to her car.

Alexis gathered her belongings while waiting for her friend's arrival.

Keaundra played it cool on the phone because she wanted to talk to Alexis face to face. Alexis didn't know it, but India had called Keaundra as soon as they had hung up the phone, and ran down the entire story about her getting beaten by Ronald with a belt. Now that she was pulling her Saturn Aura up in front of the apartment, she was ready to get at her friend for real.

Alexis walked out with a smile on her face. Keaundra smiled back until Alexis got in the car.

"Okay, bitch, what happened and I don't wanna hear no lies," Keaundra said, locking her car doors and pulling off.

Alexis closed her eyes and shook her head. "Why do I have to tell you what happened? I'm sure Big Mouth already ran the whole story down to you."

"Don't get jazzy, hefah," Keaundra said as she drove down the busy intersection that was congested with early morning traffic.

"I'm not, but somethin' that's already known leaves no need for explanation."

"I guess you just gon' be dumb all ya life, huh?"

"I guess. Look, Keaundra, all I need is a ride to work, not a lecture. Let me handle Ronald on my own." Alexis rubbed her temples as if she was suffering from a headache.

Keaundra fussed the entire ride. Alexis was happy when Keaundra finally pulled up into the dentist's parking lot. "You are so right," Keaundra said from out of nowhere. "I don't have anything else to say to yo' dumb ass about Ronald."

Alexis got out of the car and slammed the door.

Keaundra rolled down the passenger's side window. "Oh, by the way, ask Ronald when's the next time he goin' back over to Tyisha's house. Tell him he left his wallet over there!" Keaundra yelled before pulling off.

Alexis's jaw hit the ground because Ronald had told her that he had lost his wallet at the club. Alexis marched into the office and headed straight for the phone to call Ronald's no-good ass.

"Hey, Alexis." Kay-Kay smiled.

"Hey," Alexis said as she headed straight to her office and dialed Ronald's cell phone.

"Hello?" Ronald answered.

"Who the fuck is Tyisha?"

"Huh? Who is this?" Ronald asked.

"Stop playin', Ronald, and answer my question," Alexis yelled.

Ronald let out a long breath. "I don't know," he lied. "Who been tellin' you shit 'bout me now?"

"Ronald, all I want you to do is go to the house, pack your shit, drop my car off, and get the fuck outta my life!" Alexis yelled before slamming the phone down.

A couple of seconds went by and Kay-Kay's voice came across the intercom. "Alexis, you have a call on line one."

"Ask who it is."

Kay-Kay clicked over and asked the gentleman his name.

"What you wanna know my name for?" the gentleman snapped. "Just put Alexis on the phone."

Kay-Kay's voice buzzed in on the intercom again. "Look, he won't give me his name. But if you give me permission I will cuss this rude bastard out."

"What did he say to you? Never mind, just patch him through."

Kay-Kay took a deep breath and waited a couple of seconds before passing on his call.

"Alexis speaking."

"Why you hang up on me, Alexis?" Ronald yelled.

"I don't wanna talk to you."

"See, you need to stop listenin' to them bitches. They just mad 'cause they don't got no man," Ronald said, hoping to convince Alexis.

"Ronald, please just get your stuff and get outta my house."

"All right, I'ma get my stuff. When can I come see the kids?"

"Ronald, don't start that shit again. Every time I tell yo' ass to leave you wanna put the kids in it. Not this time. Shit, you won't even watch 'em when I wanna go somewhere, so what you worried about when you gon' see them for?"

Ronald became angry. "Oh, so you gon' stop me from seein' my kids?"

"Have I ever stopped you before?" Alexis yelled impatiently.

"You bet' not have no other nigga around my kids, Alexis, I ain't playin'."

"Bye, Ronald." Alexis hung up the phone feeling relieved. She stood up from her desk, straightened out her uniform, and walked out into the hallway with a huge smile on her face.

"Dang, that man got you smilin' like that? Shoot, when you first walked in the office I was halfway scared to speak to you," Kay-Kay said.

"No, that man don't got me smiling like this, I got myself smiling." Alexis was proud of the way she had handled Ronald. She had put him out a dozen times, but this time she meant it. She was not taking him back for nothing in the world. She was through, done, finished, just like all the other times!

"Girl, can you believe Alexis put Ronald's tired ass out?" India asked Keaundra.

"Yeah, I can believe it. But how many other times has she put the nigga out and end up lettin' him come back home after 'bout two weeks," Keaundra responded.

"You right, but I think she means it this time. I don't think she's gon' let him back."

"India, please. It's just a matter of time before she falls for the lies he's goin' to tell her," Keaundra laughed.

India laughed too. "Yeah, like, 'I promise I'm gon' get a job.'"

"Or this one: 'I promise things are gon' be different this time.'"

"No, this is the best of the best: 'I promise I ain't gon' put my hands on you no more,'" Keaundra said.

"I can't believe you two bitches are in here talkin' about me," Alexis said as she walked into Keaundra's house.

"We're sorry, Lexy," Keaundra laughed.

"No, y'all ain't. With friends like y'all, I don't need no enemies. Y'all are supposed to be helping me get through this, but instead y'all sitting around cracking jokes."

"We're sorry, Alexis," India laughed.

"No, y'all not. Y'all the ones who kept telling me to get rid of the nigga and now y'all sitting up here sayin' I'm gon' let him back in."

Keaundra's expression turned serious. "Don't you always?"

"That was the old Alexis," Alexis stately firmly, and with renewed confidence.

"This is the new-and-improved Alexis," India and Keaundra said, imitating Alexis's famous words.

"Fuck y'all!" Alexis screamed.

"We done heard the same thing so many times, now it's time to show and prove." Keaundra smirked.

"You will watch and see." Alexis was determined to prove her friends wrong.

"We'll see," India said.

Keaundra rolled her eyes into her head. "Yeah, we'll see."

Chapter Six

It had been three weeks since Ronald moved out and Alexis hated to admit it but she missed having him around. Ronald acted like a complete asshole sometimes, but he had a good side to him, too. It was very rare when he showed it, but he and Alexis did have some fun together. Taking the kids to the park and the swimming pool was a summer time ritual for them, when she could find him. Ronald would also take R.J. to the high school football and basketball games when he wasn't running the streets with his dudes. Alexis was starting to get depressed thinking about Ronald. She had promised herself and her best friends that she was not letting Ronald back into her life no matter what type of game he tried to run. Alexis knew she had to move on before he ended up killing her.

"Alexis, you have a call on line one," Kay-Kay said over the intercom.

"Thanks," Alexis smiled as she pushed the button to retrieve her phone call.

"What's up, girl?" Keaundra asked.

"What's up, sis?' Alexis said as she looked through some charts.

"You know what tonight is, don't you?"

Alexis thought for a minute. "Is it your birthday?" she asked, setting the charts down on top of the desk.

"Nope, try again," Keaundra toyed.

"Is it my birthday?" Alexis asked, thinking hard about what the day's occasion was.

"Nope. Try again," Keaundra teased.

"Hell, is it Christmas?"

"Nope. You give up?"

"Yes. What day is it?" Alexis chuckled.

"It's ladies' night," Keaundra sang off tune.

"And you saying that to say what?"

"I'm sayin' it so we can go get a drink."

"I don't know. I don't really feel like drinking tonight," Alexis said as she played with a strand of her hair. Plus, every time Keaundra got drunk, she started crying and reminiscing about her mother, and both India and Alexis ended up crying with her. Sometimes drinking with Keaundra could be emotionally draining.

"How you know what you gon' feel like tonight? It's nine o'clock in the morning."

"I know, I'll see," Alexis answered, still not sure.

"Come on, girl. You sound down and out. Let me and India take you out for dinner and some drinks," Keaundra offered.

"Shit, since you and India is payin' I'm game," Alexis laughed.

"Okay, then, I'll see you around eight," Keaundra said as Debbie stuck her head through the door, but quickly pulled it back when she noticed that Keaundra was on the phone.

"All right, talk to you later." Alexis hung up the phone and forced a weak smile upon her face. "I do need a drink," she said as she finished looking through her charts.

"You have a new patient out here," Kay-Kay buzzed in on Alexis's line again.

"I'll be out in a second."

"Girl, you betta hurry up 'cause this brotha is fine as hell," Kay-Kay whispered.

Alexis smiled at herself in the mirror that hung behind her chair, patted her hair down, and straightened out her jacket before walking out of the office.

"David." Alexis smiled when she saw his gorgeous face.

"Alexis?" he greeted with a smile.

Alexis was mesmerized by David's dark, sexy eyes. "Well, if you're finished with all your paperwork follow me."

"I'll follow you anywhere," David said with a sincere look on his face.

Alexis showed David that she was flattered by his comment by smiling at him. Alexis took David into a small but cozy room and began working on his mouth. She took her sweet time cleaning his already white teeth. She wanted to spend as much time as she could with this fine piece of meat she had lying comfortably in the dentist chair. She looked down into David's dark brown eyes and smiled at him.

David was one fine brotha. He was the spitting image of Columbus Short, but just a few inches taller. His skin was silky and smooth just like the caramel on an apple. His pretty white teeth lit up the room every time he smiled and you could tell by his washboard abs that he didn't miss a beat when it came to working out that well-manicured body of his. He also sported some of the deepest waves that Alexis had ever seen on top of anybody's head.

"I'm almost finished." She smiled again.

David nodded as he stared at the mark on the side of her face.

"There, all finished," Alexis said as she laid down her instruments. "I hope I didn't hurt you." Alexis handed David a cup with a sweet-smelling liquid in it for him to rinse his mouth out with.

"No, you didn't hurt me at all. As a matter of fact, this was the best teeth cleaning I've ever had." David smiled before swishing the candy-tasting mouthwash around in his mouth and spitting it into the little sink that was connected to the dentist chair.

"Good." Alexis picked David's chart up off the counter. "Follow me." David followed Alexis back out into the receptionist area. Alexis handed Kay-Kay his chart so she could add up his bill. "I'll see you in six months," she said to David.

"I was hoping I could see you tonight," David suggested.

Alexis was at a loss for words. She didn't know what to say. "I don't know, David. I just broke up with Ronald and I ain't tryin'a—"

David pressed his finger against Alexis's lips. "I just wanna take you out for a drink and maybe grab a bite to eat, that's all. Nothin' more and nothin' less."

Alexis smiled. "That's cool, I need a drink."

"Okay, then, I'll pick you up from India's house around six-thirty."

"Why you gotta pick me up over India's house? I got my own place," Alexis said, offended, like he was hiding something from someone.

"I know. I just don't want no shit to jump off just in case ya baby daddy is at your house, that's all."

Alexis smiled. "Oh, I can dig it."

"So is six-thirty okay with you?"

"Six-thirty it is." Alexis smiled widely as she watched David walk out the door.

"Oooh weeeee, he is so fine," Kay-Kay said excitingly.

"I know, girl. But you know I just broke up with Ronald so I ain't tryin'a rush into nothin'."

"Dang, girl, he only wanna take you out for a drink. It ain't like he asked you to marry him," Kay-Kay laughed.

"Hell, you never know. If you got a chance to date this dime piece, wouldn't you be tryin'a marry it?" Alexis asked playfully.

"How long you and Ronald been together and y'all still not married?" Kay-Kay joked.

Alexis shot Kay-Kay a dirty look before walking into her office and shutting the door behind her.

Alexis left work early so she could run to the mall and pick up a new outfit for her date with David. After about two hours of shopping, she finally decided on a pair of tight-fitting Platinum Plush blue jeans with the jean jacket to match. She went into Victoria's Secret to purchase a gold camisole to match her gold stiletto boots. Alexis gathered all her bags and hurried out to her car. As she loaded her bags into her trunk, she noticed a black Camry full of girls riding by her slowly. The girl on the passenger side pointed at Alexis as they crept by.

"I wonder what this is all about?" Alexis said as she got into her car and started it. "Maybe I'm just trippin'." She put on her seatbelt and looked into her rearview mirror only to see that the black Camry was behind her again. "What the fuck is goin' on?" she said aloud. Alexis unbuckled her seatbelt and got out of the car, approaching the girls. "Can I help y'all?" Alexis asked with an attitude.

The driver of the car rolled down her window. "We don't want no trouble; all we want is your parkin' space, that's all."

Alexis was so embarrassed as she apologized to the driver of the car. The girl on the passenger side started laughing as Alexis walked away.

Alexis felt stupid as she got in her car and sped away as fast as she could. She rolled down Lexington-Springmill, bumping the sweet mellow sounds of Floetry's new joint when her cell phone rang. "Hello?" she answered.

"What's up, sis, we going out tonight or what?" India asked.

"I was goin', but there's been a change in plans," Alexis said, switching lanes to get from behind this old lady who was driving thirty-five in a fifty-five.

"Come on, girl, you need to get out the house," India pressed.

Alexis began smiling. "I'm getting out the house. David is picking me up from your house at six-thirty."

"Whaaaat? I'm scared of you," India said, excited.

"Yeah, girl, he came and got his teeth cleaned this morning and he asked me out before he left the office."

"I can't believe you said yes. I thought you were still hooked on Ronald's no-good ass," India said.

"Ronald is history. I told you that. It's time for me to start living for me."

"You can't forget about my niece and nephew."

"You know they come before me, so I'm already living for them," Alexis said.

"I feel you, girl. I'm happy for you," India said sincerely.

"Thanks."

"Oh, before I go, where is David taking you tonight so Keaundra and me can watch him closely," India joked.

"Indy!" Alexis squealed.

"I'm just joking," India laughed and hung up the phone.

Alexis smiled as she drove to the daycare center to pick up the kids.

"Girl, let me tell you!" India exclaimed when Keaundra answered her phone.

"Tell me what?" Keaundra asked anxiously.

"Alexis is going out with David tonight," India said and waited for Keaundra's response.

"David who?"

"You know David. David who owns the barber shop," India explained.

"The nigga David who made them CDs for her that one time, and the same David she sported them rings around her eyes for," Keaundra said.

"You always got somethin' smart to say," India laughed. "But yeah, that's the David. He's picking her up from my house."

"Why is he picking her up from your house?"

"I don't know. I'm just glad he's picking her up."

"It wouldn't matter if he picked her up from the moon, just as long as he doesn't put his hands on her. I'm happy for her," Keaundra replied.

India smiled. "Me too."

"Oh, well, I guess it's just you and me at ladies' night tonight," Keaundra said.

"That's okay. We'll still have fun."

"I know we will, but look, I have a client waitin' on me so I"ll talk to you later," Keaundra said.

"Bye." India smiled and shook her head at the thought of her best friend going out with someone other than Ronald. She had to admit that she loved the new-and-improved Alexis. She just wondered how long it would take before the old one showed up again.

Chapter Seven

Keaundra walked through her front door, tossed her mail on the sofa, and rubbed Peaches on the stomach before heading to the kitchen. She looked into the bare refrigerator, pulled out the water jug, and turned it up.

"What you lookin' at? I'm the only one who drinks out of this jug," Keaundra said to Peaches who looked at her as if she was doing something wrong. Keaundra smiled and rubbed Peaches on the head. Keaundra checked her messages before walking into her bedroom. She listened to the message from her grandmother and decided to call her.

"Hello?"

"Hey, Gran, it's me, Keaundra."

"Now after all these years of me raisin' you, don't you think I know your voice by now?"

Keaundra rolled her eyes just like she used to do when she was a little girl. Every time her grandma would tell her to do something or say something she didn't like, she would roll her eyes so hard she would nearly knock herself out. Kenneth used to tell her that one day her eyes were going to get stuck in her head. She had quit rolling them for a long time, but after she found out Kenneth was lying, she started rolling them again, but this time even harder.

"Did ya need somethin', Gran?"

"I was just callin' to tell you that Ken-Ken is gettin' married in August."

"To who?" Keaundra asked, shocked.

"To Beverly, who else?"

Ooooh this old woman got a smart mouth! Keaundra thought. "How you know, Gran?"

"How do you think I know? If you would have been over here for dinner last Sunday, you would have known too."

"I told you I had a bit of the stomach flu," Keaundra said.

"Yeah, I know. Well, anyways, you shoulda been there; stomach flu and all," Gran said.

"So you telling me he proposed to her over at your house?" Keaundra asked her grandmother.

"Haven't you been listenin' to me, chile?"

"How come he didn't call me and tell me?" Keaundra asked.

"You know how ya brother is, maybe he wanted to tell you face-to-face."

"Naw, maybe he didn't want me to know. That's why he did it on the day I was sick."

"Chile, what are you talkin' 'bout? Do you need to go see one of them head doctors?"

"No, Gran. There's nothin' wrong with me. Kenneth just thinks he's slick, that's all." Keaundra sat down on her bed as her grandmother rambled on about how Kenneth had proposed to Beverly while they ate pound cake for dessert.

"Chile, let me tell you, it was somethin' like you see on TV. Ken-Ken was so nervous he nearly dropped the five thousand–dollar ring he bought for Beverly," Grandma said.

"Five thousand dollars!" Keaundra screamed.

"Yeah, five thousand dollars. Chile, it got enough carats in it to make Bugs Bunny sick to his stomach," Gran laughed.

"Speakin' of being sick, Gran, I don't feel too well. I'll call you back later on," Keaundra said as her head started spinning.

"You need Gran to come over and fix you some soup?"

"No, I'll be fine. I just think I'm 'bout to start my period, that's all," Keaundra lied.

"Well, baby, get up and get you some hot tea, and a heating pad, and make sure you prop your feet up, okay?"

"Okay, Gran."

"Okay, chile, but knowin' you, you probably ain't got a tea bag, a garbage bag, or no other type of bag. So when Kenneth and Beverly come over, I'll have them take me to the store so I can get you a box of green tea, all right?"

"No, I'm fine, Gran. I got some tea in the cabinet."

"Yeah, I bet. Okay, chile, I'll talk at you later."

"Bye, Gran." Keaundra was furious. How could her brother marry the same bitch he found in bed with his best friend? Keaundra dialed Kenneth's number so fast that she was amazed her fingers could move like that.

"Hey, sis, what's goin' on?" Kenneth answered the phone in his usual cheerful voice.

"No, I should be askin' you, what's goin' on?"

"What are you talkin' 'bout?" Kenneth inquired.

"You know damn well what I'm talkin' about, Kenneth. I'm talkin' about you proposing to that ho!"

"Hold on, Ke-Ke. That shit with her and Alex was three years ago. They both apologized and I forgave 'em."

"Forgave 'em? What planet are you from? How can you forgive two muthafuckas who played you for a complete fool? You trusted this nigga around your girlfriend. I remember when you used to leave them at your house alone while you went to work. Ain't no tellin' what was goin' on while you were gone."

"Ke-Ke, that's your problem, you never learn to forgive a person for their mistakes," Kenneth said.

"Now you listen here, Kenneth Rashad Davidson, I do know how to forgive people, but do you actually think I could forgive someone who fucked me over the way that Beverly and Alex done you?"

"I love Beverly, and Alex has been my boy since the first grade."

"Earth to Kenneth. Evidently neither one of them felt the same way you feel about them, 'cause if that bitch loved you back, do you actually think she would have fucked your best friend in your bed? And if Alex gave a fuck about you, do you think he would have slept with your woman, knowin' how you felt about her? Come on, Ken-Ken, be for real!"

"Beverly has changed her ways. She's in the church now and everything," Kenneth said, hoping that would change the way his sister felt about his soon-to-be wife.

"What do that mean? Some of the biggest hoes in the world go to church. Look at Lakeetha; she done slept with every deacon, junior preacher, usher, and so on in the church, and she's the preacher's daughter. So don't give me that shit about Beverly being in church makes her a changed person."

"You'll be able to tell for yourself that she's changed 'cause we're havin' a celebration dinner over Gran's house this Saturday and I want you to be there," Kenneth said.

"I'm sorry, Ken-Ken. I can't be there. I beat that bitch up for the way she treated you. I flattened all of Alex's tires and put two spoons and a bag of sugar in his gas tank for the way he did you. And you actually think I can just accept you marrying her? Next thing you gon' tell me is that you want Alex to be your best man," Keaundra said sarcastically.

"As a matter of fact, I do."

"I'll be a monkey's auntie! What the fuck is wrong with you? Gran didn't raise no fools, Kenneth, or at least I didn't think she did. But you done proved me wrong. You damn fool!"

"Call me what you want, sis, I'm still marrying Beverly."

"I can't tell you not to 'cause you're grown, but I'm gon' leave you with this: you can't turn a trick into a treat!" Keaundra slammed down the phone so hard that she chipped a piece of the receiver.

Kenneth called his sister back several times, only to keep getting her voice mail. He left message after message, but Keaundra still wouldn't return his calls. He called his grandma for some support.

"Chile, ya sister is just pig-headed! You didn't know that? Once she gets somethin' made up in her mind, the good Lord can't change it. She's been like that ever since y'all was little," Gran said.

"I know, Gran, but I thought maybe she grew up by now."

"Well, Kenneth, the girl did sleep with your best friend in your bed. How do you expect your sister to feel about a person who mistreated her only brother?"

"I don't know, Gran," Kenneth said.

"Well, you best to be tryin'a find out then. How would you feel if Ke-Ke was gon' marry a man who beat on her?"

"I would beat his ass, excuse me, his butt," Kenneth replied, angry about the thought of someone hurting his sister.

"Well, that's the same way Keaundra feels about you, Ken. She done whooped the girl's butt, and you done got back with her anyway and now you're about to marry the gal."

"Well, how do you feel about me marrying Beverly, Gran?"

"Kenneth, my son, I have done nothin' but told you and your sister the truth, whether it hurt your feelings or not, am I right?"

"Yes, ma'am."

"Hear me out then. For one, you are a grown man. You can marry Richard Simmons for all I care. There is nothin' I can do 'bout it. I don't care for that gal on account of how she did you."

"But, Gran—" Kenneth began.

"But, Gran, nothin'. Let me finish, boy. As I was sayin', I don't care for that gal, and I don't care if that gal spent the rest of her life in church, she ain't changed. See, she might fool you, but she damn sho' can't fool this old woman."

"But, Gran, you taught me and Keaundra to forgive and forget, didn't you?"

"Kenneth, I did teach y'all that. And I'm not sayin' you are wrong for forgivin' her. All I'm saying is protect your heart, baby. Because if she does anything else wrong to you, she ain't gon' hafta worry about Keaundra whoopin' that tail again, she gon' hafta worry about Gran gettin' a piece of that action."

Kenneth laughed. "Gran, what you know 'bout some action?"

"Don't let this old woman fool ya, boy. I used to get down and dirty back in my days when those old hefahs tried to get at your Grandpa Joe."

"I'll make sure I tell her that, Gran." Kenneth smiled.

"Okay, now, baby, Gran is about to watch her talk shows, so I'll talk at you later."

"Thanks, Gran," Kenneth said sincerely.

"For what?"

"For everything."

"I haven't said or done anything I wasn't supposed to."

"I love you, Gran."

"I love you too."

"Oh, before I go I have somethin' to tell you," Kenneth said.

"What is it, baby?"

"You would never have to worry about me marrying Richard Simmons. I can't stand that same red and white outfit he wears all the time," Kenneth laughed.

Chapter Eight

Alexis rushed around the house looking for her gold stiletto boot. She checked in her closet, under her bed, and she even looked in her dirty clothes basket. She started to panic because without her gold boots the rest of her outfit would be useless.

Alexis walked into her children's toy room. "Have you guys seen Mommy's other boot like this?" Alexis asked as she held up her boot.

Ro'nisha shook her head.

"Are you sure, Ro'nisha, 'cause you always wearing Mommy's shoes."

Ro'nisha shook her head no again.

"I seen your boot, Mommy," R.J. responded.

"You have? Where is it, baby?"

"Daddy cut it up," R.J. said.

"Daddy did what?" Alexis asked to make sure she heard right.

"He cut it up with a big, big knife."

"Are you sure it was this boot?" she said, showing her son the boot again. R.J. nodded.

That dirty, rotten bitch! "Thank you, baby." Alexis said to her son, and kissed him on the forehead. Alexis quickly dialed India's number.

"Hello?"

"Sis, I got an emergency," Alexis said, frantic.

"What's the matter, girl?"

"R.J. told me that Ronald cut up my other gold stiletto boot."

"You got to be joking."

"I wish I was. Now I don't have no shoes to wear with my outfit tonight. I'm 'bout to call David and tell him that I can't go."

"The hell you are," India snapped.

"Well, what am I gon' do, Indy? I need my gold boots to match my gold camisole."

"I got the same boots, Alexis. You can wear 'em."

"India, I wear a size nine and you wear a seven. So what the fuck I look like wearing your boots?"

India started laughing.

"This is no laughing matter, India," Alexis said.

"Okay, okay. What time is David picking you up?"

"Six-thirty."

"Okay, it's five forty-five. Why don't I run out to the mall and pick you up another pair of boots?" India suggested.

"India, I don't have no extra money, this is rent week. And plus, those boots cost me four-fifty. I bought them when I got my income tax check."

"Don't worry about it. I got you. Now, just finish gettin' ready for your date with David and meet me over my house."

"Thank you so much, Indy. I'll pay you back, I promise."

"Whatever! Just consider it an early birth-day present," India said before hanging up the phone.

"Happy Birthday to me, Happy Birthday. . . ." Alexis sang as she finished putting on her clothes.

"Mommy, is it your birthday?" R.J. asked, walking into his mother's room.

"No, baby, it's not Mommy's birthday. I was just singing a song."

"Oh. Mommy?"

"Yes, R.J.?"

"Is Daddy coming home tonight?"

Alexis put down her eyeliner and looked at her handsome son right in his light brown eyes. "No, R.J., Daddy is not coming home tonight, or any other night. Daddy lives with your Grandma Jane."

R.J. looked at his mommy with sad eyes. "Can I live with Grandma Jane too?"

"No, baby, you can't. Do you wanna leave me and your sister?"

"You can come too. We can even bring Ro'-nisha," R.J. said.

"No, way. I don't wanna live with Grandma Jane."

"Well, if you don't want to, I don't want to either."

"Good. Now, you, Ro'nisha and me can live here all together, by ourselves." Alexis smiled.

R.J. smiled too. "I like that."

"Okay, baby, go see what your sister is doing."

"Okay, Mommy." R.J. hugged Alexis around her legs before running off to see what type of havoc his little sister had caused.

Alexis smiled. "That boy is growing up, he is too much."

Alexis finished getting ready at six-fifteen. She gathered her children and put them in the car. She exceeded the speed limit, trying to be on time for her date. Her cell phone rang as she pulled into her mother's driveway. "Hello?"

"Alexis, are you still bringing my babies over?"

"Yeah, Mommy. We just pulled up in your driveway."

"Okay, y'all come on in."

Alexis looked in the back seat at her two sleeping beauties. She took Ro'nisha out of her car seat and carried her to the front door. Her mother was standing there to take her grand-baby. Alexis went back to the car and picked up R.J. "Damn, this boy is gettin' heavy," she said as she struggled to carry her son into the house.

"Look at Grandma's babies." Alexis's mom kissed both her grandbabies on the foreheads before they carried them off to their rooms.

"Okay, Mommy. I'll see you in the morning," Alexis said.

"You have fun. Don't come over too early, 'cause me and your father plan on taking the kids to Chuck E. Cheese."

"That's cool wit' me." Alexis kissed her mother on the cheek and walked out the door. She got into the car and drove like a mad woman. *It's six thirty-five, I hope David is running late.* Alexis weaved in and out of traffic, hurrying to get to India's house. When she pulled into the drive-way she jumped out of the car, ran to the door, and stuck her key in. She pushed open the door and went straight to the kitchen to help herself to a glass of wine to calm her nerves.

"Bitch, if you don't go out there and park your car right. You ain't the only one who has to park in my driveway," India yelled when she came rushing through the door.

"My bad. Did you get the boots?" Alexis asked anxiously.

"Nope. They didn't have no more."

"Shit!"

"Never fear, 'cause India Ariel Davenport is here," India said as she pulled out a gold boot that nearly knocked her best friend's socks off.

"Bitch, those boots are sharp! I saw those at the mall. How much did you pay for those?"

"They were on sale for six-fifty," India said.

"Six-fifty? Girl, I can't pay you no six hundred and fifty dollars back for no boots," Alexis said.

"Did I ask you to pay me back? I told you that this would be an early birthday present."

Alexis had a huge grin on her face. "India, you are too much for me." Alexis hugged her friend and gave her a wet, sloppy kiss on the cheek. Ten minutes later Alexis's cell phone rang. "Hello?"

"Hello, is this Alexis?"

Alexis had a huge smile on her face when she answered the phone, already knowing who was on the line. "Yes, it is, may I ask who's calling?"

"This is David. I'm just calling to tell you that I'm running a little late, but I will be there in the next twenty minutes or so."

"That's fine. I'll be here waiting."

"Cool, see you in a bit."

Alexis pushed the end button on her cell phone and danced around India's living room.

"Dang, what's wrong with you, ho? You act like you just hit the lottery or somethin'."

Alexis smiled and continued to dance. "It sure feels like it."

Alexis had three glasses of wine as she waited for David's arrival. She wanted to be buzzed, but not too drunk when he came. She always felt that she talked more and seemed more interesting when she had a buzz going on.

When David pulled up in the driveway, he called her cell phone to tell her that he was outside waiting.

Alexis frowned on the fact that he did not come to the door to get her. Alexis kissed India on the cheek and hurried out the door. She and David talked a lot while he drove to the nice, low-key restaurant.

David pulled into the parking lot and parked. David got out of the car, walked around to the passenger's side, and opened up Alexis's door.

She smiled as she stepped out of his brand spanking new big body Suburban. Alexis admired David's outfit. He looked very different dressed up. She was so used to seeing him thugged out in his Tims, Phat Farm, Enyce, or whatever the latest hip-hop fashion was at the time. Seeing David dressed in a cream Avirex button-down with navy blue stripes, and some navy Avirex jeans with a pair of crispy cream Air

Force Ones did something to her. Alexis felt herself getting moist at the sight of this fine brotha who stood before her. She knew she should act like a lady, otherwise she would have suggested they skip dinner and go back to her place and let her be his dessert.

"This is a nice restaurant," Alexis said as they walked in. Destiny's Child's "Cater 2 U" was playing in the background as she admired all the nice paintings of old cars on the walls. All the tables were decorated with tablecloths that had old-fashioned cars on them and they even had small gas cans with a flower in them sitting on the tables. "I've never been here before." Alexis was impressed by David's choice of restaurant. She was so used to Ronald taking her to McDonald's; she did not know how to act.

"They have really good food but a lot of people don't come here because when they look at the building it looks sorta like a run-down shack," David said as the server led them to their table.

Alexis chuckled. "I wanted to say that when we first pulled up in the parking lot, but I didn't wanna sound rude."

"People are always judging the outside of things. You should never judge the outside until you take a good look on the inside."

"Arrest me, I'm guilty." Alexis smiled as they scanned the menus.

"Welcome to Jennah's. Are you guys ready to order?" the server asked when she walked over to their table.

"Sure." David smiled. "I'll have the baked salmon."

"Would you like a baked potato or French fries?" the server asked.

"Neither. I'll just take the side salad with a squeeze of lemon juice and that'll be all."

Healthy eater. I like that, Alexis thought.

"And you, ma'am?"

"Let's see," Alexis contemplated as she tried to make up her mind between the baked chicken or the stuffed pork chops. "I'll have the baked chicken, a side salad with ranch dressing, a baked potato with lots of butter and sour cream, and a glass of Chardonnay." Alexis smiled at the server as she removed their menus from the table.

David looked over at Alexis and smiled.

"Before you say anything, I'm not the type of broad who goes to dinner with a man and just orders a salad. I have a big appetite and I'm not ashamed of it," Alexis said.

David laughed. "I like a woman with a big appetite. I'm glad you're not one of those women who goes to dinner and orders a salad, knowing damn well they be hungry as hell and then soon as they get home they run straight to the refrigerator and stuff their face."

"Well, I ain't the one," Alexis laughed.

David and Alexis talked over dinner and wine. David's cell phone would not stop ringing. Alexis tried to ignore it the first five times, but eventually it became annoying to her.

"Do you need to go make a call or somethin'?" Alexis asked.

"No, why do you ask that?"

"'Cause your phone keeps ringing and evidentally the person on the other end of that line is desperately trying to reach you."

David picked up his napkin from the table and wiped the corners of his mouth. "No, I'm fine. The person on the end of the line can wait. I'm enjoying a nice and beautiful evening with a wonderful, stunning young lady right now." David smiled.

"Thank you." Alexis blushed.

Alexis and David sat at their table long after they finished dinner. They laughed and talked about everything they could think of. David got to the point he started talking about anything just to be able to spend more time with this beautiful young woman.

"It's closing time," the server walked over to their table and said.

"Already?" David asked, looking at the time on his Movado.

"Sorry, but you guys have been here for four hours," the server laughed.

"Dang. Funny how time flies when you're having fun," Alexis said as she put on her jacket.

David shook his head in agreement. "You can say that again."

David and Alexis talked some more as they drove to India's house.

"Well, I guess I'll talk to you later," Alexis said when they pulled up in the driveway.

David looked into Alexis's sexy, light eyes. "I hope so."

Alexis stared back at David without saying a word.

Their silence was broken when India turned on her porch light and opened up the front door. "Hey, David. Oh, yeah, next time you come over here you better bring yo' butt in," she laughed.

"Sorry, that was rude of me," David rolled down the window and yelled.

"Okay, I'm going to bed now. I just wanted to be up to make sure my girl made it home safe."

"Girl, close the door," Alexis laughed.

"Good night, y'all," India yelled.

"Good night," Alexis and David said simultaneously.

"Well, I guess I better let you go. Thanks for a wonderful evening," Alexis said.

"You're more than welcome. The pleasure was all mine."

"See you." Alexis got out of the car and David got out with her.

"Let me walk you to the door," he said.

"Okay." Alexis smiled. *What a gentleman. Ronald has never walked me anywhere, but to the free clinic for a check-up for STDs he gave me.*

When Alexis and David arrived at the door, he leaned down and kissed her on the cheek.

Alexis blushed. "What was that for?"

"For being a beautiful person, inside and out," he said.

Charming. I like that. "Thank you, David."

"May I call you tomorrow after you get off work?" David asked.

"That would be nice."

"Okay, well, I'll call you tomorrow around six o'clock."

"I'll be waiting."

Alexis watched as David walked back to his car. "Damn, that nigga is so fine," she said as she walked into India's house.

"Okay, tell me what happened on your date," India said, grabbing Alexis by the arm as soon as she walked through the door.

Alexis plopped down on the leather sofa and got comfortable. "I thought you were going to bed."

"You know better than that. You know I had to find out the 411. I wouldn't be able to sleep right not knowing what all happened."

"You are so nosey, bitch."

"I know. So what happened and don't leave out nothin'!"

Alexis kicked off her boots and folded her feet under her butt. She began to smile as she replayed the night in her head.

"I'm waiting," India said anxiously.

"We ate, drank, laughed, and talked, that's it."

"Where did he take you?" India questioned.

"We went to a nice little restaurant way out somewhere, it was cozy. I really enjoyed my evening with David."

"I am so happy for you. I'm glad you enjoyed yours, 'cause I've been going crazy listening to your cell phone ring off the hook," India said.

"I accidentally left it here. Who called?"

India handed Alexis her cell phone. "I don't know. But I"ll tell you one thing, whoever it was is one desperate muthafucka'."

Alexis checked her caller ID. "Whoever it was kept calling from a private number; let me listen to my messages."

"It probably wasn't nobody but Ronald's stalking ass," India said.

"You're right. He's talkin' about he needs to talk to me, it's very important. I already know he doesn't want nothin'," Alexis said, as she deleted all ten of his messages.

"Anyways, back to the important stuff. Are you gon' see David again?" India asked while she yawned.

"I don't know, it all depends if he wants to see me again or not. I know one thing, I'm not gon' rush into nothin'." Alexis yawned too.

"You're not supposed to. Just take your time."

"He might not wanna see me after all that food I ordered," Alexis laughed.

India laughed too. "What you order, bitch?"

"Too much, 'cause I'm still full."

"That's what you get."

"Well, I'm 'bout to go home."

"I thought you were staying over here," India said.

"Girl, I got the house to myself. Tonight will be the first night that I've slept in my bed all by myself in a long time. It's gon' feel so good not having Ro'nisha's foot in my face and R.J.'s elbow in my back. I'm 'bout to enjoy myself."

"Go enjoy yourself, girl," India laughed.

"I will, trust me." Alexis stood up and gave her best friend a hug before driving home.

Alexis rushed through her front door and ran straight for the toilet. "Shit, I done pissed all over myself," she said as she squatted over the toilet seat. Alexis pulled off her clothes and walked into her bedroom, lay across the bed, and replayed the night in her head for the forth or fifth time. *I sure wish David was in the bed with me.* As Alexis drifted off to sleep with David on her mind, the phone rang, nearly scaring her to death.

"Hello," she said, looking at the alarm clock that read 4:40 A.M.

"How come you ain't been answerin' your phone?" Ronald snapped.

"Ronald, do you know what time it is?"

"Didn't you get my messages?"

"Yeah, all forty of 'em," Alexis said sarcastically.

"Well, how come you didn't call me back?"

"I was busy, Ronald, that's why I didn't call you back!"

"Busy doin' what?"

"Ronald, we are no longer together, I don't have to explain shit to you," Alexis snapped.

"You happy 'cause we're not together?"

"Ronald, look, I gotta go to work in the morning. What do you need to talk to me about?"

"I wanna know if I can come see the kids tomorrow."

"The kids are at my mom's."

"Well, I'ma pick 'em up from the daycare early," Ronald said.

"They're not going to the daycare; my mother is taking them somewhere tomorrow."

"Oh, well, can I come see you?"

"No, Ronald," Alexis said, irritated with his entire conversation.

"Alexis, can I ask you a question?"

"Yeah."

"Do you miss me?"

Alexis rolled over on her back and looked up at the ceiling. "Yeah, I do kinda miss you, but that still don't excuse that last stunt you pulled."

"I know, baby. I'm so sorry."

"Ronald, you say the same shit every time you hit me. It's time for you to start saying somethin' new."

"Alexis, I really am sorry. Since I've been over here at my mom's house, I done had a lot of time to sit back and think about how bad I treated you."

"And you saying that to say what?"

"I want you to know that I truly am sorry. Will you please forgive me?"

Alexis thought for a brief second. "I forgive you," she said sincerely.

Ronald smiled happily. He began telling Alexis about the two job interviews he had. They were having a smooth conversation and Ronald loved every minute of it. His hopes were up thinking that maybe he and Alexis would get back together like always. But this time he would treat her like she deserved to be treated . . . like always!

"That is so good, Ronald. Good luck."

"Thank you. I didn't know how to be a man until you put me out this time."

"Why this time?" Alexis inquired.

"Because I have never been away this long. So, now I realize you wasn't playing when you said I couldn't come home."

"About time. Maybe I shoulda put you out a long time ago and meant it," Alexis laughed.

Ronald laughed too. "Maybe."

"Well, Ronald, I gotta go to sleep, so I'll talk to you later." Alexis yawned.

"Later when?"

"I don't know. I'll call you tomorrow."

"I hope so, 'cause I really do miss your beautiful face," Ronald said.

Alexis all of a sudden became angry as reality set in. "You can never think my face is beautiful."

"Baby, why you say that?"

"Because if you thought my face was so beautiful, you would have kept your fist out of it!" Alexis snapped.

"Baby, I'm sor—" Before Ronald could finish his sentence, all he heard was the dial tone. "Damn!"

Chapter Nine

"Alexis, you have a call on line one," Kay-Kay buzzed in and said.

"Thank you, pass it through." She smiled, hoping that it was David.

"I thought you were gon' call me today."

Alexis's smile quickly faded when she heard Ronald's voice. "Damn, Ronald, you didn't give me time to call you. It's only nine-thirty A.M."

"I know, but I couldn't wait. I needed to hear your voice."

Alexis rolled her eyes. "Ronald, please."

"Baby, why you hang up on me last night? I called you back about five times and you didn't answer the phone."

"I know you called about five times, that's why I got these big-ass bags under my eyes, 'cause I didn't get no sleep. Look, I gotta go, I have a patient," Alexis lied.

"You gon' call me later?" Ronald asked in almost a begging manner.

"Yeah, Ronald, dang," Alexis replied.

"You promise?"

Alexis sighed heavily. "Bye, Ronald."

"Why you soundin' like I'm gettin' on your nerves?"

"Because you are, bye, Ronald." Alexis hung up the phone with a huge smile on her face. Any other time she would have been the one calling him and begging him to come see her, but now the tables had turned. *It ain't no fun when the rabbit got the gun!*

Alexis worked all day with a smile on her face.

"What's got you so happy today? It musta been your date with David," Kay-Kay said as she bobbed her head to the music that played in the background.

"That's part of it. But the other part you would not understand," Alexis said, not wanting to let Kay-Kay all up in her business.

"It's cool, girl. I'm just happy to finally see a smile on your face."

"So am I."

Keaundra moped around her house all day in her pajamas. She wasn't answering the phone for anyone; she hadn't even let the blinds up. Every time she thought about her brother marrying Beverly, she would get sick. Keaundra listened to all her messages before running herself some bath water.

"Keaundra, this is Gran, call me when you get this message."

Keaundra put her pillow over her head while her grandmother left a long, drawn-out message.

"Would you shut up already," Keaundra yelled while her grandmother rambled on. After ten hours of lying around the house and doing absolutely nothing, Keaundra finally decided to get up and fix herself something to eat. "Damn, I need to go to the grocery store," she said when she looked in the refrigerator. She opened up the cabinet, found a box of stale Wheat Thins, and ate them.

"Bitch, what is your problem," India asked as she and Alexis walked through the front door.

"What do y'all want?" Keaundra frowned.

"We wanna know how come yo' ass didn't go to work today and why you're not answering your phone," Alexis said.

"When I start needin' permission to call off work? And who pays my phone bill?"

"Bitch, don't get smart," Alexis retorted.

India intervened before things got out of hand. "What's your problem?"

Tears filled Keaundra's eyes. "I don't wanna talk about it."

"What's wrong, girl?" India asked and wrapped her arms around her best friend. Keaundra laid her head on India's shoulder and cried like a baby.

Alexis's phone started ringing; she looked at the caller ID and saw that it was David. Alexis smiled and flipped open her phone. "Hello," she answered with a huge grin on her face.

"Hey, good-looking," David said.

Alexis laughed. "Boy, you crazy."

"How was your day at work?"

"It was okay, but right now one of my girls is having a problem so I really need to call you back."

"Is she okay?"

"I don't know yet. I hope you don't mind, though."

"No, not at all. Take care of your girl and holla back at me," David responded.

"Okay, I will." Alexis pushed the end button on her phone and sat down on the sofa next to her friends.

"And I can't believe he's gon' marry her," Keaundra cried.

Alexis was lost. She did not get to hear the beginning of the conversation because she was on the phone. "Who gettin' married?"

"Kenneth," India replied.

"Well, Ke-Ke, how come you're not happy for him?" Alexis asked.

"He's marryin' Beverly." She cried harder.

"The bitch who he found in bed with his best friend?" Alexis asked, shocked.

"Yeah, she's the one," Keaundra answered.

Alexis shook her head. "Damn, that's deep."

"He wants me to accept the fact that he's marryin' that bitch. I beat that bitch's ass for him. He didn't ask me to, but I took it upon myself to do so, 'cause she disrespected him to the fullest," Keaundra said.

India rubbed the back of her best friend's head as she cried. "It's gon' be okay, Keaundra."

"No, it's not. I know she gon' end up hurtin' my brother again, but this time I'm gon' kill the bitch."

"Maybe she has changed, Ke-Ke. Just give the bitch a chance, and if you catch her slippin' an inch, then put yo' foot in her ass," Alexis said.

"I don't know, y'all." Keaundra sniffed.

"Don't do it for yourself, do it for Kenneth," India suggested.

"I don't know. It's gon' be hard."

"No one ever said it was gon' be easy," Alexis added.

"Okay, I'll try to be cordial for my brother's sake. He's having a celebration dinner over Gran's house on Saturday and he wants me there."

"Well, go then," India said.

"I'll tell you what, we'll go with you if that'll make you feel better," Alexis suggested.

Keaundra forced a weak smile. "For real?"

"You know we gotcha back," India said.

Keaundra gave each one of her friends a hug. "I don't know what I would do without y'all."

"We don't know either," Alexis and India said simultaneously.

"Now that we have that all settled, would you guys mind takin' me to get somethin' to eat? I'm starvin'," Keaundra said.

"Why don't you take your ass grocery shoppin'?" Alexis said.

"Bitch, I don't have to buy groceries, 'cause when I feed myself I have fed my entire family."

"What about this nasty black cat of yours." India grimaced.

"Don't talk about Peaches," Keaundra laughed.

Alexis and India were both happy to finally see a smile on their best friend's face. They both just prayed that it stayed that way.

Chapter Ten

Alexis lay around on the sofa watching television as her children made as much noise as they possibly could. She had a slight headache from all the yelling she had been doing all morning.

"Sit y'all asses down," Alexis screamed at the top of her lungs. Sitting up, she said, "Fine time for Mommy and Daddy to go on vacation. These kids are gettin' on my damn nerves." Alexis got up from the sofa and walked toward the kitchen.

"Mommy," Ro'nisha yelled as she ran out of her brother's room. "R.J. hit me."

"R.J., keep your hands to yourself, before I whoop you."

"She hit me first," R.J. said.

Alexis made a U-turn, peeked into her son's room and said, "Are you gettin' smart with me, little boy?" R.J. didn't respond, he just sat there and continued playing with his Power Rangers. "Do you hear me talkin' to you?" R.J. looked over his shoulder at his mother and turned back around as if Alexis had not said one word. "R.J., I'm talkin' to you."

"I heard you," he snapped.

"You betta watch that tone, young man. You only four, not fourteen, or forty." Alexis shook her head and walked away. "He gon' be just like his ignorant-ass daddy," she mumbled as she walked into the kitchen.

Alexis made lunch for her children, got them dressed, sat them down in front of the television in her bedroom, and turned on the Cartoon Network while she napped on the sofa. As soon as she had drifted off into a deep sleep, she was awakened by a loud crashing noise. She jumped up and looked around the living room.

"Ohhhh," Ro'nisha said, running out of her mother's room.

"What was that?" Alexis yelled.

Ro'nisha pointed toward her mother's room. "R.J. did it. He broke it, Mommy."

Alexis got up from the sofa and made her way toward her bedroom. When she walked into her room, she saw R.J. sitting on the floor next to her broken lamp. "How did you break my lamp, R.J.?" R.J. shrugged his shoulders. "I don't know what has gotten into you lately, but I'm 'bout to beat it right on out." Alexis stomped over to her closet and grabbed a belt.

"Oohhhh, R.J. is gon' get a whoopin'," Ro'nisha said as she watched her mother march back over to her brother.

"So?" R.J. retorted.

"Get yo' little fast ass outta here," Alexis yelled at her daughter. "Oh, so you don't care if I whoop you?" she asked her son as she towered over him. R.J. sat there and continued making his Power Rangers wrestle one another. Alexis could not believe her son was just ignoring her. She grabbed him by the arm and began whooping him. As R.J. screamed and cried, the telephone rang.

"Mommy, phone," Ro'nisha yelled from the living room, but Alexis didn't care, all she was interested in was straightening out her son.

Ro'nisha took it upon herself and answered the ringing telephone. "Hello?"

"Nisha?"

"Daddy?" Ro'nisha asked.

"Hey, Daddy's little princess. What you doin'?"

"Nothin'."

"Where's your brother?" Ronald asked.

"Gettin' a whoopin'."

"For what?" Ronald snapped.

"He broke Mommy's lamp."

"Go give yo' mom the phone," Ronald demanded.

Ro'nisha ran down the hallway with the phone held tightly in her tiny hand. "Mommy, phone."

Alexis stopped whoopin' R.J. "Who is it?" she yelled, out of breath.

"Daddy."

"What I tell you 'bout answering my damn phone, little girl? You don't pay no bills around here," she fussed as she snatched the phone out of her daughter's hand.

"I wanna go over to my daddy's house," R.J. cried.

"Shut up, you ain't going nowhere," Alexis yelled before putting the telephone up to her ear. "Hello?" she answered with an attitude.

"What the fuck you whoopin' my son for?"

"I want my daddy," R.J. cried in the background.

Alexis took the phone away from her ear for a brief second. "Shut up."

"What the fuck is yo' problem, Alexis?" Ronald asked.

"I don't have no fuckin' problem!" she snapped. "I'm just tired of your hardheaded-ass son gettin' smart with me."

Ro'nisha sat down on the floor next to her big brother. "You okay, R.J.?" she asked sincerely.

"Move!" R.J. yelled and pushed her away.

"Stop," Ro'nisha whined.

"See, that's why you be gettin' your ass whoop-ed," Alexis said, pointing at her son.

"Bring my kids over to my mom's house!" Ronald demanded. "You not gon' be over there beatin' on my shortys' like that."

"You don't run a damn thing over here, Ronald. I take care of these kids, not you," Alexis huffed.

"Just bring 'em to my mom's. I would like to see 'em."

"For what? It ain't like you live with yo' momma, nigga."

Ronald rolled his eyes and shook his head. "Who I live with then, since you know so much?"

"Tyisha."

Ronald was shocked. He didn't know how Alexis had found out about him moving in with his long time sidekick. "Who is Tyisha?" Ronald said, playing dumb.

"The same bitch who you been messin' around with for the longest time. Yo' drunk-ass momma is the one who slipped up and told me that you lived with her," Alexis replied.

"Ahhh man," Ronald laughed. "I don't know where she got her information from either, I live right here," Ronald lied. "People need to get their information right before they try to tell something on me."

"I don't know why you tryin'a deny yo' Section-Eight bitch," Alexis laughed. "The stankin' ho got three kids by four different niggas," Alexis cracked.

Ronald couldn't help but laugh himself at that one. "Man, you trippin'. I don't know what you talkin' 'bout."

"I just bet you don't."

"Are you gon' bring the kids to my mom's or not?" he said, changing the subject.

Alexis looked over at her son and then down at the broken lamp that was shattered all over the floor and said, "Yeah, I'll bring 'em over, 'cause I need a break."

"A break?" Ronald asked with sarcasm dripping from his voice. "Broad, you get a break every day the kids are always over to your parent's house. So I don't know how the kids could be gettin' on your nerves."

"I always got my kids," Alexis snapped defensively.

"Whatever! You never have the kids, and if you do, it's 'cause your parents are outta town. Where your parents now?"

"At home," Alexis lied.

"I don't believe that."

Alexis walked across the hall into her son's room and began picking him out some clothes to take with him over to his grandmother's house.

"So what you sayin', Ronald? Are you tryin'a say that I'm a bad mother or somethin'?"

"Naw, what I'm sayin' is that you need to sit yo' ass at home with the kids sometime, instead of always shovin' 'em off on your parents," Ronald stated. "Shit, they need to be callin' your mom 'Mommy' instead of 'Grandma.'"

Alexis stopped packing her son's clothes. "Well, if that's the case, they should be calling my dad 'Daddy' instead of 'Grandpa,'" Alexis shot back.

"Whatever. All I'm sayin' is that you need to let go of that nigga's dick for one day and be a mother to our children."

Alexis began gathering her son's clothes up again and placing them in his Scooby-Doo overnight bag. "What dick?"

"I know you got a nigga, Alexis. Don't play with me."

Alexis walked out of her son's room and into her daughter's room and began gathering her clothes. "I don't have nobody." She smiled. "I don't need a man in my life to make it."

"Stop the games, girl." Just as Ronald finished his sentence, Tyisha walked into the apartment with two of her girls, Ros and Khia, in tow. "I tell you what, Alexis, you betta not have no other nigga around my kids or I'm gon' beat yo' ass and then his," Ronald whispered.

"What you tryin'a whisper for? Ya hood-rat around?" Alexis said as she walked into the living room and set the children's bags by the front door.

"Naw."

"Whatever, nigga," Alexis laughed. "The kids will be at ya momma's house in about an hour."

"You gon' come in and give me some?" Ronald whispered. *Click!* "Hello?" Ronald called out, but heard nothing but a busy signal.

Tyisha walked into the kitchen where Ronald sat rolling up a blunt. "Hey, baby." She smiled down at her man.

"Hey," he said, never looking up to see the huge smile plastered all over her face.

"Who were you on the phone with?" she had the audacity to ask.

Ronald laid the blunt down and looked up at Tyisha. "Bitch, don't be questionin' me about who I'm on the phone wit'!" he snapped.

"I just asked," she said defensively.

Ronald picked the blunt back up and lit it. "I was talkin' to Alexis if you really must know."

Tyisha twisted up her face. "You talkin' about yo' baby momma?"

Ronald took a long pull from the blunt and then blew the smoke out of his mouth and nose while shaking his head yes.

"What the fuck you doin' talkin' to her?"

Ronald took one more pull from the blunt before he stood up from the table. He looked Tyisha straight in the eyes, blew the smoke into her face, and walked out the kitchen.

After Alexis dropped the children off at Ronald's mother's house, she stopped by KFC and grabbed a bite to eat before heading back home to her comfortable sofa. She grabbed the remote off the coffee table and changed the channel to Lifetime.

"Ahhhh, you hear that," she said aloud. "Peace and quiet." Just as she got comfortable and was about to take a bite out of her chicken leg, the telephone rang. "Shit," she moaned and reached over and answered it. "Hello?"

"Who the fuck is David?" Ronald shouted loudly into the phone receiver.

Alexis paused and then put her chicken back in the box.

"Hello?" Ronald yelled to make sure she was still on the line.

Alexis wiped the chicken grease on her sweats, stood, and began pacing the floor. "I'm here!" she snapped.

"Who the fuck is David?" he asked again.

"I don't know what you're talkin' about," she said smoothly. *How in the world did he find out about David?*

"Okay, keep playin' dumb with me," Ronald warned convincingly. "I already know it's the nigga who cuts R.J.'s hair."

"I don't know where you be gettin' your information from, but you need to tell them to get all the facts straight before they try to tell somethin' on me," she said, hitting him with his own words.

"Okay, smart-mouth bitch. I got my information from a reliable source."

"Who is this so-called *reliable* source?"

"You really wanna know?"

"Yeah, tell me, since your source is so reliable."

"Ro'nisha told me," he said in a matter-of-fact tone.

She talks too damn much! But that's what I get for letting her little ass answer the damn phone. Alexis became furious, not because she was mad at her daughter for running her mouth, but because her secret had been exposed. "What the fuck you over there doing, questioning my damn kids?" she hollered.

"Hell, naw. Ro'nisha brought his damn name up!" Tyisha walked into their bedroom as Ronald cussed out his baby momma. His yelling was so intense that he didn't even notice her. "So when I accused you of fuckin' that nigga, and you denied it, you really was messin' with him, Alexis." Ronald was crushed and Tyisha could hear it in his voice. Even though Ronald had been messing around on Alexis the entire time they had been together, the thought of her being with someone else made him sick to his stomach. Just as Alexis was about to tell Ronald that she didn't start talking to David until after they had broken up, he stuck his foot in his mouth. "You ain't nuttin' but a stankin'-ass ho!" he shouted. "I shoulda dogged you worse than I did, bitch!" Tyisha was frightened by Ronald's outburst. She eased her way back out of their bedroom, and stood by the door to make sure she didn't miss a word.

Alexis was shocked. Ronald had talked crazy to her in the past, but nothing could ever top the words that were popping out of his mouth at this moment.

"Bitch, that's why I cheated on yo' dumb ass the entire time I was with you," he said, hoping to hurt Alexis's feelings.

Alexis remained calm as she stood stoically in the middle of the living room. Ronald was not telling her anything she didn't already know. She just kept telling herself that one day God would send a good man her way. "Are you finished yet?" she asked in a pleasant tone.

Ronald was at a loss for words. He was expecting her to break down, start screaming and crying, but she didn't, and that made him even madder. "Fuck you, bitch! I can't believe you fuckin' my barber."

Tyisha's eyes grew big. *That bitch is fuckin' my girl, Ros, man,* she thought as she listened for more information that was pertinent.

"He only cut your hair once, and that was only because the dude who usually cut it wasn't in yet," Alexis said. "He's R.J.'s barber."

Ronald was heated because Alexis was right, so he began yelling. "Bitch, I'ma fuck you up as soon as I see you!"

Alexis shook her head before hanging up the phone, as Ronald screamed and yelled at the dial tone.

Chapter Eleven

"What's up, suga lips?" Martell said as he walked into India's condo.

"Hey, baby cakes." She smiled widely.

Martell kissed her softly on the lips. "I've missed you."

"I missed you too. What took you so long to get back home to me?"

"Oh, I had to stay an extra few days in Los Angeles to try to close a big cell phone deal," Martell said, lying down.

India straddled her man's body as he lay across her bed. "Did you close it?"

"I sure did, and to celebrate the closing of the deal I'm taking you out to dinner Saturday." He smiled.

"Martell, I already made plans for this Saturday," India said as she kissed him softly on the forehead.

"Well, cancel them. What could be more important than spending a nice quiet evening with your man?"

"Well, Keaundra asked—"

"Enough said," Martell said, cutting her off. "I shoulda known it had somethin' to do with those hood-rat friends of yours again. Now, look, India, I'm taking you to dinner on Saturday and that's that!"

"Well, what am I supposed to tell Keaundra? She really needs me."

"I fuckin' need you. Now, if you don't go to dinner with me on Saturday, than that's on you. I'll find someone who will." Martell pushed India off of him, got up, and walked out the door.

Saturday rolled around quick, a little too quickly for India's liking. She walked around the house all morning, contemplating what choice she should make. "Should I go to the party with Keaundra or should I go to dinner with Martell?" she kept asking herself. She couldn't decide, so she called the one person she knew would help her make the right decision.

"Hello?"

"Hello, Mommy?" India whined.

"Indy, my baby, how are you this morning?" her mother said in her usual cheerful tone.

"Mommy, I got a big problem."

"What is it, Indy? Do you need some money or something?"

"No, Mommy. Martell wants to take me out to dinner tonight, but I also promised Keaundra that I would go to her brother's engagement party with her. I don't know what to do," India whined.

"India, baby, that shouldn't be a hard decision to make. If Keaundra's truly your friend she should understand that your man wants to take you out to dinner."

"Mommy, I promised her. Martell gave me an ultimatum; he said if I didn't go to dinner with him then he'd find someone who would."

"India Arial Davenport, what is your problem, young lady?"

India knew when her mother called her by her full name that she meant business. "I don't have a problem, Mommy."

"You must have a problem. I don't see how choosing to go to dinner with your man over going to some engagement party with your friend is a hard decision."

"What would you suggest I do?"

"I suggest that you call Keaundra and tell her that you're not going to be able to go with her to her brother's party. And I want you to come over here and get some money so you can go to the mall and buy a nice, sexy black dress to wear out to dinner with your man," Mrs. Davenport suggested.

India let out a long breath. "Okay, Mommy, I'll be over in a bit." India hung up the phone still in the same predicament as before. She still could not decide on what to do. Martell had not bothered to call her in three days. "Maybe he doesn't wanna go to dinner anymore. That's fine with me," she said as she grabbed her car keys off the counter. As she headed to her truck, her cell phone rang. She looked at the caller ID and frowned when she saw Martell's name pop up. "Hello?"

"Hey, brown suga," he said, as if they did not just have an argument a few days ago.

Don't brown suga me, nigga! "Hey," India said in a nonchalant tone. She hoped that he would sense that she didn't want to talk to him and he would get mad and hang up on her.

"So what are you wearing tonight?" he asked.

"I don't know yet. I'm on my way to the mall." India rolled her eyes and made sure she kept all her answers short; she was still mad at him for the smart remark he had made.

"Okay, well, I'll be by to pick you up at six-thirty P.M."

"Okay." India hung up the phone and wanted to scream at the top of her lungs. She went over to her mother's house and picked up some money before heading to the mall. She shopped for hours, buying everything she would need for the night. She even bought a new panty and bra set; even though she didn't plan on giving Martell any sex, she still wanted to feel sexy. India walked through her front door at five o'clock. She listened to her messages on her answering machine while she ran some bath water. There were two messages from Keaundra, one thanking her for coming to her brother's engagement party with her, and then she had called back to thank her for being such a great friend.

India felt bad because she didn't know how she was going to tell her that she would not be able to attend Kenneth's party. She decided to call Alexis and ask her to call Keaundra and explain her situation to her, but Alexis refused. India hung up the phone and went and soaked in the tub, and hoped that she would soak away her problems.

She got out of the tub and put on her new black Gucci dress. She slid into a pair of black-wrap around Gucci stilettos and grabbed her black beaded mini micro bag out of her closet. She then sat around waiting for Martell to arrive.

Martell pulled up at exactly 6:30 P.M. He walked into the condo with a bouquette of roses and handed them to India.

"Thanks." She forced a smile, but when he turned his back, she rolled her eyes.

"You sure do look lovely," he said, eyeing her ensemble.

India returned the compliment even though she did not want to. But Martell did look good in the black, pinstriped Sean John suit he was sporting, with the white dress shirt underneath. The watch he sported from Jacob & Co. had so many diamonds in it that every time she looked at his wrist her eyes would water.

"Are you ready to go?"

India shook her head yes. She had already wasted enough of her breath talking to him. She didn't want to go to no stupid restaurant in the first place. She wanted to be over at Keaundra's grandmother's house eating some real food, with real people, with real things to talk about. But noooo, instead she had to be sitting up in some restaurant with a bunch of fake people, telling fake stories about their fake lives.

Martell began telling India about how he had settled the deal with the company in Los Angeles. She did not even bother acting interested.

"More business means more money." Martell smiled, hoping to cheer up his woman.

Money? Nigga, my daddy got more money in his piggy bank than you'll have in a lifetime, she wanted to say, but didn't. "More money, huh? That's nice. What restaurant is this way?" India asked.

"I thought I'd take you to this nice, cozy spot called Granny's Place," Martell said, trying to keep a straight face.

"It's called what?" India asked as they pulled up in front of Keaundra's grandmother's house. India smiled at her handsome man.

"We're here." Martell smiled and leaned over and kissed India softly on the cheek.

"What are we doing here, baby?"

"I thought maybe you would like to eat here with your friends instead of some place with a bunch of strangers talkin' about nothin'."

"Martell, baby, you never cease to amaze me, and that's why I love you." India leaned over and kissed her man passionately.

"I knew you wanted to be here for your friend. So I called Keaundra and asked her what time her brother's party started. You know there's nothin' I won't do for my baby." He smiled.

"I love you, Martell."

"I love you too, India Ariel Davenport."

Chapter Twelve

Kenneth and Beverly's engagement party had a nice turnout. All of their close friends and family were there to help them celebrate their special occasion. Kenneth was surprised to see Keaundra walk through the door with Alexis right behind her. He got a huge grin on his face when he saw his sister.

"Hey, sis. I'm glad you could make it." Kenneth gave her a hug and a kiss on the cheek. "What's up, Alexis?" He smiled.

"Nothin', no more." She winked. Alexis was Kenneth's first true love and the same went for her. They were each other's first everything. First kiss, first real relationship, and they even broke each other's virginity. And even though things did not work out between the two, they still had a special place in their hearts for one another.

"So you finally found someone to marry you?" Alexis smiled.

Kenneth smiled as he spoke. "Yeah, I did. Remember, you were supposed to be Mrs. Kenneth Davidson?"

"Boy, we were just kids then, we grown now. And I would have been if you wouldn't have started smelling your own ass and started screwing every bitch that had a hole," Alexis replied.

"Come on, Lexy, it wasn't even like that."

"What was it like then, Kenneth?"

"You know you're the only woman who can call me Kenneth and get away with it. For real, I got a piece of that sweet potato pie of yours and went stir crazy."

Alexis smiled.

"I had to have it at all times. When your mom wouldn't let you leave the house, I didn't know what else to do but call on someone else for it," Kenneth admitted.

Even though it had been a very long time since Alexis had any dealings with Kenneth, that statement stung a little. "It's okay, Kenneth, we were young. We live and we learn."

Kenneth gave Alexis a kiss on the cheek before walking back over to where his lovely fiancée stood talking to his best friend, Alex.

"Hi, Grandma Davidson," India said when she and Martell walked in. The house was full of people; more of Beverly's family than Kenneth's showed up for the occasion.

"Chile, I ain't seen you in a month of Sundays. How you been?"

"I've been good."

"Who is this fine piece of meat you here with?" Gran asked.

"Gran!" Keaundra shouted.

"Well, I just call 'em as I see 'em." Grandma Davidson threw her head back and let out a hearty laugh.

Martell smiled. "I'm Martell Engles." He extended his hand for Gran to shake.

She gently slapped his hand down. "I ain't one of your homeboys in the streets. I don't want no handshake; give me a hug."

"I'm sorry." Martell bent down and gave Grandma Davidson a tight hug.

"Now that's more like it. It's been a long time since this old lady had a handsome man's arms wrapped around her," Grandma Davidson laughed again.

"Gran, stop it," Keaundra laughed.

Martell and India laughed too.

"Hush up, chile. We all adults here," Grandma Davidson said as she walked away to mingle with some of the other guests.

"Y'all gotta excuse my grandmother. I am so embarrassed," Keaundra said, shaking her head.

"Don't be. Your grandmother has a lot of spunk," Martell laughed.

Keaundra, India, and Alexis stood around talking about everybody at the party while Kenneth, Martell, and some of the other men stood around and talked about sports.

"Look at that bitch over there with that cheap-ass Walmart skirt on," India said.

"It sho' is cheap," Alexis agreed.

Kenneth walked over to his sister and her friends with a huge smile on his face. "Are you lovely ladies enjoyin' talkin' about everybody?"

"Boy, shut up. We ain't talkin' about nobody," Alexis said.

"Whatever. You act like I just met you three musketeers," he laughed.

"Okay, you got us," India admitted.

"How come y'all not interacting with some of the other guests?" Kenneth asked.

Keaundra shot Kenneth a dirty look. "Don't beat around the bush, nigga. Just gon' and ask us how come we're not over there talkin' to Beverly."

"Okay, how come y'all haven't spoke to her?"

"Look, I came to this party for you, not for Beverly," Keaundra replied.

Kenneth closed his eyes and took a deep breath. "Okay, Ke-Ke," was all he could say before walking back over to the fellas to finish talking sports.

"I don't know who the fuck he think Beverly is. I ain't been talkin' to the ho, so why start now?" Keaundra snapped.

"I know that's right," Alexis and India agreed.

"Damn, that nigga is fine as hell. India is one lucky girl," Beverly said enviously, as she and her friends lusted over Martell.

"He is one fine chocolate brotha," Beverly's friend Shannon agreed. "She betta hold on to the nigga befo' I put my mack hand down on him," she said as she watched his every move.

"Okay," Beverly laughed, giving her friend a high-five.

"Kenneth is fine too," Beverly's friend Karen added. "Bitch, you 'bout to get married soon and here you are lustin' over another man. Bitches like you make it hard for a bitch like me to get a good nigga. You got one and look at you." Karen twisted up her face at her friend before walking away to fix herself a plate.

"Fuck her," Shannon shot. "Ain't nothin' wrong with lookin', as long as you don't touch," she assured her friend. "But if opportunity presents itself; you betta jump on it, girl."

If I ever get the chance, please believe I would be on him like the weave in Beyonce's head, she thought, but kept it to herself. "Girl, you know I wouldn't mess around on Kenneth."

Shannon shot her friend a dirty look. "Since when?" Shannon retorted and walked away, leaving Beverly alone as she imagined how it would feel to wake up next to Martell every morning.

The rest of the night went by pretty smoothly for the most part, other than the dirty looks that Keaundra shot Beverly from time to time. Kenneth was pleased that his sister did not get ghetto like she normally did. Even Grandma Davidson was surprised at how grown-up Keaundra acted.

"Gran, do you need any help cleaning up?" Keaundra asked as the guests started to leave.

"Naw, chile, I got it."

"You sure, Gran?"

"Yes, baby, I'm fine. G'on home and get you some rest."

Keaundra kissed her grandmother on the cheek.

"Keaundra?"

"Yes, Gran?"

"You made me so proud of you tonight."

"What was you proud of Gran?" Keaundra asked.

"I'm so glad that you didn't act a nigga fool up in here tonight," Grandma Davidson replied with a smile.

"Gran, I realized that Ken-Ken is a grown man. I can no longer fight his battles. If Beverly cheats on him again, that's between them."

Grandma Davidson smiled and gave Keaundra a hug.

Kenneth walked over to his grandmother and sister. "Thanks for coming, Ke-Ke." Keaundra didn't know what to say so she just smiled.

"So, Gran, what did you think of Mrs. Norton?" Kenneth asked.

"Chile, who is Mrs. Norton?" Grandma asked as she cleared the rest of the dirty dishes from the dining room table.

"Beverly's mom. Remember she got married again," Kenneth said.

"Oh, her? What, this make her third or fourth marriage?"

Kenneth shot his grandmother a "please don't go there" look.

"I really didn't talk to her much. But I'll tell you one thing, the apple sho' don't fall far from the tree."

Keaundra smiled. "And what do you mean by that, Gran?"

Kenneth shot his sister a dirty look.

"This woman comes in here talkin' about all these plans she has for this extravagant wedding and ain't gon' fork over one red cent. She's a user," Grandma Davidson said as she raked the remaining potato salad into a Tupperware dish.

"Gran, how can you say that about her?" Kenneth asked defensively.

"Chile, I just call 'em as I see 'em." Grandma Davidson wiped her hands on her apron and walked into the kitchen, leaving Kenneth speechless, and Keaundra satisfied.

Chapter Thirteen

Monday mornings were usually the worst for Alexis, but she had something to smile about this Monday. She had spent all of Sunday evening talking to David on the telephone. He had made her forget all about missing Ronald. They laughed and talked until they both fell asleep with the receivers still glued to their ears.

Alexis walked into the office with two big cups of cappuccino. She handed one to Kay-Kay and had one for herself. She sat at her desk with her eyes closed. She was on her way back to sleep until Kay-Kay buzzed in on her line.

"There's a delivery out here for you," she said.

Alexis opened her eyes. "From who?"

"Would you like for me to read the card and see?"

"No, nosey girl, I'm on my way out." Alexis walked out of her office into the receptionist area. There was a bouquet of beautiful pink roses sitting on the desk in front of Kay-Kay. "Those are for me?" Alexis asked, surprised. She hadn't been sent flowers since the last time Ronald put her in the hospital. Alexis picked up the card and read it aloud. "These will help chase away your Monday blues. Signed David."

"That is so sweet," Kay-Kay said. "I see somebody's been givin' it up to David."

"For your information, I have not been givin' it up to David or anybody else, thank you very much," Alexis said as she walked back to her office with a huge smile on her face. She could not wait to call Keaundra and tell her the nice thing David had done.

"Richland Bank, this is Keaundra, how may I help you?" she answered the phone, sounding all professional.

"Ke-Ke, guess what, girl?" Alexis beamed with excitement.

"What?"

"David sent me a dozen pink roses."

"Ahhh, that was so sweet of him. Do the nigga got a brotha?" Keaundra joked.

"No, but he does have a cousin named Hammer who just moved into town a few months ago."

"No, thank you. I was just joking."

"Well, girl, I gotta go. I'll see you over to India's tonight," Alexis said.

"Bye." Keuandra hung up the phone and smiled at the fact that her girl had finally found a man who did something other than put his foot off in her ass. Keaundra was outdone that Alexis had even thought about trying to hook her up with a man that neither one of them knew shit about. Alexis knew Keaundra didn't get down like that.

"Shit, Hammer could turn out to be a rapist or a serial killer for all Alexis's ass knows," Keaundra said to herself. Keaundra shook her head, laughed, and continued checking the stack of loan applications she had sitting in front of her.

Alexis and Keaundra arrived at India's house at the same time. Alexis carried her bouquet of roses while Keaundra carried a smile. As soon as they walked in, the aroma from the kitchen made their stomachs growl instantly.

"It sure smells good in here," Alexis said, setting her flowers down on the coffee table.

"It sure does," Keaundra agreed as she took her shoes off and sat down on the sofa.

"You know how I do it," India said, walking out of the kitchen with an apron on. "Awww, are these your flowers?"

"Yep."

"I'm jealous." India bent down to smell the roses before walking back into the kitchen.

"Jealous for what, hefah?" Alexis asked as she followed her friend into the kitchen.

"Cause you got roses and I didn't."

"Bitch, you got a man who owns his own cell phone company and a father who has so much money that every time he shits he can wipe his ass with a hundred dollar bill and still wouldn't be broke. They can buy you a house, a car, or anything else you want. All I got was a dozen roses," Alexis laughed.

"I'm happy for you, girl," Keaundra said, walking into the kitchen and taking a seat at the table.

Alexis smiled widely. "Thanks."

India began fixing her friends' plates. She prepared fried chicken, macaroni and cheese, green beans, and dinner rolls.

"Thanks," Keaundra said, taking her plate and setting it down in front of her to cool.

"Yeah, thanks," Alexis said, doing the same. "I been waitin' for this meal all day."

"So, when are you gon' get a man in your life?" India asked Keaundra as she sat down at the table across from her.

Keaundra rolled her eyes. "I knew this was comin'. I gotta man."

"No, a real man," India laughed.

"Fuck you, bitch. Peter is a real man."

"Peter runs on batteries, Keaundra," Alexis teased.

"That's right. And I don't have to worry about Peter cheatin' on me or puttin' his hands on me, either, now do I? And when I get tired of his ass, all I gotta do is put him back into my nightstand."

India began laughing. "Girl, you are somethin' else."

Keaundra picked up her chicken and took a bite before speaking. "I'm serious. I just don't have time for all the drama that comes along with havin' a relationship."

"I told her to let me introduce her to David's cousin, Hammer," Alexis announced.

"That would be a great idea." India gleamed.

Keaundra turned her attention to Alexis. "Do you even know what this Hammer guy looks like?"

"No, but I talked to him on the phone once and he sounds like he looks good," Alexis said, finishing off her macaroni and cheese.

"And you know if he's related to David then he has to be cute as hell," India said.

Keaundra shot India a dirty look. "Now you know damn well that ain't always the case. Look at my cousin, Darlene. The bitch is cool and all, but she looks just like a pit bull in the face."

"Not to mention the bitch smokes crack," India added with laughter.

"That broad is so ugly that you can't help but feel sorry for her," Alexis laughed as tears rolled down the side of her cheeks.

"Hold on, y'all ain't gon' be sittin' here talkin' 'bout my cousin," Keaundra tried to say with a straight face but couldn't.

"Shit, Darlene should be suing Eve for takin' her trademark," Alexis said.

"What trademark?" India asked, confused.

"The pit bull in a skirt." Alexis laughed along with Keaundra and India.

Alexis wiped the tears of laughter away from her face. "Okay, okay, enough about Ke-Ke's ugly cousin. Now let's get back to Hammer."

"What about him?" Keaundra asked.

"Well, check this out. We can all meet up at the bowling alley on Saturday," India suggested.

"Who is we?" Keaundra asked, looking at her girl as if she were crazy.

"Us ladies can meet up with David, his cousin, and Martell," India said with a huge smile on her face, hoping that Keaundra would go for it.

"I don't know, y'all," Keaundra said.

"Come on, we'll all be there." Alexis smiled widely.

"Y'all know I haven't been on a date in about three years," Keaundra said nervously.

"Well, don't think of it as a date. Just think of it as all of us gon' be there to have some fun," India replied.

Alexis smiled. "Yeah."

"What could go wrong?" India questioned.

"I guess I can go if y'all gon' be there," Keaundra said hesitantly. "But it's not a date, y'all. We all gon' be there just to have some fun, right?"

India and Alexis smiled. "Right. I'll call David and tell him that we want him and Hammer to meet us at the bowlin' alley Saturday," Alexis said, pulling out her cell phone. She hurried up and dialed David's phone number before Keaundra could chang her mind.

"Hello?" David answered.

"Hi, are you busy?" Alexis asked with a huge smile on her face and a sudden throb between her legs.

"No, not really. Why, what's up?"

"Who the fuck you on the phone wit'?" a female's voice shouted in the background. David quickly covered up the phone, hoping Alexis did not hear his ghetto ex-girlfriend shouting.

"Are you sure you're not busy? Would you like for me to call you back?" Alexis asked as she walked out of the kitchen and into the living room.

"No, no, I assure you that I'm not busy," David said, walking out of his living room and into his bedroom to get some privacy. "What's going on?"

"I was just wondering if you and Hammer had any plans for Saturday." Alexis closed her eyes and prayed that they didn't, because she knew this was the only chance she would ever get Keaundra to agree to go out on a date.

"No, we don't have any plans, why?" David asked as his ex-girlfriend beat on his bedroom door.

"Why you have to leave outta the livin' room? You coulda talk to the bitch in front of me!" she shouted, angrily.

"Who is that, David?" Alexis inquired.

"Nobody," he shook his head and said.

"Oh, so I'm a nobody now. You wasn't sayin' that last night while you was eatin' my pussy!" the female shouted.

"Broad, please," he said to his ex.

"I betta let you go, David, 'cause that female is really trippin'" Call me back when she leave."

"No. Don't pay her any attention," he pleaded.

"How can I not pay her any attention when she's shoutin' in the damn background?" Alexis grimaced. "Who is she anyway?"

"My girlfriend."

"Your girlfriend?" Alexis asked, shocked.

"I mean my ex-girlfriend," David said, correcting his mistake.

"He said it right the first time. Bitch, I am his girlfriend!" the female shouted.

"She's not my girlfriend," David said angrily.

"Look, call me back later when your company leaves." Alexis hung up the phone and walked back into the kitchen where India and Keaundra sat with smiles on their faces. Alexis couldn't tell them about the drama that was going on over to David's because she knew they would start talking shit, and then she really wouldn't be able to get Keaundra to go to the bowling alley.

"So, what did he say?" Keaundra asked anxiously.

As much as Alexis hated to lie to her girls, she had no other choice because she did not want to see her girl Keaundra disappointed once again.

"Yeah, what did he say?" India smiled.

"It's on and poppin'," Alexis said with a huge grin.

"Oh my goodness, y'all! What am I gon' wear, what am I gon' talk about? Is he gon' think I'm cute?" Keaundra asked nervously. "I don't think I can go through with this."

"Trust me, you'll be just fine. We'll get you together," India assured her best friend.

Keaundra smiled. "That's why I love y'all."

"We love you too," Alexis said, and gave her girl a hug before finishing off the rest of her cold dinner.

Chapter Fourteen

Alexis went by her parents' house and picked up the kids after dinner. She drove around the block a few times to make sure Ronald was not lurking before pulling up into her apartment complex. R.J. was in the back seat, asleep, while Ro'nisha had kept herself occupied with a toy she had gotten out of a Happy Meal.

"R.J., wake up," Alexis said to her sleeping son. When he didn't budge, she called out to him again. "R.J., honey, get up, we're home."

R.J. sat up and looked around. "Is Daddy home?" he asked in a sleepy tone.

"No, sweetie, remember what we talked about? This isn't Daddy's home anymore," Alexis said, and hoped that her son would understand.

"I want my daddy," R.J. began to cry.

"Your daddy isn't here, R.J. so get outta the car," Alexis said as calmly as she could.

"I want my daddy!" R.J. yelled.

Alexis shook her head and got out of the car. She opened up the back door, unbuckled Ro'nisha out of her car seat, and held her hand out for R.J. to grab.

R.J. sat in the car and cried. "I want my daddy. I want my daddy." Tears ran down his soft brown cheeks as he yelled the same thing over and over.

"Come on, R.J., get outta the car. Your daddy isn't here," Alexis said, trying to stay calm.

"No! I want my daddy," he yelled.

Alexis took a deep breath while Ro'nisha struggled to get out of her arms. "Be still, girl," Alexis warned. When Ro'nisha began to cry, Alexis closed her eyes and began counting. Her cell phone rang before she reached ten. She put Ro'nisha down on the ground between her legs, dug through her purse, and pulled out her cell. She checked the caller ID. "I'll talk to you later, David," she said to the phone and threw it back into her purse. She leaned into the car and yanked R.J. out by his arm.

"I want my daddy, I want my daddy, I want my daddy," he screamed louder and louder.

Alexis didn't want to make a bigger scene because her nosey neighbors were already looking out of their windows, so she leaned down and began talking to her son in a nice and calm manner. "R.J., if you stop cryin', Mommy will call Daddy when we get into the house, okay?'

R.J. stopped crying as his chest heaved in and out. "Okay." He sniffed.

Alexis picked Ro'nisha up again and they all walked into the house. Alexis did what she promised her son she was going to do, even though she did not want to. She pulled her cell phone out of her purse and dialed Miss Jane's phone number.

Alexis and Miss Jane had not gotten along since the first time Alexis had to call the police on Ronald. Even though Alexis suffered two broken ribs and a sprained ankle, Miss Jane thought that Alexis was dead wrong for getting the police involved and felt that she should have handled the situation differently. So Alexis had cut all ties with Ronald's mother except where the children were concerned. She hated the fact that Miss Jane protected her son even when he was wrong.

"Hmph! Ronald, come get this damn phone," Miss Jane hollered.

Alexis was so glad she did not have to cuss Miss Jane's drunk ass out, but she would have if she needed to.

"Hello?" Ronald answered with a smile.

"Here," Alexis said, handing the phone to her son.

"Hello, Daddy?" R.J. sniffed.

"What's up, big man?" Ronald answered.

"Can I come over to your house?" R.J. asked.

"Tell ya momma to bring you over to Grandma Jane's house," Ronald told his son.

R.J. looked up at his mother as he spoke. "Daddy said bring me to Grandma's house."

"Not tonight, honey," Alexis said as sweetly as possible.

R.J. began to cry all over again.

"What she say, man?" Ronald asked, already knowing the answer by the sound of his son's cries.

Here we go again, Alexis thought.

"Put yo' mommy on the phone," Ronald said to his son. R.J. handed Alexis the phone as he continued to cry.

"What, Ronald?" Alexis answered in a rude tone.

"How come you can't bring him over to my momma's house?" Ronald huffed.

"Because for one, it's past his bedtime and for two, your momma lives too far away."

"Well, I'm 'bout to have my uncle Johnny drop me off over there so I can see my kids, then."

Nice try, she thought. "Didn't you just here me say that it's past their bedtime?"

"Oh, so you tryin'a keep me from seein' my kids? Don't fuckin' play wit' me 'bout my kids, Alexis," Ronald warned.

Alexis chuckled before speaking. "Nigga, please. You don't give two shits about these kids, 'cause if you did, I would have never had to pay for daycare

while yo' tired ass sat at home all day playin' that
damn Playstation."

Ronald became serious. "Alexis, I really do
miss my kids." Alexis could hear the sincerity in
Ronald's voice and almost packed the kids up to
head to his mother's house just before he stuck
his foot in his mouth. "And I miss makin' love to
you, too."

"Bye, Ronald. I'll bring the kids by your mother's house tomorrow, maybe."

"How come I can't come by to see my kids
tonight?"

Alexis had another call coming in on her other
line. "I'll bring them over tomorrow. I got another call comin' in so I gotta go."

"Who is it; your boyfriend?" Ronald asked
sarcastically.

"Bye, Ronald." Alexis hung up on him and
clicked over. "Momma gon' take you to McDonald's tomorrow if you stop cryin'," she said to her
son quickly. R.J. smiled and said okay before
heading to his bedroom to play with his Power
Ranger toys. "Hello?' she answered.

"Hey, how are you?" David asked, hoping she
was not mad about his ex-girlfriend's charade
earlier.

"I'm fine," Alexis cooed, still a little upset
about the female yelling in the background earlier. Alexis wanted to cuss David out and hang

up on him, but she had no right to because they were not officially a couple.

"Sorry about earlier," David said after an awkward silence.

"What you sorry for?"

"For my ex-girlfriend acting a fool when she came to my house."

What the fuck was the bitch over your house for? "Oh, okay," she said as nonchalantly as possible. Alexis did not want David to know that she was jealous that he had another woman at his house, his ex to be exact. She wanted to be the only woman allowed at his house, the only woman kissing his soft, sexy lips, and the only woman lying in his bed taking up most of his time.

"Don't you wanna know what she was over here for?"

Hell fuckin' yeah! she wanted to say, but said, "Not really. That's y'all business."

I like that about her, David thought. "Well, I'm gon' tell you anyway."

"That's up to you" Alexis stated calmly. "You really don't have to."

"Well, I wanna tell you."

Well, hurry the fuck up before I explode then.

"She came over here to get the rest of her things. My cousin Hammer let her in, but he didn't know that he wasn't supposed to. She had been calling all day and I told her that I would drop her shit off at her apartment, but she popped up over here anyway."

"Oh," Alexis replied uncaringly.

"I don't want you to think that I'm tryin'a play games with you."

"I don't think that."

"So, enough about my ex, what do you have planned for me and Hammer this weekend?"

"I was wondering, well, me and my friend Ke-aundra were wondering if you and Hammer would like to join us at the bowling alley on Saturday?" Alexis crossed her fingers while waiting for him to answer.

"I'm game and I'm sure Hammer is too."

"How do you know Hammer is game to go to the bowling alley when you didn't even ask him?"

"Look, the way my cousin has been talkin' about gettin' some ass, I know he's game."

Alexis got heated—quick. "Hold on, nigga, who said anything about your cousin gettin' some ass from my friend?"

"No, no, I didn't mean it like that, I just know that he wouldn't mind going out with someone other than me, preferably a female," David replied apologetically.

"Ummm-hummm, you betta had meant it that way."

"Alexis, I'm for real, that's what I meant. I don't know your girl, but I do know you and I know that you wouldn't hang around someone who would give it up on the first date."

Shit, you don't know me too well then, 'cause I done gave it up on the first date plenty of times, she thought. "Okay, whatever you say. So it's on for Saturday, right?"

David smiled. "It's on for Saturday."

Alexis talked to David while she got her kids ready for bed, and before she knew it, it was going on five o'clock in the morning.

Saturday rolled around and Keaundra was more scared than anxious. She had spent all morning in the beauty shop. Once Tonya finished with her hair, Keaundra could not believe her eyes. Tonya had managed to straighten out all her natural curls and flip her hair up. Keaundra was so pleased she could hardly stop looking at herself in the mirror. She looked at her watch and decided to go all out and get her hands and feet done since she had a couple of hours before India and Alexis were to meet her at the mall to help her pick out an outfit.

She tried on about thirty different outfits that her girls picked out for her; some were too provocative while others just weren't her style. Alexis wanted her to wear a short denim skirt, and India had picked out a long denim skirt with a split that went all the way up to her crotch. Keaundra declined all the outfits before deciding on a pair of Apple Bottom jeans and an all-white T-shirt. After all, they were going bowling, not to a club. She purchased a pair of comfortable all-white Nike Air sneakers to complete her ensemble.

Keaundra finally made it home but not before stopping by Victoria's Secret for a new panty and bra set, and Bath & Body Works for some candy apple lotion and body spray. Lastly, she made a pit stop by Walmart to purchase some groceries and beverages just in case she had company later on that night. As she put away the last of the food, her phone rang.

"Hello?" she answered.

"Hey, sis," Kenneth said.

"Hey, Ken, what's goin' on?" she asked cheerfully.

"Nothin'. I just wanted to hear your voice, that's all.'

"Well, you hear it."

Kenneth sat on the phone quietly.

"Ken, are you all right?" Keaundra asked concerned.

"Yeah, I'm okay," he said, and got quiet again.

"No you're not. Ken, tell me what's the matter with you."

"I was just thinkin' about Momma, that's all."

"You miss her a lot, don't you?"

"Don't you?"

"You know I do, Ken, but she's in a better place."

"I know. It's just that today is her birthday," Kenneth said sadly.

Keaundra was so wrapped up in getting ready for her date that she had forgotten all about it being their mother's birthday. She sat down on the sofa and put her head in her hand. She couldn't tell her brother that she had forgotten all about it. Tears fell from her eyes as she sat quietly.

"Ke-Ke, are you still there?" Kenneth asked.

"Yeah . . . yeah, I'm still here," she said as the tears steadily flowed.

"Well, I was just callin' to hear your voice," Kenneth said after about five more minutes of silence.

"Okay."

Keaundra grabbed the pillow from the sofa and held it like she was trying to hold on for dear life. Ever since she and her brother were little it seemed they had been dealt a bad hand. It was bad enough having an abusive father and everybody knowing about it, but then they had to deal with being made fun of by all the neighborhood kids when their father killed their mother.

Keaundra thought about all the times she had run home from elementary school in tears. Her grandmother would wrap her arms around her and try to rock away her pain before sitting her down at the kitchen table and placing a piece of apple pie and a nice cold glass of milk in front of her. Once Keaundra made it to middle school, she made a promise to herself and to her brother that the first person who made a crack about their mother, she was going to crack their skull, and she did just that. It didn't matter how big or small, male or female, Keaundra would handle her business.

Once Keaundra got to whoopin' ass on a regular basis, everyone else got the message and quit cracking jokes because they didn't want to fall victim to the ass whoopin's she was handing out.

Keaundra looked over at her mother's picture that sat on top of her mantel. She slowly walked over, picked the picture up, and wiped the dust away from her mother's beautiful face. Keaundra admired her mother's smile and petite body. She smiled through her tears as she spoke to her mother.

"Happy birthday, Mommy. I miss you so much. I would give my own life just to have you here. You didn't deserve to die. That man who we called

Daddy took you away from us and ripped our lives apart. He caused so much pain to all of us. He's the reason why I cannot love or trust any man other than God. You don't know how hard it is to want to be loved, but be too afraid because you can't love back. It ain't fair, Mommy, it ain't," Keaundra cried. "One day I'm gon' find someone to love me and I'm gon' love him back, all because I know you would want it that way." She kissed her mother's picture and placed it back on the mantel, wiped her tears away, and began cleaning her house before getting ready for her date.

Chapter Fifteen

"Aren't you ready yet?" Martell asked India as he stood in the bathroom doorway and watched as she brushed her teeth.

"Almost," she said after spitting the toothpaste out of her mouth. Martell shook his head. "You know I gotta look good for my man."

"Yeah, but why does it take you so long to get ready? It took you three hours to put on a pair of pants, a shirt, and a pair of boots," he said with a smile plastered on his face.

"No, get it right. It took me three hours to put on a pair of black Dolce & Gabbana slacks, a cream sheer blouse by Cesare Paciotti, and my all-time favorite cream Coach boots," India bragged.

Martell playfully waved her off. "Whatever. Are you ready to go now?"

"Martell, don't get mad 'cause I'm beautiful," India joked.

"Shit, if it takes you three hours to beautify yourself, then you must be hiding somethin'."

"Somethin' like what?" she inquired as she checked her flawless makeup in the bathroom mirror.

"A whole bunch of ugliness," he laughed.

"Forget you," India laughed, punching him on the shoulder. "I can't help that it only takes you ten minutes to throw on a pair of jeans, a shirt, that watch, that whack-ass hat, and a pair of cheap tennis shoes."

"No, get it right," he said, imitating her. "It took me ten minutes to put on a pair of Five Star Vintage jeans, a crisp white button-down by Steve Madden, my watch that was made by Gucci, my white hat that was designed by Kangol, and my all-time favorite sneakers designed by Jordan," he laughed.

"Come on, nigga," India laughed as they headed out the door.

Martell unlocked the doors to his truck. He looked over at his beautiful woman and smiled.

"What are you smiling at?" she asked as she opened up the door.

"I'm the luckiest man alive," Martell said, opening up the door and getting in.

"How so?" India asked, getting in and buckling her seatbelt.

"I got my own business, a beautiful woman, and a fat-ass bank account. What more could a brotha ask for?" he said as he started the truck and backed out the driveway.

India smiled. "I guess you are one of the luckiest men in the world because you do have me."

"Well, when you gon' become my wife?" Martell asked as he weaved in and out of traffic.

"When you gon' ask me to become your wife?" India said as she checked her makeup in the sun visor mirror for the third time.

"Soon. Real soon."

"We'll see." She smiled.

"When you gon' let a brotha move in?" Martell asked before turning left on Park Avenue.

India rolled her eyes into the top of her head. *Here we go again.* "Martell, please, I don't wanna talk about that right now."

"You don't ever wanna talk about it," he said, catching an attitude. "Every time I mention us living together you try to change the damn subject."

Thank God the bowling alley is right down the street, she thought as she ignored Martell's last comment.

Martell pulled up into the bowling alley, parked the car and got out, slamming the door behind him, and leaving India sitting alone.

"Well, fuck you, too," she said to Martell, but he was already inside of the building. India checked her makeup one last time before getting out of the truck to join her angry man. Once she arrived into the bowling alley, she went straight to the bar and stood beside Martell.

"What you drinking?" he said, never making eye contact because he still had an attitude.

"I want a shot of tequila," she said, sitting on the barstool. India laid her purse on top of the bar, pulled her cell phone out, and called Keaundra's cell phone.

"Hello?" Keaundra answered.

"Where y'all at?" India asked as the bartender set her drink down in front of her.

"We 'bout to pull up right now. Is David and Hammer there yet?"

India took a quick glance around the bar. "Not yet."

"Are they in there?" Alexis asked Keaundra. She shook her head. "Okay, we're on our way in." Keaundra hung up her cell phone and waited for Alexis to park the car. She opened the door and got out. As she was about to shut the door, Alexis's cell phone rang. "Maybe that's David sayin' that they've changed their minds," Keaundra said, disappointed.

Alexis checked her cell phone. "Nope, this is Ronald's dumb ass. Go ahead and go in; I'll be in there in a few minutes."

Keaundra shook her head and smiled before walking into the bowling alley.

"Hello?" Alexis answered her phone, slightly annoyed.

"What the hell took you so long to answer the fuckin' phone?" Ronald snapped.

Alexis grimaced. "What do you want, nigga?"

"How come you haven't brought my kids over to see me?"

"I've been busy," Alexis said, licking her lips before applying more lipstick.

"Busy doin' what?"

"Busy takin' care of Alexis, that's what."

"Where you at?" Ronald asked calmly.

"Out."

"Out where and with who?" Ronald began to get agitated.

"I'm out with my girls," Alexis replied smartly, hearing the agitation in Ronald's voice.

"I think you fuckin' them bitches!" Ronald shouted angrily.

"Ronald, shut the fuck up!"

"Oh, don't act like you don't go both ways. Remember Sexy-C at the club?" Ronald smiled, bringing up old memories Alexis wanted to forget about.

"Fuck you, nigga!" Alexis hung up the phone and threw it into her purse before getting out of the car. She attempted to press the wrinkles out of her pants before walking into the bowling alley. As she sat at the bar next to her friends, her cell phone rang. She looked at the caller ID; it was David. She closed her eyes and said a little prayer before answering it. She prayed that he hadn't changed his mind, and was calling to tell her that he was running late and on his way.

"Hello?" she answered.

"We're outside. Where you at?"

"We're at the bar. Come on in." Alexis smiled before thanking God.

"What you wearing?" he asked seductively. Hammer looked over at his cousin and shook his head.

Alexis blushed. "I don't have on anything."

"Oooohhh, I can't wait to see you." David hung up the phone and got out of the car. He put his hand up to his mouth and blew into it, checking his breath. Pleased with the results, he smiled and walked into the bowling alley with Hammer behind him.

Oh, my God, Keaundra thought as she watched David walk into the bar with a dark-skinned brotha who looked like he was straight out of a fairy tale. This brotha was so fine that he had to be a mirage. Keaundra closed her eyes and opened them back up just to make sure that her mind wasn't playing tricks on her. Hammer was around six feet tall, with the body of a Greek god.

She could tell that he worked out on a regular basis by the size of those pythons that protruded through his shirt. His smooth, dark skin looked like her black silk sheets, and his lips were thick and juicy like two T-bone steaks. Keaundra imagined them locked to hers and quickly threw the thought out of her head as they approached the bar.

Alexis stood up and smiled as she greeted David. "Hey."

David smiled and gave her a tight hug. "This is my cousin, Hammer." He pointed behind him.

Hammer's pearl-white smile practically lit up the bar. "Hello," he said with his sexy, deep voice.

Keaundra was so mesmerized by this fine hunk of sweet chocolate who stood before her she couldn't even speak. All she could do was smile and shake her head. It was definitely a case of love at first sight.

"This is Keaundra," Alexis said, pointing to her friend.

Hammer smiled, pleased with the sight of this beautiful woman, and he stuck out his hand. Keaundra placed her hand in his and he turned it over, and kissed it softly. Keaundra could feel herself getting wet so she closed her legs and pressed them tightly together.

Alexis smiled because she could see how happy her friend was. She introduced David and Hammer to the rest of her friends before they all moved to a table in the middle of the bar. They ordered several rounds of drinks before going out to bowl.

Keaundra was nervous at first, but after a few shots of tequila, the nervousness flew out the window. They all laughed and talked as the girls put a whoopin' on the men. The men blamed it on the liquor, but the women knew better than that. As the night flew by and the liquor started wearing off, everyone was getting tired.

Martell checked his watch. "Well, it's gettin' late."

"Yeah," David agreed. "It's almost midnight."

"It was fun kickin' y'all asses," India laughed.

"It sure was," Alexis and Keaundra agreed.

Hammer laughed too. "Next time we gon' win."

Keaundra rolled her eyes. "Whatever."

"It really was nice meeting you all," Hammer said as he took off his bowling shoes and placed his own shoes back on.

"Same here," Martell said, giving him a firm handshake. "Come on, baby," he looked over at India and said. India grabbed him by the arm, laid her head against it, and waved over her shoulder to everybody.

Alexis watched as she and Martell exited the bowling alley. "My girl is drunk," Alexis laughed.

"You know she can't drink," Keaudra said as she buttoned up her jacket.

"She sure fooled the hell outta me," Hammer laughed.

"She was just tryin' to hang wit' the big dogs, trust me," Alexis said.

David looked at his watch. "Can I walk you to your car?" Alexis smiled and followed David out of the bowling alley.

Keaundra's nervousness flew right back into the window as she watched her friend and David walk away. All of a sudden she didn't know what to say or if she should say anything. When all of her friends were there, she knew all the right words to say, but now that it was just she and Hammer, she was dumbfounded. She fiddled with the buttons on her jacket to try to hide her nervousness. Hammer walked over to her, grabbed her hand, and smiled.

"Why you so nervous?" he asked.

"I'm not nervous," she chuckled.

"Sure you're not," he said, still holding on to her hand. "I really had a nice time with you and your friends."

"I enjoyed myself also," she said, grabbing her button with her free hand. Hammer grabbed her other hand and kissed it gently.

"Can I call you sometime?" he asked, letting go of her hands.

Keaundra smiled at Hammer. "Sure, I would like that."

"Come on; let me walk you to the car." Hammer grabbed her by the hand and lead her out of the bowling alley. When they arrived outside they noticed that David and Alexis were nowhere in sight. "That's funny, David's car was parked right over there," he said, pointing to an empty parking space.

"Well, Alexis's car is still here," she said, pointing to it. They walked over to Alexis's car and Keaundra opened up the door. The keys were in the ignition and there was a letter left on the seat, written in eyeliner.

Girl, have fun and don't do nothin' I wouldn't do, Love Alexis.

Keaundra smiled and handed the letter to Hammer so he could read it. He smiled as well.

"Well, I guess you gotta take me home," Hammer said, getting in.

I wish I could take you to my house, she thought as she walked around to the driver's side and got in. Keaundra was so nervous that when she started up the car she put it in neutral instead of drive. She pressed down on the gas and the engine revved up. She was so embarrassed as she placed the car in drive and pulled off. For a brief second, she had forgotten how to drive. She and Hammer talked as she drove. She took the long way to David's house because she wanted to spend as much time as she could with this fine brotha. When she finally turned onto David's street, they both noticed David's car in the driveway, but all the lights were out. Hammer pulled out his cell phone and called his cousin.

"Hello?" David answered out of breath.

"Why you leave me, cuz?"

David laughed as Alexis nibbled on his ear. "I didn't leave you. You got a ride, didn't you?"

"I feel you. Um, what time is yo' company leaving?" Hammer asked.

"I don't know. Why, what's up?"

"Uh, I would like to go to bed," Hammer replied.

"Oh, where y'all at, man?"

"We're outside."

"Well, come on in the house and go to bed," David said.

Hammer was really tired, but as badly as he wanted to go to bed, he couldn't mess up his cousin's groove. He didn't want David to think he was trying to cock-block. "Naw, I'm cool. I'll just get a room for the night."

"Naw, man, it ain't even like that, come on in. We not doing nothin'."

"Naw, man. Go ahead and do you. Like I said, I'll just get a room for the night," Hammer quickly replied.

"You can sleep on my sofa." Keaundra heard her voice say it, but didn't know where the words came from.

Hammer looked over at Keaundra. "Are you sure?" he asked. "I don't wanna be a burden or anything."

"Yeah, I'm sure. I don't got roaches or nothin'." *Thank God I cleaned up my house today.*

"You coming in or what, nigga?" David asked.

"Naw, I'm cool. Keaundra said I can crash on her sofa tonight," Hammer said, smiling at Keaundra.

"Straight up?"

"I'll talk to you in the morning." Hammer hung up the phone.

David rolled over, looked at Alexis, and smiled.

"What you smiling for?" Alexis asked.

"Hammer is stayin' the night over yo' girl's house."

"Whaaaat?" Alexis smiled, surprised.

"You heard me. Maybe my cousin is gon' get some ass after all," David laughed and kissed Alexis on her soft lips.

Alexis laughed before kissing him back. "Don't count on it." Alexis and David lay in the bed in each other's arms and talked until they both fell asleep.

Chapter Sixteen

Keaundra walked into her house with Hammer close behind her, and as soon as she flipped on the light, Peaches jumped up on the back of the sofa like always.

"Whoa!" Hammer said, startled. "It doesn't bite, do it?"

Keaundra laughed. "Naw, boy, she don't bite. Hammer, meet Peaches; Peaches meet Hammer." Peaches buried her head into Keaundra's stomach and she rubbed her silky, black cat like she always did. Once she stopped rubbing Peaches, the cat jumped down off the back of the sofa and ran off to pay a visit to her litter box.

"I didn't know you had a roommate," Hammer said, taking a seat on the sofa.

"Who, Peaches? She's no roommate; she's more like my child." Keaundra walked over to the coffee table, picked the remote up, and turned on the television. She flipped through the channels until she found something that she thought might look interesting to Hammer. She handed him the remote and disappeared down a long hallway that led her to the linen closet. *Thank God I washed all my clothes today.* She pulled a sheet and her best down comforter out of the closet, and smelled it before heading back toward the living room.

"Here," she said, handing Hammer the sheet and the comforter. "I forgot your pillow." Keaundra made her way back down the same hallway that also led to her bedroom. She changed into something more comfortable while she was in there.

"You have a nice house." Hammer called out as he tucked the sheet into the sofa. He admired her tiny but cozy living room. She had nice taste. She had a sage green micro-fiber sofa with the chair to match. Her walls and carpet were both light peach and she added some red here and there just to bring a little more spark into the room. She had gold picture frames on all four walls that were occupied with her and a guy who somewhat resembled her. She also had a picture framed in gold sitting on top of her mantel. Hammer thought that her fifty-two-inch plasma TV took up a lot of space, but it still looked and felt like home to him.

"Thanks," she said as she entered the living room wearing a pair of sweats, a T-shirt, and a pair of fuzzy slippers. Keaundra smiled and handed him the pillow that smelled just like Downy. Keaundra watched as Hammer removed his shoes. *Oh, my goodness*, she thought as she lusted over how big this man's feet were. She wasn't sure, but she could have sworn she felt a drop of slobber escape down the side of her mouth as she watched Hammer remove his shirt. *Look at them biceps*, she thought as she watched his every move.

Hammer smiled when he noticed Keaundra watching him. "You see somethin' you like?" he asked boldly as he neatly folded up his shirt and put it on the arm of the chair.

Keaundra laughed nervously. "Naw, dummy." She began fiddling with the string that hung from her sweats.

Hammer walked over to her and grabbed her hand.

She quickly snatched it away. "Would you like somethin' to drink?" she asked, taking a step back and looking down at the floor.

Noticing her nervousness, Hammer took her up on her offer. "Yes, please. My mouth is kinda dry." He took a seat on the sofa and pretended to be interested in the show that was on television.

Keaundra turned around and headed toward the kitchen. *Why am I so nervous?* she thought as she entered the kitchen and opened up the refrigerator. *It's not like I'm a virgin or anything. I don't know what it is.* Keaundra grabbed a can of Pepsi and called out to Hammer. "I have Pepsi, orange juice, and bottled water, which would you like?"

"I'll take a water," he called out from the living room while he got comfortable on the sofa.

Keaundra put the can of Pepsi down, grabbed the bottle of water, and took a deep breath before walking back into the living room where Hammer sat comfortably on the sofa. "Here you go." She smiled and handed him the water. "Well, if you need anything else, make yourself at home."

"Thanks." He smiled, taking the water. "I don't have to worry about Peaches attacking me while I'm asleep, do I?" He joked.

Keaundra began laughing. "Naw, man."

Hammer laughed too. "Well, I'm sure you've seen that show *When Animals Attack.*"

"Hammer, Peaches is just a harmless little kitten." No sooner did Keaundra get the entire sentence out of her mouth, than out jumped Peaches and landed on Hammer's lap.

"Whoa!" he yelled and quickly pushed Peaches off of him.

Keaundra laughed so hard, she nearly pissed on herself.

"See, I told you," Hammer said as he stood up. He was mad at first, well, more scared than mad, until he saw the huge smile on Keaundra's beautiful face. For some odd reason, her smile made his heart flutter.

"I'm sorry," Keaundra said, trying to control her laughter. "Bad cat!" she yelled, still laughing.

"You're not sorry," Hammer said as he began to laugh himself after thinking about how stupid he must have made himself look for screaming over a harmless cat.

"Yes, I am," Keaundra said. "I don't know what got into her. I've never seen her do anybody like that. She usually doesn't bother with anybody but me."

"Shit, I can't tell." Hammer looked around the room to see where Peaches had disappeared to.

"She's not gon' come back in here," Keaundra tried to assure him. "I think you scared her off."

"Fuck that, I ain't goin' to sleep! I'll just sit up all night."

Keaundra smiled in an almost laughing manner. "Would you like me to stay in here with you?"

"Please do," he said, looking around the room again. Keaundra sat down in the chair as Hammer eased his muscular body down on the sofa. He was still a little uneasy at first, but soon got comfortable once he spotted Peaches walking down the long hallway and disappearing into one of the rooms.

"You watchin' this?" she asked, pointing at the television.

Hammer shook his head and handed her the remote. His hand lightly brushed hers as she took it. The chill that went through her body the moment he purposely touched her was electrifying. She began surfing the channels as thoughts of making love to this fine, masculine man danced around in her head. She smiled at the thought and quickly passed it off as foolishness.

"What you smiling for?"

Keaundra was so embarrassed because she didn't know Hammer was watching her. "Oh, nothin'. I was just thinking 'bout somethin' that happened at work the other day," she lied.

"Let me in on it. I wanna smile too."

Keaundra smiled again as the thought raced through her mind again. "You had to be there."

"I see." Hammer turned his attention back to the television.

Keaundra watched as Hammer yawned. "You tired?"

"Not really," he said and yawned again.

Keaundra's neck and back were starting to hurt as she sat in the chair. She tried rubbing her aches away, but it didn't work.

"You wanna sit over here with me?" Hammer asked noticing her rubbing her neck and back.

"No thanks."

"Come on, I don't bite." Keaundra couldn't resist that million-dollar smile, and got up out the chair and sat down next to him on the sofa. "You feel better?"

Keaundra smiled and nodded. She and Hammer sat on the sofa watching a marathon of *Three's Company* in silence until they both fell asleep.

Keaundra slowly opened her eyes as the spring morning sun shined through her half-opened blinds down onto her glowing face. She looked over at Hammer and smiled as he rested his head on the arm of the sofa. He was still sound asleep, so she thought. *Damn, he looks like a sleeping beauty,* she thought as she attempted to get up off the sofa, but was pulled back down by Hammer's strong hand.

"Where you going?" he asked, never once opening his eyes.

"I gotta pee," she lied as she stood back up. She really wanted to go into the bathroom and brush her morning breath away just in case Hammer wanted to talk or, better yet, kiss. Keaundra was a firm believer in the old saying "you never get a second chance to make a first impression." So she couldn't have her breath smelling like "I'll be damned" and blow the chance of this fine brotha ever wanting to see her again.

Hammer lifted his head up off the arm of the sofa and opened his eyes. "Hurry back." Hammer laid his head back down and closed his eyes again.

Keaundra rushed down the hallway and into the bathroom. She grabbed her toothbrush and the toothpaste out of the medicine cabinet and began brushing her teeth. Trying to move as quickly as possible because she didn't want Hammer to think that she was in there taking a dump. She flushed the toilet so it would seem like she really did use it. She turned the water on and acted like she was washing her hands as she spit the toothpaste in the sink. She wiped the leftover toothpaste away from around her mouth as she quickly grabbed the Listerine and poured some into her mouth. She swished it around for a few seconds before spitting it into the sink. Keaundra looked at her face in the mirror to make sure her eyes weren't filled with crust, and smiled at her reflection before walking out of the bathroom and back down the hall toward the living room.

Hammer must have heard her coming out of the bathroom because once she reached the living room, he held out his hand for her to grab, still never lifting his head or opening his eyes.

Keaundra took his hand and he pulled her down close beside him. At first, she felt uneasy, but once Hammer let her know that it was safe, she snuggled up against his warm body and rested her head on his chest. She couldn't begin to remember the last time she had been with a man, and she really didn't remember it ever feeling this good.

Keaundra was on cloud nine. The feeling Hammer gave her took her places no man had ever taken her before. As she lay with her eyes closed, she felt him wrap his arm around her body and then she snuggled even closer and stayed that way until she drifted back off to sleep. As she slept, she began dreaming of Hammer picking her up off the sofa and carrying her into her bedroom, gently laying her down on the bed, and then removing her clothes while planting soft kisses all over her naked body.

Keaundra started getting wet as she watched Hammer kissing his way down her stomach, making his way to her pot of gold. Just as his tongue was about to do a swan dive into her soaking wet pussy, the telephone rang.

"Shit," Keaundra said as her eyes popped open, taking her away from her dream. She climbed off the sofa, walked into the kitchen, and snatched the phone off the hook. "Hello?" she answered with a slight attitude.

"Well, good morning to you too, cranky-ass hefah!" Alexis said into the receiver.

Keaundra's mood slightly changed. "I'm not cranky," she lied.

"Anyway, what's up? I didn't interrupt y'all gettin' y'all groove on, did I ?" Alexis asked, laughing.

"Naw, fool," Keaundra laughed as she looked around to see if Hammer was in her presence. "What type of woman do you take me for?"

"I take you for a woman who's in need of some dick!" Alexis retorted.

"Alexis?" Keaundra gasped, surprised.

Alexis began laughing. "What? Well, it's true, ain't it?"

Keaundra switched the phone from one ear to the other and leaned up against the kitchen counter. "What did you call me for anyways?" she asked, ignoring her friend's question.

"Oh, yeah," she chuckled. "David wants to know if you could drop Hammer off at home when he's ready to go. He said he would pick him up, but he has to drop his car off at the auto shop because it's making some strange clanking noise."

Keaundra pushed herself off the counter with her butt as she stood straight up on both feet. "I don't mind," she replied. "Matter of fact, I'll take him right now so I can hit the gym."

"Dang, why you tryin'a get rid of the nigga so soon? You don't like him?"

"He's cool," she whispered so Hammer couldn't hear her conversation.

"Cool? Is that all?"

"I said he's cool. What more do you want me to say?" Keaundra opened up the cabinet and grabbed a small bowl, placing it on the counter.

"I want you to tell me that you're madly in love with him. Shit, tell me somethin' other than he's cool."

"I don't know him all like that, so I can't say too much more," she said, opening up another cabinet and pulling down a box of Special K cereal and pouring some into the bowl.

"What's his favorite color? His favorite movie? Does he have any kids? Shit, girl, tell a sista somethin'," Alexis said as she lay comfortably in David's king-sized bed.

Keaundra grabbed a spoon out of the silverware drawer before grabbing the milk out of the refrigerator. "We really didn't talk much," she said as she poured some milk over her cereal.

"You mean to tell me that this man spent the night with you and y'all didn't talk much?" Alexis asked, skeptical.

"Naw, not really," Keaudra answered before sticking a spoonful of cereal into her mouth.

"So if y'all didn't talk, y'all must have fucked," Alexis said.

"What?" Keaundra said, nearly choking on her cereal.

"Well, can you at least tell a sista how big the nigga's dick is?"

"Bye, bitch!" Keaundra hung up the phone and poured the rest of her cereal out into the sink, before going back into the empty living room. *Where this nigga at?* she thought as she looked around while standing in place. *Oh, shit, he must have heard me tell Alexis that he was just cool and left walking.* Keaundra began to panic, but soon calmed down when she heard the toilet flush.

"Good morning, sunshine," Hammer said as he made his way down the hall and back into the living room.

"Good morning," Keaundra replied with a huge smile, sounding like a love-sick teenager.

"I grabbed a wash towel out of the linen closet, hope you don't mind."

"I don't mind. If you want, you can grab a brand new toothbrush out the medicine cabinet in the bathroom."

Hammer smiled at Keaundra. "That would be nice," he said and headed back toward the bathroom.

Keaundra looked at the clock that hung on the living room wall. "Nine o'clock," she said aloud.

"Huh," Hammer replied as he stopped in his tracks.

"Oh, nothin'. I was just saying the time, that's all."

"Are you keeping track of time 'cause I've been here too long or you just wanted to know the time?" Hammer asked playfully before continuing his walk into the bathroom.

"I just wanted to know the time, silly," she yelled to him as he disappeared.

Once Hammer made his way back to the living room, he smiled as he watched Keaundra fold his sheet and cover. Keaundra returned the smile when she noticed Hammer watching her. They stood in the living room smiling and staring at each other without saying a word.

After a brief moment, Hammer walked over to her, grabbed her hand, and kissed it. "Are you okay?"

Keaundra looked into Hammer's gorgeous brown eyes and shook her head yes.

"Good. Well, you think a brotha can get some breakfast?' he laughed.

"Yeah, if you cookin'."

"I don't mind. I'm a beast in the kitchen anyway," he said.

Well, what are you like in the bedroom? she wanted to ask, but didn't have the nerve. "Well, come on, beast, follow me." Keaundra led him into the kitchen, took a seat at the table, and watched as Hammer maneuvered around like the kitchen belonged to him. *Thank God I went grocery shopping.*

Keaundra and Hammer talked and laughed a lot over breakfast. They talked about everything they could think of. She found out his favorite color was blue, his favorite food was stuffed pork chops, he had no children, and no wife or deranged girlfriend who she had to worry about coming after her. This was a big plus in Keaundra's book. Keaundra found out she and Hammer had a lot in common. Both of their sets of parents were deceased, they both loved to read, and most of all, their favorite thing to do was lay around the house all day doing nothing but watching television.

Around noon, they decided it was time to drop Hammer off at home so he could get dressed. They made plans to go to dinner and a movie later that evening. After she dropped Hammer off she headed to the gym to work off some of her built-up sexual frustration. As her feet pounded on the treadmill belt, she imagined it was her pussy pounding down hard on top of Hammer's *dick.* She smiled before picking up her pace.

Chapter Seventeen

"What's up, cuz?" David asked as soon as Hammer walked into the house with a huge smile plastered all over his face.

"What's up?" Hammer answered before taking a seat on the sofa next to David.

"What's the huge smile for, man?" David asked.

"What smile?" he asked, still smiling from ear to ear.

"The smile that's tattooed all over your face. You musta got some of dat ass last night, nigga?"

Hammer laid his head back and smiled. "Naw, man, it wasn't even like that, although I probably could have if I tried."

"What, you mean to tell me that you didn't even try to dig them guts out?"

"Naw, man. We just talked, watched TV, and tried to get to know each other a little better. I don't know, man, it's somethin' about that girl that I really like."

"Y'all could have talked after you tapped that phat ass of hers," David laughed. "Well, what did y'all do for excitement last night?"

"I did get attacked by her cat." Hammer laughed a little and shook his head in disbelief.

David began laughing. "What?"

"Yeah, man, her cat jumped on my lap. That shit scared the hell outta me. I know I had to have sounded like a little bitch when I screamed." Hammer chuckled.

"You mean to tell me that yo' big, grown ass screamed because a little harmless cat jumped on your lap? Say it ain't so."

Hammer's look turned serious. "Nigga, that cat was far from harmless. That little black bitch reminded me of Cujo."

"Man, you lost cool points on that one," David said, still laughing. David picked up the remote from the coffee table and turned the television to ESPN.

"So, did you hit it last night?" Hammer asked as he focused his attention on last night's basketball scores.

David placed the remote back on top of the table before answering, never taking his eyes off the highlights. "Naw, man. It ain't that type of party. I dig her a lot, but we both just got out of a relationship so we're not tryin' to rush into anything. Besides, her ex is crazy and from the tampon that the auto body shop found in my gas tank, my ex is crazy too."

"A tampon?" Hammer asked, taking his eyes away from the television for a brief moment and staring at his cousin.

"Yeah, nigga, a tampon. Evidently the broad went nuts and thought it was a good idea to put a muthafuckin' Playtex tampon in my gas tank."

Hammer shook his head in disbelief. "Thank God I don't have those types of problems."

"No more." David smiled.

"What do you mean by that?"

"Nigga, you know Kelly's ass was crazy as hell too," David laughed.

"Kelly was crazy. But that's why I loved her so much. Something 'bout a crazy girl turns me on," Hammer replied.

"That's 'cause yo' ass is crazy too," David teased. His facial expression turned serious. "Did you tell Keaundra about Kelly yet?"

Hammer let out a long breath before answering. "Naw, man, for what?" He felt a lump form in his throat as Kelly's beautiful face flashed before his eyes. He missed his wife and son so much.

"Do you plan on seeing Keaundra again?"

"Yeah, we're going to dinner and a movie tonight."

"Do you want to take things to another level with Keaundra?" David inquired.

"Yeah, man, but you know I can't. Remember the promise I made to Kelly." Hammer said with a raised voice.

"That's why I think you should tell Keaundra about Kelly. If you like Keaundra as much as you say you do, at least you can be man enough to tell her y'all can never be anything more than friends," David explained. "Or are you gon' lead her on like you did all the others?"

"I'ma tell her," Hammer answered, getting irritated.

"Don't play with this girl's feelings, man. She's a good catch."

"Man, I have never liked a woman after only one date. But this girl has some type of an effect on me. She's different. I don't know what it is about her."

"Well, you need to tell her about Kelly then, man."

As much as he hated to admit it, Hammer knew David was right. His emotions went haywire as he thought about how Keaundra would react once he told her about his wife Kelly and the promise that he had made to her. When Keaundra first smiled at him, he knew she was something special because she made his heart skip a beat and no other woman had ever had that type of effect on him, not even his wife. His feelings were confirmed when he held her in his arms as he pretended to be asleep on her sofa. He knew she could be the one because it felt so right having her next to him. They fit together perfectly, like a missing piece to a jigsaw puzzle. Hammer knew he could easily fall in love with her, but because of a promise he had made to the only other woman his heart would allow him to love, he knew that he could never act on his feelings for Keaundra.

"I got you, man," he said, sounding depressed.

"You better, or things could get real ugly between you two." David stood up from the sofa and walked down the hallway and up the stairs to his bedroom.

I'll tell her when the time is right. Maybe I won't tell her at all, we might not last long enough for me to have to tell her, Hammer thought as he made himself comfortable on the sofa so he could take a quick nap before he had to get ready for his date with Keaundra.

"So, what restaurant is he taking you to?" India asked Keaundra as they talked on a three-way call with Alexis.

"I think we're goin' to some Italian restaurant he said had really good food," Keaundra answered happily.

"So do you like Hammer?" India asked Keaundra.

"Yes, I like him a lot. It's somethin' about that brotha that does somethin' to me. It's like he's too good to be true," Keaundra giggled.

"Oh, but when *I* asked yo' ass if you liked him, you told me that he was just cool." Alexis scowled.

"That was before him and me got to know more about each other."

"Whatever," Alexis hissed, like her feelings were hurt.

"I'm serious, Lexy. We really didn't get to know each other until he fixed us breakfast."

"He cooked breakfast, too?" India asked, surprised.

"Yeah, girl, and the brotha can throw down," Keaundra boasted about her newfound friend.

"I'm so happy for you," India said, excited.

"Now, aren't you glad we talked you into goin' out with Hammer?" Alexis added.

"I sure am. Thanks," Keaundra said. "Hang on, y'all, I got a beep." Keaundra clicked over to her other line. "Hello?"

"What's up, sis?" Kenneth chimed in.

"Hey, Ken, what's up?" she asked with her voice dripping with happiness.

"What you so happy about?" he asked, skeptical about his sister's sudden mood change.

"Hang on for a second," she said, clicking back over to her friends. "Hey, y'all, let me call y'all back."

"Is that Hammer on the other line?" India teased.

"No, it's Kenneth. I'll call y'all later."

"Tell Ken I said hello," Alexis added.

"I will. And hey, I love you guys," Keaundra said.

"We love you too," Alexis and India said in unison.

Keaundra clicked back over to her brother. "Okay. What's up?" she asked.

"Ain't nothin' up. Can't a brotha call and check up on his sister? And, furthermore, I haven't heard from you today."

"I was gon' call you. I just got caught up doing a few things."

"You sound unusually happy. Did you hit the lottery or somethin'?" Kenneth joked.

"No, I'm always happy," she lied.

Kenneth started laughing. "Please. You must be sick or somethin'."

"Anyways, how is the wedding plans coming along?" Keaundra asked.

"Now I know you're sick," Kenneth laughed.

"Kenneth? I'm serious," she shouted. "I'm tryin' to change and become a better person."

"I'm sorry, sis. It's just that a few weeks ago you were dead set against me marrying Beverly. And now, you're asking about our wedding plans, so what am I supposed to think?"

"Well, if you really must know, I met someone who makes me feel happy, and now I know how Beverly makes you feel, and I really like that feeling," she admitted.

"You mean you met a man?" Kenneth asked, shocked.

Keaundra laughed at her brother. "Yes, dummy, of course."

"What's this cat's name? What does he do for a living? Does he have a girlfriend already?" Kenneth asked, being the overprotective brother he was.

"Hammer, he's an architect, and, no, he does not have a girlfriend. *Yet*," she said.

"Hammer? What type of name is Hammer?"

Keaundra could not give her brother a straight answer, because she didn't know the answer. With all the talking she and Hammer did earlier, she never once asked him his real name. She knew good and well his government name was not Hammer. "I don't know," she admitted.

"You mean to tell me that you don't even know his real name?"

"No, I forgot to ask," she shamefully replied.

"Come on, sis. I know it's been a long time since you had a man and all, but damn, you've never walked away without knowing his real name."

"Well, I'll tell you what, when I get back from dinner tonight, I'll call you and tell you his real name."

"You mean to tell me that you're goin' out with this guy and you don't even know his real name? What am I supposed to tell the police if somethin' happens? I can't tell them my sister went out with Hammer!" Kenneth shouted angrily.

"Calm down, Ken-Ken. If it makes you feel any better, it's David's cousin," Keaundra replied nonchalantly.

"Oh, now I feel a lot better now that I know it's David's cousin," he said sarcastically. "Now, who the hell is David?"

Keaundra rolled her eyes into the top of her head because she was getting tired of Kenneth acting like her father instead of her brother. "David owns the barbershop on Park Avenue," she said, irritated.

"Well, all I know is if somethin' happens to you I'm going after David since I don't know what this Hammer guy looks like," Kenneth said in a dead serious tone. Keaundra sat silently as her brother ranted. "Do you hear me?"

"Yeah, how can I not."

"Don't get smart, girl."

"Bye, Ken."

"Hey," Kenneth called out.

"Yeah?"

"Have a good time tonight," he said before hanging up the phone.

Keaundra looked at the phone and smiled before placing it back into its cradle.

Chapter Eighteen

After an hour nap, Keaundra started getting ready for her date with Hammer. She ran some bath water and plugged in her curling iron to flip up some of the curls that had managed to fall while she slept. She then made her way to her bedroom to find something to wear. She opened up her closet; she had so much to choose from. She didn't know whether to dress sexy, casual, or thugged out, so she decided to call the one person who she knew would give her the best advice.

"What's up?" India asked when she answered the telephone.

"I need help," Keaundra said, sounding desperate.

"With what?" India asked.

"I need you to come over and help me find somethin' to wear."

"Say no more. I'm gon' stop by and pick up Lexy and we'll be over in about twenty minutes," India said happily.

"Thanks, girl."

"No need to thank me. That's what friends are for."

"Well, hurry up," Keaundra said, excited.

"I'm on my way." India hung up the phone, grabbed her keys, and called Alexis from her cell phone as she headed out the door.

Keaundra jumped in the tub. As much as she wanted to soak her sore muscles, she couldn't because she didn't want to sweat the rest of her curls out. So she took a quick wash-up and made sure she hit all the right spots, twice. She got out of the tub and dried off before making her way toward her room. She rambled around on her dresser, trying to figure out what fragrance of lotion to wear. She finally decided to wear EnJoy by Jean Patou. She rubbed it all over her body and then she put on her black lace bra and panty set. She grabbed her robe off the back of her closet door, walked into the living room, and waited for her girls' arrival. Twenty minutes later, Alexis and India burst in the door.

"Come on, girl," Alexis said, walking toward Keaundra's bedroom. Keaundra got up from the sofa and followed her friend.

"I'm about to get me somethin' to drink because I know this is gon' take awhile," India said, walking into the kitchen.

Alexis rambled through Keaundra's closet, pulling out many different clothes and laying them on the bed. "Here, I like this," Alexis said, holding up a short, black Gucci dress.

"She can't wear that," India said, walking into the room and munching on a bag of Doritos.

"And why not?" Alexis asked.

"Because, she's going to dinner and a movie, not to dinner and a club," India replied smartly.

"So?" Alexis argued.

"This is a dress that you wear when you're going to look for a man, not when you have a man with you," India explained with her mouth full of chips.

Keaundra looked at Alexis and nodded, letting her know that she agreed with India.

"Fine, then. You come find her somethin'." Alexis pouted and took a seat on the bed.

"No problem." India wiped the leftover cheese from the Doritos on her pants before walking over to the closet and pulling out a cream organza halter pants suit with the short jacket to match and put it up against Keaundra's body. Her smile assured India that she was pleased with the pick. India also pulled out a pair of cream and gold Sergio Rossi boots with the stiletto heels and the wrap around straps and handed them to Keaundra. Keaundra's smile grew even wider. India dug deeper into Keaundra's closet and pulled out a gold clutch purse, while Alexis dug through Keaundra's jewelry box and found some gold jewelry to set the magnificent ensemble off that India put together.

"Now you know you gon' have to take off yo' panties and bra," Alexis said.

"I do know that much," Keaundra said as she removed her panties and bra and slipped into her outfit. She put her boots on and looked at herself in the mirror.

"Damn, bitch, you look good," Alexis shouted.

"I told you I could put her an outfit together," India bragged.

"You sure did one helluva job," Alexis agreed happily.

Keaundra didn't know what to say. All she could do was smile at the reflection in the mirror.

"Girl, Hammer ain't gon' be able to keep his hands off of you tonight." Alexis grinned.

"That's the whole idea," India said with a devilish grin.

"You so nasty," Keaundra giggled.

"I don't got Martell wrapped around my little finger for nothin'," India said.

"You got that right," Alexis agreed.

After Alexis helped Keaundra curl her hair and apply a little bit of eyeliner to bring out her eye color, she and India made their way home and left Keaundra alone to wait for her date.

When her friends left, Keaundra went into
the kitchen to get a glass of wine to try to calm
her nerves. Every time she heard a car come by,
she would rush to the kitchen window to see if
the car had stopped in front of her house. *Calm
down, girl*, she told herself as she sipped on her
Riunite.

Two glasses of wine later, there was a knock at
her front door. Keaundra took a deep breath and
looked at herself in the mirror that hung from
the living room wall before going to the door.
"Who is it?" she called out.

"It's me, Hammer."

Keaundra unlocked the door and pulled it
open. The sight that stood on the other side of
the door nearly floored her. Hammer stood there
looking like a nice piece of chocolate cake. He
was dressed in a freshly pressed pair of Sean
John jeans, a crisp pair of white, green, and yellow Air Force Ones, and a white, green, and yellow Sean John button-down shirt. You could tell
that he hadn't too long gotten out of someone's
barber chair because his haircut was as fresh as
the cool Spring air.

"Damn, you look good," Hammer said as soon
as he stepped into the doorway.

"Thank you, and so do you," Keaundra replied
bashfully. *Thank God for my girls*, she thought

as Hammer eyed her like a hungry wolf. "Are you ready?" she asked, breaking his stare.

"As ready as I'm gon' get." Hammer held out his arm for her to take. Keaundra grabbed his arm with one hand and her clutch with the other and they made their way to his car.

Hammer hit the button on his key ring that unlocked his silver beauty. He opened up the passenger's side door for Keaundra and waited patiently as she got in before he closed her door and made his way around to the driver's side. He got in and started up the car. The engine was so quiet, you couldn't even tell that the car was on.

"Nice car," Keaundra said, admiring the plush leather seats.

"Thanks," he said as he pulled off. Steely Dan's "Do It Again", played calmly while they rode. "Are you comfortable?" Hammer glanced over at Keaundra and asked.

Keaundra smiled. "Yes, very." She sat back and enjoyed the music along with the ride until they pulled up into a nice little Italian restaurant.

"We're here," Hammer announced, as if Keaundra didn't know.

"We're here," she repeated. Hammer got out of the car, walked around to the passenger's side door, and opened it up for her. He held out his hand for her to grab. She took his soft hand

and he helped her out of the comfortable seat. "Thanks." She smiled, pleased with his manners.

Hammer hit the button on his key chain to lock the doors on his brand new Audi S8. Once they arrived inside the restaurant, Keaundra looked around, amazed at how beautifully decorated the place was. The walls were decorated with pictures of different Italian dishes painted on them. The tablecloths had the exact same décor. Each table had a vase with the most beautiful flower arrangement in them and each arrangement was different. Gentle Italian music flooded the restaurant speakers. Keaundra did not recognize any of the music; it was not something she was used to hearing, or something she enjoyed hearing. She was just glad that she only had to listen to it for a couple of hours.

"Do you have a reservation?" the server walked over and asked Keaundra and Hammer.

"Yes. Donye' Woods," Hammer replied.

Donye' Woods, Keaundra thought. *Now I know his real name.* "Excuse me, ma'am, can you please tell me where the bathroom is?" Keaundra asked the server as she led them to their table.

"Sure, it's right over there," the server said, turning around and pointing to the left of them.

"Thank you. I'll be right back," she said to Hammer.

"Hurry back," he said. Hammer watched Keaundra's backside as she walked.

Keaundra stopped and turned around to see if he was watching. She smiled once she realized that he was, feeling like the chick did in *Waiting to Exhale*. Keaundra switched so hard she damned near threw her hips out of socket.

Once inside the bathroom, Keaundra pulled out her cell phone and called her brother. "Hello," she whispered when he answered.

"Keaundra?"

"Yeah, it's me."

Kenneth began to panic. "Why you whispering? Are you okay, sis? You don't need me to come and get you, do you?"

"Naw, I'm fine. I was just callin' you to give you Hammer's real name."

Kenneth smiled. "Okay. What is it?"

"Donye' Woods," Keaundra said proudly.

"Donye' Woods, huh? How do you know that's his real name? How do you know he's not making that up?" Kenneth asked suspiciously. "Did he show you some identification? Hell, even if he did, the ID still could have been fake."

Keaundra rolled her eyes into the top of her head. "Bye, Kenneth," she said, and hung up the phone before her brother could say another word. Keaundra looked at herself in the mirror, applied more lip gloss, and headed out of the bathroom.

Hammer had a huge smile on his face upon Keaundra's return. Keaundra began to get nervous all over again. She picked up her menu and pretended to read it. Hammer could sense her nervousness so he sparked up a conversation.

"So, what would you like to drink?" he asked, scanning over the menu as if he hadn't seen it a million times before.

Keaundra was unsure, as she had never heard of any of the wine choices. She was so used to drinking the White Zinfandel that she occasionally purchased from Walmart, that she was oblivious to anything else. "I'm not sure. What are you having?" she said, not wanting Hammer to know she was clueless when it came to the wine selection.

"I'm having the—"

"Are you guys ready to order?" the server walked up and interrupted.

Hammer laid the menu down on the table and looked up at the server. "I'll take a glass of Amarone," Hammer replied and looked over at Keaundra, waiting for her to order.

"Good choice," the server said and looked down at Keaundra and waited patiently as she pretended to think about on what she should order.

"Um, I'll just drink the same thing he's drinking."

"Let's just get the bottle then, please, and we'll be ready to order when you come back," Hammer said. Hammer waited until the server left the table before speaking. "Are you familiar with the wine?"

"Not at all," she admitted.

Hammer smiled. "Well, you made a really good choice. Amarone is from the Veneto region of Italy. It's made from grapes that are dried to concentrate their juice, and believe me, it gets better with age."

Keaundra was impressed by Hammer's knowledge about the wine. "You seem to know a lot about wine."

"Actually, I do. I've always been infatuated with good wine. As a matter of fact, I go to South Carolina every year to the Charleston Food and Wine Festival."

"Interesting," she said, intrigued by the fact that this young fine black brotha knew about something other than what the latest rap song was or when the next pair of Jordans was coming out. "So, do you stay with family while you're in South Carolina?"

"No, I normally get a room at the Wentworth Mansion."

"A mansion, huh?" Keaundra shook her head in approval, impressed by Hammer's taste.

"Yeah, it's a nice place to stay. The rooms start out at three hundred and ninety-five dollars a night, though, and you only get a three night minimum." As he finished his sentence, the server walked over to their table carrying the bottle of wine and two wine glasses, and set them down on the table.

"Are you guys ready to order yet?" the server asked.

Hammer cleared his throat. "Yes, I'll start off with a bowl of *zuppa vera contadina*." Keaundra looked at him like he was crazy. She tried to figure out what he had just ordered as he spoke to the server as if Italian was his native language. "And for my dinner I'll have the *pollo alla scarpariello*." After he finished his order, Hammer handed the server his menu and waited for Keaundra.

Keaundra had never been to an Italian restaurant, let alone eaten any Italian food other than spaghetti and lasagna, so she played it safe, not wanting to make a fool of herself and order something she wasn't too familiar with. "I'll just have the spaghetti," she said. *I can't go wrong with that*, she thought as she handed the server her menu. The server took the menu and headed off toward the kitchen to place their orders.

Hammer smiled as he admired Keaundra's beauty.

"What?" Keaundra asked shyly, and shifted in her seat.

"Nothin'. I'm just admiring your beauty, that's all." Hammer could tell that Keaundra was getting nervous, so he changed the subject. "Do you like to travel?"

Keaundra took a sip from her wine glass before answering. "I don't travel much because there's nowhere I really wanna go."

"What? There are a million places you should wanna go. I thought all women like to travel," Hammer chuckled.

"Do you like to travel?" Keaundra shot back.

"Do I? I love to travel. It's nothin' for me to take off and go to a place like Rhode Island and stay at the Manisses on Block Island where there's nothin' but beaches, two hundred-foot cliffs, and freshwater ponds." Hammer's face lit up like a Christmas tree as he spoke about some of the places he had traveled. "Or a beautiful place like Ashland, Oregon. That is one of the most romantic towns in the Northwest."

Keaundra felt a twinge of jealousy at that remark, wondering if he had visited that place with a woman by his side. "The place is known for its art, theater, and good old spring water. But believe it or not," he continued, "my favorite place to travel to is South Dakota in February. Strolling through the tropical paradise does something to the soul. Being surrounded by exotic butterflies at Sioux Falls Sertoma Butterfly House is so amazing."

Keaundra listened as he talked about places she didn't even know black people lived let alone traveled. "The goldfish pond is so relaxing and the most exciting part about the whole trip is if you wear bright colors, you'll attract the Lepidoptera."

I'm not even sure what a Lepidoptera is, but I know this brotha has a lot of class, he's intelligent, he's been to a lot of places, and his conversation holds my attention. He's also cute, he has a sense of humor, and he has a real job. He's exactly the type of man I need in my life.

Keaundra actually found herself enjoying talking with Hammer about the different places he had been. Hammer was not like any of the other men she dated in the past. They only talked about money, drugs, cars, and how phat her ass was. The server brought them their food and they ate while Hammer continued taking Keandra's mind to places where she had never even dreamt of going.

Chapter Nineteen

"Thanks for a wonderful evening," Keaundra said as Hammer pulled up into her driveway.

Hammer put the car in park and looked over at Keaundra with a smile on his face. "No, thank you. It's been a long time since I have really enjoyed myself." Kelly's face flashed into his mind. Hammer closed his eyes for a brief second, cleared his throat, and continued speaking. "I'm glad you enjoyed yourself too. I tried not to talk too much, but you see it didn't work," he laughed.

"That's okay, I really enjoyed listening to your conversation," she said, sincerely. "You're a very intelligent man."

This time Hammer was flattered. No woman he had ever dated had complimented him on his mind, only his body, his looks, or how big his manhood was. Hammer could sense that some of the women he conversed with were intimidated by his conversation; he didn't feel that with Keaundra. He knew she hadn't the slightest idea what he was talking about sometimes, but she acted interested and she asked questions and Hammer liked that about her.

Growing up, Hammer's 4.0 grade point average along with being on the honor roll every semester made him stand out in school. Hammer found out quick that girls didn't want to date a nerd, or a brainiac, which he was often called. All they ever went after were the stars of the football team or the captain of the basketball team; it was never the guys in the chess club or on the debate team. So Hammer tried out for the football team. It took one good tackle and getting the wind knocked out of him before he realized this was not the sport for him. He then tried out for his favorite sport, basketball, and made the squad, but soon gave it up once he found out that basketball practice would interfere with his Spanish club meetings.

Hammer smiled widely. "Thank you. I'm glad you enjoyed listening to me."

"I have to admit that a lot of the things you talked about, I didn't know anything about," she said honestly with a slight laugh. "But I like to learn about different things and I love to stay 'in the know,' so to speak."

"I sensed that I lost you a few times in my conversation," he chuckled. "But you caught up real quick."

A yawn escaped Keaundra's mouth from out of nowhere. She was so embarrassed. "Sorry."

"Am I boring you that much?" Hammer asked playfully.

"No, not at all. It's just that I'm a little tired."

"Well, I better let you go so you can get yourself some sleep," Hammer said, not really wanting their night to end.

I don't want to go, she thought. *I want you to come in with me and make wild, passionate love to me.* "Okay," She smiled with tired eyes.

"Let me walk you to your door." Hammer turned off the car and grabbed the keys out of the ignition.

Keaundra sat and waited for Hammer to come around to the passenger's side to open the door. He held out his hand for her to grab. As they walked toward the porch, Keaundra looked up into the sky and noticed one of the brightest stars she had ever seen in her life. She smiled and closed her eyes and mouthed the words, Thanks, Mom.

Keaundra felt in her heart that the star was her mother shining down on her and that gave her a sense of peace, strength, and courage. Keaundra pulled her house keys out of her clutch and turned to Hammer and asked, "Would you like to come in?"

"I don't know. Is Cujo in her cage?" he joked.

"Cujo?" Keaundra laughed. "Peaches is harmless." Keaundra stuck her key into the lock and opened the door.

"Yeah, that's what you said last time and look what happened," he said as he followed Keaundra into the house.

Keaundra flipped on the light switch and just like clockwork, Peaches came walking down the hallway and jumped up on the back of the sofa for her head and belly rub.

Hammer shook his head, hurried past Keaundra and her cat, and took a seat in the chair. After Keaundra rubbed her cat down for a few minutes, Peaches jumped down off the sofa and sashayed her way back down the hallway.

"You and that cat," Hammer said, laughing.

"Make yourself comfortable. I'm goin' to change my clothes." Keaundra made her way down the hallway and into her room. She kicked off her shoes. "Oooohhh, my feet are hurting." Keaundra took a seat on her bed for a few seconds to give her feet a quick rest. She then stood and removed all her clothes.

"Excuse me," Hammer said, startling Keaundra. Keaundra turned around in shock. She took her hands and attempted to cover her naked body.

"I'm sorry," he said, embarrassed, and turned his back. *Damn, she got a bad-ass body.*

"No, you're all right," Keaundra said, shocking herself with her boldness. She let her hands fall down to her sides as she made her way over to her closet with confidence and grabbed her robe off the back of the door. "Did you need somethin'?"

"I was wondering if you had some Tylenol or somethin' for a headache," he said with his back still turned.

"You can turn around and talk to me, Hammer. I do have my robe on," she chuckled.

"Oh." Hammer smiled and turned around to face Keaundra.

Keaundra brushed past him, intentionally touching him while making her way to the bathroom to retrieve the Tylenol. Keaundra rambled through the medicine cabinet until she found some pain pills. She looked at the date on them to make sure they were still good, because she was guilty of keeping things that were way past their expiration date. She walked out of the bathroom and back to her bedroom. Hammer was standing patiently in the same spot that Keaundra had left him in.

"Thank you," he said, stealing a feel of her hand as she handed him the bottle of pills.

"You need some water to take those, don't you?"

"Not really, but some water would be nice." Hammer followed Keaundra out of her room and toward the kitchen. She grabbed a bottle of water from the refrigerator and handed it to him. "Thanks," he said, opening the water.

Keaundra watched as Hammer opened up the pill bottle and shook two pills into the palm of his hand. She then watched as he popped them in his mouth and took a long drink of water. *Damn, he even makes drinking water look sexy*, she thought as she eyed his full lips wrapped around the rim of the bottle. Hammer finished off his water and handed the empty bottle to Keaundra. "Thanks," she said sarcastically.

"You can't say I never gave you anything."

Keaundra sucked her teeth. "Come on, crazy, and let's go see what's on TV." Keaundra walked out of the kitchen with Hammer in tow. She took a seat on the sofa and Hammer sat down next to her. She picked up the remote and began surfing through the channels.

"Right here," Hammer said, grabbing her hand.

Keaundra looked at Hammer like he was crazy. "What's this movie?"

"What? You mean to tell me that you have never seen *Claudine*? This movie is a classic," he said, excited.

"I'm afraid not. Who's in it and what's it about?"

"You mean to tell me that your grandmother never had y'all watching these kinda movies?"

"I was never interested in watching TV; all I ever wanted to do was follow my brother and his friends."

"This movie was made in 1974 and it stars James Earl Jones, who plays a garbage man, and Diahann Carroll, who plays a part-time house-keeper who's on welfare," he explained. "With six kids," he added.

"So is it a love story or what?"

"Yeah, kinda like the ones y'all females be watching on Lifetime, only the black version." Hammer went on about the movie for a few more minutes before they began watching it.

"Dang, Diahann Carroll is a whore in this movie," Keaundra said after watching a love scene between her and James Earl Jones.

"Why you say that?" Hammer asked, his eyes still glued to the television screen.

"She slept with that man and she doesn't even know him. Hell, this is their first date, at least make the brotha wait a month or two before you start giving up the panties."

Hammer smirked and turned his attention toward Keaundra. "So you telling me that you've never given it up on the first date?"

"No, I haven't. I don't get down like that," Keaundra said proudly.

"Like what?" he asked, wanting to get deeper into her head.

"Like that," she said, pointing at the TV screen. "I like to take my time and get to know the brotha a little before I jump in the bed with him."

"So you've never had a one-night stand before?" Hammer inquired.

"Yes . . . I mean, no," Keaundra stammered.

"Make up ya mind."

"I didn't plan on it being a one-night stand, we went out a couple of times, had sex once, but after the nigga said somethin' I didn't appreciate, I never fucked with him again after that night," Keaundra stated, becoming uncomfortable.

"So the answer is yes, you have had a one-night stand before?"

"That's not what you would call a one-night stand," she said defensively. "We did go out a couple of times."

"You had sex with the guy one time?"

Keaundra nodded.

"And after he pissed you off, you never had sex with him again, right?"

Keaundra nodded.

"Well, it sounds to me like you had a one-night stand before." Hammer smiled victoriously.

Keaundra sucked her teeth. "Whatever. Call it what you want."

"I am," Hammer laughed. "And I'm calling it a one-night stand."

Keaundra rolled her eyes playfully. "Be quiet, I'm tryin'a watch the movie."

Hammer smiled at Keaundra. "Whatever you say."

Hammer put his arm around Keaundra; she snuggled up close to his body, and this time she wasn't nervous all. In fact, she loved every minute of it and felt she could get used to it.

Chapter Twenty

The day was unusually warm for the end of March. David decided to take off work early so he could enjoy the nice weather. He also wanted to surprise Alexis for lunch. David finished his last customer's head, swept up the hair, and walked into his office to grab his jacket. He noticed his message line blinking on his phone and hesitated to answer it. He already knew it was nobody but his ex-girlfriend, Rosalind. She had been calling the shop all day, but he had been telling the other barbers to tell her he was not in.

David shook his head, taking a seat in his big comfortable chair behind his desk. He reluctantly pushed the play button and listened to his messages. He had tons of messages from his mom telling him to call her. He had been meaning to return her call, but every time he planned on it, something else came up.

The last three messages were from Rosalind. The first one was her telling him how sorry she was for putting the tampon in his gas tank.

The second one was her telling him how much she loved and missed him. David let out a long breath. The final message was her telling him she had something very important to tell him. She said that it was a matter of life or death. David heard the urgency in her voice and decided he would call her after he came back from lunch, just in case she was just trying to pull another one of her foolish stunts. He put on his jacket, said good-bye to the other barbers, and headed out the door.

David got in his car and checked his image in the mirror. "Flawless as usual," he said with a smile to his reflection. He popped in the new Donell Jones CD and pulled out of the parking lot, bobbing his head as the music soothed his eardrums. He kept looking in the rearview mirror. He could have sworn that someone was following him.

To make sure he wasn't going crazy, David took a right at the light, and so did the black Camry. David went down two more blocks and took a left and so did the black Camry. "I wonder who this muthafucka' is following me," he said to himself. Just as David pulled over to the curb, the person in the Camry put on their blinker and turned up into a driveway. He watched as a female he had never seen before emerged from the car.

"Damn, they live this way," David laughed at himself, feeling embarrassed. He shook his head and pulled off. Before going to the dentist office where Alexis worked, David stopped off at a small flower boutique and picked up a single red rose; he was really falling for Alexis. As David pulled up in the half-empty parking lot he spotted Alexis sitting at a picnic table, talking to the receptionist as she puffed on a cigarette.

Alexis waved the smoke out of her face and smiled when she saw David's car pulling up.

"Girl, what is he doin' here? I didn't see his name in the appointment book," Kay-Kay said after she blew out her cigarette smoke.

"I don't know," Alexis said, still smiling. Alexis waited patiently as David parked his car and got out. He walked toward them with the single red rose in hand. Alexis could feel chills going up and down her spine as she watched this smooth brotha glide her way.

"Hey," he said once he reached the picnic table where she sat. David handed her the rose. "This is for you."

"Thanks." Alexis put the rose up to her nose and sniffed the pleasant aroma. "What are you doin' here? I didn't know you had an appointment today."

"I don't. I just stopped by to see if you wanted to go to lunch."

Alexis looked at her watch. "My lunch break is over in twenty minutes. Where can we go in that short period of time?"

David thought for a second. "You'd be surprised."

"I can't, David. Maybe some other time."

Kay-Kay shot Alexis a crazy look. "And why not?"

"You know my next appointment is in thirty-five minutes."

"I'll tell you what: if you go to lunch with me, I'll have you back in thirty-four minutes." David smiled, showing off his pearly whites.

Alexis looked at Kay-Kay as if she was asking for her approval. Kay-Kay nodded. "Go on, I'll tell your patient you're running late. Shit, either the bitch will wait or she can take her ass somewhere else."

Both David and Alexis laughed. "Okay, I'll be back soon as we're finished with lunch." Alexis waved good-bye to Kay-Kay as she and David made their way to his car.

Kay-Kay waved back and watched as they pulled away. She took a few more drags off her cigarette before putting it out in the ashtray. She got up from the picnic table and began walking toward the door but stopped as she saw a black Camry with dark tinted windows speeding into the parking lot.

A high yellow girl with shoulder-length hair got out of the car. She ran her fingers through her hair, fixed her clothes, and walked toward Kay-Kay.

"Hello," Kay-Kay said.

"Is this the office of Dr. Gavenstein?" The high yellow girl asked rudely.

No, this bitch did not just come up here and not speak back, Kay-Kay thought. Kay-Kay didn't want to get ghetto with the girl, being she was at work, so she tried to keep it professional as possible. "That is what this big old sign says," Kay-Kay said, pointing.

The high yellow girl looked Kay-Kay up and down before proceeding to the door. *The bitch ain't even all that pretty*, she thought as Kay-Kay followed suit and walked in behind her.

The girl signed her name on the chart and looked around the office as if she was looking for someone. Looking frustrated, she picked up an old *Essence* magazine from the shelf and took a seat.

This has to be the bitch that David's fuckin' 'cause she is the only black girl up in here. I know David ain't started messin' with no white girls, she thought as she flipped through the pages.

Kay-Kay frowned as she walked to her desk. She deliberately took her time getting settled as the girl sat waiting impatiently with her legs crossed. Kay-Kay watched as the girl tapped her foot to the music that came from the speakers. The girl looked up from her article, caught Kay-Kay staring at her, and cut her eyes. Kay-Kay smiled before picking up the chart to see what the patient's name was.

I know this bitch don't call herself picking with me? Smiling and shit, Rosalind thought. *I guess that's her little way of rubbing in the fact that she's fuckin' David. If I wasn't on probation for kickin' David's door off the hinges, I would beat that ass!*

"Does this say Rosalind Mitchell?" Kay-Kay asked.

Rosalind let out a long breath. "Is the dentist ready to see me yet?" she asked with an attitude.

Damn, this bitch act like she knows me or somethin'. Boo, I'm not the one fuckin' yo' man if that's your problem, but I sure hope you find out who she is so you can lose the attitude, Kay-Kay wanted to say badly. "Are you a new patient?" Kay-Kay asked, already knowing the answer.

Rosalind rolled her eyes. "Yes."

"Oh, well, I need you to fill out these forms." Kay-Kay smiled as she turned around and walked over to the filing cabinet where they kept all the forms.

"You should have given me the forms as soon as I walked in and signed my damn name!" Rosalind snapped at Kay-Kay. Kay-Kay turned back around with the same smile on her face, walked over, and handed Rosalind the forms.

Rosalind snatched the forms from Kay-Kay's hand and went and sat back down and began filling them out.

Rude bitch, Kay-Kay thought as she sat down and began flipping through some charts on top of her desk.

As soon as Rosalind finished filling out the forms, she got up from her seat and walked over and threw the forms on top of the counter, causing them to fall on the floor.

Kay-Kay's mouth flew open in amazement. She got up from her desk and bent down to pick up the forms. She looked up at Rosalind for one brief second and saw the mischievous grin plastered all over her face.

Yeah, bitch, I know you fuckin' David and if wasn't for my girl, Tyisha, fuckin' ya baby's daddy, I would have never found out about you. Rosalind stared at Kay-Kay with an evil stare.

Just as Kay-Kay was about to start calling Rosalind every name in the book, Dr. Gavenstein came out of his office.

"I'm ready for my next patient," he said as he looked down at Kay-Kay, who was still trying to gather all of the forms. "I see you had a little accident here," he chuckled as he turned and walked back toward his office.

Kay-Kay stood up and laid the forms on top of her desk. "Rosalind, follow me," she said as she ate crow. *This bitch betta be glad my rent is due in two weeks or I woulda cussed this stankin'-ass ho out,* Kay-Kay thought as she led Rosalind into Dr. Gavenstein's office.

"Please, take a seat right here," Dr. Gavenstein said to Rosalind.

Rosalind took a seat in the oversized chair and looked up at Kay-Kay and smiled victoriously. Rosalind knew she was getting to Kay-Kay.

Just as Kay-Kay was about to leave the office, Linda, one of the other dental hygienists, came in to assist Dr. Gavenstein. She smiled at Kay-Kay as she walked by. "Oh, Kay-Kay," Linda called out. Kay-Kay stopped and turned around.

"Yes?"

Kay-Kay? Rosalind was confused. *I thought the bitch David was fuckin' name was Alexis,* Rosalind thought as she sat with her mouth wide open while Dr. Gavenstein examined her teeth.

"Alexis's one o'clock cancelled."

Kay-Kay smiled. "All right, thanks," she said and continued on her way.

Damn, all this time I been trippin' on the wrong bitch, Rosalind thought as she lay in the

chair feeling dumb as hell. After Dr. Gavenstein
was finished with Rosalind, he suggested that
she come back to get two fillings. Rosalind knew
after the way she acted, she would never return
to this dentist office again. She reluctantly followed Linda out to the receptionist area. She
held her head down in embarrassment as Kay-
Kay flipped through the chart to read the dentist's notes.

"I see the doctor would like you to come back
in two weeks. What's a good time for you?" Kay-
Kay said as politely as her voice would let her.

Rosalind nodded. "I'll call you and let you
know what's a good time for me," she said as she
made out a check for her co-payment. Rosalind
never made eye contact with Kay-Kay as she
made her way out of the office quickly. She got
into her friend, Tyisha's, car and began banging
on the steering wheel.

"Stupid, stupid, stupid!" she said aloud. "How
could I have been so stupid?" she asked herself
as she sat in the car. "I failed this time, but one
thing for sure and two for certain, I will find out
who this Alexis bitch is that's fuckin' my nigga."
Rosalind started up the car and pulled off. As she
made a right out of the parking lot, David and
Alexis pulled in, but Rosalind was so distracted,
she never even noticed.

Chapter Twenty-one

For the past couple of months Keaundra and Hammer had been seeing a lot of each other. Going to the movies, out to dinner, or just sitting at her house laughing and talking had become an every-weekend ritual for the two. Keaundra was really feeling Hammer and he was feeling her as well. Keaundra was more than ready and willing to take their relationship—if that's what you could even call it—to another level, but it seemed as if every time they even came close to becoming intimate, Hammer froze up. She was confused, but kept convincing herself that Hammer didn't want her just for sex, he wanted more from her and that's why he wanted to wait. But after a while, she began thinking there was something wrong with her, but after looking at herself in the mirror a few times, she thought with her good looks and great body, it had to be something more. She needed to get to the bottom of Hammer's problem and fast, because it had been three long, excruciating years since the last time a real man had been between her thighs, and Lord knew it was due . . . way over-due!

"Girl, you mean to tell me every time Hammer comes to your house all y'all do is kiss?" Alexis said as they sat around India's living room after their weekly dinner.

"Yep. That's it," Keaundra answered.

"Dang. You can't even give that old pussy away," India cracked up laughing.

"Fuck you, bitch," Keaundra laughed, but had thought about what her friend had just said. "Y'all, what's wrong with me?" Keaundra's facial expression became serious. "Am I not pretty enough? Am I too fat? It has to be some reason why Hammer is not tryin'a make love to me."

India was shocked. "He ain't even tried?"

"Nope, the closest thing we get to fuckin' is when he's fingering me."

"Maybe he has a little dick and is embarrassed to pull it out in front of you," Alexis said, trying to give her friend a ray of hope.

"Naw, that's not it, 'cause sista done felt the dick and it's far from little and almost close to being way too big," Keaundra bragged.

"Maybe he's gay," Alexis replied.

Keaundra and India shot her a dirty look.

"What? You never know."

"Maybe he's a virgin," India shouted.

"Shit, that nigga ain't hardly a virgin."

"How do you know?" India and Alexis asked at the same time.

"Imagine if the nigga can make a bitch cum with a kiss, what type of training do you think he has with his dick?"

"True dat," Alexis said, giving Keaundra a high-five.

"Sit down, R.J., and Ro'nisha," Alexis hollered at her children who played loudly in India's bedroom.

"Okay, Mommy," the children hollered back and continued making a lot of noise.

"Leave my babies alone and let them play," India said.

"Okay, bitch, when they break somethin', don't come lookin' for me to pay for it, 'cause I'm broke."

"Whatever they break, trust, it is replaceable," India replied.

"Well, since you feel like that, let me have that crystal jewelry box," Keaundra said with a smirk.

"Bitch, please, Martell would kill me if I gave that away."

"Just tell him the kids broke it," Alexis retorted.

Just when India was about to respond, Keaundra's cell phone began to ring. She smiled widely, letting her friends know that it was Hammer on the line.

"Hello?" she answered in a cheerful tone.

"How are you doing?"

"I'm fine. How about yourself?"

"I'm good."

Alexis and India made faces at Keaundra as she talked on the phone.

"Go on," she whispered to her friends as she attempted to keep a straight face.

"I'm about to head over to the gym with David. I was just calling to let you know I wanna do somethin' when I come over tonight."

Keaundra was all smiles as she spoke. "Do somethin' like what?" she cooed.

"You'll see. It's somethin' I should have done a long time ago."

Keaundra was so happy she could barely think straight. "Okay. Well, I'll see you tonight at seven then."

"All right, talk to you later."

Keaundra hung up the phone, letting out a loud scream while kicking her feet.

"What the fuck is wrong with you?" Alexis asked.

"Are you all right, Auntie Ke-Ke?" R.J. ran out of India's room and asked.

"Yeah, she's good. Now go on back in the room with your sister," Alexis said and turned her attention back on Keaundra.

"What the fuck did that nigga say to you on the phone to make you scream like that?" India asked.

"He said he wanted to do somethin' with me tonight."

"And?" Alexis and India asked.

"He said it was somethin' he should have done a long time ago." Keaundra was all smiles.

"Uh-oh, my girl 'bout to finally get her some dick tonight." Alexis smiled happily for her friend.

"Yeah, about time. I guess the nigga couldn't hold off any longer," India added.

Keaundra stood up from the sofa. "I gotta go. I gotta go home and get ready for tonight," she said anxiously.

"Yeah, go home and douche that stanky pussy," Alexis joked.

"Yeah, and while you at it, get the vacuum cleaner and clean all them cobwebs out of it," India teased.

"Fuck the both of you bitches, I'll call y'all tomorrow." Keaundra smiled as she picked up her purse and car keys, and headed home. She was ecstatic Hammer finally decided to give her what she been longing for since the first night they spent together. So actually, Keaundra really was a lot like Diahann Carroll was in *Claudine*, but without the six kids.

"Chile, ya sista sho' has been a lot nicer since she's been seein' that Hammer guy," Grandma Davidson said to Kenneth.

"I have to agree with you on that, Gran. Can you believe she and Beverly are goin' out to pick out wedding decorations, *together*!"

"I know it. Baby, when Keaundra told me that, I nearly fell outta my recliner. That Hammer must really be puttin' it down on her."

Kenneth's eyes widened. "Gran, watch yo' mouth. What do you know about somebody puttin' it down?"

"Boy, you think ya grandma is a virgin or somethin'? I had four kids, so somebody was puttin' it down, either me or ya granddaddy. I would like to think it was me," Gran said, smiling.

"Gran, you are sick." Kenneth pretended to be sick to his stomach. "Let's not talk about you and Granddad, let's stick to Ke-Ke and Hammer."

"Have you met him yet?"

"Not yet, Gran. She said she was gon' bring him to my wedding."

"What? That's a few months away," Grandma Davidson shouted. "How come she's waiting so long to bring him around?"

"Gran, I'm gon' keep it real with you, you know how you always embarrassing people, especially ya grandchildren?"

"I don't be embarrassing y'all."

"Yes, you do. Just like when I first started dating Beverly, you told her that I pissed in the bed until I was twelve."

"Did I lie?"

"No, but you still didn't have to tell her that. I was so embarrassed."

"Well, excuse me for tellin' the truth."

"Remember what you told Ryan Anderson, the boy who used to live down the street from you had that major crush on Kay-Kay?" he continued.

"Naw, refresh my memory."

"Well, when him and Kay-Kay was going to the movies, you told him he better not go in the house, 'cause they had roaches and to shake his coat out before he got back in his car." Kenneth laughed as he remembered the look on Ryan's face.

"Did I lie?" Grandma Davidson asked again.

Kenneth laughed. "Naw, but Ryan never did pick her up for the movies."

"Well, it wasn't my fault that Paula's house was nasty and full of them bugs," Gran said, laughing.

Kenneth shook his head. "You are somethin' else, Gran."

"Grandma just likes to keep it real, that's all."

"Shall I go on?"

"Naw, point well taken." She smiled at her handsome grandson. "What you doing over here anyways?"

"Oh, a brotha can't come see about his ol' girl?"

"I got yo' ol' girl," Grandma Davidson laughed.

"Naw, but for real, I came over to talk to you about somethin'." Kenneth took a seat on the coffee table across from where his grandmother sat in her favorite recliner.

Grandma Davidson had seen the serious look that crossed her grandson's face and sat back in her recliner to listen, hoping and praying to God Beverly had not done anything to hurt him.

"Gran, you know I'll be married soon," he started.

Grandma Davidson shook her head and held her breath. "And we'll probably be starting a family sometime in the near future."

Grandma Davidson patiently hung on to every word Kenneth said.

"So I've decided to have Beverly a house built from the ground up. I want a nice, big, four-bedroom house, with a finished basement, first-floor laundry room, a top-of-the-line kitchen with every stainless steel appliance you can think of, and an office for myself," he said, waiting for his grandmother's reply.

Grandma Davidson sighed. "Lord, and I thought you was 'bout to tell me that Beverly cheated on you again."

"No, Gran, I told you she's a changed person. So what do you think?"

"I don't know if she's a changed person," Grandma Davidson replied.

"I'm not talkin' about Beverly, I'm talkin' about what do you think about the house?"

"Oh. Well, son, I think it's a wonderful idea. What woman wouldn't want a nice big house, with every stainless steel appliance you could think of. But I got one question."

"Yes?"

"Who in the hell gon' cook on all those appliances? 'Cause if I remember right, you told me Beverly can't even boil an egg without messin' it up," Gran, said laughing.

"I'm gon' be the one doing all of the cooking, 'cause Bev can't cook."

Grandma Davidson shook her head. "What a shame. I feel sorry for y'all kids. What are they gon' eat?"

"They'll eat, Gran."

"Yeah, a peanut butter and jelly sandwich. Can she make one of those?" Kenneth shot his grandmother a dirty look. "What? I'm just askin'."

Kenneth smiled at his grandmother. "Yes, Gran, she can."

"Sign her tail up for cookin' classes. Hell, if you wanna save money, make the chile watch Emeril or Rachel Ray. Now they always got some good recipes on their shows," Gran said seriously.

"Okay, Gran. Well, here's what I wanna know—" Kenneth started to say.

"You need some decorating tips?" she said, cutting him off. "'Cause you know ya grandmother is good at decorating a room," she said, looking around her living room.

"I can't tell. 'Cause you done had this same furniture in here since the dinosaurs roamed the earth," Kenneth joked.

"You got jokes." She playfully slapped him on the arm.

"I'm just kiddin', but for real, just listen to me." Kenneth cleared his throat and began speaking again. "Well, my lease is up in a couple of weeks and I sure don't wanna stay with Beverly's mother, so I was wondering, could we stay here until the house is finished?" Kenneth closed his eyes and waited for his grandmother to fly off the handle and start shooting cuss words his way.

Grandma Davidson looked at her grandson like he was crazy. "What? You mean to tell me that you wanna stay here? In my house with all the furniture that's been here since dinosaurs roamed the earth?" she teased.

"Gran, I was just playin'," he opened his eyes and laughed.

"Boy, you know you more than welcome to come here. I wouldn't let you stay with Beverly's mother, even if you wanted to."

Kenneth smiled and gave his grandmother a hug.

"But I'll tell you what, if that girl gets out of line with you one time, her ass is gon' be out there on the curb before you can say the word boo, you feel me?"

"Yes, Gran." Kenneth gave his grandmother another hug and kissed her on the cheek.

"Now run to the store and get ya grandma some Aleve, I got a pounding headache."

Kenneth did what was asked of him and hurried to the corner store. He was so happy his life was finally coming together again. He thought after the devastating loss of his parents, and the shocking moment he walked in and found Beverly in bed with his best friend, his life would never get any better, but he was wrong; Everything was finally coming together. From this day forward it would be all good . . . or would it?

Chapter Twenty-two

Keaundra rushed through her front door, throwing her purse and keys down on the sofa, and making her way to her bedroom. She was moving so quick, she didn't even notice Peaches on the back of the sofa waiting for her belly rub. Keaundra took off her clothes and put on something more comfortable. She walked out into the hall and opened the linen closet, pulling out her brand new sheet set with the comforter and dust ruffle to match. She wanted everything to be perfect for tonight.

Once she finished cleaning her room, she went into the kitchen to pull out some pork chops to thaw. She decided instead of their usual pizza, she would cook Hammer's favorite meal. While she ran the meat under hot water to thaw it, she walked into the living room to turn on some music to get her hyped up. She was finally getting some dick, some real dick. Keaundra smiled to herself and walked down the hall toward her bedroom.

She opened up her nightstand drawer and pulled Peter out. She took the top off the box. "Well, Peter, I will no longer be needing you," she said to her handy-dandy vibrator, and tossed him in the waste paper basket. She took some old papers from the drawer, crumbled them up, and threw them on top of Peter to keep him hidden from Hammer. She walked back into the kitchen to begin preparing her meal.

After she got the pork chops in the oven and the vegetables cooking on low, she decided it was time for her to get ready. She went into the bathroom and ran some water. She poured some bubble bath in the water and began undressing.

As soon as she put one foot in the water to test its temperature, the phone rang. "Imagine that," she said as she made her way to the kitchen to get the cordless. She looked at the caller ID and rolled her eyes. "Hello, Gran," she answered.

"Hey, chile, what you doin'?"

"I'm standing in the kitchen buck naked."

"Oh, girl, you so silly," Grandma Davidson laughed. "What you doin' for real?"

Keaundra laughed too. "I just told you, Gran."

"Oh, you were serious?"

"Yeah, I was." *Dessert*, she thought as she took a Jell-o cheesecake out of the cabinet.

"Is Hammer in the kitchen with you?" Grandma Davidson asked on the sly.

"No, Gran, he's not here yet."

"Oh, well, me and ya brother was talkin' about you today."

Keaundra leaned her naked behind against the refrigerator and leaned her head to the side while the phone rested between her shoulder and ear. "Talkin' about me for what?" Keaundra asked curiously.

"We were just sayin' how happy you are with this Hammer guy."

Keaundra smiled at the sound of his name. "Yes, Gran, I am happy, very happy." Keaundra opened the oven door, checked on the pork chops, and stirred the vegetables.

"Well, I'm happy for you and Kenneth is too."

"Thanks, Gran." Keaundra made her way back toward the bathroom as her grandmother bragged about the house Kenneth was getting built from the ground up. "That's nice, Gran," she replied as she soaked in the hot water.

After about fifteen more minutes of her listening to her grandmother ramble on about her next-door neighbors and her sudden headaches, Keaundra decided to get off the phone. "Well, Gran, I'll talk to you later, I need to start getting ready for my date."

"Okay, baby. I can't wait to meet Hammer. He really has changed you into a better person.

The way you act now he must be living up to his name."

"Huh? What you mean by that?" Keaundra asked, confused.

"*Hammer* must really be poundin' the hell outta yo' puss—"

"Gran!" Keaundra shouted in shock, cutting her grandmother off. "You are so nasty," Keaundra laughed.

"What? Grandma's just keepin' it real . . . that's all."

Keaundra shook her head and hung up the phone. Then, she finished taking her bath and put on some sweats and a T-shirt until it was closer to Hammer's arrival. Next, she finished preparing the meal and cheesecake before calling her girls to calm her nerves.

"Did you tell her yet?" David asked Hammer as he stood over him, spotting him as he bench-pressed the hundred and fifty pounds of heavy weights.

"Naw, man, not yet," he said as he exhaled.

David looked down at his cousin and shook his head. "Man, you gon' fuck around and hurt that girl's feelings."

Hammer slammed the bar down into its resting place. Making such a loud noise, it caught some of the other patrons' attention. Sitting up on the weight bench he placed his head in his hands.

"I know, man. That's why I'm gon' tell her tonight."

David tapped his cousin's leg and motioned for him to scoot over. "How do you think she's gon' take it?"

"I don't know, man. I hope she understands."

David shook his head in disgust. "What?" Hammer inquired.

"Nothin', man. Just nothin'." David said angrily and got up from the bench, walking toward the locker room.

Hammer sat on the bench, confused. He didn't know what was ailing his cousin, but he had so much on his mind at the moment, he really didn't care. Hammer sat staring into space for a few minutes before getting up and following his cousin into the locker room. After a quick shower, he got dressed. He was hoping David was still lingering around the gym like always, but he wasn't. With his mind clouded with what and how he was going to break the news to Keaundra about Kelly, Hammer made his way to his car.

After hanging up the phone with Keaundra, Alexis and India sat around laughing and talking about how happy they were for her. Once the children had played until they tired themselves out, India decided it was time for them to have a drink. She walked into the kitchen, grabbed two champagne glasses, brought them back into the living room, and set them on the table. She walked over to the liquor cabinet and pulled out a fresh bottle of Wrothram Pinot. She filled Alexis's flute to the rim and did the same for hers.

"Toast," they both said as they held up their glasses.

"To friendship and relationships," India said. Alexis nodded her head in agreement as their glasses clinked together.

"Ummm," Alexis moaned as the smooth taste of the wine tickled her taste buds.

"You can say that again," India seconded.

"Where did you get this from?" Alexis asked before taking another sip from her flute.

India took another sip from her glass before answering. "Martell bought it for me. He said we were going to celebrate the next deal he closes."

Alexis set her half-empty glass down on top of the coaster resting on the coffee table. "Well, why are we drinking it then?"

"Girl, please. It ain't like we're drinking it all. They'll still be some left for me and Martell to celebrate with."

Thirty minutes later, Alexis and India had finished off the entire bottle of wine.

"So much for you and Martell's celebration," Alexis slurred as she poured the last few drops into her glass.

India shrugged her shoulders. "Oh, well. I guess we'll have to celebrate with somethin' else," she giggled.

"You don't have a choice," Alexis said before finishing off her drink. "Too bad it's all gone."

"I know. I better throw the bottle away before Martell decides to pop up." India laughed.

"Too late." Alexis giggled as Martell walked through the front door. "Hello," Alexis spoke, but Martell kept right on walking.

"How rude," India looked over at Alexis and said. "Martell, Alexis spoke to you." Martell stopped, turned, and looked at India and then at Alexis, nodded his head in an upward motion, and continued walking toward the bedroom.

Alexis's cell phone rang and she checked the caller ID. "This is Beverly," she said for no reason in particular before answering the call.

India stood up and walked into the kitchen to throw the wine bottle away. As she made her way back into the living room, she heard Martell let out a loud sigh as he walked out of her bedroom.

He walked into the living room shaking his head. He looked at both women with a disgusted look on his face and proceeded into the kitchen, and that's when all hell broke loose.

"What the fuck is this?" Martell shot out of the kitchen and yelled as he held up the empty wine bottle. India had a dumb expression on her face as he stood there with the bottle held up in the air.

"Beverly, I'll call you when I get in the car," Alexis said, pushing end on her cell phone. She scrambled to get her shoes on her feet before disappearing down the hallway to retrieve her children.

"What?" India asked as if it was no big deal.

"What the fuck you mean, what?" Martell snapped. "How come y'all drank the damn wine you and I was supposed to celebrate with?"

India could tell Martell was furious. "Calm down, Martell, it was only a bottle of wine, damn," she huffed, rolling her eyes.

Martell let the empty bottle fall to his side. "You just don't get it, do you?" Martell looked at Alexis and grimaced as she and her children walked into the living room.

"I'll call you later," Alexis said to India, avoiding eye contact with Martell as she opened up the front door.

India stood up from the sofa and walked over toward the door. "Okay, girl, don't forget." India bent down and kissed each of her godchildren on the forehead. "Auntie will see y'all later." India watched as her friend and godchildren safely got into the car. She closed the door and turned around to what seemed like a raging bull. Martell was still standing in the same spot, looking mad as hell.

"Are you gon' answer me or what?" Martell shouted and walked toward India's bedroom.

"Look, Martell, you gon' hafta calm down if you want an answer from me," India hissed as she followed him into her room.

"Okay." Martell stood as calmly as he possibly could.

India looked Martell dead in the eyes as she spoke. "Alexis and me drank the wine because we were celebrating."

Martell turned up his face. "Celebrating what?" he said in a raised tone. "What the fuck was so important you and your hood-rat-ass friend had to drink the muthafuckin' bottle of wine I spent my hard earned money on for us, me and you, India, to celebrate with?"

"We were celebrating our friendship and our relationships," India said smartly.

"Puhleeze, India. I really can't believe you. First, I come home and find you and that bitch drinking the wine I bought for us," he said, beating his chest.

Nigga, please, this is not your home, she thought as she watched Martell overreact about a bottle of wine.

"Secondly, I come into the bedroom to lay down, and find not one but two crumb snatchers spread out all over my damn bed."

That is not your bed, she wanted to say, but kept her mouth closed.

"Chip crumbs, Kool-Aid glasses, and God knows what else all around the room. If the bitch gon' come over, the least you can do is make the ho control her muthafuckin' triflin'-ass kids, India," Martell shouted.

"Hold up," India said, holding up her hands. "You are not about to be talkin' like that about my godchildren. They are children, Martell, for heaven's sake," she huffed.

"Look, I keep tellin' you I'm gettin' real fed up. I can't take it no more." Martell balled up his fists and began shaking them. "I better get outta here before I do somethin' I might regret later." Martell walked out of the bedroom and into the living room and stood there.

India followed him, only because all the excitement on top of the buzz she had from the wine was making her horny, so she couldn't let Martell leave, at least not until he gave her a nut. "Where you going?" she whined.

"I'm going to my place," he said, never turning around as he made his way toward the door.

"Why?" she whined again. "I don't wanna be home alone."

Martell stopped in his tracks but still never turned to face her.

"I want you to stay with me."

"Why? You don't give a fuck about me. You care more about your friends and their children than you do me!" Martell snapped angrily.

India walked toward Martell and placed her hand on his strong shoulder. "That's not true, Telly." India knew she was getting through to him by the way his tense body had softened up.

Martell knew India only called him Telly when they were sexing or she wanted to be sexed. It had been awhile since he had been between his woman's legs; two weeks to be exact, so he let go of his anger and grabbed the hand that rested on his shoulder. He kissed it softly as he turned around to face her. A smile crept across her lips.

"Baby, why you always puttin—" Martell started to say.

India placed her index finger up to Martell's lips. "Shhh," she said, shaking her head. She held on to his hand and led him back into her bedroom. She walked him over to the bed. 'Sit down," she commanded, and like a child obeying his parent, he did so. She began removing her clothes, slowly, but seductively.

Martell could feel his nature rise as he watched his brick house undress.

"You like?" she asked, with the sexiest look on her face.

Martell was so turned on he couldn't speak. All he could do was nod.

"Good," she said as she removed the last of her attire. She walked over to him and began unbuttoning his shirt. Martell sat there, helpless, as India removed the rest of his clothes with little assistance from him. India could tell by the eight-inch ruler that stuck out from between his thighs that Martell was turned on big-time.

Martell attempted to suck one of India's perky breasts but she stepped back. "Slow down, baby," she purred. India kissed Martell from the top of his fresh haircut down to his chest. She got down on her knees in front of him and took his manhood into her warm, moist mouth.

"Mmmmm . . ." Martell moaned in pure ecstasy as India began putting in work. India's head bobbed up and down while she sucked the electricity out of Martell's body. With his eyes glued shut, he grabbed the top of her head and began pushing it up and down. India didn't mind at all, in fact, it turned her on even more because that let her know she was working her man's magic stick like a nine-to-five. Once Martell was about to cum, India pulled back.

"My turn," he said as he stood up from the edge of the bed. Martell picked India up and began kissing her hard, but passionately. He gently laid her on the bed and spread her legs. India closed her eyes and held her breath, preparing herself for the ride Martell was about to take her on. He lowered his head between her legs, just close enough for her to feel his warm breath on her clit, and flicked her little man in the boat with his tongue once, and that damn near sent her over the edge.

Martell lifted his head so he could see her fuck face then lowered his head again, but this time he just wanted to take in the aroma of her fresh Brazilian-waxed pussy. He began teasing her with his tongue. He started licking the inside of her thighs and it was driving her bananas. India raised her hips off the bed, trying to guide Martell's wet tongue to her throbbing pussy, but he kept avoiding her advances as he continued teasing her.

"Telly," she moaned almost in a begging manner.

"Calm down, baby, I got this," Martell said before he gave in and gave his woman what she wanted.

"Yesssss," she squealed as Martell ate the memory card out of her.

As India lay shaking, Martell reached over and pulled a condom from her nightstand drawer. As much as he would love for India to be the mother of his firstborn, he knew she wouldn't let him go up in her raw for all the tea in China. Martell placed the condom on his fully erect manhood and plunged into India like a diver. They made love in every position possible until they were both exhausted. Martell rolled over and fell asleep as India lay wide-awake with a huge smile on her face. "India, you have done it again," she said before snuggling next to her man and drifting off to sleep.

Chapter Twenty-three

Keaundra made sure that everything was perfect for Hammer's arrival. The table was set beautifully. Her mother's candle burned in the center of the table as the bottle of White Zinfandel chilled in ice. The pork chops and vegetables had turned out just the way she wanted. She took the rolls out of the oven and placed them in the breadbasket her grandmother had given her for Christmas one year.

Keaundra walked around the house and made sure every light was off. The only light she wanted shining was the light from the twenty-something candles she had burning. Walking into her bedroom to make sure everything was intact. She laid two condoms on top of her nightstand, but not wanting to be thought of as desperate, even though she was. She decided to place them under her pillow.

Keaundra looked at herself in the mirror one last time. She admired her body as she sported a red lace negligee, with the robe to match. She even went as far as putting on a pair of red pumps, because that's what she'd always seen in movies. Keaundra glanced over at the clock on her nightstand and her heart began to beat faster as seven o'clock crept up on her. She paced the floor until she heard the doorbell ring.

"Oh, no, he's here." Keaundra gave herself a last once-over before turning off her bedroom light and walking into the living room to open the door.

When Keaundra opened up the door, Hammer was surprised to see all of the lights off. "Your electric got turned off?" he joked as he walked into the house.

"Naw, silly," she laughed nervously.

As they got closer to the light from the candles, Hammer noticed the sexy ensemble Keaundra was wearing. "Damn," he said out loud, meaning to say it to himself.

"You like?" Keaundra turned in a circle and asked.

Hammer gazed at Keaundra through the candlelight. "You look good, girl."

"Are you ready to eat?"

"I sure am," Hammer said. "Is the pizza here already?"

"There's been a change in plans. We're not eating pizza tonight," Keaundra said softly.

"What's on the menu?" Hammer followed Keaundra into the kitchen.

"Your favorite."

"Smells good." Hammer took a seat and watched as Keaundra prepared their plates. He waited for Keaundra to take a seat and he grabbed her hand. "Let's pray." Keaundra bowed her head as Hammer said the prayer. After their amens, they both began eating the deliciously prepared meal.

Hammer and Keaundra laughed and talked over dinner and after dessert, Keaundra cleared the dishes with Hammer's help and they moved the after party to the living room sofa. Hammer stared into Keaundra's eyes as the fire from the candles flickered. They both sat in silence, savoring the moment. Keaundra stared back with confidence. She wanted Hammer as badly as she thought he wanted her. He touched a curl that hung loosely from her hair. She leaned in for the kill.

Hammer leaned in also, but stopped himself. "Wait, Keaundra," he said, sitting back and taking a deep breath. "I can't do this."

"What?" Keaundra asked, confused.

"I . . . I can't do this . . ." he stammered.

Keaundra leaned over and turned on the lamp that sat on the end table. "What type of game are you playin'?"

"Game? I'm not playin' no games with you."

"I don't understand, Hammer. If you can't do this, why did you call me earlier and told me you wanted to do somethin' you should have done a long time ago?"

Hammer hung his head. "Damn."

"Damn what?" Keaundra asked in a need-to-know tone.

"I didn't mean for it to sound like I was coming over here for sex, even though I want nothin' more than to make love to you. I just can't."

Keaundra was so embarrassed, she wanted to die. She attempted to close her robe before she spoke. "Look, Hammer, what's goin' on?"

Hammer interlocked his fingers before he began speaking. "Keaundra I came over here to tell you somethin' that I should have told you a long time ago. I'm sorry if I misled you."

"You what? What do you have to tell me?" Keaundra stood up from the sofa and looked down at him. "Oh my God, don't tell me you're gay," she said with a serious look.

Hammer couldn't help but laugh. "Hell naw, girl, I'm far from a fag."

"I don't see anything funny, Hammer. What did you come over here to tell me?" Keaundra placed her hands on her hips and waited for an answer.

"Please, sit down," he said, grabbing for her hands.

"No!" she said, snatching her hands away.

Hammer stood up too and looked down at the floor.

"The least you can do is look me in my face."

"You right." Hammer looked into Keaundra's eyes, knowing he was in love with her, but also knowing there could never be anything between them because of his promise to Kelly.

"I'm waiting," she said with her hands still on her hips.

Hammer took a deep breath. "Keaundra, I like you a lot. Matter of fact, I think I'm in love with you." Keaundra wanted to shout and jump for joy because she felt the same way, but she held off the celebration until Hammer was finished saying what he came to say. "But, we can never be anything more than just friends."

"Just friends, huh?" she repeated, shocked.

"Yes, just friends."

"This is real fucked up!" she shouted. "And why is that? You already got a woman? Shit, nigga, I know you not married? What the fuck is going on?" Keaundra felt like her heart stopped beating for a brief second.

Hammer hung his head again. Keaundra's voice cracked and tears filled her eyes as she spoke. "So you lied to me? You are married?" Keaundra asked through tears.

Hammer lifted his head and saw the tears streaming down Keaundra's face and his heart broke into a million tiny pieces. The last thing he had wanted to do was hurt her.

"It's not what you think, Keaundra."

"It's not what I think? Nigga, you're married! Get the fuck outta my damn house!" she said, pointing to the front door.

"Keaundra, let me explain," he pleaded. Hammer grabbed Keaundra by both of her hands, but before he knew it, she was going off like a mad woman.

"Get the fuck out," she cried as she began wailing on Hammer. She swung with all her might. She took all the hurt she had built up in her out on Hammer. She swung and screamed with all her might, taking all her hurt and frustrations she had built up inside her out on Hammer. He attempted to block her blows, but most of them connected.

"Let me explain, Keaundra," he said as he tried to duck and dodge her powerful punches.

Keaundra took a break from swinging just to talk. "Get the fuck out of my house, Hammer!" she shouted, out of breath.

"I'm not leavin' until you calm down and let me explain."

"I don't wanna hear shit you gotta say. Hammer, please just get out." Keaundra looked at Hammer as the tears flowed freely, shook her head, walked into her bedroom, and slammed the door behind her.

Peaches jumped up on the back of the sofa and purred. Hammer took a deep breath before rubbing Peaches's head.

Hammer waited a few seconds before walking to her bedroom door. He knocked softly, but she didn't answer. He knocked again. Hammer wanted to open the door and go in and plead his case, but he was no fool. He couldn't take the chance of walking in and getting rolled out on a gurney, so he played it safe. All he could hear were muffled cries as he placed his ear against the door to see if he could hear any movement. Hammer waited by the door for about five more minutes to see if Keaundra was going to come out. When he finally realized she wasn't coming out, he shook his head.

"Keaundra, I love you," he said as tears filled his eyes. Hammer walked away from her bedroom door and out of the house.

Once Keaundra heard the front door close, she waited a few minutes to see if Hammer had really left. She stood up from her bed and peeked out of her bedroom door. She looked down the hall and watched as Peaches sashayed her way toward her. Peaches walked into Keaundra's room and jumped up on her bed.

Keaundra shut her door, sat down on the edge of her bed, and began rubbing Peaches. She couldn't wait to call her girls and tell them what just went down, but first she had some business to take care of. She reached down in the waste paper can, pulled Peter out, and wiped him off with her hand.

"Oh, well, Peter, I guess it's me and you again," she said to her vibrator. Keaundra shooed her cat off the bed and lay back with her legs spread open as wide as they would go. Tears began flowing down the side of her face as she put Peter in his favorite place and let him take her to complete ecstasy.

Hammer walked into the house and slammed the door behind him. He looked in the living room where David and Alexis sat watching a movie.

David smiled toward his cousin, but his smiled faded as soon as he saw the sadness in his eyes. "How did it go?"

Hammer looked at David and then at Alexis and continued walking to his bedroom. Hammer sat down on his bed, held his head in his hands, and looked down at the floor.

"Why did I have to make such a silly promise to my wife," he said aloud. Tears began to burn Hammer's eyes as he thought about the last day he has spent with his wife. How weak and frail she had looked as she lay in the hospital bed six months pregnant and deteriorating from the brain cancer that ate away at her.

Kelly was the only woman who Hammer loved almost as much as his own mother. Despite her selfishness, unpredictable mood swings, and her conceited ways, Hammer still adored his wife. Hammer loved Kelly so much that as she lay on her death bed, she made him promise he would never replace her with another woman.

Out of love and respect he held for his wife, Hammer agreed. Unfortunately, Kelly did not make it out of surgery alive, and the promise he made to her he would later regret.

Hammer could no longer stay in his and Kelly's house, so his cousin David suggested he sell the house and move in with him. Hammer sold all he could and what he could not sell, he gave away. The only memories he wanted of Kelly was the ones he held in his heart. He never really was himself again until he met Keaundra. She brought something out of him that had been bottled up for the past year, causing him to constantly battle within himself about the promise he'd made to his late wife. Hammer knew if he wanted any kind of

future with Keaundra, he would have to deal with
his conscience and try to repair the damage he
had caused.

Chapter Twenty-four

Martell already made up in his mind the next time India put her friends before him, he was leaving her for good. Martell was fed up with playing second in India's life. He had plenty of women throwing the pussy at him, but turned it down, well, except for the couple of hotties he hooked up with while he was away on his business trips. Martell didn't consider it cheating because the women he messed around with lived in different states.

India turned out to be just what his mother told him she was; a spoiled little bitch who had to have her way at all times. As much as Martell hated to admit it, he had let it get way out of hand. If he had put his foot down like he was supposed to in the beginning of their relationship, he wouldn't be going through the stuff he was going through with India now. Martell was through kissing India's ass. From now on, it was his way or the highway and he meant it.

"Baby, could you please do me a favor this weekend?" India asked Martell as she got dressed for school.

"Anything for you, baby cakes." Martell smiled as he admired his woman.

"Keaundra—"

"I ain't doin' shit for that bitch," he spat, cutting her off. "I don't even like that ho, so why would I do anything for her?"

India sighed as her eyes rolled into the top of her head. "If you would let me finish, you would know I don't want you to do anything for Keaundra, it's her grandmother who needs the help."

Martell's entire attitude changed. "Oh, what does *she* need done?" Martell liked Gran because she was as real as they came.

India buttoned up her House of Dereon jeans. "Her air conditioner went out last summer and she needs someone to look at it." India slid her feet in her Jimmy Choo pumps. "You know she's too old to be sittin' in a hot house all summer."

"It ain't even summer yet."

"It's the end of May and plus, Gran likes to get things taken care of beforehand."

"Don't Kenneth and his fiancée live with her now?" Martell asked with a slight attitude.

"Yeah, but Kenneth's out of town." India walked over to the mirror on her dresser and applied some

Vaseline to her lips. "He won't be back until Monday night."

"Tell her I'll be over Sunday. I have to go out of town Friday night and I won't be back 'til Saturday evening," Martell said, getting out of bed.

India smiled, admiring her man's large package as it swung from side to side as he walked over to her. "You know she be in church all day on Sundays," India said, smiling.

Martell hugged India around her waist, pushing his half-erect manhood against her backside. "That's my only free day, baby."

"Calm down, tiger, I'm already running late for school," India laughed as she struggled to get out of Martell's grasp.

"Seriously, Sunday is the only day I can make it." Martell picked his pants up from off the floor and put them on.

"Then Sunday it is. Shit, Beverly will be there, so she can let you in," India stated in a matter-of-fact tone.

"That's cool," he said, putting on his shirt.

India grabbed her backpack off the chaise, kissed Martell on the lips, and walked out of her bedroom.

"See you later," he said before India walked out of the house.

"See you." India closed the door behind her and headed to her truck.

"I love that girl," Martell said aloud as he finished getting dressed.

India's cell phone rang as she weaved in and out of traffic. "Hello?"

"Girl, I need a huge favor," Alexis said into the phone. "It's an emergency."

"What you need?" India asked as she looked in her rearview mirror at the cop car that pulled out behind her.

"I need for you keep the kids Sunday evening," Alexis asked desperately. "I would ask my parents, but they are out of town and Keaundra is goin' somewhere with Beverly."

"Sure, I haven't got anything planned for Sunday, so tell my godchildren I said we'll rent movies and pop some corn."

"Thanks, Indy, you are the best."

"Just what do you got planned anyway?"

India could tell Alexis was smiling. "Well, David is planning a romantic evening for us."

"So in other words, y'all are gon' finally have sex?" India joked.

Alexis giggled. "Yes, girl, it is gon' finally happen and I can't wait!"

India found a parking space and shut her truck off. "Well, as much as I would love to chat, I can't because I'm running late for class." India opened up the truck door. "So kiss the kids for me and tell them I'll see them Sunday."

"Thanks again, India," Alexis said gratefully.

"No problem. That's what friends are for." India hung up the phone and hustled to class. As she reached her psychology class, a text message came across her cell phone:

> Sun, me n u out 2 dinR, won't t8ke no 4 answer, love Telly.

India smiled. "My man is so romantic," she said as she made her way to her seat. "Shit," she shouted before sitting down.

"Are you okay, Ms. Davenport?" the professor asked.

"Yeah, I'm fine." It had just dawned on India that she had just promised Alexis that she would babysit for her on Sunday, so dinner with Martell was going to have to be postponed. "Here we go again," India mumbled as she pulled her psychology book out of her backpack.

Keaundra woke up exhausted. Ever since Hammer's confession, she had done nothing but cry. If she heard a slow song on the radio, she would cry. If she watched a movie she and Hammer had watched together, she would break down and cry, and every time she had to use Peter, she would cry because it was a toy and not Hammer. She didn't want to leave the house, but she had promised Beverly weeks ago she would go with her to buy all of the bridemaids' shoes. So she peeled herself out of bed and stumbled to the bathroom. She looked at herself in the mirror and noticed the big dark rings underneath her eyes.

"Girl, you look a hot mess," she said to her reflection. Tears flowed down her cheeks as she stood feeling sorry for herself. Keaundra turned on the water in the shower and got in, letting the water run down her body as thoughts of Hammer invaded her mind. She couldn't get him out of her head.

After showering, she threw on a pair of old jeans and a tank top, and pulled her growing hair up into a ponytail. Keaundra picked up the phone, dialed her grandmother's number and told Beverly to be ready she was on her way. Keaundra got into her car and put her seatbelt on. She turned the radio on before backing out of the driveway. Mary J. Blige's "I'm Goin' Down" came on. She had never paid any real attention to songs that came on the radio, but since she and Hammer had split, it seemed to her that every singer was singing about her life.

Keaundra pulled up into her grandmother's driveway. She was so exhausted from all the crying she had done in the past couple of weeks, she couldn't even get out of the car. She blew the horn a few times and waited for Beverly to come out.

Beverly came to the door and held up her index finger. "Hang on, I'm comin'."

Keaundra smiled, not really wanting to. "You betta hurry up, bitch, before I leave yo' ass," she said aloud.

After a few seconds, Beverly came out the door dressed in a nice, casual outfit. It was too white-girl for Keaundra's taste, but it was okay for Beverly, being that she was mixed anyway.

"Hey, girl," Beverly said, getting into the car. Her spirits were high. She had finally gotten one of the most important people in her soon-to-be husband's life to forgive her for her wrongs, and that had her excited. She began talking just like old times, not wanting to think about a couple of years back when Keaundra had got in that ass for messing around on her brother. Beverly was glad that she and her future sister-in-law were about to spend some time together. All she really wanted was for Keaundra to see she was a changed person and everything in her life now revolved around God and her brother.

"Hey," Keaundra said in a melancholy tone.

"Are you okay?" Beverly asked, noticing her lack of enthusiasm.

"Yeah, I'm fine. I'm just goin' through somethin' right now." Keaundra pulled out of the driveway and drove down the street. "Where we goin' first?"

"I thought maybe we could go to the Shoe Department, then maybe Macy's. We'll just play it by ear, okay?"

Keaundra nodded in agreement.

Beverly didn't know if she should cross the line, but she tried her luck anyway. The worst that could happen was Keaundra would cuss her out. "Is it Hammer who has you bothered?" she said, waiting on a royal tongue lashing for trying to get in Keaundra's business. Keaundra and Beverly talked, but they were nowhere near cool.

Keaundra needed someone to talk to before she exploded. She talked to India and Alexis about Hammer from time to time, but didn't really want to keep bothering them with her problems since they were both occupied with their men. "Yeah, we're goin' through somethin' right now."

"Would you like to talk about it?"

"Sure, why not." Keaundra pulled into Starbucks for a much needed cup of coffee. The women placed their order, went outside, and took a seat at a table on the patio. Keaundra began feeling a little better after a two-hour talk with Beverly.

"Well, are you ready to go find some shoes?"

"Yep. Let's go." Keaundra stood up, smoothed out her clothes, and walked to her car. She looked back at Beverly and smiled.

"What?" Beverly asked, smiling.

"You're glowin'. Are you pregnant?" Keaundra asked, opening up the car door and getting in.

"No. I can't have kids, remember?" Beverly opened up the car door and got in as well.

"Oh, yeah, that's right. I'm sorry."

Beverly had way too many abortions in her younger days and it had messed her body up. The doctor told her after her fifth abortion the chances of her ever being able to conceive were slim to none. Beverly hadn't cared then, all she knew was that she definitely didn't want a child, not knowing each time if Kenneth was the father or not.

"That's okay," Beverly said, teary eyed.

Keaundra started up the car and pulled out of the Starbucks parking lot. Another one of Mary J.'s songs came on the radio. "Dang, they just played a Mary J. Blige song on my way over to Gran's house."

"Maybe it's her birthday or somethin'," Beverly responded as she bobbed her head to the beat.

"Yeah, maybe. This is my jam and from this day forward, it's my theme song, too." Keaun-

dra sang along as Mary sang "Enough Crying."
She sang loud and off-key, but she didn't care
because the lyrics were lifting her spirits. She
pulled into the mall parking lot and she and
Beverly got out. The ladies walked into the mall
like two best friends. They laughed and talked
as they shopped for any and everything Beverly
wanted, thanks to Kenneth's American Express
credit card, which had no limit.

Kenneth wanted his fiancée to have the perfect wedding, and told her to make sure she got
everything she'd ever dreamt of having for her
wedding and Beverly was doing just that. She
went all out. She bought twenty-dollar candles
for all thirty tables, she got books of matches
with their names engraved on the front cover,
and she even went as far as buying a two-hun-
dred dollar set of flutes for them to toast with.
You name it, Beverly bought it, not to mention
the new wardrobe she bought to take with them
on their two-week honeymoon to Belize.

"Aren't you finished shoppin' yet?"

"Just about," Beverly said as she looked at the
Dooney & Bourke purse selection.

"We came to the mall to get shoes for the
bridesmaids' and you have bought everything
except shoes," Keaundra laughed.

"Yeah, shoes. I need shoes to go with my outfits."

"Not shoes for you, silly, for us." Keaundra followed Beverly over to the shoe section and began checking out the shoes for all the girls.

"I like these," Beverly said, holding up a six-inch heel.

"For who? Us or a stripper?" Keaundra joked.

Beverly set the shoe back down. "Pick a shoe out you think would look cute with y'all dresses."

Keaundra browsed around all the shoes. "I like these white ones." She picked up the shoe and showed Beverly.

"So do I." Beverly walked over to Keaundra and took the shoe from her hand. "Let's get 'em."

"They're white though." Keaundra grimaced.

"That's okay. We can get 'em dyed."

"Yeah, I never thought about that."

Beverly called the saleswoman over, pulled out a piece of paper with all the sizes of the girls in the wedding, and asked the saleslady to get them for her.

"I hope they got Kay-Kay's size," Keaundra laughed. "She's my cousin and all, but baby girl got some big feet to be a lady." Beverly didn't comment even though she had thought the same thing. Instead, she came in Kay-Kay's defense. "Her feet ain't that big. She only wear a size ten."

"Girl, a ten is big for a female. I tell Kay-Kay that all the time," Keaundra laughed.

The salesperson brought all of Beverly's shoes up to the register with the help of another girl. "Here you are," she said as she began ringing up the sale. "Will this be cash or charge today?"

"Charge," Beverly said proudly. She whipped out Kenneth's American Express card like it belonged to her. As much money as she spent today, you couldn't tell her it wasn't.

Keaundra was exhausted and hungry. She wanted to get away from the mall—fast. "Let's go get some lunch."

"That sounds like a good idea to me," Beverly said as they headed out of the mall. They decided on Chinese food. Once seated, they began laughing and talking, and Keaundra noticed how much Beverly smiled every time she talked about Kenneth. Keaundra had been skeptical at first and thought maybe Beverly was just marrying her brother for his money, but the more she listened to her, the more she realized Beverly really did love Kenneth. Satisfied and ready to forgive and forget, now all Keaundra had to do was try to talk her grandmother into doing the same thing, which she knew would be tougher than leather.

Chapter Twenty-five

David was sitting around the house watching the highlights from the hockey game before getting ready for his romantic evening with Alexis, when the telephone rang. He was so into the fight that broke out on the ice; he didn't even check the caller ID before picking it up like he normally did. It had become a ritual lately for Rosalind to continuously blow up his house, cell, and the shop phone. It became a must to always check the caller ID.

"Hello?" he answered, eyes still glued to the television.

"David?" Rosalind asked, surprised that David had answered the phone.

David became irritated just hearing Rosalind's voice. "What do you want, girl?" He started to hang up the phone, but figured he might as well get it over with since she had him on the phone, or she would never stop calling.

"How are you?"

"Rosalind, what is it? I'm busy," he lied.

Rosalind really didn't want anything other than to be back in David's life. He had caught her off guard when he answered the phone, so she didn't have time to make up a story. She had to think quickly. Her mind took her back to the time when she watched an episode of *Diff'rent Strokes*. Kimberly and Willis had conjured up a story to get Muhammad Ali to come visit Arnold under the pretense that this was his dying wish.

"David, I got cancer," she blurted from out of nowhere. Rosalind had made up some lies in the past, but she had shocked herself with this one.

David snapped his attention away from the television. "Are you sure?" he asked, knowing that she was capable of coming up with some wild and crazy stories.

"Yes, David, I'm sure," Rosalind stated morosely.

David began feeling sorry for the woman that he swore he never wanted anything else to do with. He had watched his own father die slowly from the same disease and still felt the loss, so to hear that someone he once cared about had the same ugly disease, softened his heart a little.

"Where's the cancer at, if you don't mind my asking?"

"Cervical—just like my mom," she lied.

"Damn, it must be hereditary or somethin'," David said, saddened by the fact that Rosalind had the same disease that took her mother away also. David knew Rosalind could be psycho at times, but he didn't believe she would ever play with something so serious.

Rosalind couldn't believe that David was actually buying her story, so she really began playing the role. "Yeah, it is," she said, sounding depressed. "That's why I've been tryin'a get in contact with you, but you never returned any of my calls."

David could hear the hurt and pain in Rosalind's voice. "I'm sorry, Ros, I just thought . . . never mind," he said, stopping in mid-sentence. "Just know that I apologize." David really did feel bad. He didn't know what to say next so he said the first thing that came to mind. "Do you need anything?"

Yeah, nigga, I need you to come over here and fuck the shit outta me. "No, I'm fine," she sighed. "Well, I was just calling to let you know I won't keep bothering you."

David really felt bad. He sat quietly on the phone. "Hey, Ros," he called out.

"Yeah, David," she answered as if David was now getting on her last nerve. Rosalind had a smile on her face the entire time and hoped that David couldn't tell.

"If you need anything, please don't hesitate to call." David felt a lump forming in his throat.

"Are you gon' answer the phone?" she asked, sarcastically.

"Yeah, girl," he laughed.

"Okay, David, I'm feelin' tired so I have to go now." Rosalind hung up the phone and danced around the living room like she had just hit the jackpot. "Nigga, I knew I would get you back in my life one way or another," she said aloud. "Watch out, Alexis, 'cause Rosalind is back!"

Rosalind hurried to the Internet to do some research on cancer. She wanted to know every symptom and every medicine that was given to cancer patients; she even went as far as locating some Hospice houses around Ohio. Rosalind began feeling bad about telling such a drastic lie to get David back in her life and felt even worse for telling him that her mother had passed away from cancer just so David would think they had something in common. It had been so long ago when she had told that lie, she had forgotten all about it. Even though her mother was alive and kicking somewhere in a crackhouse, she was dead in Rosalind's eyes.

Chapter Twenty-six

India had put off telling Martell that she was babysitting for Alexis until the day of. Martell and India had lay around the house all morning until the late afternoon. They were worn out from all the lovemaking they had engaged in the night before. India knew she had to put in work and lots of it because once Martell found out that she couldn't make it to dinner, *again,* the shit was gon' hit the fan. India put it down raw and uncut on Martell. She did things to him that she never imagined doing to any man. She licked every part of his body, not missing a spot. She tried to tire him out to the point that he wouldn't want to leave the house.

"What you gon' wear tonight?" he asked India as they lay face-to-face in her bed.

India didn't answer; she began kissing his chest and made her way down to his stomach. She then put his now erect manhood between her lips.

"You haven't had enough of yo' daddy yet?"

"Not yet," she said between licks and sucks. India's chocolate cave got soaking wet as she listened to Martell moan. She was working hard to please her man and even harder to make sure he went to sleep after she was finished. After an hour of sweaty lovemaking, Martell did just what India wanted him to do; he fell straight to sleep.

"Yes," she whispered and climbed out of the bed to take a shower. India showered, dressed in some sweats and a T-shirt, and waited patiently for her godchildren to arrive. As soon as Alexis dropped the kids off, India sat them down in front of the television and ordered *Transformers 2* on the Demand channel.

"I'm hungry, Auntie India," R.J. whined.

"Okay, I'll order a pizza. Now, Auntie needs you guys to be very quiet, okay?"

Both children while India went into the kitchen to order the pizza.

After a two-hour nap, Martell woke up feeling refreshed. He felt India's side of the bed, realizing it was empty; he climbed out of bed in search of his woman. He put on his boxers and walked out of the bedroom and just stood in the doorway once he noticed Alexis's two rug-rats.

India looked up from the television and smiled at her man, hoping he would smile back, but the

look on his face let her know that wasn't happening.

"You never answered my question," he said,
ignoring her smile and never taking his eyes off
the children as he spoke.

India became nervous, knowing all hell was
about to break loose. "What question, honey?"

"The question was, what are you wearing to
dinner tonight?"

"R.J., take your sister and go wait in Auntie
India's room for me, okay, sweetie?"

"But I wanna watch *Transformers*," he whined.

"Me too," Ro'nisha added.

"You can, just as soon as I finish talkin' to
Uncle Martell."

"How come y'all can't go in your room and talk
so we can keep watchin' TV?" R.J. asked smartly.

"Boy, get outta here!"

"Come on, doo-doo head," R.J. said, grabbing
his sister by the hand and pulling her toward
India's room.

India waited until the children were out of
sight before she began speaking. "Martell, honey,
I had promised Alexis I would keep the kids for
her right before I got your text message," India
said, bracing herself because she knew things
were about to erupt.

"So how come you waited all week to tell me if you already planned on not goin' to dinner with me?" India had no explanation. She shrugged her shoulders. "Shruggin' ain't a good enough reason."

"I don't know," she said in a child-like tone.

"How come her muthafuckin' parents or Keaundra couldn't keep 'em?" he shouted.

"Shhh, lower your voice, Martell, the kids are in the other room."

"I don't give a fuck!" he snapped.

"Her parents went out of town and Keaundra went shopping with Beverly," India tried her best to explain, hoping that he would understand, but as usual, he didn't.

"Man, I can't do this shit no more," Martell said as he made his way toward India's room to pack his clothes.

"What are you talkin' about now, Martell?" India asked as she followed close behind.

Martell began grabbing his clothes out of the closet and tossing them on the bed. "You guys go back in the living room and finish watching *Transformers*," India said to the children.

"Yessss!" R.J. ran out the room with his little sister on his heels.

"Every time I wanna spend some quality time with you, you always got somethin' else to do, India." Martell started grabbing his shoes from under her bed, and jewelry and cologne off the dresser, and throwing them on top of his clothes. He grabbed India's Louis Vuitton luggage and began packing his belongings.

She wanted to ask, *Where you going with my luggage?* but didn't.

"I'll drop your luggage back off," he said, reading her facial expression. Once Martell got everything he could into the suitcases, he grabbed his keys off the nightstand. "I'll come back for the rest later." Martell grabbed the suitcase and walked out of India's bedroom.

"So what you sayin', Martell, it's over?" India asked just to make sure she hadn't misunderstood the words that were coming out of his mouth.

"You figure out the *Blue's Clues,*" he said and walked out the front door; slamming it behind him.

"No, this nigga didn't," she said, shocked.

Martell wondered if he was doing the right thing by walking away. He turned around and looked back at the house before continuing his walk to his car. He shook his head, got in the car, and started it up. As he backed out of the driveway, he decided to go ahead and give India one last chance to change her mind about going to dinner before he called it quits. He pulled out his cell phone and dialed her number.

India was sitting watching television when her telephone rang. She looked at the caller ID and smiled. India knew that Martell couldn't resist her. She had heard he was finished too many times before. She didn't believe him then, just like she didn't believe him now. "Hello?" India answered in a cocky kind of way.

"I'm goin' home to get dressed, and when I get back, you better be dressed for dinner. So call me and let me know what it is." Martell hung up the phone without giving her a chance to say anything.

India looked at the phone in shock before placing it back in the cradle. "Fuck you, nigga, I told you I was babysitting," she said, and sat back on the sofa and continued watching the movie with her godchildren.

India was stressing Martell out big-time. He didn't know what to do about this situation. On one hand, he wanted to leave her alone, but he couldn't stand the thought of her being with someone other than him. On the other hand, he wanted to make their relationship work because behind her bitchy ways, there was a sweet person just waiting to come out. Martell was confused. So instead of going home right away, he drove around listening to the mellow sounds of Boney James and tried to get his mind right.

"Shit, I gotta go put that air conditioner in for Gran," he said, almost forgetting. He made a U-turn in the middle of the street and headed over to Gran's house. He bobbed his head as Boney James tickled his eardrums. As soon as he pulled up in Gran's driveway his cell phone began to ring Bow Wow and Ciara's "Like you," letting him know it was India. He smiled. "Hello," he answered, trying not to sound mad anymore.

"Martell, you told me to call you to tell you what it's gon' be."

"Yea."

"Well, I'm babysitting so we are gon' hafta' go out to dinner some other time."

"I'm cool." Martell hung up the phone and threw it on the passenger's seat. He didn't want India to know it, but he was furious. Martell slammed the car into park, got out of the car, and slammed the door before making his way up to the porch. Once he reached the porch, he rang the doorbell and waited for someone to answer.

After a few seconds of waiting, Beverly came to the door wearing nothing but panties and a bra. "Damn," Martell said unknowingly. "Sorry."

"You all right, come on in," Beverly said, opening up the screen door. "Excuse me, but it's too damn hot in here to have on some clothes."

Martell stepped into the house. "Damn, you sure y'all don't have on the heat?"

Beverly walked over to the thermostat. Martell's eyes watched every switch in her hips. "When I got back from shopping I checked to see if the heat was on, but it wasn't, see?" she said pointing.

I can see just fine from over here, he thought. "Well, let me get started. Can you show me where the air conditioner is?"

"It's in the other room." Beverly led Martell into the living room. "Here it is, right here."

Martell walked over to the air conditioner and removed it from the window. "Let me go to my trunk and get my tools."

"You ride around with tools in a nice car like that?"

"I keep my tools with me. You never know what might happen," he said as he walked out to his car. Once he made it back in, he noticed that Beverly had pulled a chair up next to the air conditioner. Martell smiled at her and began unscrewing the back. "Is Gran still at church?"

"Yep, she sure is." *Damn, this nigga is fine,* she thought as she stared at him. *I would love to have a piece of that. Come on, Beverly. You are about to marry Kenneth and he's all the man you need.* Beverly watched as the sweat began pouring from Martell's face. She imagined run-

ning her lips up and down his cheeks, using her
tongue as a sponge. "You thirsty?" she asked,
standing up. Martell wiped the sweat from his
brow.

"Yeah."

Beverly walked toward the kitchen. She knew
Martell, or any man for that matter, couldn't resist watching all that action she had in the back,
and she was right, Martell's eyes were stuck like
glue. "Shit," Martell squealed as blood squirted
from his finger.

"You okay?" Beverly turned back around and
asked.

"I cut my finger on this loose piece of metal,"
he said as he applied pressure to his wound.

"Here, let me see," she said, grabbing a hold of
his hand. "Let's go into the kitchen to rinse this
off." Martell followed Beverly into the kitchen.
She turned the water on and let it run for a few
seconds. Martell hesitated at first. "Come on,
chicken. It won't hurt," Beverly joked. Martell
stuck his finger under the water and watched as
the blood washed down the drain.

"Do you have any Band-Aids?" he asked, looking at the deep cut on his finger.

"Nope, sorry, but I got somethin' else that will
make it feel better." Beverly gently grabbed his
hand and kissed it softly, like a mother would
do her child, making Martell's manhood jump

a few times. "There. You feel better?" she asked seductively.

Martell shook his head.

"Do you need me to kiss it again?" she asked, praying that he said yes.

Surprising them both, Martell nodded.

Beverly smiled and grabbed his hand again, but this time she turned that motherly kiss into some freak-type shit. She stuck his finger in her mouth and sucked on it just like the professional dick sucker she was.

Martell's ruler stood at full attention. He snatched his finger out of her mouth. "I better finish my work," he said, taking a step back.

Beverly smiled at Martell. "I'm sorry if I offended you."

Martell leaned in close to Beverly's face. "Don't be sorry, be careful," he said, looking down at his fully erect love muscle.

Beverly giggled and walked over to the cabinet, watching Martell the whole time as she got a glass out. "Would you still like somethin' to drink?"

"Sure." Martell watched closely as Beverly made her way to the refrigerator.

"What would you like?" She began naming everything they had.

You on a platter, he wanted to say. "I'll just take some water."

Beverly grabbed the pitcher of water out of the refrigerator and began filling up the glass. As she was turning around to hand him the water, the glass accidentally slipped out of her sweaty palm. "Shit!" she yelled as the glass hit the floor.

Martell began to laugh.

"What are you laughing at?"

"I see I'm not the only clumsy one here." He continued to laugh as Beverly got down on all fours to clean up the mess she made. Martell got down on the floor with her and began helping to pick up the glass. Beverly looked up and catching Martell staring at her. She smiled and stared back. Martell leaned in and parted Beverly's lips with his tongue and she didn't resist; in fact, she took control.

Beverly was all into the kiss before she realized what she was doing. She quickly backed away from Martell and stood up, touching her lips as if to see if they were still there. She walked over to the table, took a seat, and held her head in her hands.

Martell got up off the floor, walked over to her, and put his hands on her shoulders. "I am so sorry. I really don't know what got into me," he said, embarrassed.

Beverly looked up at Martell with a slight smile on her face. "Don't be sorry, be careful."

Chapter Twenty-seven

Keaundra was exhausted from all the shopping she and Beverly had done earlier. All she wanted to do was take a hot bubble bath and lay her tired bones down. She needed to go back over to Gran's because she had forgotten to get her shoes for the wedding. She had planned to drop them off to get dyed, but once she made it home, there was no way she was going anywhere but to bed. As she got out of the tub, her telephone rang. She started not to answer it, but answered it anyway just in case it was an emergency.

"Hello?"

"What's up, Ke-Ke?" Kay-Kay asked.

"Not shit. 'Bout to lay my tired ass down."

"Did you and Beverly go shopping today?"

Keaundra put on her pajamas and lay down in her bed. "Yep, and I'm tired." Peaches jumped up in the bed with Keaundra.

"Did she get our shoes?"

Keaundra yawned. "Yeah, but they're white so we have to get 'em dyed peach."

"That's cool. Do you have the shoes at your house?"

"Nope. I forgot to get 'em from Beverly." Keaundra yawned again as she rubbed her cat's fur.

"Shit, I'm 'bout to go get mine and drop 'em off at the shoe store before they close."

"The wedding is three months away. Why you gettin' 'em dyed so soon?" Keaundra asked.

"You know I don't like to wait 'til the last minute to do nothin'," Kay-Kay responded.

"Would you get mine too then and drop 'em off?"

"I sure will." Kay-Kay hung up the phone, grabbed her car keys, and made her way out to her car. She drove fast because the stores closed at six o'clock on Sundays. Kay-Kay pulled up in her grandmother's driveway next to a brand new Porsche.

Um, I see Gran got company. I wonder if it's a man, she thought as she opened up her car door. Reaching the porch, she looked back at the car once more. *Well, whoever it is got to have a lot of money to be ridin' in a whip like that.* Kay-Kay started to knock on the door but decided against it and went ahead and used her house key. She walked into the front room and didn't see anybody. *Huh, I wonder where Gran is.*

Just as Kay-Kay opened up her mouth to call out her grandmother's name, she heard loud moans. *Oh, my goodness, I know Gran is not up in here gettin' her groove on.* She followed the moaning that led her toward the kitchen. She peeked around the corner, but all she could see was some well-built black man towering over her grandmother, pounding her as if he was taking all of his frustrations out on her. Gran's legs rested on his strong shoulders as she called out to the Lord.

Damn, he has a nice body and a cute ass to be an older man. Kay-Kay's eyes did a complete search of his entire backside. Feeling a slight thumping sensation between her legs as she watched this man use his dick like a jackhammer digging the hell out of her grandmother's hole. *This old cat got some skills.* She thought about turning around and sneaking back out the door, but opportunity wouldn't let her. She was about to get her one and only shot at embarrassing Gran just like she had done her countless times growing up. Memories of Ryan Anderson popped into her head. *Payback,* she thought as a smile crept across her face. She giggled quietly, stood in the doorway, and called out to her grandmother.

"Gran." Kay-Kay's eyes widened as the man she thought was old turned out to be some young cat and that Gran was actually Beverly! The young cat quickly pulled up his pants as

Beverly jumped down off the table and ran out of the kitchen. Kay-Kay grimaced, grabbing her stomach as if she was about to become sick. She looked at the fine brotha before backing out of the kitchen. The dark-skinned brotha made his way past Kay-Kay and out the front door.

Kay-Kay wanted to beat the shit out of Beverly. For one, Beverly had disrespected her cousin, Kenneth, again, and for two, disrespecting the table that she ate at every Sunday. Kay-Kay didn't know what to do so she decided to leave, but she knew she would get even with Beverly somehow, for Kenneth's sake.

Kay-Kay got in her car, started it up, and backed out of the driveway as fast as she could. She wanted to get away from there, and fast, feeling angry and betrayed. She did not want to be the bearer of bad news but she couldn't allow this bitch Beverly to get over on her cousin again. Kay-Kay knew she would make Beverly pay some kind of way she just had to figure out how! Kenneth had been through so much in his life already; finding out about Beverly would probably send him over the edge. Tears flowed from Kay-Kay's eyes as she drove home with thoughts of payback dancing around in her mind.

Chapter Twenty-eight

David moved the coffee table from the middle of the living room and spread a blanket on the floor. He filled the picnic basket with finger sandwiches, grapes, strawberries, three kinds of cheeses, assorted crackers, and a bottle of champagne. He lit vanilla scented candles and placed them all around the room.

David had been looking forward to this night for quite a while and wanted everything to be perfect. But ever since Rosalind had called and sprung the news on him about her illness, David couldn't focus on anything other than Rosalind's well-being. Even though he had no intention of ever getting back with Rosalind, David still cared about her. She had a lot of good qualities that would make some man happy, but it definitely wouldn't be him.

At first, David had tried to overlook her insecure ways. He understood that she had been hurt many times in the past by the men she chose to associate herself with, but instead of leaving the

baggage at the door, she had carried it into their relationship.

After a while, David finally admitted that things weren't going to work out between him and Rosalind because her insecurities were getting way out of hand. One time he walked in on her sniffing his underwear to see if she could smell another female's vagina. Other times when he would have to work late, he would see her car riding by the shop to see if his car was there. Another time she even went as far as requesting a printout of his cell phone bill. When David confronted Rosalind about all this, she acted as if what she was doing was completely normal. The final straw was when David found the tape recorder under his car seat; he knew he had to get away from her fast and for good.

Alexis made sure that when she got dressed, her clothes were easily accessible. It being the first part of June made it just that much easier for her to wear next to nothing. She didn't want to dress too scantily so she put on a pair of white, sheer gauchos, a white halter that accentuated her flat abs, and a pair of white Chanel flip-flops. She made sure her white Chanel purse included all the right necessities: a few Summer's Eve wipes, a bottle of FDS spray, and a toothbrush, just in case

the night's forecast called for a little freakiness, and the most important items of all, condoms.

Alexis checked out her flawless image in the mirror as she applied some strawberry Lip Smacker to her juicy lips. She puckered her lips and kissed the air before heading out the door to her car. Once inside her car, her stomach filled up with butterflies. She felt like a virgin who was about to get her virginity taken all over again. While driving to David's house she listened to *The Best of Aretha Franklin* to try to calm her nerves. Once she pulled in David's driveway, she noticed that it looked awfully dark in the inside. She slowly got out of the car and knocked on the door. David opened it up with a huge smile on his face.

"Hello," he said, holding the door open for her to enter.

"Hello to you." She smiled, noticing the sweet scent of vanilla. Alexis followed David into the living room. He sat down on top of the blanket and motioned for her to do the same. "This is nice," Alexis said, admiring the way David had set up the little picnic area for them. No one had done anything this romantic for her in a very long time. Ronald's idea of romance consisted of taking her out to dinner and her paying for it. Alexis wanted to scream, but didn't want to let

on that she wasn't used to being romanced out of her mind.

David was trying his hardest to stay focused on Alexis, but he just could not shake the thought of Rosalind.

"Are you all right, David?" Alexis asked as she noticed him staring off into space.

"Yeah, I'm all right," he answered sullenly.

David and Alexis enjoyed their little picnic, but from time to time, she would catch him staring off. Alexis even caught him doing it a time or two while she was talking. She began to feel like he didn't want to go through with their night. Alexis hoped that David didn't turn out to be just like his cousin Hammer.

"Are you sure you're all right?" Alexis asked again, annoyed that David really wasn't into anything that was going on around him.

"Yeah, why do you keep askin' me that?" David never even noticed that Alexis had been watching him when his mind started to drift again.

"It seems like your mind is occupied with somethin' else." Alexis stood up from the blanket. "Look, we don't have to go through with this tonight. Maybe I'll see you some other time."

"Nonsense," David said, standing up too. "We are gon' go through with this tonight." He sat back down and pulled her down with him.

"Well, what's on your mind then?"

David had been honest with Alexis from the jump and he wasn't about to start telling lies now. He took a deep breath before speaking. He looked her dead in the eyes. "Alexis," he said, taking her hand into his, "Rosalind called me tonight."

David had Alexis's full attention. She hung on to every word that came out of his mouth.

"She told me that she has cancer."

"Okay, and?" she stated bluntly.

"It's just bothering me 'cause I know she's scared. It's the same disease that took her mother's life."

No, this nigga ain't up here feelin' sorry for his ex-girlfriend on the same night I'm supposed to give him some ass. "So you still care about her?" Alexis braced herself for the truth.

"No, I mean, yeah, I do care about her, but as a friend," David explained in hopes of being understood. Alexis looked at David upside his head. "What?" David asked innocently.

"Nothin'," she said, standing up and throwing her purse on her shoulder. "Look, I'ma holla at you when you get your emotions together."

David stood up and tried to protest. "What are you talkin' about?" David gently grabbed Alexis by both wrists. "I got my emotions together. It ain't like I said I wanna marry the girl."

"Like I said, holla at me when you get your feelings in order." Alexis yanked her wrists away and walked out the front door to her car.

David stood in the doorway, confused about what just went down. He was too out done to chase her. He decided he would let her cool down before he called her because there was nothing worse than being cussed out by an angry black woman.

"Shit, sometimes honesty don't get you nowhere," he said, slamming the door as Alexis pulled out of the driveway. "It must be in the air." David blew out the candles and continued talking to himself. "First Hammer and Keaundra, now me and Alexis." David was disgusted. He cleaned up the picnic area, washed up the few dishes in the sink, and went to take a cold shower.

As Alexis drove home, she realized how much she had overreacted. "It ain't like the nigga said he was in love with the broad," she said. "At least he was man enough to keep it real with me, somethin' Ronald never did." Alexis pulled her cell phone out of her purse and dialed David's phone number to apologize for acting like a complete ass. He answered on the first ring.

"Hello?"

"David, I apologize."

David was not used to a woman admitting to being wrong. He was speechless. "It's okay. I apologize too."

"For what? You didn't do anything but keep it real with me and I like that about you."

David smiled. "That's the way I would like to keep it, if you don't mind. I feel that if I need to hide somethin' from you, then I don't need to be with you."

Alexis was really feeling David's philosophy. "I'd like it like that." Silence fell between them. "Would you like for me to come back over?"

"Please, I'll be waiting."

Alexis smiled and hung up the phone. She did a U-turn in the street and headed back over to David's to finish what they had started.

Chapter Twenty-nine

Gran stood over the stove stirring a pot of greens as Beverly sat sulking at the kitchen table cutting celery and onions for the potato salad. Her helping Gran was not by choice but by force.

"When you gon' get yourself a job?" Gran looked over at Beverly and asked.

Beverly rolled her eyes. *Here we go again*, she thought as she continued chopping the celery like she didn't hear her.

"Did you hear me?" Gran asked loudly.

"I'm startin' school in the fall."

Gran laid the big wooden spoon in the spoon holder that sat on top of the stove, wiped her hands on her apron, and turned to face Beverly. "Now, chile, you have been sayin' that same mess since I met you and you ain't even went as far as signing up for no type of classes."

"Excuse me?" Beverly asked indignantly.

"What did you do, sneeze or somethin'? You heard what I said." Gran opened up the oven door to check on her cornbread. She closed the oven door and continued talking to Beverly. "You young girls nowadays kill me. All y'all lookin' for is for some man to take care of y'all and give y'all a wet ass." Gran shook her head in disgust. "Y'all act like y'all so scared to do somethin' for your-selves."

"I'm not afraid to do anything for myself," Beverly huffed, defensively. "I can take care of me."

"Well, why don't you?" Beverly looked at Gran like she was stupid. "Baby, you don't even have a black pot to piss in."

"What?" Beverly snapped before laying the knife down on top of the cutting board.

"Everything you have has been given to you by your parents or my dumb-ass grandson." Gran was becoming angry because she knew that Beverly wasn't doing anything but using her grandson, but he was too blinded by love to even notice.

This old bitch has got a lot of nerve, Beverly thought as she sat there with a dumb look on her face. "Gran, I don't think you know what you're talkin' about."

"Beverly, I'm from the old school, so don't get it twisted." Beverly wanted to laugh at Gran's hip lingo, but didn't. "I can see through you like a piece of plastic. You might have my grandson all confused in the head, but I'm hip to you."

"What are you talkin' about?" Beverly began getting nervous. Beverly wondered if Gran knew that she had fucked Martell on top of her kitchen table, or if she was just talking like most older people do.

"You want my grandson to marry you so he can take care of you, that's what I'm talkin' about."

Beverly was relieved when Gran didn't mention Martell's name.

"You and ya momma think y'all slick. She tryin'a push you off on my grandson so she don't have to take care of yo' grown tail no more."

Beverly had heard enough. She couldn't take any more of the brutal tongue lashing that Gran was handing out. She stood up from the table and pushed her chair in. Gran was so mad she began shaking.

"I love Kenneth." Beverly raised her voice just enough to let Gran know that she didn't know what she was talking about.

"That's why you've been sneakin' your conniving tail off to the doctor, gettin' them fertility shots in hopes of my grandson gettin' you pregnant so he will never leave you. Is that what you call love?" Gran said angrily.

Beverly couldn't say a word because everything Gran was standing in front of her saying was true. She did love Kenneth with all her heart and didn't want him to leave. She knew if she could get pregnant again, he would stay with her for sure, even if he did find out about Martell. "What were you doing in my room rambling through my stuff?" Beverly said, becoming angry.

Gran's eyes bucked as she walked a little closer to Beverly. "Look here, chile." Gran pointed her finger in Beverly's face. "Don't nothin' in this house belong to you; everthing that's brought in here belongs to me. If you want to put claims on it, then put it in your own house, 'cause this house here," Gran said, looking around, "belongs to me! So I'ma let you in on a little secret, there is not a room in this house that I'm not allowed in, you understand me?"

"Yeah, whatever."

Just as Gran was about to cut into her for that smart remark, she had another dizzy spell. Gran grabbed her forehead and fell back against the counter.

Beverly panicked and ran over to help Gran. "You all right, Gran?"

Gran had been having dizzy spells for the past couple of months but hadn't told anyone, because she was too afraid Kenneth and Keaundra might make her go to the hospital. Gran hated hospitals just as much as she hated liver.

"Get off me, chile, I'm fine." Gran shook Beverly away from her, walked back over to the stove, and picked up her wooden spoon to stir the greens.

Beverly walked out of the kitchen and into her bedroom. She sat on the bed and waited for Kenneth to arrive home from work. She lay across the bed, and was flipping through the channels when she drifted off to sleep.

Kenneth came in from work, walked straight into his bedroom, and set his briefcase down. He looked down at his sleeping beauty and bent down, planting a kiss on her cheek. Beverly looked up at him and smiled. She rubbed her eyes as she sat up on the bed to give Kenneth the grapes on Gran. Soon after Beverly filled him in on his grandmother's dizzy spell, Kenneth went straight to her room, walking in without knocking first.

Gran was sitting on her bed watching the finale of *American Idol*. "You don't know how to knock?" she asked without looking up, already knowing it was her grandbaby.

"Naw, my knockers are broke," he teased before giving her a warm kiss on the cheek. Kenneth took a seat on the edge of his grandmother's bed. "What's up?"

"Your head is in my way, that's what's up." Gran attempted to look around Kenneth's head to see the television.

"What did you do today?" Kenneth asked in a roundabout way.

"Would you get to the point so I can finish watchin' *American Idol?*"

Kenneth smiled at his grandmother's bluntness. "Beverly told me what happened in the kitchen today."

"Did she?" Gran asked without any feeling whatsoever.

"And I don't like it one bit, Gran."

"I don't care what you like, boy. I'm the king and the queen of this castle."

Kenneth gave her a confused look. "What does a dizzy spell have to do with you being the king and the queen of this castle?"

"Oh, my bad. It was nothin'," she said, pretending to watch television.

"So just how long has this *nothin'* been goin' on?"

"A couple of days," Gran said, stretching the truth a little.

"Whatever, Gran. This could be somethin' serious. When was the last time you been to see a doctor?"

"It's been awhile and plus, I don't need no doctor tellin' me what's wrong with me. I already know what the problem is."

Kenneth looked around his grandmother's room. "I don't see a Ph.D. hanging on your wall anywhere."

"Don't get smart, boy. You know I hate doctors and hospitals and all that stuff." Gran shivered at the thought of going to a doctor.

"Look, Gran, there could be somethin' seriously wrong with you. So I really think you should make an appointment. Keaundra and me need you, so promise me you'll make an appointment with your doctor tomorrow."

Kenneth hit his grandmother with his sad, puppy dog eyes so she had no choice. "Okay, I promise."

"Okay, now. I'm gon' have Beverly tell me if you made an appointment or not." Kenneth stood up from his grandmother's bed.

"You need to have Beverly take her tail out and find a job," Gran said while she watching her television program. Kenneth shook his head and smiled before walking out of his grandmother's room.

Chapter Thirty

Kay-Kay was sitting at her desk staring into space when Alexis walked through the door. Alexis walked past her and said good morning. Kay-Kay didn't respond. Alexis knew something had to be on her mind because Kay-Kay's mouth never stopped running. She was forever keeping Alexis posted on the latest gossip.

"You okay?" Alexis asked. Kay-Kay looked up at Alexis and shook her head. "What's the matter then?"

Kay-Kay's eyes began to water. "I don't wanna talk about it."

"Girl, don't do that right here," Alexis said, looking around the office at the other women who were starting to notice the tears that had begun falling down Kay-Kay's cheeks. "Come into my office."

Kay-Kay got up from her desk and followed Alexis.

"Close the door."

Kay-Kay took a seat at Alexis's desk and wasted no time talking. "Somethin' is goin' on in someone's life who I'm real close to and I know if I tell 'em that it will kill 'em. I know they need to know, but I don't want to be the bearer of bad news." Tears flowed freely from her eyes. By the time Kay-Kay broke down and told Alexis what she had walked in on, Alexis was almost in tears herself.

Alexis paced back and forth as she spoke. "I can't believe that dirty bitch did it to him again. Who was the nigga she was fuckin'?"

"I don't know. Some dark-skinned cat. He was fine as hell."

"We gon' hafta tell Keaundra," Alexis said. "You know she ain't gon' waste no time beatin' that bitch's ass."

"That's what I'm afraid of."

"We are gon' hafta just pray on the situation," Alexis said to Kay-Kay.

"It's gon' take a lot more than prayer to keep Keaundra from killin' that bitch. Matter of fact, it's gon' take Jesus himself to keep her off of Beverly."

"You already know," Alexis laughed. "We might hafta take up a collection to get her ass outta jail."

Kay-Kay sighed heavily. "I know. I just feel sorry for Ken-Ken 'cause he's a good man."

"Last of a dying breed," Alexis added. Alexis looked at the clock and then at Kay-Kay who was hurting for her cousin. "Don't worry, girl, by the end of the day, trust me, I will come up with somethin'."

"Are you sure?"

"I'm sure."

Kay-Kay and Alexis went on with their day as Alexis racked her mind trying to come up with a way to tell Keaundra without Keaundra getting herself into a world of trouble. But knowing Keaundra, that was going to be easier said than done.

Hammer had been working out for two hours. He was losing it. He couldn't eat, sleep, or think straight. All he could do was keep wondering what Keaundra had been up to. He felt like a teenage boy in love for the very first time. No woman had ever made him feel this way, not even Kelly.

During the week, Hammer occupied his time with work, and on the weekends he worked out in an attempt to keep Keaundra off his mind. He missed everything about her from her smile to the way her cute little nose wrinkled up when she got mad. Every time Alexis came over to see

David, he wanted to ask her about Keaundra, but didn't want to come across desperate.

Hammer got up early one morning and promised himself that he wasn't going to sleep until he at least attempted to get Keaundra back. He ate a bagel, drank a glass of orange juice, and headed out the front door. He stretched, put on the headphones to his iPod, and began jogging with no destination in mind.

Two hours later, he ended up at the music store. He purchased a CD before jogging a couple blocks down to the flower shop and buying fifteen dozen roses of varying colors. He had the florist send them to Keaundra's job along with the CD. He spent a lot of money, but Keaundra was well worth every dime. Hammer walked out of the flower shop feeling fresh and revived. He looked up at the sky and said, "Sorry, Kelly, but I gotta let you go. Keaundra is not taking your place, baby, it's more like she's taking your space."

All of a sudden the wind began to blow. Hammer didn't know if that was a sign from Kelly giving him the go-ahead or telling him to go to hell. Either way, Hammer was determined to get Keaundra back. He put his headphones back on and jogged all the way home with a smile on his face.

Chapter Thirty-one

"You have a call on line one," said Kay-Kay's voice on the intercom.

Alexis was busy looking at some very important charts so she had no time for personal calls at the moment. "Take a message," she said, pressing the intercom button and never taking her eyes off the chart.

"Will do." Kay-Kay clicked back over and asked the caller to leave a message.

"Who is this, Kay-Kay?" India asked.

"Yes. Who is this?" Kay-Kay asked.

"This is India. Can you please tell Alexis to get her ass on the phone?"

"Please hold." Kay-Kay clicked over and buzzed back in on Alexis's phone.

"Didn't I ask you to tell whoever it is to call back?"

"I tried to tell India, but she insisted you get your ass on the phone," Kay-Kay said with a slight chuckle.

"Okay, patch her through." Alexis continued looking at the chart while she waited for her call. "That's it," she said to herself. She could stop racking her brain on how to tell Keaundra about Beverly and this mystery man. She knew if she told big mouth India, it was sure to get back to Keaundra. "Hello?" Alexis answered in her most pleasant tone.

"Next time tell Kay-Kay when I call to put you on the phone, no matter what," India said with a slight attitude.

"You got that comin'. Anyway, what's up?"

"Girl, I gotta get somethin' done to my hair," India started in. "It's June and this humidity is eatin' my shit alive." India ran her fingers through her thick mane as she spoke.

This girl called me at work to talk about her hair. You gotta love her.

"I hear they got a new hair salon opening up on the north end of town called Loose Endz. I might give them a try," India rambled. "But you know I can't just have anybody playin' up in my hair."

"I know that's right. Anyway, before you go on about your hair, we need to have an emergency dinner tonight."

India could hear the urgency in Alexis's voice. "What's the scoop?" India asked, needing to know.

"That's the whole purpose of the emergency dinner." Alexis took the phone away from her mouth and laughed because she knew India was about ready to explode.

"You know I can't wait until later on, Lexy. Just tell me now," India whined.

"No, 'cause you might tell Keaundra and I don't want her to know until later." Alexis smiled as her best friend fell right into her little trap.

"Uhnnh uhhh, I won't tell her, I promise," India said as she crossed her fingers.

"You better not tell, India," Alexis demanded in a serious tone while a smile was plastered on her face.

"I won't. Now gimme the grapes."

Alexis closed her eyes, took a deep breath, and let it out slowly. "Beverly got caught fuckin' on top of Gran's kitchen table."

"What the hell you just say?"

"You heard me."

"Wait a minute." India climbed out of the bed slowly, trying not to wake Martell. He had showed up the night before to talk and their conversation had ended with them in the bed. She walked into the master bathroom and quietly shut the door behind her. "Okay, now who caught her and who was the dirty low-down-ass nigga she was fuckin'?" India wanted to know everything from the beginning to the end.

"I can't tell you who told me, and the person doesn't know who the nigga was."

India let the lid down on the toilet and took a seat. She propped her feet up on the tub and shook her head in disbelief. "That's a damn shame. What did Kenneth say?" India checked out her fresh pedicure while she waited for Alexis to answer.

"Kenneth don't know."

"Poor Kenneth." India really did feel sorry for Kenneth because she knew how good a man he was. He treated his women with nothing but love and respect, and any woman who had the chance to be with him was more than lucky. If she didn't know any better, she would have sworn that Kenneth and Martell were related in some way. She felt lucky as hell to have an honest and loving man like Martell in her life. "Boy, I might hafta call my pops to retain him once Keaundra finds out, 'cause I know she gon' kill that bitch."

Alexis laughed.

"What's so funny, Lexy, I'm serious."

"Keaundra ain't goin' to jail; I hope. We just gon' hafta talk some sense into her."

India scratched her head and chuckled. "You'd be better off talkin' to a brick wall."

"Man, you can say that again."

"Bitches kill me," India blurted out from nowhere. "They get a good man and don't know how to treat him."

"Hush truth," Alexis agreed. "Well, I got work to do, somethin' you don't know anything about. I'll see you tonight at dinner."

"Okay. Oh, before you go, what's on the menu for tonight?" India stood up from the toilet seat, walked over to the bathroom door, and stopped.

"I don't know. It's your turn to host so you choose."

"Red Lobster it is," India said as she opened up the bathroom door and walked back over to the bed, where the love of her life lay sound asleep.

"Fine with me, and don't forget; if Keaundra call don't say a word," Alexis reminded her friend.

"I won't."

Yeah right, Alexis laughed to herself as she hung up. Alexis pushed the button on the intercom, "Mission accomplished," she said to Kay-Kay.

Kay-Kay smiled and shook her head.

India hung up the phone and climbed back into bed next to Martell. She tossed and turned as the news about Beverly played with her mind. She wanted to call Keaundra, but she had promised Alexis that she wouldn't. All of a sudden she became like a feind needing his last and final fix. She had to call Keaundra. She picked up her phone and dialed Richland Bank as fast as her fingers would let her.

"Hello, Richland Bank, this is Keaundra, how may I help you?"

"Ke-Ke?" India whispered.

"India?"

"Yeah, it's me. Hang on." India climbed back out of bed and walked back into the master bathroom. "Okay, what you doin', girl?" India asked as she sat back on top of the toilet seat.

"Workin'. Somethin' you don't know nothin' about," Keaundra laughed.

"Ha ha ha, very funny," India said, pretending to be hurt. "Anyway, Bernie Mac, we are havin' dinner tonight and Red Lobster is on the menu."

"I can't tonight. Beverly and me have to go get our dresses altered."

"I can't believe you of all people is gon' turn down Red Lobster just to go get a stupid dress altered. You can do that anytime."

"Indy, you know this wedding is very important to my brother and he wants everything to be perfect for his bride to be."

"Hmph, after I tell you what I heard about this broad, there might not be a wedding." India knew she wasn't supposed to open her mouth, but she couldn't help it. Her best friends already knew this about her. India began to wonder if that was the reason Alexis had told her about

Beverly, so she could be the one to run back and tell Keaundra.

Keaundra laid the loan application she had in her hand down on the desk. "What is she supposed to have done now?" Keaundra asked, rolling her eyes.

"She got caught fuckin' on Gran's kitchen table," India blurted out.

Keaundra got real quiet. She had to think about what had just come out of India's big mouth. "Who caught her?" Keaundra asked with a contorted face. "Gran sure didn't and I know if Kenneth caught her, he would have called and told me by now."

"I don't know. They wouldn't give me all the information just yet."

"People are always tryin'a hate on somebody," Keaundra hissed. "Muthafuckas need to mind their own damn business."

"So what, you don't believe it?"

Keaundra chuckled, not because something was funny, but because she knew that whoever told India this shit was doing nothing but lying on her sister-in-law-to-be. "All I'm sayin' is people are jealous of Beverly and Kenneth's relationship because he is a good catch and they might just want him for themselves. So they tryin'a start shit to try to break 'em up."

India couldn't believe her ears. "I know you ain't insinuating that I'm jealous of Kenneth and Beverly's relationship are you?"

"I mean, if you believe Beverly is bold enough to do some shiesty shit like that up in Gran's house, then, yeah, you fit in that category," Keaundra stated smartly.

India was outdone. This was the same person who ripped Beverly a new asshole a couple of years back when Kenneth caught her fuckin' his best friend in his bed. Now she's sitting up there protecting her like she's some type of Virgin Mary or something.

"Bitch, there is no reason at all for me to be jealous of Beverly's relationship. I can get anything I want from my man. I want for nothin', don't you ever forget that!" India was furious. "You damn right I believe the bitch was fuckin' on Gran's table, that ho ain't changed. She got yo' dumb ass brainwashed into thinkin' she has." India got up from the toilet seat and peeked out the door to make sure she hadn't woken Martell up with all the yelling she was doing. He was still sound asleep.

Keaundra knew she was dead wrong for calling her best friend a hater. She was way out of line so she did the womanly thing and apologized. "I'm sorry, Indy, for callin' you a hater." India smacked her lips. "It's just I see a big change in Beverly, that's all. Do you accept my apology?"

India twisted up her lips. "I guess so." India was still scorned by her best friend's remark. "I'm about to get off the phone, but first I'ma leave you with this," India said. "If you think you see a change in Beverly that's on you, but if I were you, I would invest in a pair of glasses." Without leaving room for Keaundra to comment on her smart remark, India hung up the phone.

India walked back out of the bathroom and climbed into bed with her man. She snuggled against him. He wrapped his strong arm around her and pulled her closer to him. She thanked the Lord as they became one. She kissed him gently on the lips and smiled as she admired his handsome face. *I'm so glad that I'm not in Kenneth's shoes right now. Thank God I don't hafta worry about my man out fuckin' around with these hood-rats. Humph, what man in his right mind would wanna lose India Ariel Davenport?* India smiled at the thought before drifting off to sleep with her man's arm wrapped around her.

Keaundra shook her head in disbelief. She wanted to call Beverly and ask her about India's accusations, but decided against it. The last thing Keaundra wanted was to cause havoc between Kenneth and Beverly a few weeks before their wedding. Why bother calling with such nonsense? Keaundra continued working as the thought of Beverly having sex on Gran's kitchen table stayed on her mind.

Chapter Thirty-two

Keaundra arrived at work unusually early. She could have slept in for an extra hour or so, but didn't. Since she didn't have Hammer to talk to on the phone while she got ready for work like she was used to doing, there was no use. Keaundra showered, got dressed, and grabbed herself a cereal bar on the way out the door. When she arrived at the bank, she met the branch manager, Angela, on the walk.

"Good morning," Angela said cheerfully.

What the fuck this bitch so happy for this damn early in the morning? "Morning," Keaundra replied in one of the driest tones.

Angela stuck the key in the lock and turned only her head around to look at Keaundra. "What are you doing here so early?"

Open the damn door you nosey-ass bitch! "I have some work I need to catch up on."

"Oh," Angela replied as she unlocked the door.

Keaundra walked in after Angela and headed straight to her office, closing the door behind her. She sat behind her desk, turned on her computer, and waited for it to boot up. She looked over at the picture that she and Hammer had taken at the mall, and began feeling sad. Ever since Keaundra and Hammer's friendship fell apart, her entire world had been turned upside down. She never smiled much, she alienated herself from her family and friends, and there wasn't a night that passed when she didn't cry herself to sleep.

Alexis and India did their best to keep Keaundra's mind occupied, but her friends were little help; she still wasn't happy. Keaundra became nauseated at the thought of Hammer being married to someone other than her. She got up from behind her desk and opened her office door to let in some fresh air. By that time, the other women who worked at the bank began scurrying in.

Debbie, Keaundra's secretary walked in the bank and looked over at Keaundra. Debbie looked up at the clock before checking her own watch. "I thought I was late or somethin'," Debbie chuckled. "I'm not used to seein' you here this early. The coffee will be ready in just a few," Debbie said as she made her way over to the bank's waiting area.

All the smiling faces were enough to make Keaundra want to throw up, but the sound of Debbie's voice took the cake. Keaundra shook her head, disgusted by the sight, and slammed her office door. She walked over to her desk, took a seat in the chair, and began looking over the work that should have been finished weeks ago.

Keaundra kept watching the clock on the wall; the day was dragging by slowly and she couldn't wait until five o'clock. She would've left early, but she was already way behind at work. Keaundra had Debbie sending all of her calls to her voice mail, no matter who it was. She wasn't in the mood to talk to anyone.

Debbie tapped lightly on Keaundra's office door and waited to be invited in.

"Yes," Keaundra answered as politely as possible, just in case it was her boss on the other side of the door.

Debbie stuck her head in. "There's a delivery guy out here to see you."

Keaundra wasn't expecting any packages from anyone. "Send him in." Debbie motioned for the delivery guy to come into the office. In walked this short, chubby, white man holding two bouquets of roses in each hand. Keaundra smiled as she stood up from her chair and walked over to retrieve the flowers. "Who are these from?" she asked no one in particular.

"There's more where those came from," the delivery guy said, disappearing back out of the office door to get the other thirteen dozen roses and the CD. Keaundra's eyes lit up each time the delivery guy brought in more flowers. He handed her the small package that was wrapped neatly in heart designed wrapping paper. There was a note stuck to the front of it that read: *Play number 6.* The roses were causing a big commotion among the women in the bank, as they looked on with jealous smirks on their faces.

"I wonder who sent me all of these flowers," Keaundra looked over at Debbie and said.

"Here's a card right here." Debbie said, pulling out a card from one of the bouquets and handing it to Keaundra. Keaundra opened up the card and began reading it to herself.

> *I know you are still mad at me, but if you would have let me explain.*
>
> *The night I walked out of your house, my life was filled with so much pain.*
>
> *Without you in my world, my life is incomplete.*
>
> *Please forgive me because with love my heart cannot compete.*
>
> *Love conquers all and it definitely rules my world.*
>
> *What I'm trying to say in my corny little poem is will you do me the honor of becoming my girl?*
>
> *Donye' "Hammer" Woods*

Keaundra tried her hardest to hold back the tears as she read the card but couldn't. The tears flowed freely. Keaundra had never had a man send her flowers before, because she had never let anyone other than Hammer into her space. She had always kept men at an arm's length to keep from getting her heart broken. She had shared everything with Hammer, from stories about her abusive father to the night she was told about the death of her mother.

After the crowd of envious women went back to work Keaundra closed her door and opened up the package. She walked over to her desk and popped the CD into the boom box that sat on top of her desk, and pushed the button until she got to song number six. She sat in her big comfortable chair and clasped her hands together as she admired her flowers. She was confused as ever. Keaundra closed her eyes and bobbed her head as Robin Thicke's "Lost Without You", soothed her eardrums. She smiled and picked up the phone to call Hammer to thank him for the flowers, but immediately slammed the phone back down.

"Fuck that," she said. Keaundra stood up from her chair and paced through her office. "That nigga thinks 'cause he sent me fifteen dozen roses and this old-ass CD that I'm supposed to just forgive him." Keaundra grimaced. "Shit, it ain't like the nigga forgot my birthday or some simple shit like that. The muthafucka is married."

Keaundra looked over at all the beautiful flowers that Hammer had sent and wanted to walk over and knock each and every one of them over, but she would have to clean up the mess, so she didn't.

"If you're lost without me, go find your wife!" Keaundra walked over to the boom box and slammed her finger down on the stop button. She took a seat in her chair and held her head in the palms of her hands, shaking her head vigorously. "What am I gon' do? I love Hammer, but I refuse to let myself get involved with a married man."

Keaundra started feeling sick all over again. She took a deep breath, pushed play on the boom box, and began catching up on her work, while her head bobbed to the sweet melody.

Chapter Thirty-three

"Comin'," David yelled at whoever was ringing his doorbell. He opened the door to Rosalind standing on the front porch. "Rosalind?" he questioned. "What are you doin' here?" David was surprised because he hadn't seen or heard from her in a grip. Rosalind stood before him looking famished, with her lips looking like she had just finished eating an entire box of powdered doughnuts. She wore a big T-shirt, ripped jeans, and a baseball cap, which was uncanny, because Rosalind was always dressed to kill.

"I had to drive myself to chemotherapy and on my way home I got tired, so I stopped over here. I hope you don't mind."

David opened the screen door for Rosalind to enter. "No, I don't mind at all."

She walked in and looked around as if she were in a foreign place. She wanted to make sure that nothing had changed, and it hadn't. "I hope I'm not interrupting anything."

"Don't be silly, girl. We still friends, aren't we?"

"Of course," she said while yawning. "I don't wanna just barge in on you."

"That's okay."

"I can barely keep my eyes open," Rosalind said, hoping David would fall for her game.

"You can rest in my bed." David immediately took Rosalind by the arm and led her to his bedroom. He helped her lay down, took her shoes off, and stacked them neatly in front of the nightstand. David threw his comforter over her body, kissed her on the forehead, and began walking back out of his room.

David and his mother watched cancer slowly eat away at his father's pancreas and there was nothing they could do about it. They had done all they could to make sure that his father lived out his last days enjoying himself, so if he could help it, he would do the same for Rosalind.

"David," Rosalind called out.

David turned to face her. "Yes."

"Thanks."

"No problem."

Rosalind waited for David to exit the room before sitting up in his big comfortable bed. She had a huge smile on her face as she looked around the bedroom. "It's just a matter of time before I'm back in this bed permanently," she said to herself.

Rosalind's plan was going as smooth as a baby's bottom. She lay back and stared up at the ceiling until she drifted off to sleep.

Two hours later Rosalind woke up feeling refreshed and revived. She climbed out of bed, stretched her arms, and set out to find David. "Ummm," Rosalind moaned as she walked toward the living room. The smell of food being cooked made her stomach growl. Rosalind began scheming on how to get a dinner invite. "David," she called out.

David came out of the kitchen with an apron on, wiping his hands. "Yes."

"Thanks again," she said. "I'm about to go on home."

"Not before you eat."

Rosalind smiled. "I don't know, David."

"You hafta stay. I cooked your favorite meal. You can still eat, can't you?"

"Yeah, at least until the doctors tell me otherwise."

"Then it's settled. Dinner will be ready in no time," David said happily.

Rosalind pretended she was thinking about staying. It was already a part of her plan to spend as much time with David as she possibly could. "I guess I can stay."

David smiled. "Good, now make yourself at home while I finish preparing dinner." Rosalind took a seat on the living room sofa, making herself at home just like she was told, as David vanished back into the kitchen.

After David finished cooking, he fixed each of them a plate of catfish, homemade macaroni and cheese, and fresh collard greens. They sat and talked as they ate. David wanted to learn as much as he could about Rosalind's disease. He promised her that he would do his best to make sure she took good care of herself, so she could live a long and prosperous life. Rosalind agreed to let him do just that. After they ate they went into the living room to watch television. They began reminiscing about the fun times they used to share together.

"Are your knees still ticklish?" Rosalind asked.

"What do you think?" he asked and blocked his knees with his hands to keep Rosalind away from them.

"I think they are," she said, and broke through his barrier and began tickling his knees. He laughed as he tried to get her hands away from him. As they struggled, playfully, David accidentally knocked off Rosalind's baseball cap.

They both stopped. Rosalind grabbed her hat and put it back on in a hurry. David was shocked to see the bald spots scattered all over her head. "I didn't know," David said, embarrassed.

Rosalind stood up from the sofa and pretended to be embarrassed. "It's from the chemo," Rosalind said, avoiding eye contact as she spoke. "That's why I wear this baseball cap."

David stood up from the sofa and lifted her chin with his index finger. "You're still beautiful to me," he said. "Don't let anyone tell you anything different, you hear me?"

Tears swelled up in Rosalind's eyes. "You're not just sayin' that, are you?"

"Have I ever lied to you?" Rosalind shook her head. "I wouldn't start now." David stared into Rosalind's eyes. His heart went out to her because of the way she described the cervical cancer to him, her chances of surviving were slim to none, and she looked so sick and helpless. David stared into Rosalind's eyes and leaned in to kiss her, but was interrupted by the doorbell.

Shit! Rosalind thought.

David let out a nervous chuckle and stepped back. "I better get that." David made his way to the door, not bothering to check to see who it was. He opened up the door and Alexis stood on the front porch wearing a long trench coat. David thought it was rather odd, being that it was hot as hell outside. "Hey." He smiled at the sight of his lovely friend.

"Hey."

David opened the screen door to let Alexis in. "What you doin' in my neck of the woods?"

"I lost somethin'," Alexis said as she stepped into the foyer.

"What did you lose?" David had a confused look on his face. He didn't remember running across anything that belonged to Alexis.

"My clothes." She smiled mischievously and opened up her trench coat, revealing her lace, fire-engine red Victoria's Secret panty and bra set.

"Damn!" he snapped. David's manhood instantly stood at attention as he admired Alexis's body. She could have passed for a centerfold model with no problem; she was built to a T. She didn't have the body of a woman who had two children; there wasn't a stretch mark or blemish anywhere on her.

"David, are you okay in there?" Rosalind asked, walking into the foyer where David stood, drooling over Alexis.

David was so mesmerized by Alexis's beauty, he had forgotten all about Rosalind being in the other room. "Oh. Yeah, I'm fine," he stammered.

Who the fuck is this? Rosalind thought. *I've seen her somewhere before.*

Alexis quickly snatched her coat closed. "I didn't know you had company." *I've seen her somewhere before*, Alexis thought.

"Alexis, Rosalind. Rosalind, Alexis," he said.

Oh, so this is what Alexis look like? Awkward silence filled the foyer. Rosalind and Alexis both stared at David as if they wanted him to make a choice on who should stay and who goes. Rosalind felt embarrassed by the way she was dressed, standing in front of David's new piece and looking like shit.

Rosalind couldn't compete with Alexis, not at this particular moment, so she decided to be the one to tap out. "Well, David, I better be goin'. Thanks again for letting me sleep in your bed and for fixing me dinner." Rosalind knew exactly what she was doing. She knew if she couldn't get to Alexis one way she would get to her another.

Alexis's stare could have easily burned a hole in the side of David's head. David knew Alexis would be upset after hearing his ex had slept in his bed and he cooked dinner for her. Even though he had done nothing wrong, he knew Alexis would feel differently.

"No, boo-boo, you stay. I'ma leave, 'cause evidentially I'm the one in the way here." Alexis opened up the front door. She was so mad she wanted to scream, but she kept her composure.

She didn't want David's ex to know how ghetto she really could get, so she kept it cool.

Yeah, scram, Rosalind wanted to say.

"Alexis, you don't hafta leave," David said, grabbing her hand.

Let the bitch go, Rosalind thought.

David didn't want Alexis to leave. He wanted to spend time with her, and had a feeling tonight would have been the night he finally got to get between them thick thighs. The last time they were together things didn't pan out because he couldn't get Rosalind off his mind. Even when Alexis had returned to his house after storming out, he still couldn't focus on anything other than Rosalind's illness. They had decided to just hold one another until they fell off to sleep.

"Naw, it's cool. Just call me when your company leaves," Alexis stated.

Who said I was goin' anywhere?

David didn't want to start an argument so he agreed to do what Alexis asked. He watched as she made her way to her car and pulled out of his driveway like a deranged lunatic. He wanted to run after her, but figured with Rosalind still being there, she wouldn't listen. David watched until Alexis was out of sight before closing the front door. He shook his head and turned around. Rosalind was standing behind him looking like a lost puppy.

"I'm sorry," Rosalind said. "I hope I didn't cause too much trouble between the two of you."

David forced a smile, wrapped his arm around Rosalind's shoulder, and led her back into the living room to finish watching television.

Alexis damn near ran to her car, jumped in, and pulled off like she was Jeff Gordon. She weaved in and out of traffic as she made her way home, cussing all the way. Once pulling into her apartment complex, she noticed that the maintenance man hadn't been by to fix the lights her neighbor's kids had broken. As she was pulling into her assigned parking space, it dawned on her where she had recognized Rosalind from.

"That's the bitch who was on the passenger's side of that black Camry the day I made an ass of myself at the mall. It sho'll is," Alexis said aloud, shaking her head.

"Hey, shorty," she heard a voice call out from the darkness, breaking her train of thought. Alexis ignored the cat-call and continued on her way. She mumbled profanity about David, Rosalind, and the lazy maintenance man on her way up the walk.

"Oh, you just gon' ignore me?" the same voice hollered out.

Alexis stopped and turned around. She couldn't see anything. All she saw was the fiery orange tip of a cigarette. Whoever it was was sitting on the hood of a car that was parked right next to hers. Alexis was so caught up in cussing David, Rosalind, and the maintenance man out, she hadn't even noticed him.

Alexis stopped and turned around. "Look, I think you got me confused with someone else," she said and continued walking. Her instincts told her to look back and as she did so, she could see the fire from the cigarette slowly coming toward her. She sped up her pace.

"Oh, now you don't know me?" the male's voice asked.

Alexis fumbled for her house key. She had so many keys on her ring, she didn't know which was the right one. She looked around to see if she could see anyone, but couldn't. Normally, her nosey-ass neighbor, Ms. Ruth, would have been in the window peeking out the blinds, but her apartment was pitch dark. Finally, Alexis found the right key and stuck it in the lock. She turned it and ran in, but before she could get the door closed all the way, the man had stuck his foot in the door, blocking it from closing.

"Get the fuck away from my door," Alexis screamed as loud as she could, hoping someone would hear her. Sweat was pouring from her forehead and her heart was beating fast as she put as much pressure on her front door as possible.

"Damn, baby, it's been that long," the man said as he blew the cigarette smoke through the crack of the door, making Alexis cough.

"Please, leave me alone," Alexis begged realizing what she was wearing. *Shit, I done made it real easy for this man to rape me*, she thought as she pushed hard on the door with all her might.

It was somewhat strange that the man on the other side of the door didn't try to force entry. He could have easily pushed the door open and raped, robbed, and killed Alexis, leaving her dead body on the floor for someone to find. Instead, he just stood with his boot stuck between the door and the frame.

Alexis's mind raced as she contemplated her next move. Just as she came up with a plan to make a mad dash to the kitchen and grab a knife, the man revealed himself.

"Alexis, this Ronald, let me in, girl," he laughed.

"Ronald?" Alexis asked, skeptical. She was still pushing up against the door.

"Yeah, it's me."

"Nigga," she yelped and opened up the door. Ronald flicked his cigarette in the yard and stepped into the apartment. "What's so funny? You had me scared as hell," she said, feeling a little more at ease, knowing it was Ronald and not some serial killer.

"Help me, help me?" Ronald laughed, imitating his best scared white woman's voice.

"I didn't say no shit like that," Alexis laughed, playfully punching him in the shoulder.

"You might as well have."

"Anyways, what brings you over here? The last time I talked to you, you was cussin' me out."

"I know. My bad," Ronald said apologetically. Alexis rolled her eyes and smacked her lips. "For real, I'm sorry."

Alexis walked through the apartment and turned on the television. "The kids aren't here," she said, flipping through the channels. She took a seat on the sofa and looked over at Ronald. "You scared to sit down? I don't got roaches."

"I didn't know if I was still welcome here or not." Ronald took a seat on the sofa and looked around the living room.

"You're not, but you're here so you might as well stay for a little while," she said, and besides, she wanted the company.

An hour later Ronald had gotten comfortable as he and Alexis talked. He told her about his new factory job and complained about his hourly wage, but told her he would continue to hang in there until he found himself something else. He also told her about the car he bought off Tyisha's uncle for three hundred dollars. It wasn't much but it got him back and forth to work. It definitely got him to his weed customers. Ronald bragged about not taking a drink in nearly three months. Alexis was so proud of the father of her children. She was beginning to look at Ronald differently; he was definitely growing up and would finally make someone a good man.

"Why you still got that coat on in the house?"

"Oh, I forgot all about it." Alexis smiled as she began unbuttoning it. She took it off and went to hang it on the coat rack.

"Damn, where you comin' from dressed like that?" Ronald asked. "I know you don't got your job back at the strip club, do you?"

Alexis put her hands on her shapely hips. "Naw, fool. Even though I do still got what it takes to be a stripper," Alexis said as she turned her back to Ronald and made her butt cheeks clap together like old times.

Ronald's love muscle jumped in the air as he watched her ass jiggle like Jell-o. "Yeah, you do still got what it takes," he agreed.

"Whatever. I had to run to the store real quick," she lied. "And I didn't feel like puttin' on no clothes so I went in my panties and bra."

Ronald didn't remember seeing her get out of the car with a bag, but he left it alone.

"I'll be back. I'm about to go put somethin' on," she said, walking toward her bedroom.

"No, don't." Ronald jumped up from the sofa and walked over to Alexis. He got close enough for her to feel his warm breath on her neck. He wrapped his arms around her waist and pulled her close to him.

"Move, Ronald," Alexis said as she struggled to get his arms from around her.

"Stop fightin'," he said, kissing her neck, making her pussy lips throb as moisture seeped through her tight walls.

"Boy, gon'." Alexis closed her eyes and rolled her neck back. She was enjoying the softness of Ronald's lips. "You got a woman at home," she moaned.

That didn't stop Ronald; he began kissing her lips. His tongue explored the inside of her mouth as his hands grabbed her firm ass. It had been a while since Alexis felt this good. She wanted Ronald to stop, but at the same time she wanted him to fuck the shit out of her. Ronald picked her up and carried her to her bedroom. Without hesitation, he laid her down on the bed, moved her bra up, and began sucking her hard nipples. He went from one to the other, licking and sucking them like chocolate-covered strawberries. Alexis started feeling guilty as Ronald removed her panties and did a swan dive into her wetness with his tongue. For the past few months, she had belonged to David and only David, but tonight she belonged to Ronald because David had Rosalind to keep him company.

Chapter Thirty-four

"What are you wearing to Kenneth and Beverly's dinner party?" India looked over at Martell and asked.

Martell sat up in the bed and gave India a look of confusion.

"Ken and Beverly's dinner party, remember?"

"Oh, um, I don't know if I'm gon' be able to make it," Martell stammered.

"Why not, Martell?" India whined as she got undressed to shower. "You know I've been lookin' forward to goin' to this dinner for weeks now." India walked over and grabbed her robe off the chaise that sat in the corner of her bedroom.

"I have got a business meeting next Saturday."

India shook her head and walked toward the bathroom. Before entering, she turned around and said, "That's funny that you never mentioned a business meeting until now. I think maybe you don't wanna go to the party with me."

Martell climbed out of bed. "I do wanna go with you, but I told you I will be out of town next week." Martell made his way over to his woman.

India rolled her eyes. "Shit, you a grown man, if you don't wanna go just say so."

Martell wrapped his arms around India's naked body and rocked her from side to side. "Baby, you know I'll go to the moon with you if you asked me to."

India smiled happily. "Good, then it's settled, the party starts at six." India stood on the tips of her toes, kissed Martell on the lips, and continued her walk to the bathroom.

What the fuck did I just do, Martell thought as he stood dumbfounded. India had just tricked him into going to a party he had no business showing his face at. Martell made his way over to the closet and waited until he heard the water come on before reaching into the back of the closet and pulling a dusty shoebox out. He wiped away some of the dust before opening it, and pulled out a pack of cigarettes and a book of matches.

Martell shook one of the cigarettes out and lit it, put it up to his lips, and took a long drag from it. He held the smoke in his mouth for a few seconds before blowing it out. His mind raced just thinking about showing up at a party given by the man whose fiancée he had fucked in *his* grandmother's house.

Martell walked over to the window and raised it up. He took one last drag from the cigarrette before flicking it out the window. He then walked over to India's dresser, grabbed a bottle of perfume, and began spraying it to cover up the smell of the cigarette smoke.

Martell made up his mind. He was going to march right into the bathroom and put his foot down. He was going to tell India that he was not going to no damn dinner party next Saturday. He really didn't want to miss this meeting. Martell thought long and hard about sending someone in his place, instead of upsetting India or possibly making her suspicious. *Maybe it won't be so bad going to the party, My infidelity hasn't come to light yet, and maybe it won't. I just have to keep my woman as happy as possible, just in case my dirty little secret does come out. She would be hurt, but we would be able to go on just as if nothing happened.* Martell was pleased with his plan. He walked into the bathroom as India sang one of Whitney Houston's old songs off-key. He took off his boxers and slid into the shower with his woman. India smiled and Martell kissed her soft lips.

"I was thinkin' that maybe we can go out ring shopping today after I leave the office," Martell said with a smile.

"For real, Martell?"

"For real, baby."

India wrapped her arms around Martell and he hugged her back. She looked up into his eyes. "I love you, Telly."

"I love you too, India Ariel Davenport."

"I know," she replied before they began kissing passionately. Martell then turned India around and she placed her hands on the shower wall as he entered her from behind. She began pushing against Martell's long, thick meat. Martell stroked hard and deep as his manhood worked itself in and out of India's sacred paradise. They moved rhythmically as the water from the shower beat down on their bodies.

"I'm about to cum," Martell grunted as he held tightly onto India's waist. The thought of being up in his woman raw excited Martell even more. India moved her hips like Patra as Martell moved violently in and out of her.

India was into it just as much as Martell. "Don't cum in me," she moaned, fucking up Martell's groove.

Damn, Martell thought as he pulled out just in the nick of time, squirting all over her back. Martell forced the rest out with his hand before stepping out the shower, leaving India alone to wash away the babies he had just left behind.

Chapter Thirty-five

Keaundra, Alexis, and India sat around India's condo. They laughed and talked about everything that had been going on in their lives. Keaundra bragged about all the roses that Hammer sent her and India chatted about the three-sixty Martell had done. She was telling her best friends how they had begun making wedding plans. India showed off the three-carat diamond that Martell had given her the night before.

"Oh my goodness," Alexis said in awe. "Girl, I have never seen a rock that size before in my life."

"Me either," Keaundra added. "Shit, my roses ain't got nothin' on that ring."

India cheesed but soon became serious. "I don't know, y'all. There's something behind Martell's sudden change in attitude," she said, skeptical.

"Why does there have to be somethin'?" Keaundra asked. "How come the brotha can't just be tryin'a change?"

"The nigga told me to call y'all and invite y'all out to dinner on him," India stated. "Now, tell me what y'all think about that."

"He has a motive," Keaundra and Alexis said simultaneously.

"That's what I thought. I just gotta find out what it is." Just when Alexis was about to give her opinion, Martell walked through the front door.

"Hey, ladies, what's goin' on?"

Keaundra and Alexis looked at each other before responding.

"Hey," Keaundra replied. Alexis hesitated but spoke once Martell smiled at her.

"Where y'all goin' to eat at?"

"I was thinkin' we could go to Olive Garden," India answered.

"Olive Garden sounds good." Martell looked at Alexis and Keaundra and waited for a response but got none. Both Keaundra and Alexis were outdone with his mood change. It wasn't long ago they were bitches and hood-rats, but now he was acting like they had been the best of friends for years. Martell took his wallet out of his back pocket and handed India two crisp hundred dollar bills. "Is this enough, baby?"

India took the money from his hand. "Yeah, it's enough." India smiled at her man before he began walking toward her bedroom. Martell stopped and turned back around. "You ladies have a good evening," he said and proceeded on his way.

Keaundra waited until she heard India's bedroom door close. "What the fuck is wrong wit' that nigga?" she asked, surprised. "You need to take that nigga to the doctor, 'cause he gots to be sick."

"I'm hip," Alexis agreed. "Why is he being so nice all of a sudden?"

"See, I told y'all," India responded quietly. "He has somethin' on his mind because I smelled cigarette smoke yesterday when I got out of the shower."

"What does cigarette smoke have to do with anything?" Alexis asked.

India had a dead serious look on her face as she spoke. "Martell only smokes when somethin' bad is really bothering him. The nigga got somethin' on his mind and I need to get to the bottom of it."

"I don't give a fuck what the nigga's problem is. I can deal with him just as long as he keeps payin' for a sista to eat," Keaundra laughed.

"I'm wit' you," Alexis agreed, giving Keaundra a high-five.

"Me too. Now let's go eat," India laughed as she and her girls made their way to her truck for a fun-filled night of food, drinks, and excitement, thanks to Martell.

All that week David had been spending all of his time with Rosalind. According to her the cancer was starting to spread, and David wanted to make her last few months on earth as happy as possible. Picnics in the park, long drives to the lake, or just relaxing were David's ways of showing Rosalind how much he cared.

Rosalind was enjoying every minute she spent with David; she wouldn't have cared if he took her out to a field and had her shoveling shit, just as long as she could spend time with him. It wouldn't be long before her and David would be rolling around in the sheets, making hot, passionate love like old times. She had to take things slow because she didn't want David to get suspicious of anything. She didn't mind taking her time. If she didn't have anything else, she sure had plenty of time on her hands.

David had tried calling Alexis a few times, but she never returned any of his calls. He missed Alexis a lot but decided to deal with her at a later date.

Alexis planned on returning David's phone calls eventually. Right now, she was enjoying every waking moment she and Ronald had been spending together. They had even talked about getting back together and becoming a family again. Alexis thought hard about the idea and happily agreed because she missed having a man around the house. There was no one to share her happy news with; she couldn't dare tell India and Keaundra about her and Ronald, not yet anyway. She knew she was going to have to put the news on her girls slowly, that's why she had to make sure her affair with Ronald stayed a secret, for now.

"Baby, I'm leaving for work," Ronald tapped Alexis on the shoulder and whispered. Alexis rolled over and slightly opened her eyes and smiled. Ronald leaned down, kissed her, and headed to his car.

Alexis drifted back off to sleep only to be awakened by the ringing telephone. "Hello?" Alexis answered, still half asleep.

"Bitch, where you been all week?" Keaundra snapped.

"And why haven't you returned any of our phone calls?" India chimed in on the three-way call.

Alexis sighed deeply. "I've been busy," was all she could manage to say.

"Busy?" Keaundra snapped.

"Busy doin' what?" India asked.

"Busy doin' shit I need to get done around my house, if y'all bitches don't mind."

"Well, excuse the fuck outta us," India retorted.

"You are still gon' bring yo' busy ass to the dinner party, aren't you?" Keaundra asked.

"You know I'ma be there for you, girl," Alexis assured her best friend.

"I don't know, you got a bitch wondering," Keaundra laughed.

India started telling her girls about the house she and Martell had looked at. She told them he had even taken her to pick out any car on the lot. India felt like the luckiest woman in the world. Martell was definitely making her happy; he had her floating on cloud nine. She had even been letting Martell make love to her without protection.

For the first time in India's life, she had let her guard down and let Martell take total control of her heart. Martell was happy as well, because his plan appeared to be working. Nothing and no one could come between him and his woman now.

Chapter Thirty-six

Saturday took forever to roll around. India could hardly wait until the dinner party; she was dying to show off her new outfit. As she stood in the mirror admiring her new hairdo, Martell walked into the bathroom. She turned around and smiled at her man. Martell forced a weak smile before lifting up the toilet seat and taking a piss. India could tell that Martell had something on his mind; she just didn't know what.

"Are you okay?" India asked Martell. Without making eye contact, Martell nodded and flushed the toilet. India watched as Martell washed his hands, walked out of the bathroom, and stood in the middle of her bedroom floor. Martell was nicely dressed. He had on a pair of black Red Monkey jeans with red and white Japanese embroidery on both back pockets, a white, red, and black button-down, with a pair of old-school Jordan number fives.

India walked out after her man and placed her hand on his shoulder. "Why you so tense?"

"I'm cool," he said and walked out to the living room.

I look too damn good for you to be fuckin' up my night, India thought as she grabbed her beaded clutch out the closet. *So whatever is botherin' you, get over it or stay yo' black ass at home.* India made sure all of her windows and doors were locked before she and Martell headed out to his Porsche. Martell was quiet the whole drive to Gran's house. India knew that Martell was stressed out. She wanted to be there for her man, but at the same time, she didn't want to take the risk of asking him what his problem was, and starting an argument and stressing herself out as well. She decided to wait until the next day to find out what was ailing him. Once they pulled onto Gran's block, there was not a parking space in sight. Martell ended up parking at the end of the street.

"You look nice," India looked over at Martell and said.

"Thanks," he said in one of the driest tones.

Ain't this about a bitch! This nigga didn't even tell me how good I look. That's okay, I know I got it going on, India thought as they walked up to the front door and rang the doorbell.

India walked through the door with Martell trailing behind. She stepped on the scene wearing a light pink silk backless Christian Dior top with the plunging V-neck that ended just underneath her belly button and a pair of cream, silk Venta Bottega short shorts. India's calves stuck out like a sore thumb as she stepped gracefully in her Christian Louboutin espadrilles with the straps wrapped all the way up her firm thighs. India lit up like a Christmas tree as her ears, neck, and wrist glistened from all the diamonds she had on.

Martell smiled as he noticed his dime piece catching the attention of every man in the house, young and old. He watched as wives grabbed their husbands by the hand, pulling them close to their sides, and mothers covering their young sons' eyes to keep them from watching India's round backside.

India noticed some of the women turning up their noses while others whispered as she walked by. She was way too confident to let the envious women stop her shine. She lived by the old saying, beauty queens walk on the red carpet. But she walked on toilet paper because she was definitely the shit! India kept her composure, held her head up, and continued to search for her friends.

Alexis and Keaundra stood watching as India and Martell got held up by one of Gran's long conversations.

"They look so cute together," Alexis said to Keandra.

"Who?" Kay-Kay intervened as she came out of the kitchen holding a pan of Gran's good, old-fashioned cornbread.

"India and Martell." Keaundra pointed.

Kay-Kay looked. "Oh, my fuckin' goodness," she said.

"What's wrong with you?" Alexis asked, confused.

"That's him," Kay-Kay said, looking like she had just seen a ghost.

"Him who?" Keaundra asked.

"The nigga standing over there with India," Kay-Kay said, pointing with her head.

"That's Martell. What about him?" Alexis snapped.

"Oh my goodness, is that India's boyfriend?" Kay-Kay's heart sank when both Keaundra and Alexis nodded. "That's the nigga I caught fuckin' Beverly on Gran's table."

Alexis and Keaundra looked at each other.

"You lyin'," Alexis said as her heart pounded like a drum.

"Get the fuck outta here," Keaundra said, waving her hand The sincere look on Kay-Kay's face made Keaundra a believer. "Are you sure, Kay-Kay?" Keaundra said, hoping it was a case of mistaken identity.

"Of course I'm sure. How in the world could I forget an ass like that?" Kay-Kay said, replaying the day she saw Martell from behind as he banged the hell out of Beverly.

"Wow!" Keaundra stated, feeling sick to her stomach.

"That's him, I know it is."

Alexis and Keaundra shook their heads, disgusted by the thought.

"That's what the nigga been stressin' out about," Alexis said.

Keaundra shook her head in disgust. "He was so worried about India finding out, that's why he's been so nice to us," she added. "That low-down ass, nigga."

"Let me go put this cornbread on the table before Gran have a fit," Kay-Kay said. "But I'll be back, 'cause I know the shit is about to hit the fan."

"Girl, you wearing the hell outta that outfit," Keaundra said as soon as India and Martell walked up.

"Ain't she?" Alexis added with a smile.

India smiled as she turned to show off her entire ensemble. "Thank you. Y'all look good too."

"Hello, ladies," Martell spoke with a smile.

Alexis and Keaundra had to bite their tongues because the last thing they wanted to do was cause a scene. They nodded and turned their attention back to India. India thought it was somewhat odd for her friends to brush Martell off like they did, but she let it go.

"Hey, India," Kay-Kay said as she walked back over to where the ladies and Martell stood. Kay-Kay smiled at Martell mischievously.

"Martell, this is Kay-Kay, Keaundra's—"

"Go in the kitchen and get the rest of the meat," Gran yelled at Kay-Kay. Kay-Kay rolled her eyes and smacked her lips as she marched into the kitchen to do as she was told.

Martell knew he recognized that face from somewhere, he just couldn't think of where. He wondered if she was one of his many out-of-town one-night stands. India rambled on about all the "hatin'–ass" women in the house as Martell racked his brain about where he knew this woman's face from.

"That's it," Martell said. Keaundra, Alexis, and India turned their attention toward Martell. "I'm sorry," Martell chuckled nervously. "I just thought about something I needed to get done." Martell began feeling uneasy. Sweat beads formed on his forehead as he remembered exactly where he knew Kay-Kay from. "I have to go to the bathroom," he said to no one in particular.

"It's up the stairs and to the right," India said, smiling at her handsome fiancé.

"Thank you." Martell excused himself and made a mad dash for the stairs. As he reached the top of the stairs, Beverly and Kenneth were coming out of one of the bedrooms.

"Hey, man," Kenneth smiled and stuck out his hand for Martell to shake. Martell nonchalantly took his hand and shook it firmly.

Beverly nearly passed out; the last place she expected to see Martell was at her dinner party.

"Look, baby, it's Martell," Kenneth said, nudging Beverly as if she didn't see him standing in front of them.

"I see," Beverly said with little enthusiasm. "I forgot somethin' in the room." Beverly walked back into her bedroom and leaned her back up against the door. *What the fuck is this nigga doin' here?* she thought as her heart raced.

Martell and Kenneth stood out in the hall and talked about the Cavs while Kenneth waited for Beverly to come out of the room. After ten minutes of conversation, Kenneth decided to wait for his lovely wife-to-be downstairs.

Martell made his way to the bathroom and took care of his business. After he finished washing his hands, he walked out into the hallway. Beverly was leaned up against the wall. Martell smiled.

"What the fuck are you doin' here, Martell?" Beverly whispered. "You got a lot of fuckin' nerve showing up at *my* dinner party."

"India tricked me into comin' and, besides, I missed you," Martell said, stroking the side of Beverly's cheek with his finger.

"Oh, stop it, Martell," Beverly hissed, pushing his hand away. "It's only been two days since you've last seen me."

"I know, baby, but those two days seem like an eternity."

"Pull yourself together, Martell," Beverly said, smacking her lips. "Don't go gettin' sloppy on me now."

Martell took a step closer to Beverly. "But I need you."

Beverly held her hands up to stop him. "Don't do this, Martell; you know I"m gettin' married in a couple weeks."

"I know, but we've had so much fun together these last few weeks. I see that bitch caught us is here; I thought you were gon' handle that?"

"Calm down, nigga, I got her under control. You don't hafta worry about that money hungry bitch sayin' nothin'."

"How do you know she won't start runnin' her mouth? You said yourself she has one of the biggest mouths in town."

"Yeah, well she also has expensive taste and spends more than she makes, but don't worry money talks." Beverly winked.

"That's my girl." Martell quickly brushed his lips across Beverly's.

"We better get downstairs before people start missin' us," Beverly stated.

"I know," Martell agreed. "You go first."

Alexis and Keaundra spotted her as soon as she hit the bottom step. They looked at each other, then back at India as she continued talking about how some of the women in the party were dressed. A few minutes later, Martell came down the stairs and walked toward the ladies. Once again, Alexis and Keaundra looked at each other and shook their heads.

"Oh, hey, baby," India said once Martell made it over to them. "What took you so long in the bathroom?"

Martell grabbed a hold of his stomach and said, "It musta been that Mexican food we had for lunch."

"Coulda been."

Keaundra and Alexis were ready to explode and Martell knew it. Maybe it was the look of disgust plastered all over their faces.

Keaundra grimaced. "I need some air."

"Me too," Alexis agreed as she and Keaundra walked away, leaving Martell relieved and India confused. India turned, looking at Martell for an answer, and all he could do was shrug his shoulders.

Alexis and Keaundra avoided India and Martell the entire night. Every time India and Martell would walk over to them, Keaundra and Alexis would stop talking and walk away. India was so fed up with feeling like her so-called best friends were among the other hatin'-ass females at the party, she and Martell decided to turn it in early.

India was quiet on the way home, but Martell was talkative as ever. He was glad to get away from the party. He was getting tired of seeing Beverly and Kenneth all wrapped up in one another like two love-sick teenagers. India couldn't figure out why her girls treated her like a stepchild. She began thinking that maybe they were jealous because she was there with her man, and they had no one by their sides, but erased that from her mind because her girls were not that shallow. Something was bothering them; she just didn't know what.

Alexis and Keaundra felt bad about how they treated their girl, but every time India made her way over to them, Martell was right on her heels. So to avoid creating havoc at Kenneth's dinner party, they just avoided both of them.

Chapter Thirty-seven

That night after the party, Keaundra helped her grandmother clean up the house along with Kenneth and Beverly. Beverly tried numerous times to hold a conversation with Keaundra, but was ignored each time. Kenneth was about to check his sister's behavior but decided to keep his mouth closed. Keaundra finished the last of the dishes, kissed her grandmother on the cheek, and headed toward the door.

"You all right, Ke-Ke?" Gran called out before Keaundra opened the door.

Keaundra turned around and smiled at her grandmother with tears in her eyes and nodded yes.

Gran walked over to her granddaughter and wrapped her arms around her just like she used to do when Keaundra was a little girl. Keaundra felt safe and secure just like she used to. She wanted to burst into tears, but she knew she had to stay strong for Kenneth, and Gran, but mainly for herself.

"You know if you need to talk I'm here for you," Gran said.

"I know, Gran," Keaundra replied, shaking her head knowingly. "I'll call you tomorrow." Keaundra gave her grandmother a kiss on the cheek.

"You do that, so I can find out why you didn't bring Hammer over here to meet me."

Keaundra smiled, shook her head, and headed out to her car. She knew she had a lot of explaining to do to her grandmother about her situation with Hammer, and she felt guilty about not telling her sooner. She knew if anyone could give her some good advice, Gran would be the one, because she was gon' give it to her raw and uncut!

Beverly was upset about Keaundra ignoring her. Just when things started looking up between them, Keaundra started acting funny all over again. Kenneth decided to take his soon-to-be wife on a long walk to clear her mind of his sister's *Sybil*-like ways. Beverly changed into something more comfortable while Kenneth went in to the kitchen to tell his grandmother where he was going.

"Hey, old lady," Kenneth joked when he walked in to the kitchen.

"I got yo' old lady," Gran laughed and playfully slapped him on the arm.

"Me and Beverly 'bout to go for a walk, we'll be back in a couple of hours."

"All right. Y'all be careful out there. You know it's a lot of lunatics in the area."

"They better be worried about me," Kenneth said as he did a bad impression of Bruce Lee.

Gran laughed. "Boy, you silly."

"We'll be back." Kenneth kissed his grandmother on the cheek and disappeared out of the kitchen.

"That's one crazy boy," Gran said, laughing. Gran began feeling tired on top of having a throbbing headache, so she decided to leave the rest of the cleaning until morning. She pulled a glass out of the cabinet and filled it up with water, and made her way to her bedroom.

Gran sat down on the edge of the bed and grabbed the bottle of Aleve off of her nightstand. She struggled to open up the bottle. After a few unsuccessful attempts, she walked back into the kitchen to get a dishrag to help her loosen the cap. Once she reached the kitchen, her head began spinning and Gran collapsed on the kitchen floor.

Kenneth and Beverly returned home after about a two-hour stroll. Kenneth was happy that Beverly was feeling better. He was exhausted and was getting ready to turn in.

"Thank you." Beverly smiled at her husband-to-be.

"For what?"

"For everything."

"You deserve everything I do for you and more."

"Do you want anything out of the kitchen before we go to bed?"

"Please, bring me a bottle of water."

"Anything for you." Beverly made her way to the kitchen and when she got in there she saw Gran lying on the floor with blood running from her head. "Kenneth, come quick," she yelled at the top of her lungs.

"What's wrong?" He panicked, running toward the kitchen. He nearly passed out when he saw his grandmother laying on the floor with blood everywhere. "What happened to her?" he screamed and knelt down beside Beverly and Gran.

"I don't know," Beverly cried. "Call an ambulance!"

"Nine-one-one, what's the emergency," the dispatcher answered.

Ten minutes later, Kenneth watched as the paramedics worked on his grandmother. He didn't know what they were doing; all he could do was hope that whatever it was would save her life. He climbed into the back of the ambulance as they hauled his grandmother off to the hospital. It dawned on him when they pulled up into the hospital parking lot that he hadn't even called his sister to tell her what had happened. As they rushed her down a long hallway where Kenneth wasn't permitted to go, he went to the pay phone and called his sister.

"Hello?" Keaundra answered, still half asleep.

"Ke-Ke, Gran is in the hospital," Kenneth said quickly.

Keaundra sat up. "What happened to her?" Before Kenneth could answer his sister, she had thrown the phone down on the floor and began getting dressed.

"Hello?" Kenneth called out. "Hello?" He got no answer because his sister was already on her way out the front door.

When Keaundra got to the hospital, Kenneth was standing out front, waiting for her. She ran over to him and they hugged. Neither one of them said a word, they just cried in each other's arms. Once the tears slowed, they walked into the hospital's waiting area to join the rest of the family and friends who were arriving. No one was permitted in Gran's room until the doctor was finished running tests on her. Beverly sat holding Kenneth's hand. The sight alone made Keaundra want to walk over and beat Beverly's ass. Under different circumstances, she would have done just that.

Hours later, Kenneth, Beverly, and Keaundra were the only ones still at the hospital; they refused to leave. Kenneth insisted Beverly go home to get some rest. Beverly stood up and kissed him on the top of his head before leaving.

Early the next morning, Keaundra and Kenneth were both still sitting in the hospital waiting area. The doctors still hadn't found out what was wrong with Gran. Keaundra remembered drifting off to sleep around 3:00 A.M., but Kenneth hadn't let his eyes close for a second. Keaundra woke up and looked over at her brother.

"Still no news?" she asked in a groggy tone.

Kenneth shook his head. He turned his attention toward his sister. He could see the weary look on her face. "Why don't you go home and try to get some rest. You look tired."

"I ain't leavin'," Keaundra contested.

"Look, if anything changes, I'll call you."

Keaundra hesitated for a minute. She did need to get some rest. Trying to sleep in those hard hospital chairs had put a lot of strain on her back, plus, she had some important business she needed to handle while she had the chance.

"Okay, but call me if anything changes, please," she said as she stood up from the uncomfortable chair.

"I will, sis." Kenneth stood as well, gave Keaundra a hug, and sent her on her way.

Keaundra cried her eyes out on her way home. She pulled into her driveway, left the car running, and ran into the house. She walked into her room, opened up the closet door, and pulled out a shoebox. The box contained a .38 revolver. She opened up the barrel to make sure it was loaded, and it was. She grabbed the biggest purse she owned and put the gun in it before heading back out to her car.

Keaundra felt like she was losing her mind as she drove. Thoughts of Hammer, Kenneth, and Gran ran through her mind. Tears streamed down her face as she drove to her destination with only one thing on her mind: murder.

Once Keaundra pulled into Gran's driveway, she sat there for a minute, contemplating her next move. One minute, she was amped and ready to go in for the kill, and the next, she was ready to make a U-turn and go back home. She sat and thought for a few more minutes before coming to the conclusion that she couldn't let Beverly or anybody else hurt her or her brother again. Keaundra threw the purse strap on her shoulder and got out of the car. She used her key to let herself in.

"Ken, is that you?" Beverly called out from upstairs.

Keaundra waited a couple of seconds before responding. "Naw, it's me, Keaundra."

Beverly came down the stairs and stood at the bottom of the steps staring at Keaundra.

"What's up?"

"What's up wit' you?" Beverly snapped, still mad about how Keaundra treated her the night before.

"So, you got somethin' you wanna tell me?"

"Somethin' like what?" Beverly replied with an attitude.

Keaundra pulled the .38 revolver out of her purse and pointed it at Beverly. "Somethin' like why you fuckin' Martell?"

Beverly's eyes nearly popped out of her head. She couldn't believe Kenneth's sister was standing in front of her pointing a weapon in her face. Beverly was no fool though, she knew Keaundra meant business from start to finish. So she did what was expected—she began to cry.

"Save the tears, bitch," Keaundra snapped. "You wasn't cryin' when you was fuckin' on Gran's kitchen table, now were you?" Beverly was scared to answer. "Were you?" Beverly shook her head , which for some strange reason made Keaundra madder. "Bitch, I shoulda' known yo' tramp ass hadn't changed." Tears formed in Keaundra's eyes once again. "I can't believe you was still gon' let my brother marry you, knowing damn well you're messin' around on him." Tears fell as she stared at Beverly. Keaundra gripped the handle of the gun tightly as she thought about how devastated Kenneth was going to be once he found out that Beverly had been cheating on him again. "Why, Beverly?"

Beverly shrugged as the tears steadily flowed.

"Why do you continue to hurt the only man who gives a fuck about you?" Keaundra screamed.

Beverly shrugged again. "Answer me, bitch. Don't talk to me with your shoulders."

"I don't know why," Beverly wailed.

"I'll tell you why—because you a ho, that's why. You have always been one and you gon' die one." Keaundra cocked the hammer back on the gun.

"Please don't kill me," Beverly begged. "Please, please, I'll tell you whatever you wanna know." Beverly's voice was full of fear.

"Start talkin'." Keaundra stated with the gun still pointed. "And if I even think you lyin' to me, I'ma kill you on the spot." The deranged looked in Keaundra's eyes let Beverly know that Keaundra meant every word she said. Beverly swallowed hard before she began spilling the beans.

Beverly began explaining how she was checking Martell out at her engagement party. And when she ran into him at the grocery store, he asked for her phone number, claiming he needed a female's point of view on what they expect from their man. When they exchanged numbers, he started out calling for advice when he and India were having problems. Then the calls progressed to them spending hours on the phone.

She then went on to tell Keaundra how Martell asked to take her out to lunch a few times and she accepted. Tears blurred Keaundra's vision as Beverly explained the sickening details on what transpired the day Martell came over to fix the air conditioner. She even told the part about how she agreed to pay Kay-Kay a thousand dollars a month to keep her mouth shut. Keaundra didn't think it was possible, but she became even angrier.

Keaundra wanted to shoot Beverly and then go shoot Kay-Kay for betraying her own family. She thought back when India had tried to tell her and became mad at herself. Beverly kept her eyes glued to the gun as she went on with the story. She told Keaundra that since she knew the money would keep Kay-Kay's mouth closed, she continued sleeping with Martell. Keaundra's finger itched to pull the trigger just to watch the look on Beverly's worthless face. Keaundra cried for her brother as Beverly cried for her life to be spared.

Keaundra took her free hand, wiped the tears away, and looked Beverly straight in the eyes.

"This is what you gon' do, bitch, and I'm not askin' you, I'm tellin' you. You gon' call this wedding off, 'cause I can't sit back and watch my brother give you everything under the sun while you fuckin' around on him behind his back."

"The wedding is a couple weeks away," Beverly said, cautiously.

"So the fuck what!" Keaundra yelled.

"What about all the guests we invited?"

"What about 'em? You betta' call 'em and tell 'em that the wedding has been postponed to a later date."

"What about all the money we spent on the honeymoon, the decorations, and the rest of the stuff?"

"You didn't spend a dime. And while you're wasting your time worrying about the petty things, what about Kenneth and how he's gon' feel?" Tears clouded Keaundra's vision as she thought about how hurt her brother was going to be once he found out that Beverly wanted to postpone the wedding.

How Kenneth would feel hadn't dawned on Beverly until Keaundra mentioned him.

"I never wanted to hurt Kenneth, honestly."

"You not gon' hurt him. You gon' help him by tellin' him you want to postpone the wedding. And I'm gon' help you by not tellin' him about you and Martell; he's been hurt enough."

All Beverly could do was shake her head in disbelief. She had fucked up and this time she knew there was no fixing it. She had lost the only man whoever truly loved her.

Keaundra lowered the gun to her side, looking at Beverly as if she were a piece of shit. She walked toward the front door. Keaundra put the gun back in her purse and placed her hand on the knob, but before she opened the door, she turned back around to face Beverly.

"Oh, by the way, I want you out of my grandmother's house . . . today!" Keaundra proceeded to walk out the front door with a crooked smile on her face.

Chapter Thirty-eight

Ronald woke up bright and early and cooked breakfast for his family. He made pancakes, bacon, eggs, and freshly squeezed orange juice. He fixed everybody's plates and set them on the kitchen table, checking to make sure everything was perfect before leaving the kitchen.

"Get up, sleepy head," he said to Ro'nisha when he walked into her bedroom. She opened her eyes and smiled at her daddy, which made Ronald feel good on the inside. "Come on." He held out his hands and Ro'nisha climbed into her daddy's arms as he carried her across the hall into her brother's room. "R.J., get up, man." Ronald laughed as R.J. squeezed his eyes closed, pretending as if he were still asleep. "Get up, boy, you ain't asleep."

R.J. laughed as well and jumped up. "I tricked you, didn't I, Daddy?" R.J. smiled while his big brown eyes lit up.

"You sure did, big man. Are you hungry?"

"Starvin'."

"Well, go in the bathroom and wash your face and help your sister wash hers."

Ronald put his daughter down. R.J. and Ro'nisha ran out of the room and down the hall to do what they were told. His last stop was Alexis's bedroom. He walked in and stood in the doorway, watching as Alexis slept. He smiled before walking over to her and pressing his lips against hers.

Alexis opened her eyes and smiled. "Good mornin'."

"Mornin', sunshine. I fixed breakfast."

"You did?" Alexis asked, surprised. She could not remember the last time Ronald had cooked for her and the children. "Let me wash my face and I'll be in the kitchen." Alexis yawned before getting out of bed. Ronald just stood staring. "What?"

"Nothin'. I love you."

"I love you too, Ronald," Alexis said on her way to the bathroom.

After they finished breakfast, Ronald cleared the table and began washing the dishes while Alexis went to get the children dressed. He had made plans to take Alexis and the children to the Columbus Zoo for a fun-filled day, and all expenses were on him.

Alexis couldn't pass up a chance for Ronald or any man spending his money on her and the children. While Alexis was in the middle of giving Ro'nisha a bath, her cell phone rang. She hopped up and ran into her bedroom to get it; the last thing she needed was for Ronald to answer it and it be Keaundra or India on the other end. She wouldn't know how to explain Ronald answering her phone. Alexis felt bad that she still hadn't told her girls that she and Ronald had gotten back together. Every time she thought she was ready to tell them, she came up with a reason not to.

"Hello?" Alexis answered.

"Alexis, Gran is in the hospital," Keaundra stated.

"What's the matter with her, Ke-Ke?" Alexis asked as she walked back into the bathroom to finish giving her daughter a bath.

"Kenneth just called me and said she had a massive stroke. She's still in a coma."

"Ahh man, Keaundra. I'm sorry to hear that. Are you at the hospital?"

Tears formed in Keaundra's eyes as she spoke. "Not yet, but I'm on my way back there."

"I'm 'bout to finish gettin' the kids dressed then I'll meet you there."

"Okay."

"Have you called India yet?" Alexis asked as she picked her daughter up out the tub and wrapped her in a *Blue's Clues* bath towel.

"I've been callin' her all morning, but she's not answering."

"I'll stop by her house on my way to the hospital."

"Thanks, girl."

"See ya in a bit." Alexis hung up the phone, walked into her room, and began getting her daughter dressed. After doing the same for her son, and herself, she headed into the living room where Ronald sat watching television. Alexis knew she had promised Ronald that she would go to the zoo with him, but Keaundra needed her.

"Oh, you dressed already?" Ronald asked, looking up from the program he was watching.

"Um, yes, but, Ronald, there's been a change in plans."

Ronald raised both brows. "What's the change?"

Here we go. "Keaundra's grandmother had a stroke last night so I'm goin' up to the hospital to sit with her." Alexis braced herself and waited for Ronald to blow up like he used to.

"Okay, that's cool. We can go to the zoo another day. Go'n up to the hospital 'cause Keaundra needs you," Ronald said sincerely.

What the fuck? Ronald being caring and understanding of someone else's feelings, especially Keaundra's? This has to be a dream. "Okay, baby, thanks." Alexis gave Ronald a peck on the lips. "I'll try not to be gone too long," she said, grabbing her car keys off the coffee table.

"Take yo' time. I'll take the kids to McDonald's for lunch."

Alexis had to give Ronald another kiss, but this time it was long and passionate.

"Wow!" Ronald said when he broke loose from the lip lock Alexis had him in. "What was that for?"

"If you only knew," she replied with a huge smile. Alexis floated out to her car on cloud nine. Once she pulled out of the parking lot, she made herself a promise that she would tell her best friends about her newfound relationship with Ronald. Regardless of what they had to say, she and Ronald were a couple, a happy one, at last.

Alexis pulled into India's driveway and parked behind Martell's Porsche. She pulled out her cell phone and dialed India's phone number. After getting no answer, Alexis got out of the car and rang the doorbell. She waited a few minutes before letting herself in with her key.

"India?" Alexis called out. When she didn't get an answer, Alexis began searching the house. Her first stop was the kitchen. Alexis frowned when she walked in on India and Martell having breakfast.

"How come you haven't been answering your phone?" Alexis started in. "You cut the ringer off or somethin'?"

"Nope." India kept her eyes glued to her plate.

"Well, how come you didn't answer it then?"" Alexis snapped.

"I didn't feel like it," India snapped back.

"My, don't we have an attitude this morning. What's wrong with you?"

"I should be askin' you that question," India replied nastily.

Alexis knew where this was going. India must have still been upset about how she and Keaundra treated her at the dinner party. "Be mad later, but right now I need you to go get dressed."

"For what? I ain't goin' nowhere with you," India replied snottily. Martell loved the way his woman stood up to her friend.

"Whatever. Just get dressed 'cause we need to meet Keaundra at the hospital."

India's mood mellowed out quickly. "What's the matter with her?"

"It's not her, it's Gran. She had a massive stroke last night."

"Oh, no." India gasped as tears filled her eyes. "Is she gon' be okay?"

"I don't know. She's still in a coma."

"A coma?" India asked, scared.

"Yes, so go get dressed so we can meet Keaundra at the hospital."

As India was about to walk out of the kitchen, Martell called out her name. "India?" India stopped and turned around, but didn't open her mouth. "What about the movie we were supposed to go see today?" he asked selfishly.

"Did you not just hear what Alexis said? Gran is in the hospital." India was disgusted by Martell's selfishness.

"Fuck that!" he snapped angrily.

Alexis and India both shot Martell a death stare. He pushed himself away from the table and threw his plate in the sink without emptying it first.

"You always puttin' them bitches before me," he shouted.

"I knew it wouldn't last," Alexis said, shaking her head.

"Martell, listen to how you sound. Keaundra's grandmother is lyin' up in the hospital and you're worried about a damn movie."

"I'll just find someone else to take then," he said, hoping he could get India to change her mind about going to the hospital, but instead he only made her angry.

"Do that," she spat and walked out of the kitchen to go get dressed.

"Take Beverly," Alexis said, winking with a smirk, and followed India.

Martell was so outdone by Alexis's remark, he couldn't even open his mouth with a come back. *How in the hell did that bitch find out about me and Beverly.* Martell began to panic. *Beverly told me she had everything under control. Oh my God.* Sweat beads formed on Martell's head as he paced the kitchen floor while trying to figure out how Alexis had found out about him and Beverly. *So if Alexis knows, I'm sure Keaundra knows too. I just can't figure out why they haven't told India yet. God, please don't let them bitches tell on me. I don't wanna lose India.* Martell prayed silently as he waited for India and Alexis to leave. Once he heard the front door close, he hurried out of the kitchen and into the bedroom. He went straight to the closet, reached for his shoebox, pulled out his pack of cigarettes, and smoked until he became nauseated.

As Alexis and India pulled into the crowded hospital parking lot, Alexis's cell phone began to ring. She checked the caller ID and smiled when she saw the familiar number.

"Hello?"

"How are you?" the caller asked.

The sound of his voice sent electric waves through her body. "I'm fine and you?" Alexis couldn't believe David still made her feel like she had butterflies in her stomach.

"Better now that I hear your voice," David replied honestly.

Alexis giggled like a school girl. "Whatever." India rolled her eyes and pointed toward the hospital to let Alexis know that she was going in without her. Alexis nodded and continued her conversation. "Long time no hear from."

"I know. You kicked me to the curb," he laughed.

Alexis laughed too. "Whatever, David. What's up?"

"Nothin'. I was just callin' to check on you, that's all."

"Thanks."

Silence fell between the two.

"Well, maybe one day you'll let a brotha take you out to lunch or somethin'."

"That'll be nice," Alexis agreed, forgetting all about Ronald. Alexis thought her feelings for David were long gone, especially since she and Ronald were back together, but she was wrong.

"What are you doin' tomorrow?"

"I really don't know because Keaundra's grandmother had a stroke so me and India are up at the hospital with her."

"Ahhh, sorry to hear that. I'm gon' hafta tell Hammer," David said regretfully.

"Yeah, do that."

"Is she gon' be okay?"

Alexis let out a heavy sigh. "I don' know. I hope."

"Yeah, me too. Tell Keaundra I said I'll keep her and her grandmother in my prayers."

"Sure will." Alexis and David talked a few minutes longer. Before saying their good-byes, Alexis promised David that she would call him the next day to make plans for their lunch date. She hung up the phone with one of the biggest smiles on her face and walked into the hospital to find her friends.

Chapter Thirty-nine

Kenneth finally took a chance on going home after sitting with his grandmother for two straight days. By the time he pulled into the driveway, Kenneth was completely exhausted. He turned off the ignition, laid his head back, and closed his eyes for a brief moment. When he finally pulled himself together, he got out of the car. He looked over where Beverly's Avenger was normally parked and smiled. He figured she had gone out for a few last-minute wedding preparations. He unlocked the front door and headed straight to his bedroom.

Kenneth walked in, tossed the keys on the nightstand, and immediately plopped down on the bed. He removed his shoes and lay back. Once his head hit the pillow his eyes slowly closed but opened right back up once he thought about the important phone call he needed to make to the contractors. Beverly had changed her mind on the color of the living room and the master bath again. He looked over at the dresser as he lay in thought and noticed Beverly's side of the dresser was completely empty.

"That's strange," Kenneth said. The more he stared at the empty space on the dresser the more his stomach began to turn. Kenneth climbed out of bed, walked over to the closet, and pulled open the double doors. Beverly's clothes were gone. The only sign of her belongings ever being there were the plastic hangers she had left behind. "What the fuck?" Kenneth asked, puzzled. He then walked over to the dresser and began pulling open drawers only to find them empty as well.

Kenneth's heart began to race with anxiety as he made his way over to the nightstand to retrieve the cordless phone. He dialed Beverly's cell phone but it went straight to the voice mail. He then dialed Mrs. Norton's house and his heart slowed down a pace or two as soon as Mrs. Norton answered the phone.

"Hello?" Mrs. Norton answered in the most pleasant tone.

"Is Beverly there, Mrs. Norton?" Kenneth started in.

"Um." Mrs. Norton hesitated while looking in Beverly's direction. Beverly was in the background shaking her head and hands. "No, she's not. Would you like to leave a message?" she continued.

"Mrs. Norton, I know Beverly is there. Tell her to get on the phone," Kenneth said, agitated.

"Kenneth, I don't wanna get in the middle of y'all's business. Just know that when Beverly is ready to talk, she'll call you," Mrs. Norton explained and then hung up.

"Stankin' bitch!" Kenneth yelled as he pressed the redial button on the phone. His chest tightened when no one answered the phone. Kenneth had left so many messages on the voice mail it wouldn't take anymore. He slammed the phone down, grabbed his keys, and headed to his car. He pulled out of the driveway and put the pedal to the metal as he headed over to see Beverly.

Kenneth didn't have the slightest idea why Beverly moved out. He knew that they hadn't had a fight, he hadn't cheated, he gave her any and everything she wanted, so she had no reason to leave. Kenneth was confused and he wanted some answers. Once he turned onto her mother's street, he instantly spotted Beverly's car parked in the driveway next to her mother's Chrysler 300.

Kenneth pulled in behind Beverly's car and got out. He walked up to the door and began knocking. When he got no answer, he began knocking a little harder. Kenneth waited a few more minutes and began knocking again. He became angry when no one answered and began pounding on the door like the police. Kenneth became angrier each time his knuckles connected with the big wooden door.

"Beverly, I know you're in there," he began yelling. "How you just gon' up and leave me? I didn't do shit to you!"

"Beverly, why don't you go out there and talk to him," Mrs. Norton whispered to her daughter.

Tears filled Beverly's eyes as she spoke. "I can't, Ma."

"Why not?" Mrs. Norton asked, confused. "You guys are supposed to be gettin' married in a couple of weeks. It's obvious the man wants to spend the rest of his life with you. What could he possibly have done that you can't even talk to him?" Mrs. Norton believed that Kenneth was truly in love with her daughter; he had to be, in order to take all the shit Beverly had put him through. "The man gives you everything, I mean everything, Beverly. Kenneth loves you," she stressed.

"I love him too, Ma. It's just too complicated to explain." The tears fell from her eyes as she spoke.

"Well, whatever it is you're mad at him about, let it go and make up with him," Mrs. Norton said angrily.

The thought of Keaundra pointing that gun in her face flashed into Beverly's mind and gave her the chills. "I can't."

Mrs. Norton shook her head in disgust. "Suit yourself. You're the one missin' out on a good thing, and when he finds someone else, you'll regret ever playin' with that man's emotions," Mrs. Norton said before walking away from her daughter.

Beverly knew her mother was right. Just the thought of Kenneth being with another woman made her sick to her stomach. She wanted nothing more than to stay with Kenneth, but he had already told her if she ever cheated on him again, he would never forgive her. She was in a no-win situation. Besides, she had no choice but to let Kenneth go if she wanted to live. Beverly knew Keaundra all too well to think she was playing about killing her, or at least trying to.

After about ten more minutes of pounding, Kenneth realized that no one was going to answer the door. Hurt and defeated, he walked to his car and drove home. Kenneth walked through the door, went back to his room, and cried himself to sleep.

David had a huge smile on his face when Rosalind walked through the door. He was dancing around the living room like he had just hit the jackpot.

"What you so happy for?" Rosalind asked, walking in with her hands full of groceries.

"Oh, nothin'." David took the bags from her hands and carried them into the kitchen.

"You must be happy about somethin', you smiling and dancing around the room," she stated as she followed him into the kitchen.

David rolled his eyes. He didn't want to seem mean to someone who claimed to be dying, but ever since he let Rosalind back into his life, she had been smothering his every move. If he went to the bathroom, she was right there by the door. If he went to the store, when he returned, she wanted to know why it took him so long. When he went to work, she would pop up on the job and just sit around. Rosalind was getting on his last nerve, but he didn't have the heart to tell her.

"Why can't I just be happy about nothin'?" David asked.

"You're happy about somethin' and I would like to know what so I can be happy with you."

You wouldn't be happy if I told you why I was happy, he thought as he stared at her in disbelief. "I'm just happy, leave it at that." David walked out of the kitchen, leaving Rosalind alone.

Rosalind soon followed. "Happy about what, David?" she continued picking.

David let out a long breath. "I'm just happy, damn!" he said, walking down the hall toward his bedroom.

"It has to be a reason." Rosalind followed close behind.

I'm happy because the woman I want to be with has agreed to go out to lunch with me, okay, are you happy now? "Let it go, Rosalind, please." Rosalind was driving David insane. He wanted to scream, but was too afraid that she would ask questions when he was finished.

Rosalind placed both hands on her hips and said, "Oh, so you can't tell me what you happy for?"

"Rosalind, I'm happy because I'm alive. I'm happy because I own my own house, car, and business. I'm just fuckin' happy, dammit!" he said and walked into the bathroom, closing and locking the door behind him.

Rosalind stood in disbelief. She couldn't believe David had just talked to her like that. Rosalind walked out into the hall and began knocking on the bathroom door. "David, are you in there?"

David wanted to bang his head on the bathroom door. "Rosalind, just leave me alone, please," he practically begged.

"Okay, fine. I still think there's more to why you're so happy and it's okay that you don't wanna share it with me." Rosalind walked away from the bathroom door, figuring she had pestered David long enough.

"Calgon, take me away," David said quietly.

"I'm tellin' you man, I be wantin' to choke the broad out sometimes," David said to Hammer as he sat in the barber chair getting a line up.

"Man, she can't be that bad."

"You just don't know the half of it. She's driving me crazy."

"Well, tell her to kick mud then," Hammer suggested.

David sighed. "That's just it, I can't."

Hammer shook his head. "Well, you just gon' hafta deal with the shit she's puttin' you through then."

"Man, I'ma end up in the pen if she doesn't move out," David said, shaking his head.

"How did she end up moving in anyway?" Hammer leaned his head over to the side while David lined up his sideburn.

"Man, I let the broad spend the night once and after that she began moving her shit in, piece by piece," David said, annoyed.

Hammer laughed. "That's how it usually works."

"Man, this ain't no laughing matter."

"I'm sorry, dog, it's just that for Rosalind to be so-called sick, she still got hella game," Hammer said, laughing.

"I know. I'm beginning to think she's startin' to take my kindness for weakness."

"Oh, you think?" Hammer said sarcastically. "Man, you just gon' hafta break down and tell her."

"I know. I know."

Hammer admired his fresh fade and nicely shaved face in the mirror before continuing. "Well, act like you do."

David began sweeping up the hair around his barber chair. "I'm gon' tell her tonight. Shit, I'm tired of feelin' like I really owe her somethin'."

Hammer nodded in agreement. "Yeah, man, she's startin' to treat you like you're a part of a peonage."

David stopped sweeping and gave his cousin a look of confusion. "A what?"

"A peonage. You know, a system of forced labor, a form of involuntary servitude to a creditor until the debt is fulfilled," Hammer answered smartly.

David shook his head and laughed. "I forgot that my favorite cousin was a genius."

"Whatever," Hammer replied. "Don't hate 'cause I'm smart."

"I ain't hatin'. Anyways, I'ma tell her, I promise."

Hammer climbed down out of the barber chair and turned toward David. "You betta 'cause it's getting close to the first of the month and the rent is almost due." Hammer fell out laughing as he made his way out the shop's door.

"Very funny, nigga, very funny." David continued sweeping up the hair on the floor. Once he finished, he sat down in the chair and began putting a plan together on how to tell Rosalind that he needed his space, but before he could get his plan all mastered out he heard the bell chime that hung above the door. David looked up as Rosalind made her way over to him.

"Hey, baby." She smiled.

David closed his eyes and shook his head. "Fuck!"

Chapter Forty

A week had passed and Gran's condition took a turn for the worse. She went from being in a coma to being placed on a respirator. Seeing her lying there in a vegetative state with tubes running out of her body brought tears to Kenneth's and Keaundra's eyes every time they walked into her hospital room. The doctors were giving Gran little to no hope at all. The only thing they had to rely on was prayer.

Kenneth took a leave of absence from work to stay by Gran's side, just like she had done for him and his sister. Keaundra couldn't afford to take a leave from work, but she made sure she went to the hospital every day after work to sit and visit with her grandmother.

Keaundra walked into the hospital, stood by the nurse's station, and watched as the doctor walked out of her grandmother's room. She waited a few minutes, pulling herself together before walking in.

Kenneth sat next to Gran's bed rubbing her hand when Keaundra walked into the room. He looked up and smiled.

"Hey," she said with a weak smile as she looked over at Gran.

"Hey."

"How is she? I just seen the doctor leaving out of here, what did he say?" she asked, hoping to hear some good news.

Kenneth's eyes instantly filled with tears. "Sit down, Ke-Ke," Kenneth said in a somewhat demanding tone. Keaundra obeyed as she reluctantly sat down at the foot of her grandmother's bed.

Kenneth sat in complete silence as he stared somberly at his sister.

"What is it, Ken? What did the doctor say?" Keaundra asked impatiently.

"He said that Gran's CAT scan showed some signs of bleeding. They hafta run some more tests on her."

"What?" Keaundra gasped. "What's causing it?"

"They really don't know, but they're tryin'a link it to her being a severe diabetic."

Keaundra heard her brother clearly, but for some odd reason she couldn't comprehend what was coming out of his mouth. "So what does that mean?"

"Gran should have been on insulin a long time ago, Keaundra, to keep her diabetes under control." Kenneth paused for a second and looked down at the floor. "They said she might have to get both of her legs amputated," he continued.

Keaundra hopped off the end of the bed and stood over her brother. "Who is this *they* you keep talkin' about?" I know you're not talkin' about the doctors. They're not God, Kenneth, so what do *they* really know," Keaundra pressed. Kenneth didn't have a definite answer for his sister so he remained quiet.

"Calm down, Ke-Ke."

"What do you mean calm down? We can't just sit back and let them start chopping things off of Gran," Keaundra said angrily.

"I know, Keaundra. I know."

"What do you think she'll say when she wakes up and she's missing both of her legs?"

"She'll go off." Kenneth chuckled a little at the thought of his grandmother raising hell about her legs being cut off.

"You damn right she will."

Kenneth turned to face his sister. The look on his face scared her. "What other option do we have?"

Keaundra shook her head. "I don't know, Ken. I just don't know."

Kenneth and Keaundra sat next to Gran's bed
and talked for hours. Kenneth had decided to
have a family meeting the following day to let the
family know what was going on with Gran and to
ask for their input. At first, Keaundra was dead
set against letting the rest of the family have
any input on what happened to Gran, since they
rarely ever came to visit her. Gran's own children
hardly ever came by, but Kenneth convinced Keaundra after his lecture about family needing to
stick together.

The nurse walked in around seven o'clock to
draw blood from Gran's arm. Keaundra stood up
from her chair and turned her back. She couldn't
stand the sight of the big, long needle being
pushed inside her grandmother's vein. "I'll call
you later on," she said to her brother.

"You okay?" Kenneth stood up and asked.

"Yeah. I just need to get out of here, plus, I got
somethin' I need to take care of."

Kenneth kissed his sister on the forehead.
"Okay then, call me later."

She smiled at her handsome brother and
said, "I will." Keaundra took one last look at her
grandmother before walking out of the hospital
room. Once she got into the car, her cell phone
started ringing. "Hello?"

"Where you at? We sittin' over here waiting
for you," Alexis started in.

"I'm coming. You know I had to stop by the hospital to check on Gran."

"How is she?" Alexis asked cautiously.

Keaundra took a deep breath before speaking. "I wish I knew."

"Sorry."

I'm on my way. Don't start eatin' without me."

"We won't, but hurry up," Alexis said before hanging up the phone.

Keaundra was so distracted on her drive over to India's house that she nearly caused two car accidents. She couldn't stop thinking about how her life would be if Gran didn't make it. She knew that if Gran did pass away, their lives would never be the same. Gran had been with them for what seemed like a lifetime. Without her, Kenneth and Keaundra would have nothing.

Thoughts of Hammer also danced around in her head; she had started missing him more and more with each passing day. Keaundra also worried for India and how she was going to react once she found out about Martell and Beverly. She knew her friend all too well to know that it was not going to be easy for India to get over Martell. She remembered how long it had taken her to get over Jerry, her first high school boyfriend. For eight long months, India cried each and every time she had seen something that reminded her of Jerry.

***

"About time," India yelled from the kitchen when she heard her friend coming in the door.

"Ahhh shut up," Keaundra yelled back as she made her way toward the kitchen. Keaundra sat down at the kitchen table as Alexis put a plate of food down in front of her. India had made steak, baked potatoes, homemade rolls, and a salad. "Damn, girl, it sure smells good."

"You know anything I cook is good," India bragged before they all bowed their heads in prayer.

The three friends laughed and talked over dinner. Alexis and Keaundra decided they needed a drink to muster up enough nerve to tell India about Martell.

"Come on, y'all, let's go in the living room to see what Martell has in the liquor cabinet," Alexis suggested and stood up from the kitchen table.

"You remember what happened the last time we drank Martell's liquor," India joked, standing up from the table as well.

They all walked into the living room. India walked over to the liquor cabinet and pulled out a bottle of Perrier-Jouët champagne. She grabbed three glasses and the corkscrew from the top shelf, carried them over to the coffee table, and set them down.

"Okay, bitches, now y'all wanna tell me what this emergency dinner is all about?" India asked while uncorking the top of the champagne.

Alexis and Keaundra looked at each other nervously. India could sense the uneasiness. "Spit it out," India said as she filled each of the glasses up.

Alexis picked up her glass and took it to the head and so did Keaundra.

"Come on, y'all," India whined and waited for her friends to began speaking. "I waited until we finished dinner; now tell me what's goin' on."

Alexis cleared her throat as she grabbed the bottle and refilled her glass. "Well," she said, taking a sip, "this dinner is about . . ." She took another sip.

"Come on, Lexy, stop playin' and tell me what the fuck is goin' on."

"What she's tryin'a say is that this dinner is about Martell," Keaundra cut in.

"What about Martell?" India asked, skeptical.

Keaundra and Alexis looked at each other.

"Quit playin' and tell me what's up with Martell."

"Martell is fuckin' around with Beverly," Keaundra blurted quickly.

"Run that by me again?" India replied.

"Martell is fuckin' around with Beverly," Alexis repeated slowly as if India were hard of hearing.

"Bitch, please, Martell is not fuckin' around with Beverly. So stop playin' and tell me what's really going on."

"No, for real. Martell is fuckin' around with Beverly," Alexis said.

India's adrenaline began to rush. "How the fuck y'all know that?"

India began to perspire as Keaundra began to speak. "Martell is the nigga that Kay-Kay caught fuckin' Beverly on Gran's kitchen table."

India's eyes began to water. "Y'all tell me y'all playin' wit' me." Tears began to roll as she waited for her friends to yell, Psych!

"I wish we were," Alexis stated sadly.

India knew about the women Martell messed around with while he was out of town on his so-called business trips, because she had figured out the code to his voice mail and checked his messages from time to time. Different females were constantly leaving messages. India never told her friends about the women because not everything that is known is meant to be spoken about, even with her best friends. But India never thought in a million years that he would be bold enough to mess around so close to home.

"I can't believe this shit," India said, shaking her head. "I shoulda known somethin' was goin' on. That's why the nigga started smokin' cigarettes again, his conscience was eatin' his black ass up. All this time the nigga that was caught fuckin' Beverly was right under my nose."

Alexis and Keaundra sat in silence as India spoke. "And here I thought I had me somethin' good, but it turned out I didn't have shit but a no-good, lyin'-ass nigga. He ain't nothin' but another Jerry."

I hope we ain't about to go through another Jerry episode, Keaundra wanted to say but decided to keep it to herself only because she knew her friend was hurting.

"So what you gon' do?" Alexis cut in on the conversation that India held with herself.

India shrugged. "I'm gon' do what I always do. I'm gon' hold my head up high and step. What else can I do?"

"I feel you, girl." Alexis smiled.

"If the nigga want a bitch like Beverly, he can have her. That's just like trading a Benz for a moped. So I ain't gon' worry about it, I'll find me somebody."

"You sure will," Keaundra agreed.

"You too good for him anyways," Alexis added.

"I know," India agreed, sounding as if her confidence had been shot.

"Just know that we got ya back," Keaundra assured her friend.

"Thanks." India refilled her glass and held it up for a toast. Keaundra and Alexis looked at each other, confused. "I would like to make a toast," India said, wiping her tears away with her free hand.

"To what?" Keaundra asked, surprised.

"To freedom and friendship."

The three friends held up their glasses and made a toast, took a sip from their drinks, and set their glasses on top of the coffee table. India looked over at Keaundra and asked the question that Keaundra would have rather avoided.

"What did Kenneth say about all of this?"

Keaundra held her head down. "He doesn't know."

"What? It's bad enough you kept it from me as long as you did, now you mean to tell me that you haven't even told Kenneth yet?" India said, shocked.

Keaundra picked her glass up off the coffee table and looked India straight in the eyes. "No, I haven't told him and I'm not gon' tell him either."

India was confused. "Why not?"

"Because, my brother has been hurt enough and I refuse to add fuel to the fire." Tears filled Keaundra's eyes as she thought about her brother and all the pain he was left to deal with throughout his life. "It's just best that he doesn't find out."

Alexis sat in silence as India and Keaundra talked back and forth.

"Let me ask you a question," India said. "If Kenneth doesn't know about Martell and Beverly, why did they postpone the wedding?"

Keaundra and Alexis both began laughing as Keaundra explained to India what went down at Gran's house the day she went over there with her gun. She told her how she made Beverly tell people that the wedding was postponed instead of cancelled so no one would get suspicious. Keaundra also told India about how Kay-Kay had been extorting Beverly.

That night the three friends' bond grew even tighter as they sat around sharing laughter and tears. India knew that tonight was the end of Martell and the beginning of her. She was so hurt after hearing the news about Martell cheating, but she refused to let their breakup effect her like the one she had with Jerry. India kept her head up as usual and kicked it with her girls. She knew from experience that men come and go, but her true friends would have her back forever.

Chapter Forty-one

Alexis woke up early the next morning with a hangover. She dragged herself out of bed and walked into her son's room only to find him missing. Alexis ran over into her daughter's bedroom to see if he was in there, but she was gone also. She called out for Ronald but didn't get an answer. She walked into the kitchen to see if they were in there, but all she found was a note from Ronald.

> *Good morning, sunshine,*
> *You were sleeping like a baby so I didn't want to wake you. I fed the kids, got them dressed, and dropped them off at the daycare so you could take your time getting ready for work. See you when I get home.*
> *Love Ronald*

Alexis was outdone with how Ronald was continuously stepping up to the plate being the man and father she had always wanted him to be. She smiled as she grabbed a bottle of water out of the refrigerator and popped the cap. She took a long swig as she walked back toward her bedroom. Alexis lay back down for a few more minutes of rest. She was in love and it was a must that she shared it with her girls. She wasn't about to hide her relationship anymore.

Alexis climbed back out of bed, grabbed the phone and dialed Keaundra's phone number, but the call went straight to her voice mail. Hanging up she then called India, and the same thing happened. She put the phone back on the charger and began looking for something to wear to work. As Alexis showered, she imagined how her girls would react when she told them about Ronald being back in her life. The longer she thought the more doubt set in. Alexis began wondering if the calls going straight to voice mail were a sign to keep her relationship with Ronald quiet a little longer. She finished showering, got dressed, and headed out for work.

Keaundra couldn't sleep after she got home from kicking it with her girls. All she kept thinking about was how the family meeting would turn out. She hoped and prayed that the family's decision concerning Gran was a positive one,

but knowing them, this meeting would be nothing but chaos. Keaundra dreaded the turnout
and tossed and turned until she finally fell off to
sleep. Her ringing phone startled her awake. She
looked at the clock and her heart began pounding because people only called at three 'o clock in
the morning when something bad has happened.

Keaundra grabbed the phone off the nightstand and checked the caller ID. David's number
showed up. She knew that it could have only
been Hammer calling. Keaundra wanted to answer it but she also needed to get some sleep
so she could be well-rested and alert in order to
face her dysfunctional family. Once the phone
stopped ringing, she took the phone off the hook,
and turned her cell phone off before drifting
back off to sleep.

India woke up and looked around her bedroom. All she could hear was the irritating sound
of the phone letting her know that it was off the
hook. She could hear the shower running so that
indicated that Martell was there. India instantly
got an attitude when she looked down at her
body and found herself completely naked.

*How come the nigga couldn't take a shower
over Beverly's house?* she thought as she climbed

out of bed, grabbed her robe, and put it on. India walked over to the closet and began taking all of Martell's things out and laying them on the bed. Martell walked out of the bathroom just as India finished gathering all of his things.

"What's goin' on?" he asked, confused.

"What does it look like?"

"It looks like you packing my stuff."

"Damn, you intelligent."

"Where am I going?"

"I don't know, but you got to get the fuck up outta here," India snapped.

Martell grabbed India by both of her arms. "What's the matter with you? We made passionate love all night and now you puttin' me out?"

"Let me get this straight, we made love all night?"

"Yeah, don't you remember?"

"Only thing I remember about last night was drinking two bottles of your champagne. I don't even remember when my girls left. Shit, I don't even remember how I got in the bed."

"I carried you. Now can you tell me what's going on here?"

India stared at Martell as if he were crazy. "You tell me what's going on, *Martell*."

"I don't know what you talkin' about," he said as he began getting dressed. Martell knew just what India was talking about. He rode by the house last night and saw Alexis's and Keaundra's cars so the only thing she could have been talking about was Beverly, but he wasn't about to admit to anything.

"Oh, so you don't know what I'm talkin' about?"

"Naw," he replied nonchalantly while continuing to put his clothes on. Martell let out a nervous chuckle. "What lies did ya girls fill ya head up with now?"

"Just the one about Beverly."

"Beverly?" he said. "What about her?"

"Oh, so you didn't get caught fuckin' her over on Gran's table?"

Martell's face twisted up as if something smelled bad. "Hell, naw. Who told you that shit? Somebody's lying on me!"

India chuckled out of anger. "Nigga, so you gon' stand here in my face and say that somebody's lying on you?"

"Yeah," Martell answered without hesitation. "Ain't nobody told you that shit but them jealous-ass bitches, Alexis and Keaundra."

"Well, who do you think told me about Kenya from Washington, Diane from Michigan, and Joy from Atlanta?"

Martell's eyes widened. He was in shock. He didn't know how India found out about all of them.

"Yeah, I knew about them, Martell, but I didn't care because those were bitches you spent your time with when you were out of town and believe it or not I could deal with that. But I can't and won't deal with you fuckin' a bitch that lives in the same city as me. Not only the same city, but she was supposed to marry my best friend's brother. Now how fucked up is that, Martell?"

Martell couldn't say a word. He had been busted. He looked at India with sorrowful eyes. He knew he had hurt her, but what hurt him even more was she showed no signs of it. "I'm sorry," he finally said.

"I am too," India said walking into the living room and slamming her bedroom door behind her tears filled her eyes but she refused to let them fall, not now, not ever. The tears she cried last night with her girls would be the only tears shed for the pain Martell had caused. Breaking up with Jerry had taught her something about pain. It hurt when it first happens, but it doesn't last forever. India sucked up her tears and walked back into her bedroom, watching as Martell stuffed his things into garbage bags. He stopped what he was doing and looked over at her, wanting her to say something to let him know that she still loved him and wanted to work through this. But she didn't; instead, her words stung.

"Don't watch me, keep packing your shit so you can get the fuck up outta here!" she said coldly. "And don't leave nothin'!"

Martell shook his head and continued packing. He had filled four trash bags; he grabbed two, and carried them toward the door. India grabbed the other two and followed him. Martell opened the door and stepped out on the front porch. He turned to look at India and prayed that she could see the pain in his eyes. He wanted her to see that he was sorry and that if she gave him another chance, he would never mess around on her again, not even on his business trips. He didn't know what to say so he said the first thing that came out of his mouth.

"I'll call you later, okay?" he said before realizing how dumb he sounded.

"Don't bother, I don't have time for no counterfeit-ass niggas in my life," she replied and slammed the door. India smiled as she walked to her bedroom and climbed back into bed. The smile remained on her face as she drifted off to sleep.

Chapter Forty-two

The morning crept by like a snail as Keaundra sat at her desk going over a pile of loan applications that should have been finished days ago. The sad part was she would have put them off a little longer if it weren't for her boss breathing down her neck to have them finished by the end of the day. As hard as she tried, Keaundra couldn't concentrate on anything other than the hands on the clock.

Keaundra was anxious to get to the family meeting to see what her money hungry aunts and uncle had to say. If they had any indication that Gran was leaving them anything in her will they would pull the plug on her with a quickness. Keaundra felt it was unfair that Gran's children would be a part of making the decision on whether Gran lived or died. They only came around when they needed to borrow money, a place to stay, or a nice hot meal.

Keaundra chuckled as she thought about how Gran always ranted and raved about her children.

"Out of four children only one wanted something out of life other than a handout, and the good Lord took her away and left me with three knuckleheads," was Gran's famous saying. Gran was disappointed in her children. None of them kept a steady job.

Gran's oldest son, Joe, was a stone-cold drunk who hustled on the pool table at the neighborhood bar. He had so many children by so many different women, if he even thought about getting a real job, child support would be standing in line with him at the bank waiting for him to cash his check. Gran's middle child, Paula, took care of an elderly lady and her husband. Word on the street was that Paula was taking care of the lady's husband in more ways than one. That's how she kept her rent and bills paid. If it weren't for the goodness of welfare and Section 8, Gran's youngest daughter, Bonita, would be broke and homeless. Forty-eight years old with six children, the youngest being three, Bonita's philosophy was, "Why get a job when you can have the government taking care of you for at least the next fifteen years?"

Keaundra shook her head, disgusted by the fact these people were a part of her family. As the day ended, Keaundra managed to finish all of her work. She dropped the applications off at her boss's office and headed over to Gran's for a fun-filled day of nothing but drama.

Alexis was just about to walk out of the dentist's office when her cell phone rang. She pulled it out of her purse and checked the number. When she didn't recognize the number she started to put it back into her purse but went ahead and answered it.

"Hello?"

"Hey you," said a deep voice.

"David?" Alexis asked.

"Yes, it is."

A smile crept across Alexis's face. "What's good?"

"You."

"What made you call me?" she asked playfully.

"I was wondering if you were ready to take me up on my offer?"

"What offer?"

"When I offered to take you out to lunch."

Alexis looked up at the clock on the wall. "It's past lunchtime."

"Well, we'll just turn lunch into dinner if that's okay with you," he said, hoping she would say yes.

"Yeah, that'll be nice."

"It's set then. Would you like me to pick you up or do you want to meet me?"

Alexis almost made the mistake of telling him to pick her up, but remembered that Ronald had moved back in. "I'll meet you, 'cause I have to stop by my parents' house later on," she lied.

"That's cool; meet me at Jennah's."

Alexis thought it was romantic that David wanted to meet at the same restaurant where they shared their first date. "What time?" she asked, smiling.

"Eight o'clock?"

"Eight it is. See you then."

David hung up the phone with one of the biggest smiles on his face and began humming as he swept up the hair around the barbershop.

Keaundra pulled up in front of Gran's house, threw her purse over her shoulder, and got out. She could hear loud talking, almost like arguing, as she approached the porch. When she let herself in, she could hear Paula and Bonita fussing about something. Keaundra made her way to the living room where everyone else was.

Kenneth sat over in Gran's recliner with his eyes closed as Paula and Bonita argued over who was keeping Gran's plants and silverware if she didn't make it, while Uncle Joe was in the background ranting about taking the sixty-one-inch television that Kenneth had bought Gran for her birthday. Keaundra couldn't believe her ears. Here were Gran's children arguing over her things as if she was already gone.

"I can't believe y'all sitting up here arguing over Gran's things like she's already dead!" Keaundra shouted in disbelief. The family got quiet, becoming embarrassed by Keaundra's statement.

Kenneth opened his eyes and looked over at his sister. "What's up, sis? They have been arguing ever since we got here."

"They in here arguing about what they takin' if Gran passes away." Keaundra took a seat on the sofa next to Paula.

Kenneth shook his head. "Let's get on with this meeting so we can get it over with." Kenneth stood up from the recliner and walked into the middle of the living room.

"I agree, 'cause I gotta work overtime tonight," Paula said.

"It must be Mrs. Black's bingo night," Bonita smirked.

"Fuck you, Bonita, and you need to mind yo' own damn business!"

"Shit, you act like what you doing is a secret," Bonita said.

"Worry about yourself and all them damn kids."

"No, you need to be worried about why ya son can't keep his black ass out the penitentiary. The nigga must be institutionalized or his ass is gay."

"No, you didn't call my son gay." Paula screamed.

Keaundra sat back and laughed as her aunts ripped into each other. She found it to be pure entertainment just like when she was a little girl. Believe it or not, that's how Keaundra first learned to cuss, listening to her aunts arguing.

Paula and Bonita never got along as long as Keaundra could remember. They were always arguing and fighting about something. They never had one kind word to say about each other and they always expected Gran to choose sides. Gran would just shake her head and say they acted more like enemies than sisters.

"Can y'all please settle down," Kenneth interrupted. Paula rolled her eyes at Bonita as Kenneth began to speak. "We know Gran's condition, right?" Everybody nodded. "We all need to come to some type of agreement on what needs to be done if Gran makes it out the hospital, and we need to start making preparations if we decide to take her off life support."

The room got quiet for a moment as everyone went into deep thought.

"I suggest that if Momma makes it through, I should be the one to move in with her so I can take care of her," Paula suggested.

"Humph, Mr. Black must be gettin' tired of payin' fo' that old used-up pussy of yours," Bonita retorted.

"Bitch, I'm sick of yo' mouth!" Paula stood up and shouted.

"Well, what you gon' do then?" Bonita stood as well. Keaundra cracked up as she waited for them to start throwing blows.

"Y'all come on, damn!" Kenneth said, agitated with all the bickering.

"Well, I think I should be the one to move in here with Momma," Bonita said. "Being that I am her favorite."

"Where you and all them damn kids gon' sleep? Y'all need a mansion," Paula laughed.

"That was a good one." Uncle Joe laughed too.

"Anyways," Kenneth continued while cutting his eyes at Uncle Joe for encouraging them, "if it comes to that I'll just hire a nurse to be here with her around the clock."

"Well, before y'all start packin' y'all shit and start moving in," Uncle Joe said to his two sisters, "when I talked to the doctor today he said Momma is getting worse."

Keaundra was unaware of what Joe was talking about. She looked to her brother for an answer and he confirmed what Joe said by nodding.

"Why don't we just face it, Momma will never make it home," Paula said. "So we might as well gon' and pull the plug."

"What?" Keaundra asked, surprised.

"She's got a point, Keaundra," Uncle Joe said, cutting in before Keaundra could tear into her aunt. "Momma can't make it without the respirator, so we might as well gon' and take her off instead of racking up all those hospital bills."

Keaundra looked at her brother, not understanding how the people whom Gran called her children could sit up and say to remove her from the only thing that was keeping her alive. "Do you hear the shit they're sayin'?" she asked Kenneth as if he weren't sitting in the same room with them.

"I agree with Joe and Paula," Bonita said. "I don't like seeing Momma lying up in the hospital with all those damn tubes running out of her."

"If God wants her with Him, let Him take her on His own," Keaundra spat.

"Keaundra, everybody has already agreed on taking Momma off that machine," Paula said.

Kenneth was hurt.

"Kenneth didn't say nothin'. So don't go putting words in my brother's mouth."

"What's your decision?" Joe asked.

Kenneth was stuck. On one hand, he agreed with his sister, but on the other, he understood where his aunts and uncle were coming from. "I don't know, y'all. I need to sleep on it."

"We need to come to some type of agreement before we all leave here today. It don't make no sense for Momma to keep lying up in that hospital like some damn vegetable," Paula said.

"The sooner she's dead, the quicker y'all think y'all can get ya hands on her stuff," Keaundra spat.

"How could you say that, Keaundra?" Bonita asked. "You act like she's not our mother, too."

"Y'all never acted like she was y'all momma. All y'all ever did was use her for everything she was worth." Tears streamed down Keaundra's cheeks as she spoke. "I never saw any of y'all sittin' up at the hospital for days at a time, not even goin' home to wash yo' ass like me and Kenneth did."

"I—" Bonita attempted to explain but was cut off.

"Come on, y'all. We not gon' get anything accomplished by pointing out who did and didn't do what," Joe said, feeling guilty as charged.

Everybody waited for Kenneth's answer. He wanted nothing more than to keep Gran around as long as he possibly could, but he knew in his heart that Gran would want him and Keaundra to take her off life support, instead of having her lay up in a place that she hated so much. Kenneth took a deep breath.

"I agree," he said as the tears filled his eyelids.

"With who?" Keaundra asked with a smile, already knowing the answer. She just wanted her aunts and uncle to know that her twin brother felt the same as she did.

Kenneth dropped his head. "With them."

Keaundra nearly went into shock. She couldn't believe her brother agreed with removing Gran from the respirator. Kenneth couldn't look his sister in the face because he felt and she looked as if he had betrayed her. "Fine, y'all go ahead and do what y'all do, but don't expect me to be a part of it!" Keaundra yelled angrily. Keaundra stood up from the sofa and walked toward the door.

"Keaundra!" Kenneth called out, but she ignored him as she made her way to her car. Kenneth ran out on the porch and called to his sister again. "I'm doin' it for Gran."

Keaundra never even bothered to turn around; she got in her car and pulled off as fast as she could, never looking back.

Chapter Forty-three

Alexis prayed as she drove home from work that Ronald wouldn't be there when she got there. All she wanted to do was rush in, grab something to wear for her dinner date, and head over to India's to get dressed. As soon as Alexis pulled up into the apartment complex, she spotted Ronald's beat-up car.

"Shit," she said as she got out of the car. She tried to come up with an excuse to leave as she made her way up the walkway. The aroma of something cooking smacked her dead in the face once she opened the door. Alexis leaned over and turned the ringer off on the phone in the living room. She then threw her purse and keys on the sofa and made her way to the kitchen.

"Hey, baby." Ronald turned around and smiled. *When did this nigga start cookin' dinner? All I ever known him to make was breakfast.* "Hey. What ya cookin'?" she asked as she walked over to the stove to peek in the pot.

"Hamburger Helper," he said proudly, as if he had just prepared a gourmet meal.

Alexis wanted to laugh but didn't. *It's a start*, she thought as she took a seat at the table. "Where the kids?"

"I asked your parents if they could keep them tonight so me and you can have a romantic evening together."

Ain't this 'bout a bitch! You wanna have a romantic evening on the same night that David is takin' me out to dinner? "Oh, baby, that's so sweet. But I promised Keaundra that I would go up to the hospital with her to sit with her grandmother," she lied. Alexis quickly said a prayer asking God to forgive her for using Gran in a lie.

Ronald turned around and looked at Alexis. Alexis just knew by the look he shot her way that he was about to explode, but Ronald smiled. "That's cool. At least have dinner with me and when you come from the hospital we can watch the movies I rented."

Alexis was surprised once again by how calm Ronald was. "Sounds good to me," she said as Ronald began preparing their plates. Alexis hurried through dinner. As Ronald washed up the dishes, she was in her closet looking for something nice to wear. Once she found the perfect outfit for the occasion, she stuffed it in a duffle bag and tossed it out her bedroom window. She then showered and got dressed in a pair of sweat-pants and an oversized T-shirt. She brushed her hair into a ponytail, turned the ringer off on the phone in the bedroom, and made her way into the living room where Ronald sat on the sofa watching television.

He looked up and smiled at her when she walked in. "You look comfortable."

"I'm only goin' to sit at the hospital, how do you want me to dress? In a pair of stilettos?" she joked.

"If you dressed in some heels, I would think you were goin' somewhere other than the hospital," Ronald reached up and grabbed Alexis by the waist and pulled her down to him.

"Somewhere like where?" Alexis straddled Ronald's body and kissed him softly on the forehead.

"Somewhere with another nigga," he said as he cupped her firm ass in the palms of his hands.

"Nigga, please, you know you're the only nigga for me," she said as she climbed off his lap.

Ronald playfully slapped Alexis on the backside. "I betta be."

"I'll see you later on." Alexis blew Ronald a kiss and headed out the door.

"See ya," he said, turning his attention back to the basketball game that was playing on television.

Alexis was all smiles as she walked out of the house. She couldn't believe how easy it had been for her to get away. She grabbed her duffle bag from the front yard and made her way to her car. Once she got in, she called India to ask her to plug in the flat iron so she could straighten out her hair. Alexis already knew India was about to be asking a hundred and one questions, so she hung up before India could start in order to get her lies together.

"The next song I'm about to play is an old-school cut," the deejay said in a deep, sexy voice. "'Lies', by En Vogue."

"That's my cut." Alexis smiled as she turned up the radio and began bobbing her head to the music. Alexis had heard this song many times before, but this was the first time she actually listened to the words they were singing. It dawned on her that these women were also singing about her and all the lies she had been telling to Ronald and her best friends. She started feeling disgusted with herself and the secret life she had been living. The lies and secrets she was keeping from the people she claimed to love were taking a toll on her mind, body, and soul, and it took En Vogue to make her realize it.

"Damn, this has to be another sign," she said, as she continued to make her way over to India's house. "I gotta come clean with everybody, about everything. That's the only way I'm gon' be able to look at myself in the mirror. But first, I got a date to get ready for," she said and turned the radio up as loud as it would go to keep from letting her conscience get the best of her.

"Keaundra, we decided to remove Gran at eight o'clock tomorrow morning," Kenneth said into the answering machine.

"So soon?" Keaundra asked as if her brother was going to answer her.

"We would like for you to be there with us, Ke-Ke. As a family," he continued.

"Fuck family," Keaundra yelled at the phone.

"Call me, Ke-Ke, I wanna know if you're all right." Kenneth waited a few seconds before hanging up the phone.

Kenneth waited five minutes before calling his sister back. "Ke-Ke, pick up the phone, please," he begged.

Keaundra lay there in her bed staring up at the ceiling while stroking Peaches. Kenneth waited a few more seconds. "Sis, I understand how you're feelin'. I'm hurt too, but we need to do what's right for Gran." Kenneth paused. "I wish you would pick up your phone and say somethin'," Kenneth said angrily.

Keaundra knew that her brother wasn't going to stop bothering her so she rolled over and grabbed the phone out of the cradle. "You want me to say somethin' Kenneth?" she asked, snottily.

Kenneth was glad that his sister decided to pick up his call. "That would be nice."

"Well, hear this, stop callin' my fuckin' phone," she snapped and hung up before Kenneth could respond.

Kenneth was surprised by the way Keaundra had just spoken to him; she had never talked to him like that before. He was shocked; he couldn't help but stare at the phone in disbelief. Hurt, Kenneth didn't know what else to do. He knew that Keaundra was tough to deal with sometimes, but the situation with taking Gran off of life support was taking its toll.

Kenneth decided to leave his sister alone for now, and take a nap. He would get through to his sister, one way or another, even if it meant he had to go over and drag her butt out of the house and up to the hospital to be with him and the rest of the family. Kenneth began praying; he prayed for strength because he knew that once Gran was gone, she would take a big part of him with her. He needed to stay strong for himself, as well as Keaundra. Tears streamed down his cheeks as he drifted off to sleep and began dreaming.

Chapter Forty-four

Keaundra tossed and turned all night. She couldn't sleep knowing that in a few hours, her malicious family would take her grandmother away from her. Keaundra also felt bad about how she had talked to Kenneth earlier. She wanted to call him and apologize, but it was much too late; she would have to wait until the next morning.

Keaundra wished her brother could understand why she couldn't be up at the hospital with them, watching them remove Gran from life support. She didn't want to be anywhere around her aunts and uncle while they shed fake tears, but Keaundra also knew she couldn't let them pull the plug without saying good-bye to Gran first. She climbed out of bed and put her clothes back on. She walked into the living room and grabbed her keys before heading to her car.

Keaundra was actually going to say good-bye to her grandmother, forever, and that tore her world apart. Pulled into the hospital parking lot, she wiped away her tears as she got out of the car. Her heart beat hard as she made her way to the elevator. Keaundra's hands were shaking so much, she could barely press the floor number on the elevator wall.

Once she made it to the third floor and the elevator doors swung open, Keaundra slowly stepped off. It seemed like it took her forever to make it down the hallway, she felt like she was walking the "Green Mile." The nurses smiled as Keaundra walked past their station. She returned the smile and walked into her grandmother's room. There was Gran, lying in her bed looking as peaceful as ever, and Keaundra smiled as she took a seat next to her bed.

"Hey, Gran," Keaundra said in an upbeat tone. She paused as if Gran was going to speak back. "You know Kenneth and your children plan on taking you off this machine," she said in a teary voice. The only sound that came from Gran was the annoying beeps from the loud machine she was hooked up to. Keaundra laughed as she heard Gran's voice in her head, fussing and carrying on like she used to do. "Gran, I don't want them to take you away from me. But everyone seems to think that it's best that we pull the plug. They all have their reasons why, but I say we should leave you on here, just in case you come through. I need you, Gran."

Keaundra stood up from the chair and kissed Gran on the cheek. Keaundra stared down at her and it looked as if she had aged ten years within the past few weeks; she didn't look like the same sassy lady she was used to seeing. Her smooth skin was now full of wrinkles, her lips were dried out, and her hair was falling out in patches. Keaundra couldn't stand seeing her grandmother look this way, so she knew she had to let her go, in peace.

"Gran, I thank you for trying to stick around for me and Kenneth and for raising us to be the respectable children that we've grown to be. I know your body is tired, and I know that you need to rest now." Keaundra kissed her grandmother one last time, sat back down in the chair, and grabbed hold of her hand. She closed her eyes and hummed one of Gran's favorite songs by Donnie McClurkin. Tears fell steadily as Keaundra began to sing the words aloud.

We fall down but we get up
We fall down but we get up
We fall down but we get up, oh yes
For a saint is just a sinner who fell down,
But we get couldn't stay there and got up . . .

Keaundra felt Gran squeeze her hand, and she continued singing through tears as machines began beeping and Gran flatlined. Nurses ran into

the room and began working on Gran as Keaundra sat in the chair, still singing.

"We've lost her," one of the nurses finally said.

"We're sorry, we did all we could," another
nurse said.

Keaundra opened her eyes. "Bye, Gran." Keaundra smiled slightly, knowing that her grandmother was now resting in peace, without the
help of Kenneth and her ungrateful children.

Kenneth smiled in his sleep as he dreamed. He
dreamt that he and Keaundra were outside playing in Gran's front yard. They were both dressed
in their Sunday best, waiting for Gran to come out
of the house for church just like they used to do
when they were little. After they had played a few
games of Freeze Tag and Mother, May I, Gran finally came out of the house and stood on the front
porch. Kenneth and Keaundra were both amazed
at how nice she looked, standing there dressed
in all white, looking like the beautiful angel she
was. They both began pressing the wrinkles out
of their clothes, just like Gran had taught them,
and looked up at her and smiled. Gran gave them
a smile of approval.

"You ready, Gran?" Keaundra asked. Gran
stood staring at her precious grandbabies with

a huge smile on her face and made her way off the porch.

"Come here," Gran said to her grandchildren. Kenneth and Keaundra obeyed and walked over to their grandmother. Gran knelt down in front of them. "I'm goin' to church by myself, but I want you two to take care of each other while I'm gone, okay?"

"But, Gran, we wanna go to church, too," Keaundra whined.

"Now, stop that whining, girl," Gran said and stood up. She then fixed Kenneth's tie and rubbed the top of Keaundra's head. "Now, like I said, you two take care of each other while I'm gone, you hear?" Kenneth and Keaundra nodded. They watched as Gran made her way down the walk and a van appeared out of nowhere.

The doors swung open and Gran climbed in. She rolled down the window, smiled, and waved as the van drove off.

"Noooooo," Kenneth shouted and woke up, still yelling. His heart beating fast, he rolled over to grab the phone. "Man, that was a crazy dream," he said as he dialed Keaundra's number.

"Hello?" he heard someone call out.

"Hello? How did you get on the line and the phone didn't ring?" he asked.

"Ken, she's gone."

"That's crazy, I just picked up the phone and you're on it," he said, not paying any attention to what Keaundra had just said.

"Did you hear me, Ken?"

Still dazed from the nap he took, Kenneth had to ask. "Who you talkin' about?"

"Gran. She passed away about ten minutes ago."

Kenneth felt his air supply being cut off by the huge lump that formed in his throat. Tears burned his eyes as he tried to hold them in. "How?" was all Kenneth could muster up to say.

"The right way,'" Keaundra replied. "The right way. . . ."

Keaundra spent the next hour or so at the hospital meeting and greeting family and friends. Reminiscing and listening to stories made Keaundra feel good about being the granddaughter of a woman who was well-loved and respected by everyone. Keaundra kept a close eye on Kenneth, who sat tucked away in a corner all by himself. She went over and checked on him a few times and each time he assured her that he was fine, but Keaundra knew better. He was good at hiding his feelings, which wasn't good, because it often led to violent outburst. Keaundra recalled numerous occasions when Kenneth would get so angry that he would go off and tear up his room. He would tear posters off the walls, rip clothes out of the closet, flip over his mattress while crying the entire time. It used to scare Keaundra to see her brother act that way. Gran would just wait until he was done having a fit, as she called it, before calling him into the kitchen and giving him his favorite dessert.

When Kenneth was done eating, Gran would then give him a big hug and send him off to clean up his room. Keaundra could even remember Gran helping Kenneth clean up his mess a time or two. Their father, who was very strict and abusive, used to tell Kenneth as a young boy that real men don't cry. Kenneth, who looked up to his father, had tried his best to live by that, causing him to hold in his anger until he couldn't take it anymore.

Keaundra tore herself away from a conversation she was holding with one of the church mothers and tried calling Alexis's cell phone a few times to no avail. She ended up leaving her a message. She then called India with the bad news. India was devastated; she rushed up to the hospital to be by her best friend's side. After everyone had left the hospital, Keaundra followed Kenneth over to Gran's house to get things situated. They needed to write out the obituary, make funeral arrangements, and go through Gran's file cabinet to gather all of her life insurance papers.

"That's one thing I loved about Gran," Kenneth said as he pulled all the labeled manilla folders out of the file cabinet. "She always kept her stuff in order."

Keaundra chuckled. "She sure did." Keaundra's eyes wandered to the sealed envelope Kenneth held in his hand. "What's that?"

"This here?" he asked, holding up the envelope. "This is Gran's will."

"I know Bonita and them can't wait until the will gets read," Keaundra said as she sorted through some of Gran's paperwork.

Kenneth placed the envelope on top of the dining room table. "As a matter of fact, I need to contact Gran's attorney later on because I don't want no mess when it's all said and done."

"I feel you on that." Keaundra sat silent for a few minutes. "I wonder who she left the house to."

"I don't know, Ke-Ke. Let's just hope whoever she left it to takes good care of it."

"I know, 'cause Gran and Granddaddy worked hard to buy this house." Keaundra looked around the room at all the upgrades that had been done since she was a little girl living there.

Kenneth looked over at his sister. "You wanna know who's gettin' what?"

Keaundra smiled mischievously. "Yeah, let's find out." Keaundra watched as her brother opened up the sealed envelope.

Kenneth began reading the will. The more he read the wider his eyes got. "Hell naw!" he shouted, excited.

"What?" Keaundra asked before jumping up and looking over his shoulder. "Dang!" Keaundra smiled with big eyes. "Gran left everything to us. The house, the money in her savings account, all her insurance money, plus her stocks and bonds," Keaundra exclaimed.

Kenneth set the will on the table and sat back with a smile on his face. "Wait 'til Bonita, Paula, and Joe get wind of this," Kenneth said, laughing.

Keaundra smiled as she spoke. "Man, I know. They gon' be heated when they find out."

"What can we say? Gran was the one who left us everything so they can't be mad at us," Kenneth said.

"What we gon' do with the house?"

"I don't know. We both already have a house so maybe we can rent this one out."

"Uhhnn-uhhh, we ain't having nobody living up in here messing up Gran's house."

Kenneth laughed. "You crazy."

"Since you and Beverly ain't gettin' married now, how come you don't just move in here," Keaundra suggested.

Kenneth sighed. "You got a point there. I can put my house on the market once they get it finished and just continue to live here."

"Well, Ken-Ken, it looks like you're the new owner of this house," Keaundra said, happily.

Kenneth and Keaundra stayed up the rest of the morning finishing off everything that needed to be done. Once they were done, Keaundra decided to go home and get some rest.

"Kenneth, I apologize for the way I talked to you yesterday," she said as she stood from her chair.

He smiled at his sister with tired eyes, letting her know that everything was cool between them.

Keaundra walked over to her brother and kissed him on the cheek before heading out the door. The sun was rising as Keaundra made her way to her car. She walked slowly as she listened to the birds chirping a melodic tune while the neighborhood dogs tried to out bark one another. She looked up at the sky and smiled.

Alexis woke up to the sound of the birds chirping. She jumped up and looked around. Her surroundings were unfamiliar until she looked over at David who was sound asleep in the driver side of his car. Alexis smiled before the beep from her cell phone's voice messaging startled her. She became nervous because she knew Ronald had to have called her at least a hundred times. She didn't know what she was going to tell him when she got home, but she would think of something; she always did.

Alexis prayed as she strolled through her missed calls list that Keaundra or India hadn't popped up at her apartment. She knew they couldn't get through if they had called because she had turned the ringers off on all the phones. She pressed in her pass code and listened to her messages. There were six messages from Ronald asking her if she was okay. The final message rocked her entire world and made Alexis gasp for air, instantly waking David up.

"You okay?" Alexis was speechless. All she could do was shake her head from side to side. "What's the matter, Alexis?" David asked, worried.

Alexis's eyes filled with tears. "Keaundra's grandmother passed away."

David sat straight up in his seat. "Man, I'm sorry to hear that," he said sympathetically.

Alexis felt like shit as she dialed Keaundra's phone number. If she hadn't agreed to take a drive out to Mifflin Lake with David after dinner, she would have been there for her best friend. She had been so caught up with being with David again, she had ignored all her phone calls. Alexis had checked her caller ID while she and David sat on the hood of the car looking out at the water, but she didn't want to have to explain to Keaundra where she was or who she was with, so she had let it go to her voice mail.

"Hello?" Keaundra answered, sounding as if her nose was clogged up.

"Ke-Ke? I'm sorry," Alexis cried into the phone. "I took two Tylenol PMs so I didn't hear my phone," she lied. David looked at Alexis like she was crazy.

"Why, Lexy? Why God have to take my grandmother away from me?" Keaundra wept. "She was all I had."

"I don't know, Ke-Ke," Alexis said as she began crying. "It's a reason for everything, Keaundra. God had His reason on why he took Gran." Alexis hoped her friend could find some comfort in her words.

It hurt David deeply to see Alexis cry. He stepped out of the car as he felt his eyes tearing up.

"She was all I had though, what am I gon' do?"

"No, Ke-Ke, you got me, India, and Kenneth."

"You don't understand, my life is over."

"Don't say that, Ke-Ke. You need to be strong for Kenneth. You have to be the backbone he needs."

"I don't know how," she said.

"Yes, you do, Keaundra. You have always been the strong one. I'm on my way over there, okay?"

"Okay." Keaundra sniffed and hung up the phone.

Alexis got out of the car and walked over to David, who was leaned up against a tree. He held his arms open for her to enter his space. He wrapped his strong arms around her body and rocked her as she cried into his chest. David laid his cheek on top of her head and rubbed her back.

After about five minutes of crying out all the pain she felt for her friend, Alexis removed her head from David's chest. "I'm sorry," she said, wiping the tears away.

"It's okay."

"No, I'm really sorry."

David looked confused. "For what?"

"For all the snot I got on your shirt," she laughed as the tears slowed.

David laughed as well. "That's okay, I'll just put it in the cleaners and send you the bill," he joked, hoping to lighten the mood a little.

Alexis smiled. "Can you please take me to my car? I need to go check on Keaundra."

David held out his hand for Alexis to grab. "Let's go." Alexis grabbed hold of his hand and followed him back to his car. Alexis sat quietly as David drove. She closed her eyes, lay her head back on the headrest, and enjoyed the rest of the ride.

David pulled into the parking lot of the restaurant so Alexis could get her car. "Wake up, sleepy-head."

Alexis sat up and stretched her arms out in front of her. "Man, I don't even remember fallin' asleep. Thanks for a wonderful dinner and an even better night," Alexis said.

David smiled. "You're more than welcome."

Alexis opened the door and stuck her foot out on the pavement. "Hey?" David called out. Alexis turned to see what he wanted and was greeted by his soft lips on top of hers. Alexis didn't fight the feeling, in fact, she stuck her foot back into the car as their tongues did the Superman.

"Well," Alexis said, licking the moisture from her lips. David smiled as Alexis got out of the car and walked over to her vehicle. She turned around and waved.

"Ummp, ummp, ummp," Alexis said, flattening down her hair and getting into her car. As she drove, her cell phone began to ring. She looked at the caller ID and hesitated, but only for a second, already coming up with a lie. "Hello?" She sniffed as if she was crying.

"Baby, you okay?" Ronald asked, concerned.

"No."

"Where are you?" Ronald started getting nervous. It wasn't like his baby to stay out all night, unless something major was wrong.

"I'm still at the hospital with Keaundra. Her grandmother passed away this morning."

"Ahhh nawww, baby," Ronald said sympathetically. Even though he did not care too much for Alexis's friends, he still felt bad for Keaundra's loss. "I'm sorry to hear that."

Alexis sniffed. "I'll make sure I tell her you said that."

"Well, go ahead baby and comfort your friend, I'll see you when you get home," Ronald said soothingly.

"Okay."

"I love you, baby."

"I love you too," Alexis replied and hung up the phone. "Man, I'm good!" She smiled as she pulled into Keaundra's driveway.

Chapter Forty-five

The morning of the funeral, Keaundra took her sweet time getting dressed. She never thought she would live to see the day that she would actually be burying her grandmother. Keaundra knew her grandmother had to go someday, but she always had this crazy thought she would live forever. Tears blurred Keaundra's vision as she neatly pulled her hair up into a bun; she wiped her tears away and finished getting ready.

Twenty minutes later, Kenneth came walking through her door. "Hey, sis," he said as he walked into her bedroom and kissed her on the cheek. "I used my key to let myself in."

A weak smile crept across Keaundra's face. "That's cool."

"The limo is outside waiting for us. Oh, your aunts and uncle are out there too."

Keaundra rolled her eyes before taking one last look at herself in the mirror, then following her brother out to the limo. The driver was waiting by the back door to let them in. Keaundra slid into the car, instantly catching an attitude as she laid eyes on her grandmother's children.

Kenneth got in and sat in the seat next to his sister. The tension in the car was so thick, you could have sliced it with a knife.

"Morning," Joe said to Keaundra.

"Good morning," Keaundra replied dryly.

"Good morning, Keaundra," Bonita and Paula said simultaneously as they enviously stared her up and down.

"Morning," Keaundra said with little enthusiasm. Kenneth grabbed hold of his sister's hand and held on to it.

The ride to the church was a silent one. Once they arrived at the church both Keaundra and Kenneth were amazed at how many cars occupied the entire area. Cars were parked all up and down both sides of the street, along with the grocery store that was adjacent to the church. Not to mention the church's parking lot was so full, people had made their own parking spots so they wouldn't have to walk a mile to the funeral.

Kenneth and Keaundra walked into the church, hand in hand. The church was packed. There was still a line of people trying to get into the church as Keaundra and Kenneth maneuvered their way in. Keaundra knew by the turn out of people that her grandmother was loved. She could feel her knees getting weak as she and the rest of the family were ushered up to the front of the church. Tears came as she laid eyes on Gran's cream casket with all the many wreaths of flowers surrounding her.

The usher motioned for Keaundra to take her seat, but she had something else in mind. She walked up to the front of the church and stood in front of the casket. She laid her hand on top of Gran's; they felt cold and clammy. Keaundra smiled pleasantly as she looked down at her grandmother, who was all dressed up in a cream ensemble that she had picked out. She had thought it would be nice if her clothes matched her casket. Sonya, Keaundra's hair stylist, had put big, pretty curls in Gran's hair to cover up the patches of missing hair, and Nikki, a professional makeup artist Keaundra went to school with, had worked her magic on Gran. She had her looking like Lena Horne did in *Stormy Weather*. This was how Keaundra was used to seeing her grandmother.

Keaundra bent down and kissed Gran on the cheek before walking toward her seat.

Alexis and India sat a few rows behind Keaundra. Their hearts went out to their best friend as they watched her. They both noticed Keaundra's eyes fixated on something as she made her way back over to her family. Alexis and India turned around to see what had her attention. David and

Hammer were coming through the door and both men were dressed nicely and looking yummy as ever. Alexis smiled as she nudged India.

"Ouch," India whispered.

"Sorry," Alexis chuckled. The ladies turned back around as Reverend Powell was entering the pulpit. Alexis turned around and snuck another quick peek at David. She knew it was the wrong time and place for her to start thinking about sex, but the thought of going back and jumping on top of David and riding his love muscle crossed her mind a time or two. Alexis felt her panties starting to get wet so she focused her attention on the reverend while he gave the eulogy.

Keaundra sat in a daze as the reverend spoke about how loving Gran was. Her mind wandered back to the days when she, Kenneth, and Gran used to spend a lot of time together doing family things. Friday was game night. They each took turns picking a board game to play. Monopoly always seemed to be the pick of the week. Saturday was movie night. Gran would take them to the video store and let them each pick out a movie before going home to sit in front of the television with a big bowl of popcorn; meanwhile, Gran would be in the kitchen preparing the meal for the next day. Sunday, of course, was the day they would all go to church, come home, and wait for the rest of the family to show for Sunday dinner. Keaundra smiled at the thought of how much fun they used to have together.

Kenneth looked over, noticing the trance-like state Keaundra was in, and grabbed her hand. They sat hand in hand for the rest of the funeral. Kenneth broke down the moment the funeral director closed Gran's casket. The reality set in that this would be the last time he laid his eyes on his grandmother.

Keaundra couldn't stand seeing her brother cry. She watched as the pallbearers slowly walked in harmonic steps as they carried Gran away. Keaundra closed her eyes and shook her head. In a blink of an eye, Gran's cream-colored casket had disappeared into the back of a long black hearse. Gran was gone, for good.

Keaundra picked at the food on her plate while everyone else stood around the basement of the church laughing and talking. She was amazed at how all these people could still smile while her grandmother was lying in the cemetery. Keaundra instantly became angry with everyone inside the church.

"You okay?" India walked over with a plate of food in her hand and asked.

"I'm all right," Keaundra responded while rolling around a dry meatball with her fork.

"You sure? 'Cause you don't look like it."

"I said I'm cool," Keaundra snapped.

"Excuse me for askin'," India said and continued eating.

"Girl, I'm sorry, for snapping at you."

"It's okay. I understand."

"Where's Lexy?"

"Over there talkin' to David and Hammer," India replied, nodding her head in their direction. "It was nice of David and Hammer to come pay their respects," India said with a mouth full of food.

"Yeah, it was."

"Look at Alexis over there smiling all hard and shit," India laughed.

"India, we *are* in a church," Keaundra reminded her.

India chuckled. "Oh, yeah, I meant to say and stuff."

Keaundra turned sideways in her chair and watched as Alexis held a conversation with David and Hammer. Keaundra nearly fell out of her chair when Kenneth walked up to David and gave him a firm handshake.

"'Sup man?" Kenneth asked and then turned his attention toward Hammer, nodding.

"This my cousin, Hammer," David said.

"What's up," Hammer said, sticking out his hand.

So this is Hammer. "'Sup," Kenneth replied, giving him a firm handshake. "I finally get the chance to meet the man who keeps a smile on my sister's face."

Hammer had a skeptical look on his face. "Who's your sister?"

"This is Keaundra's twin brother, Kenneth," Alexis intervened.

"Okay," Hammer said, smiling. "Nice to finally meet you too." Hammer was happy to hear that he kept a smile on Keaundra's face.

Keaundra watched as her brother held a conversation with her ex and wondered what they were talking about. Seeing Hammer's face for the first time in ages confirmed that she missed him more than she thought, and that she still loved him.

"I'm 'bout to go check on my girl," Alexis told David.

"I'll go over with you," David offered.

"Come on." Alexis smiled and held out her hand for David to grab.

"You okay?" Alexis asked Keaundra once they made it over to her.

"I'm cool."

"Sorry about your loss," David said and gave Keaundra a hug.

"Thank you," she replied as she hugged him back while peeking over his shoulder at Hammer.

Hammer finished his conversation with Kenneth before walking over to where David sat talking to Alexis, India, and Keaundra.

"Hey, India," Hammer said.

"Hey, Hammer." India smiled.

Hammer looked over at Keaundra. He tried reading her face before he spoke, but went ahead and took his chance. "Hello, Keaundra," he said, stepping toward her and wrapping his arms around her shoulders, giving her a tight squeeze. Hammer could feel his manhood start to rise, so he quickly stepped back before he embarrassed himself.

Keaundra wanted to melt as she rested her head on Hammer's chest for the few seconds he held her. Her heart did a dance as she inhaled Hammer's fragrance.

"I'm sorry about your loss."

"Thank you," Keaundra replied gratefully.

"Well, cuz, we betta get goin'. I gotta take Moms to the airport," David said.

"Let's roll, 'cause you know you better not keep Moms waiting," Hammer laughed.

Hammer and David said their good-byes. Keaundra could tell Hammer had something he wanted to say to her, but he kept it to himself and walked away. Part of her wished Hammer would have said what was on his mind; maybe it would have given her the closure she needed to move on with her life.

Hammer was mad at himself for not letting Keaundra know how he was feeling, and almost turned back, but he decided this wasn't the time or place, and plus, David was on a time schedule. What he wanted to say to Keaundra would have to wait until some other time.

Once Keaundra made it home from the funeral, she didn't want to be bothered with anyone. She put on an oversized T-shirt, big, fuzzy slippers, and popped herself some popcorn. She grabbed the remote and got comfortable on the sofa and channel surfed. She got excited because one of her favorite movies was showing on TV One.

"Ooohhh, *Carmen Jones*, this is my movie," she said as she put the remote down beside her. Keaundra was well into the movie when she was disturbed by a knock at the front door. *Who could this be this late at night?* Keaundra set the bowl of popcorn down on the floor next to the sofa. "Who is it?" she called out. She could have sworn the person said "Hammer." "Wishful thinkin'," she chuckled as she walked toward the door. "Who is it?" she asked again.

"It's Hammer."

"Hammer?" she asked, confused. Keaundra opened the door and there stood Hammer looking even better than he did at the funeral. He wore a light blue Sean John button-down, navy blue Sean John jeans, and a crispy pair of white and navy blue Air Force Ones. *Oh my goodness*, she thought before she exhaled. Keaundra began fidgeting with a few lose strings on the bottom of her T-shirt. Hammer grabbed her hand and stepped into the doorway.

"What's up?" he asked.

"What's up with you?"

"Why haven't you returned any of my calls?"

"I've been busy," she replied as she began fidgeting again.

"I see I still have that effect on you?" Hammer joked.

Keaundra rolled her eyes. "Whatever," she said, smacking her lips. "What do you want?"

"I need to talk to you."

"'Bout what?"

"About us."

"I thought we already talked before. Hammer, there is no us, you have a wife." The thought of

Hammer being connected to someone else made Keaundra's skin crawl. Keaundra walked away. The pain she felt the last time Hammer was over began to come back. Keaundra took a seat on the sofa.

"Keaundra, I need you to know the whole story behind my wife." The word wife made Keaundra cringe.

"What more do I need to know about her, Hammer? She's your wife for goodness sake!" Tears clouded her vision.

"Please just let me explain," Hammer said in a somewhat begging manner.

"Explain for what? Just get out of my house, dammit!" Keaundra stood up from the sofa. She couldn't take the pain any longer. She walked over to the door and opened it. "Please leave," she shouted as the tears flowed.

Hammer grabbed the door and slammed it shut. "I'm not leaving this time, not without explaining myself. Now sit yo' ass down and listen," Hammer demanded.

"Hold up, nigga, this my house," Keaundra stated while wiping away her tears.

"I don't give a damn. You gon' listen to me." Keaundra was shocked because she had never seen this side of Hammer before. He was actually turning her on with the demanding tone he was using. Keaundra slowly took a seat on the sofa and waited for Hammer to begin speaking.

"Keaundra, Kelly is my wife, true enough." Keaundra was about to open her mouth but Hammer shut her down. "I loved that woman to death and no one can take that away from me. I had promised Kelly on her death bed that I would never replace her, and I had planned on doin' just that, until you came into my life." Keaundra was touched. "Keaundra, you made me realize that I can love again. I fought with myself many nights because I thought if I fell in love with you, which I did, Kelly would never forgive me. But Kelly's gone and she's not coming back." Tears formed in Hammer's eyes as he poured his heart out to the woman he now loved. "So it wouldn't be fair to me, or you, if I kept that selfish promise I made." Keaundra didn't know what to say.

"I didn't know, Hammer." Keaundra began crying.

Hammer sat down on the sofa next to Keaundra. "Didn't know what? That I loved you?"

Keaundra was embarrassed by what she was about to say. "I didn't know Kelly was dead."

"If you had let me explain that night I came over here, you would have."

"I'm so sorry, Hammer," Keaundra said sincerely as the tears flowed steadily.

"There's no need to apologize. I got you now and with me is where I want you to stay." Hammer wiped away Keaundra's tears.

"You a little bossy, don't you think?" she teased.

"Very." Before Keaundra saw it coming, Hammer's lips were pressed against hers. Hammer kissed Keaundra intensely.

Keaundra took a step back and looked down at the floor.

"Did I do somethin' wrong?" Hammer asked and lifted her chin with his index finger.

"No . . . no, you didn't," she stammered. "It's just that—" Before Keaundra could finish her sentence, Hammer's lips were pressed up against hers again. Keaundra submitted and kissed him back. She wrapped her legs around his waist as he lifted her up off the floor and carried her down the hallway to her bedroom. Keaundra's entire body trembled with each step. Once they made it to her room, Peaches jumped off the bed and ran out the door.

"That damn cat," Hammer said as he gently laid Keaundra on the bed. He removed her big fuzzy slippers and tossed them on the floor. It had been a long time since Keaundra had a man between her thighs, other than Peter, and he was not a real man. As she lay trembling as if it were her first time, Hammer pulled her shirt over her head. Hammer then pulled her pajama bottoms off and tossed them to the side, smiling at the sight before him.

Hammer removed his own clothes before climbing on the bed. He lay next to her and began caressing her milk chocolate mounds. Keaundra let out soft and sexy moans, which drove Hammer wild. It had been a long time for him as well, and he wanted to take things slow to keep from embarrassing himself by cumming too quickly.

"You okay?" Hammer asked. Keaundra was in pure ecstasy. She slowly nodded. Hammer took his finger and removed Keaundra's panties. He kissed her from her forehead to her perky breasts. She moaned with each tender kiss. He took his tongue and circled around each one before moving his way down her stomach and sticking his tongue into her belly button. Keaundra's body shook like a pair of dice. She had never felt such an electrifying feeling before in her life. Hammer spread Keaundra's legs with his face before diving in. The tongue work Hammer was putting down was better than any she had ever experienced, but she was anxious to feel him inside of her. After making Keaundra cum back to back, Hammer guided his Mandingo warrior to the place it longed to be.

"Ohhhh," she moaned, in ecstasy and pain.

"You okay?" Keaundra nodded.

"You kinda tight." Keaundra took that as a compliment.

Hammer entered Keaundra gently. He started out slow as he got her tight walls open, moving like the professional that he was. Each stroke was rhythmically in tune with hers as Hammer stroked long and deep. Hammer was doing his thang, but Keaundra wasn't no ho, either. She climbed on top of Hammer and rode him like a true cowgirl. They sexed in every position they could possibly think of; they even made up a few of their own. After hours of love-making, both Keaundra and Hammer were completely exhausted as they held on to one another before drifting off to sleep.

The next morning before Hammer went home, he and Keaundra had agreed on trying to build a relationship. Keaundra was happy because she had finally found a real man to share her life with, and Hammer was relieved that he could finally put Kelly behind him and move on with his life.

Chapter Forty-six

As the summer turned into fall, Alexis's life began to fall apart little by little. All the lies she had been telling to everyone began to catch up with her and all the games she played were starting to play with her. She could hardly stand herself. Even sneaking around with David behind Ronald's back was getting old. Alexis didn't know if it was the way David held her after sex or the way he looked at her as if she was the only woman that mattered in his life, but there was something about him she could not shake. The more time she spent with David, the less she cared about Ronald and his needs.

Ronald sensed the change, and the more Alexis pushed him away the harder he fought to make things right between them. Alexis knew she was not being fair to either, and in order for her to get her life back, she would have to leave David alone. It was the hardest decision Alexis had to make but she knew it was the right thing to do. She was going to focus on making things right between her and Ronald.

Alexis was in the kitchen cooking Sunday dinner before Ronald got home from work, so all he could do was shower, eat, and relax. She also planned on dropping the kids off over at her parents' house for a few hours after they ate so she could give her man what he'd been longing for. She planned on making this a night to remember. She looked over at the dozen roses that Ronald had brought home the day before and smiled. Making up her mind right then and there that she would call David and break it off. Alexis walked over to the wall and picked up the phone. Regret swept over her like a warm summer's breeze as she dialed his number.

"Mommy, I'm hungry," R.J. ran into the kitchen and whined.

"Okay, Daddy will be home in about an hour then we can eat, okay?" She smiled down at her son while hanging up the phone.

"That's a loooong time."

Alexis opened the cabinet door, grabbed a box of chocolate chip cookies and gave her son four cookies. "Here's two for you and give two to your sister."

"Thanks." R.J. smiled happily before running off to share with his little sister.

Alexis picked the phone up a second time and began dialing David's cell phone number when the doorbell rang.

"Mommy, somebody's at the door," R.J. yelled.

"Hello?" David answered.

"Hey, we need to talk."

"Is everything okay?" David whispered.

What this nigga whispering for? Oh, Rosalind must be somewhere around, she thought as the doorbell rang again.

"You want me to git it, Mommy?" R.J. screamed.

"Naw, boy," she yelled back. "Look, I'll call you back later." Alexis hung up the phone on David, wiped her hands on her apron, and walked out of the kitchen. "Stop jumpin' on my sofa, boy," she yelled at her son as she walked past. "Get out my damn shoes, girl," Alexis hollered at her daughter as she stomped around the living room in a pair of her stilettos.

Alexis opened the door and stared into the face of a young, pregnant girl with a black eye and busted lip. Alexis had never seen Tyisha before but had a gut feeling that this was who was standing before her. "May I help you?" Alexis asked with an attitude.

"You don't know me, but I'm Tyisha," the girl replied.

Alexis leaned up against the door frame and smirked. "I figured that much," she said sarcastically. Tyisha shot Alexis a confused look. "I could tell by your black eye and busted lip, I know Ronald's work when I see it."

Tyisha felt ashamed and less of a woman as she lifted her hand to feel her swollen face. "Oh, this. Yeah, uh, I fell," she lied.

"Honey, you can save that, 'cause I used to tell that same lie when Ronald was whoopin' my ass too."

"He didn't mean to do it," Tyisha replied, defending the father of her children.

"He never does. You musta just tripped and landed on his fist," Alexis spat harshly.

"Look, I didn't come over here to go 'round and 'round with you about Ronald. And I sho' didn't come over here to be judged; my parents do enough of that." Alexis could see the hurt in Tyisha's eyes as tears glazed her vision.

Alexis's heart softened as the painful memories of being judged by her parents and her girls came rushing back. Being called stupid for staying with a man who claimed to love you but would put his hands on you in a heartbeat. Alexis was always forced to choose between Ronald and her family, and of course, Ronald was always the chosen one. To this day, Alexis regretted ever choosing Ronald over her family and friends.

"I'm sorry," Alexis said sincerely. "I'm not tryin' to judge you, 'cause I been in your shoes before."

Tyisha was skeptical of Alexis' apology but let it go.

"Would you like to come in and sit down," Alexis asked.

"No, thank you. My cousin is waiting for me in the U-Haul," Tyisha said, pointing behind her.

"You moving?"

Tyisha didn't know if she could trust Alexis to keep a secret, but she took her chances anyway. "Yep, to Atlanta so I can start braiding hair."

Alexis gave Tyisha a crazy look. "I guess."

"Please don't tell Ronald," Tyisha said nervously.

"Don't worry, I won't," Alexis promised. "I'm just glad you're strong enough to walk away and not stick around for the next ass whoopin'."

"You're still wit' him."

"No, hun, he's with me. I've learned my lesson about niggas. I might look like Converse, but believe me baby, I'm Nike all day long," Alexis replied.

"Okay," Tyisha laughed and held up her hand for a high-five.

Alexis hand connected with Tyisha's as Ro'nisha ran up and grabbed her by the legs. "Mommy, who is this?"

"This is Tyisha, sweetie," Alexis said, smiling.

"She got a baby in there," Ro'nisha pointed to Tyisha's round belly and said.

"Yeah, that's your little . . ." Alexis looked at Tyisha for an answer.

"Sisters. I'm havin' twins in less than six months."

"Those are your little sisters."

"R.J. those are my sisters in there," Ro'nisha screamed excitedly as she ran over to her brother.

"She's pretty," Tyisha smiled. "I hope my daughters come out lookin' like her." Tyisha stared behind Alexis and watched as R.J. and Ro'nisha played together. "Well, I better get goin'. We have a long ride ahead of us."

"Yeah, you do. Be safe."

"I will." Tyisha turned to walk away as Alexis began closing the door.

Alexis snatched the door back opened. "Tyisha," Alexis called out.

Tyisha stopped and turned back around. "Yeah?"

"You never told me the reason you came over here."

"Oh, yeah," she chuckled. "To give Ronald this." Tyisha pulled a wad of money out of her purse and handed it to Alexis. "Tell him the answer is no, I will not let him pay me to keep my mouth shut about the babies."

Alexis was confused. "Won't you need this money for the babies?"

"No thanks. Ronald has given me enough," she said, rubbing her swollen eye and busted lip. "I don't want anything else from him." Tyisha turned and walked away, leaving Alexis floored. She wanted to call Tyisha back and ask if she and Ronald had been sleeping together since they had gotten back together, but the answer was evident. They had been back together for a little over four months and Tyisha was three months pregnant.

Hurt, Alexis closed the door and walked back into the kitchen. She grabbed the roses from the vase and threw them in the trash can. She packed the children some food in a Tupperware bowl before dropping them off at her parents'. Once Alexis made it back home, she had less than twenty minutes to get a plan together. She had always thought of herself as a quick thinker so she knew that she would come up with something. Alexis went into her bedroom and packed all of Ronald's belongings before dragging them by the front door. She went to the hall closet and pulled out a steel bat, sitting it next to the sofa just in case he wanted to get stupid. Thirty minutes later, Ronald came walking through the door, smiling.

"Hey, baby," he said. His smiled slowly faded as he noticed his stuff sitting by the door. "What's goin' on?"

"You tell me." Alexis threw the wad of money at Ronald and watched as it went all over the place. "The money is from Tyisha."

Ronald bent down and picked up the bills. "Oh, so you gon' believe that stank bitch over me?" Ronald screamed angrily.

"That's it! That's the Ronald I know. Get mad, nigga," Alexis taunted.

"Fuck you, bitch!" Ronald shouted and walked toward Alexis with pure fire in his eyes. The same fire she remembered before he broke his foot off in her ass.

Alexis reached down, grabbed the steel bat, and stood in a batter's stance. "Bitch, if you take another step, I'm gon' knock yo' head off yo' shoulders and kick it out the front door." Ronald was shocked as he stopped in his tracks. This was the first time Alexis had ever threatened him. Alexis's words were dripping with poison as she spoke between clenched teeth. "Nigga, leave my key, get yo' shit, and go."

Ronald picked up all he could and turned to look Alexis dead in the eyes. His cold stare gave her the chills because it was a look she had never seen before. Alexis wasn't about to back down; she still would have taken his head off with no problem. "I'ma get you, bitch," he spat before walking out the door. He had said those exact words many times before, but this time Alexis knew he meant them.

Alexis waited until she heard his car start up, and ran over and put the chain on the door. She walked over to the sofa and sat down. She wanted to call India and Keaundra to tell them what just went down, but couldn't. Instead, Alexis grabbed her keys and hurried to her car just in case Ronald was lurking somewhere. Pulling out of the apartment complex as if someone was chasing her, continuously looking in her rearview mirror to see if Ronald was following her. She felt at ease once she pulled into her parents' driveway. Alexis pulled out her cell phone and called into her parents' house.

"Hello?" her mother answered.

"Open the door, Ma," Alexis said, still a little spooked.

"You here to get my babies already? I'm not ready for them to leave."

"Don't worry we not leaving yet, matter of fact, we gon' stay over here a couple days so you can spend time with ya grandbabies."

"Is everything okay?" Alexis's mom asked, sensing nervousness in her daughter's voice.

"Yeah . . . yeah, everything's cool. It's just that they're exterminating our apartment complex.

So we need to stay over here for a few days, that's all," Alexis lied.

"That's fine. Come on in, baby."

"I'll be in in a minute."

Alexis pulled herself together before getting out of her car. She looked behind her one last time before walking into her parents' house, because the last words Ronald said to her had her shaken.

Chapter Forty-seven

"Mommy, I can't do anything with my hair," India whined into the phone receiver.

"India, baby, you have long, pretty hair, I'm sure you can come up with something," Mrs. Davenport said.

"I've tried everything and nothing seems to work," she huffed. "I'm just gon' get some scissors and cut it all off."

"Don't you dare, India Ariel Davenport," her mother said in a threatening tone.

"Well, what else can I do with it?"

"Make an appointment with someone," Mrs. Davenport suggested.

"I refuse to let just anybody play up in my head," India said.

"Well, throw the mess up in a ponytail then," Mrs. Davenport laughed.

"Mommy, that's not funny," India pouted.

"Well, baby, just try that new hair salon on the north end that you talked about a while ago."

India smiled. "I guess it wouldn't hurt."

"Well, baby, I have to get ready for my tango class, so I will talk to you later."

"Love you," India said.

"Love you too," Mrs. Davenport said before hanging up the phone.

India grabbed her keys and purse and headed to her truck. Her home phone rang as she was locking the door behind her. India didn't bother going back in to answer it, because nine times out of ten it was Martell. He had been calling her at least fifteen times a day, begging her to let him back into her life. Every time she turned him down, he would get mad and threaten her. Martell even offered a couple of times to send India and her friends on an all expense–paid trip to Paris if she gave him another chance. After India refused his offer, Martell called her every name in the book; he even made up a few of his own. India just laughed at his childish temper tantrum and hung up on him.

India bobbed her head to the music as she drove to the salon. Once she pulled into the parking lot, she noticed how packed it was for a Thursday. India got out of the car and walked up to the door, looking around in the window to see if she could see a sign that said "walk-ins" welcome, but she didn't. India pushed opened the door and walked up to the receptionist desk smiling.

"Welcome to Loose Endz, who is your appointment with?" the receptionist replied.

"I don't have one. But I would like to make one."

"With whom?" the receptionist asked politely.

India looked around the nicely decorated hair salon. There was a daycare to the right of her, full of screaming children. India smiled as she watched some of the children play on the little plastic slide. The walls were painted off-white with a mauve border all around the room, and pictures of all the hair stylists were neatly hung in a row.

"I don't know. I've never been here before. Who's the best?"

"Let me see what kind of hair you workin' wit," the receptionist said, walking from behind her desk. She grabbed a few pieces of India's hair, examining it. "Oh, you have that good stuff. Are you mixed with something?"

How rude, India thought as she shot the receptionist an "I know you didn't" look. "I'm black, thank you."

"Oh, no need to get offended, honey. I just asked because different hair stylists deal with different types of hair. You see Nona over there," the receptionist said, pointing to a short, dark-skinned girl with Kinky Twist in her hair, "her speciality is braiding and locks. Now, Pinky over there," she said, pointing to a tall, skinny male with "homosexual" written all over his body, "he specializes in quick weaves and up-dos. Girl, he is the bomb! Now, I recommend Flower over there," she said, pointing to a pretty, light-skinned lady with a nicely done quick weave that hung to the middle of her back. "She deals with the good-haired women. She can cut, style, perm, and do anything else you need done. She's one of the top stylists here at Loose Endz and she owns the joint."

"I think I'll go with Flower then." India smiled.

"Good choice. So, when do want your hair done?" the receptionist asked as she walked back behind her desk to retrieve the appointment book.

"Does she have any openings today?"

"Depending on what you want done."

India watched a young lady walk past her with a short, but jazzy, hairstyle. "I want it all cut off," she said, not knowing where those words came from.

"Huh?" the receptionist asked to make sure she heard India right.

"I want it all cut off," India said again.

"Okay. Hang on." The receptionist walked over to where all the stylist were working their magic on clients with long hair, short hair, good hair, and good and nappy hair. India watched as the receptionist whispered something to Flower and pointed over at her. Flower squinted her eyes to see if she recognized the face. India threw her hand up and gave a friendly wave. Flower nodded and went back to working on her client's hair.

"She said give her about ten minutes and she'll be with you," the receptionist walked back over to India and said. "You can have a seat in the waiting area."

India smiled. "Thank you." She walked into the waiting area, grabbed an *Essence* magazine, and took a seat. Occasionally she looked up at the big, forty-six-inch plasma TV they had in the waiting area that was showing a bootlegged copy of *I Can Do Bad All By Myself*.

"India," the receptionist called out.

Dang, it's been ten minutes already. India watched as some of the other ladies shot her dirty looks as she walked by. She didn't know if it was because she looked better than they did or because some of them had talked about being in the waiting area for over an hour and she only had to sit a little under ten minutes.

"Hello," India said to everyone before sitting in Flower's chair.

"Hello. I'm Flower." Flower stuck her hand out for India to shake.

"I'm India." India responded by shaking Flower's hand.

"India, that's a very pretty name."

"Thank you."

"So what would you like done to your hair?"

"I want it all cut off."

"What?" Nona gasped. "Girl, you got some beautiful hair. Why you want it all cut off?"

"This ain't for no nigga, is it?" Flower asked.

"No. I don't do anything for a man unless I want—"

"Girrrl, you know some women will do almost anything just to keep a man," Pinky added his two cents, cutting India off.

"Won't they," Nona agreed. "I got a cousin who takes the cake. This bitch, eat, sleep, shit, and breathes, just to keep a nigga happy. And the ho don't mind payin' a nigga either." Nona shook her head, disgusted.

"Girl, my cousin Jasmin was messin' around wit' this one cat, and she found out he was cheatin' on her ass," Aletha, another stylist, added to the conversation. "So the dumb bitch got pregnant on purpose by the nigga, thinkin' he was gon' change."

"Did the baby change him, girl?" Flower asked.

"Girrrl, three kids later the nigga still out there messin' around with anything in a short skirt," Aletha shouted.

"Say it ain't so," Nona laughed as she pretended to do the Holy Ghost dance.

India listened as each of the stylists tried to out-gossip one another. India thought it was crazy how they stood around and put people's business out in the open without even thinking about it.

"Girl, that ain't nothin' compared to my cousin, Rosalind. This bitch wanna be with this nigga named David so bad, she been pretendin' like her ass got cancer," Flower laughed.

"David who?" Nona asked.

"You know the David who owns the barber shop on Park Avenue."

"Whaaat?" Shawny, another stylist, laughed as well.

"Girl, yeah, the bitch is pitiful," Flower continued.

India listened as Flower went on about how her cousin did research on the Internet about cancer so she could be up on all the different treatments and medicines that cancer patients take. India was taking it all in, *every ounce.*

"Girl, you mean to tell me she got this nigga thinkin' her ass is dyin'?" Pinky asked. Flower nodded.

"What she gon' do when the nigga find out she ain't sick?" Shawny asked.

"Girl, that ain't no business of mines. The only advice I gave her was to be careful," Flower said, laughing.

Ain't that about a bitch! India thought as she listened. *So Rosalind's ass really ain't sick.*

"Honey, that bitch is desperate for a man," Shawny added.

"She sho' is," Pinky agreed.

"Y'all don't tell nobody though, she don't want nobody to know," Flower requested as she added Wrap Lotion to India's hair.

Too late for that. Shit, you done told half the hair salon. India made a mental note as she sat under the hair dryer to never let Flower know any of her personal business.

Two hours later, India walked out of the hair salon, leaving all her long, pretty hair behind. Flower had given India a signature style. Once she finished perming, cutting, and shaping India's hair, Flower had worked up on a masterpiece. India had found herself a new hair stylist. She was happy about her transformation, but she was even more excited about the juicy gossip she had for Alexis.

Chapter Forty-eight

"What, bitch? You lyin'?" Alexis squealed as she, India, and Keaundra sat in Keaundra's kitchen eating Red Lobster and sipping champagne. "You sure we talkin' about the same Rosalind and David?" she asked again, just to make sure. "And by the way, I love your hair," she slid in.

"Thanks."

"Come on, girl," Keaundra laughed. "You know she's talkin' about the same David and Rosalind."

"I just want to make sure before I bust this bitch's bubble."

"Girl, bitches just don't know a good thing when they got one," India said.

"They sho' don't," Keaundra agreed.

"Listen at you. You got a good-ass man on yo' side," Alexis said.

Keaundra smiled. "He is good, ain't he?"

"So you gon' tell him?" India asked, changing the subject.

Alexis shrugged. "I don't know. Wouldn't that be like hatin'?"

"Shit, we all can't be playas, we do need some haters in the world, so why not be one of 'em," India joked.

Keaundra laughed. "I heard that."

"I might as well, huh?" Alexis laughed. "If it were her, I bet you she would tell on me." Alexis wasn't sure if she was going to tell David about Rosalind's scam. She didn't want to think about it anymore so she changed the subject. "How has Kenneth been since, you know, Gran and Beverly?"

"He's been tryin' to cope. He started going back to Joyce, the psychiatrist we used to see after we lost our parents." Keaundra felt bad for her brother. "They put him on Adivan for his depression and gave him Rozerem to help him sleep."

"Damn, that's deep," India said sympathetically.

Kenneth let himself into his sister's house. He heard the three ladies giggling in the kitchen. He started to let his presence be known, but he wanted to hear what they really talked about when they were together.

"Shit, I woulda gave Kenneth some," Alexis said. "You know I still got a little crush on your brother."

"You nasty thang, you," Keaundra laughed as she playfully swatted at Alexis.

Kenneth grinned as he leaned up against the living room wall and continued listening as they put him on a pedestal. "Now, Kenneth is a prime example of a good man," India said. "He don't mind takin' care of his woman."

"He sure don't. Even when we were kids, he did things for me that no other teenage boy woulda done," Alexis added. "I remember when I had that job at McDonald's and I would come home from a long day at work, he would rub my back and my feet. That man was good to me, I swear," Alexis said proudly.

Kenneth smiled and was about to walk into the kitchen until Keaundra mentioned Beverly's name. He wanted to know how his sister really felt about Beverly before he told her the good news about them working through their problems and deciding to go on with the wedding. Eventually he would marry Beverly and Kenneth wanted nothing more than his sister and the woman he loved to get along. They were the only two people he had left in this world.

"Beverly had the world, but she fucked up when she started fuckin' around on Kenneth," India said. Kenneth's smile slowly faded.

"Yeah, with Martell of all people," Alexis said.

Tears formed as India thought about her ex-man sexing Beverly.

Kenneth wanted to confront them because he wanted them to be lying, but instead, he snuck back out the door with his hopes and dreams shattered.

"You betta not cry," Keaundra warned.

India smiled as a tear escaped one of her eyes. "I'm not. Neither one of them is worth my tears."

"I'll drink to that," Alexis said, raising her champagne glass.

"You'll drink to anything, bitch," India laughed as they all touched glasses.

After a couple hours of laughter and girl talk, Alexis and India decided it was time for them to go home.

"Y'all sure y'all gotta leave now?" Keaundra whined.

"Yeah, girl, I gotta put my kids to bed," Alexis said.

"And I gotta get up early for class," India added.

Keaundra said good-bye and watched as both of her friends pulled off before going to the kitchen to clean up their mess.

India's phone rang as she walked in the door. She walked over and looked at the caller ID. Of course, it was Martell, again. Once the phone stopped ringing, India took it off the hook and went to bed. No sooner did she fall into a deep, comfortable sleep, than the ringing of her cell phone woke her up. "Damn!" she shouted angrily before grabbing her cell phone off the nightstand, throwing it across the room and shattering it against the wall.

Alexis argued with herself the entire drive to her parents' house about calling David. She didn't want to hate on Rosalind, but at the same time, she didn't want Rosalind playing David for a fool. Alexis pulled up into the driveway, shut the engine down, and pulled her cell phone from her purse. She dialed David's cell number and waited for him to answer.

"Hello?" he answered, still half asleep.

"David, we need to talk," Alexis stated quickly.

Chapter Forty-nine

Kenneth took two Rozerem sleeping pills and one Adivan that his psychiatrist had prescribed him, ignoring the directions that firmly stated to take only one, and he still could not sleep. He kept tossing and turning, thinking about Beverly and Martell and hoping Keaundra and the others were wrong. Thoughts of how, when, and why Beverly had cheated stayed on his mind. He climbed out of bed and went downstairs to the refrigerator. He grabbed a bottle of Budweiser, popped the cap, and drank it straight down. He tossed the bottle in the sink before grabbing another one and doing the same. Fifteen minutes later, Kenneth had drunk a whole six-pack by himself. The effects of the beer and medicine must have been working because Kenneth started feeling sleepy all of a sudden.

"I need to talk to Beverly," he slurred as he walked over to the phone and dialed her cell phone number. He let it ring until the automated voice message came on. He dialed the number three or four more times, getting madder each time no one answered. He threw the phone and ran back upstairs, grabbed his keys off the nightstand, and his Tech nine from the closet. Kenneth took the steps two at a time and ran out of the house; leaving the front door open. He jumped in his car and drove to Beverly's mom's house like a drunken lunatic, dipping and dodging in and out of traffic.

Once he pulled up in the driveway, he didn't see her mother's car and remembered that her parents had gone out of town for the weekend. Kenneth got out of the car and tucked his nine in his pants. Deciding not to knock, he went around to the back of the house. He found an old bucket and turned it upside down in front of the dining room window.

The neighborhood dogs barked as Beverly sat on the edge of the bed, reading a paper she had received in the mail from her OBGYN, and listening to 93.1 FM on the radio. She hated being home alone, but since her mother and stepfather decided to go to Memphis for the weekend, she had no choice.

Kenneth fell off the bucket a few times before finally getting the window pried open. He climbed in.

Beverly thought she heard noises and peeked out the window. She felt at ease once she saw that it was her neighbors going into their house. She sat back down on the edge of the bed and continued reading the paper. A smile crept across her glowing face until she was startled by a voice behind her.

"How come you didn't answer your phone," Kenneth slurred.

"How did you get in here?" Beverly asked, standing up. "You know it's after midnight and my parents wouldn't like it if they knew you were here this time of night."

"Answer me, dammit," Kenneth shouted, ignoring her last comment.

Beverly stared at Kenneth like he was crazy. He looked like he had been up smoking crack for three days straight. His eyes were bucked and bloodshot while globs of foamy white stuff were stuck in the corners of his mouth.

"Why didn't you answer the damn phone, Beverly?" Kenneth asked as he paced back and forth.

"I didn't hear it, Kenneth," she answered, terrified. "It's on the charger in the living room."

"Did you have a nigga over here, huh? Is that why you didn't answer the phone?"

"No, Kenneth, I told you I didn't hear it. You know I don't want nobody but you."

"That ain't what my sister and her friends said," he said, getting madder by the second.

"What did they say, baby?" she asked nervously.

"They said you was fuckin' Martell. Now, bitch, tell me the truth!" he shouted and pulled the gun from under his shirt.

"Oh my God, Kenneth, what's wrong with you?" Beverly asked, scared.

"Bitch, I'ma ask you one more time. Was you fuckin' Martell?" he asked between clenched teeth.

"No, baby, I wasn't fuckin' nobody," she lied, hoping her lie sounded convincing.

"Why would my sister say some shit like that if it wasn't the truth?"

"I don't know, Ken, you know your sister does not like me," Beverly cried with fear.

"I think you lyin'. Take off your clothes," Kenneth demanded while pointing the gun at Beverly.

Beverly was confused and moving slow. She didn't know what was the matter with him; he was acting possessed.

"Hurry the fuck up, bitch!"

"Here, baby, I got somethin' to show you," she said holding out the letter she received from the OBGYN. Kenneth smacked the paper out of her hand. Beverly ducked as the gun waved around in the air. "You want some water, baby?" Beverly asked, hoping he would say yes so she could make a run for it.

"Did you ask Martell if he wanted some water after he got through fuckin' you?"

Tears flowed down Beverly's cheeks. "I didn't fuck Martell, Kenneth."

Kenneth walked over to Beverly and wiped away her tears with the same hand he held the gun in. "Ahhh, don't cry, baby," he said calmly. Beverly's body shook as she felt the cold steel brush against her cheek.

"Why you cryin'?" Kenneth asked in a calm voice. He was back to the old loving and caring Kenneth she was used to.

"I'm scared," she said through tears.

"You scared of me, Beverly? What did I do to make you scared of me?" Kenneth became angry again. "I can't fuckin' believe you're scared of me. Was you scared of Martell when he was fuckin' you?"

"I didn't fuck him," she shouted, hoping the neighbors would hear her and call for help.

"Who you yellin' at, bitch?"

"I'm not yellin," she cried as her chest heaved up and down.

"Didn't I tell yo' ass to take your clothes off?"

Beverly didn't respond, she just shook her head and began getting undressed.

"Lay down. I 'bout to fuck you like the ho you are."

"Kenneth, don't call me that," Beverly cried.

"Lay down, ho." Beverly obeyed Kenneth and finished getting undressed. Kenneth pulled his pants down around his ankles, and climbed on top of Beverly and began fuckin' her as hard as he could, never letting go of the gun.

"You're hurtin' me," Beverly whimpered. "Please stop, I'm pre—" Before she could finish her sentence, Kenneth had smacked her across the face with the gun.

"Shut up and enjoy this dick." Beverly was in great pain. There was not a bit of moisture coming from anywhere except for the tears that slid down her face.

Kenneth looked down at Beverly and imagined a seductive smile on her face and then he imagined Martell on top of Beverly, fuckin' her brains out. "Oh, you liked how Martell was fuckin' you, bitch? Martell fuck you betta than me, ho?" he shouted as he continued to ram his dick inside of her.

"Kenneth, please stop," Beverly pleaded as the tears flowed.

"Fuck you, ho," he shouted before putting the gun right between her eyebrows. "Should I kill you?" Kenneth asked feeling Beverly's body tremble. Beverly shook her head vigorously from side to side. "I think I should," he said, and pulled the trigger. Kenneth continued fuckin' Beverly until he exploded inside of her. "There I'm all done." He rolled off her, wiped the sweat off his face and looked down at her.

"Get up, bitch!" Blood dripped from the right side of Beverly's face. "I said get up." Kenneth hit Beverly across the head with the gun. "Oh, you don't hear me now," he shouted and continued beating her over and over with the gun. Kenneth freaked out when he realized there was blood gushing from Beverly's head. "Oh my God, what have I done?" Kenneth began crying. "I can't believe I killed her. Beverly, baby, get up. Please get up, baby, I'm sorry!" In an instant, Kenneth's whole mood had switched again. "Now, bitch, if I can't have you, nobody can," he said coldly and spit in Beverly's face. Kenneth pulled his pants up and sat on the edge of the bed. He picked up the letter she had tried to show him and began reading it.

Dear Ms. Mason, we are sending you the results of the bloodwork that we performed on you on 10/07/09. The results of all the STDs are negative, but your HMG shows that you are pregnant. Please make an appointment for further prenatal care.
Sincerely Dr. Waltz

"Oh my God, Beverly, we about to have a baby," Kenneth said while looking back at Beverly. He rubbed her belly as he spoke. "I'm about to be a father." Kenneth heard police sirens as he smiled at the wall. "Probably ain't even my baby, bitch." Kenneth stood up and pointed the gun at Beverly. "Is it? I didn't think so," he spat and let off two more rounds into Beverly's stomach. "I wonder where the police is goin', baby," he asked Beverly as he heard the sirens roar. Kenneth walked over and looked out the window at all the flashing lights. "Get up, baby, and come look. They're outside our house."

"Put down your weapon and come out with your hands up," one of the many police officers yelled.

Kenneth looked over at Beverly. "They comin' for me, baby. What am I gon' do?" Kenneth stood over Beverly's lifeless body, bent down, and kissed her. "I love you," he said and took a seat next to her. He looked over at the wall and smiled while hallucinating about seeing his mother, father, and Gran waving him over to them. "Here I come, just hold on don't leave me," he said and began crying. Kenneth placed the gun in his mouth, closed his eyes, and pulled the trigger. It was over all in an instant.

Chapter Fifty

Keaundra's head lay comfortably in Hammer's lap as they watched *Harlem Nights* on television. Hammer brushed her hair while they enjoyed the movie. She yawned as the credits started rolling.

"It's gettin' late," Hammer said, looking at the clock on the cable box.

"I know, it's after midnight," she said, sitting up. "And we both have to work early in the morning."

Hammer yawned. "I know." Hammer laid the brush on the coffee table and stood up. "Aren't you gon' at least walk me to the door?"

"You know the way," she joked playfully.

Hammer smiled. "Get up here." Keaundra held out both of her hands and he pulled her up to him.

"Oh my God," Keaundra grabbed her head moaning in agony.

"Damn, baby, I didn't mean to pull you that hard."

Keaundra took a seat on the sofa and held her head in her hands for a few seconds.

"I'm sorry," Hammer said again.

"No, it's not that. I just got a really bad headache all of a sudden."

Hammer sat down on the sofa next to Keaundra and wrapped his arm around her shoulders, pulling her close to him. "You need me to get you some Tylenol?"

"No, I'm okay now."

"That's not good. You need to make you a doctor's appointment," Hammer suggested.

"It's more to it then that. I need to call my brother and see if he's okay," Keaundra said, grabbing her cell phone off the coffee table and dialing Kenneth's number. Keaundra began to worry when there was no answer.

Hammer could see the fear in Keaundra's eyes. "You okay?"

"I just got this strange feelin' that it's somethin' wrong with my brother."

"Huh?" Hammer asked, confused.

"I'm tellin' you, there's somethin' wrong with Kenneth." Keaundra stood up and began pacing the floor as she dialed Kenneth's cell phone and home phone repeatedly.

"Just calm down, baby. How do you know somethin' is wrong with your brother?"

"We're twins, Hammer, and sometimes we can feel one another's pain. That headache wasn't a coincidence, it was my brother, I just know it."

"It's almost like telepathy, but a little deeper," Hammer replied, trying to make sense of Keaundra's intuition.

"Yeah, a lot deeper." Keaundra desperately tried to reach her brother. Keaundra threw the phone on the sofa, grabbed her keys, and opened the door. "I'll be back," she looked back at Hammer and said.

"Where you going?"

"To my brother's house."

"Wait, I'll go with you." Hammer followed Keaundra to her car. Keaundra was a nervous wreck the entire drive. She yelled and screamed at cars to move out of her way as she exceeded the speed limit.

"Somethin' isn't right, Hammer." Tears filled Keaundra's eyes as she pulled into the driveway and noticed Kenneth's car was gone. She found her house key, got out of the car, and walked up the drive.

"Why you say that?" Hammer asked nervously.

"Because, it's almost one in the morning and he's not home. Kenneth is normally home and in bed no later than ten o'clock."

Once Keaundra and Hammer reached the porch, Keaundra broke down when she saw the front door was left open. "Oh my God, Hammer, my brother," she cried. Hammer didn't know what to say or do. He didn't know whether to try to calm Keaundra down or call 911. Keaundra walked in the front door and called her brother's name. "Kenneth," she called out, getting no answer. "Ken-Ken, answer me, please," she cried, running from room to room. When she finished checking the entire house, she knew what she had to do. Keaundra held her hand out. "I need to use your phone." As Keaundra began to dial, a police cruiser pulled up into the driveway. Keaundra knew right then that something terrible had happened to her brother.

The officers got out of the cruiser and walked up the drive. Keaundra and Hammer met them on the front porch. "Can I help you," Hammer asked, knowing Keaundra was in no shape to be answering questions.

The tall, white officer cleared his throat before speaking while his partner stood back, letting him do all the talking. "Do you know a Kenneth Davidson?" he asked. Keaundra could not answer; all she could do was nod.

"He's her brother," Hammer responded.

The officer turned his attention toward Keaundra. "I'm sorry, ma'am, but there's been a terrible accident." Keaundra still did not respond. She stared at the officer, waiting for him to tell her what had happened to her brother. "I'm afraid your brother was involved in what looks like a murder-suicide."

The officer continued bearing his bad news, but all Keaundra could hear were words that sounded like Charlie Brown's teacher. Keaundra's entire body went numb and without warning, she was out like a light.

"Call an ambulance, quick!" Hammer screamed.

Keaundra woke up and looked around. It took her a few minutes to get her eyes focused, and when she did the first two faces she saw were India's and Alexis's.

Keaundra forced a weak smile. "What you two bitches doin' in my bedroom?" she said, still groggy from the medicine that dripped intravenously through an IV. "Why y'all cryin'?" she asked when she noticed the tears running from their eyes.

Alexis and India were speechless. They didn't know how to tell Keaundra that her twin brother had killed Beverly and taken his own life as well.

"What's the matter with y'all?" Keaundra asked, becoming irritated when no one answered.

Alexis and India remained quiet.

Hammer walked back into the room. He had been standing in the hall trying to pull himself together.

"Can you tell me what's the matter with these two hefahs?" she asked Hammer as he came closer. Hammer's eyes were puffy and red. "What's wrong with everybody?" Keaundra became alarmed as everyone stood around her crying.

"Ke-Ke," India spoke. "Kenneth is . . ." she continued but the lump in her throat wouldn't allow her to finish.

"What's the matter with Kenneth, India?" India just stared at Keaundra. "What the fuck is wrong with my brother?" Keaundra looked over at Alexis and yelled.

Tears flowed freely from Alexis's eyes as she spoke. "Sweetie, he's gone."

Keaundra struggled to pull herself into an upright position. "Gone where? What the fuck is goin' on here," she asked, realizing she wasn't at home in her own bed. "Where the fuck am I?" She looked down at the IV in her hand and snatched it out. "I wanna see Kenneth now," Keaundra demanded.

"Sweetie, Kenneth shot Beverly and then himself," Alexis said through tears.

Keaundra looked at India and then at Hammer for confirmation. They both shook their heads in agreement.

Keaundra attempted to get out the bed. "Baby, please lie down," Hammer replied, placing his hands on her shoulders.

"Get your hands off me," she said. "Where's my brother, y'all? Quit playin' with me."

"He's gone for real, baby," Hammer said through tears. He wrapped his arms around Keaundra's body as she cried like a newborn baby. "Get the fuck off of me," she screamed, fighting to push Hammer away from her. Hammer attempted to grab her again, but she pushed him away.

"Ke-Ke, calm down, please," Alexis cried as she rubbed Keaundra's shoulder.

Keaundra knocked Alexis's hand away from her. "Get off me! Please tell me y'all lyin'," Keaundra begged.

"Baby, I wish we were," Hammer replied. Hammer took a chance and wrapped his arm around Keaundra again.

She grabbed his shirt, pulling him closer to her, and cried. "Why, God?" she wailed. Alexis and India were torn as they had to stand by watching their best friend weeping from her soul.

"Is everything okay in here?" the nurse questioned, walking into the room.

"Get the fuck outta' here," Keaundra screamed.

"Ma'am, please calm down," the nurse replied.

"Fuck you, bitch," Keaundra shouted, moving toward the nurse.

Hammer grabbed Keaundra by the arm and pulled her back, hugging her.

Keaundra kicked and screamed as she tried to get loose from Hammer's tight grasp.

"Is everything all right in here?" one of the hospital security guards burst in the room and asked. He looked like Old Otis off *Martin*. He sported a big, drippy Jheri curl, thick, pop-bottle glasses, and three tarnished gold teeth in the front of his mouth.

"Everything's okay," India responded, wiping tears away from her face.

Alexis and India walked over to Hammer and Keaundra and wrapped their arms around both of their bodies. They stood in a group, crying, for what seemed like forever.

"Why, y'all, why my brother?" Keaundra cried.

"We don't have the answer to that question, baby," Hammer replied.

"I'm ready to go home," Keaundra said.

India looked over at the nurse. "She needs her discharge papers."

"Dr. Lee said she has to stay here for at least twenty-four hours for observation," the nurse replied.

"That's fine," Keaundra said, wiping away her tears. "I don't need no papers tellin' me when I can leave, hand me my clothes."

"But, ma'am, you can't leave without being discharged," the nurse stated.

Keaundra began putting on her clothes. "Watch me."

"But ma'am," the nurse contested.

"But ma'am my ass, I'm going home."

After convincing the nurse to talk to the doctor about releasing Keaundra, India had to promise the doctor that she would make an appointment for Keaundra with her family physician for a check-up.

The sun was shining bright when Keaundra finally made it home. She walked in the house with Alexis, India, and Hammer behind her. Peaches jumped up on the back of the sofa for her belly rub, but Keaundra ignored her and continued walking to her bedroom. Alexis rubbed Peaches for Keaundra and took a seat on the sofa.

Keaundra lay across her bed and stared at the ceiling as she tried to decipher what would make her brother lose his mind and kill Beverly and then himself. She knew Kenneth had a bad temper, but what could Beverly have done to push him over the edge? To make him snap? Without the answers to her questions, Keaundra took two muscle relaxers and cried herself to sleep.

When Keaundra finally woke up from her nap, it was well after 5:00 P.M. She looked beside her at Hammer, lying there asleep, and noticed India and Alexis lying fast asleep on the floor. Keaundra couldn't help but smile, because she knew even though she had no more close family left in her life, Alexis, India, and, prayerfully, Hammer had her back. Keaundra had turned off the ringer to her phone before falling back off to sleep, so she knew she was going to have a million and one messages from family and friends. She looked over at the blinking light on her answering machine and shook her head. As she began checking her messages, the automated voice gave her the date first. "First unheard message sent today, September fourteen," the voice said.

"Oooohhhhh my God," Keaundra screamed at the top of her lungs, making Alexis, India, and Hammer nearly jump out of their skin.

"What's wrong, baby?" Hammer asked as his heart beat like two twelve-inch speakers in the back of a Pinto.

Keaundra began screaming bloody murder as the tears ran like Niagara Falls. Keaundra cried

until she stared gagging. She jumped up, ran
into the bathroom, and hugged the toilet as tight
as she could. Keaundra vomited so much there
was nothing left in her to throw up but the acid
in her stomach. "Please, God, tell me why?" she
screamed between coughing and gagging.

"What's wrong with her?" India asked confused.

Alexis shrugged her shoulders. They both looked over at Hammer but he appeared just as lost.
They walked out in the hallway and stood in the
bathroom doorway.

"Oh my goodness," India gasped.

"What?" Alexis and Hammer asked, simultaneously.

India thought for a moment and tried to figure
out what else could be the matter with Keaundra.
"Oh my goodness! Today is the anniversary of
her parent's death," India said, shocked.

"It sho' is," Alexis added with wide eyes.

Hammer couldn't do anything but shake his
head. "How ironic," he said before walking into
the bathroom with Keaundra. He grabbed a towel
off the rack and wiped her mouth before helping
her back to her bedroom. Hammer guided her to
the bed and helped her lay down. He positioned
himself behind her so she could use his body as
a pillow. He began massaging her scalp while
singing a song by John P. Kee. Hammer's voice

Keaundra held onto Hammer's free hand and cried herself back to sleep.

was so strong and melodic as he belted out the words. Alexis, India, and even Keaundra were amazed at how beautiful his voice was.

Chapter Fifty-one

"Here you go, baby," Rosalind said as she walked into the living room with a plate of turkey bacon, egg whites, and grits.

David was in the process of tying up his shoes and looked up at Rosalind and returned her smile. "Is that for me?" he said as he sat upright on the sofa.

Rosalind smiled proudly. "Yep. Sure is."

"What did I do to deserve breakfast?" he asked, taking the plate of food from her hand.

"For last night." She grinned deviously.

"I did put it down, didn't I?" he bragged with a mouth full of food.

"Yeah, you sure did." Rosalind sat down on the sofa next to David and wiped a crumb from the side of his face. "I love you, baby."

David ignored her words while finishing off his breakfast. As soon as he scraped off the last spoonfull of grits, he handed Rosalind the empty plate.

"Did you hear what I said?"

David wiped his mouth. "Go get Daddy some orange juice." Rosalind smacked her lips and rolled her eyes before standing up from the sofa. She shot David a dirty look and headed toward the kitchen. "Hey," he called out.

Rosalind turned around and grimaced. "What?"

"When's the next time you go to the doctor?" he asked nonchalantly.

Rosalind was caught off guard by David's question. The entire time she was claiming to have cancer, he had never once asked anything about her doctor's appointments, other than how they went. "Why?" she asked nervously.

"I just wanted to know, 'cause I want to go to the next one with you." David spoke as calmly as possible, even though his blood was boiling on the inside.

"For what? I mean, okay," she said and continued on her way to the kitchen.

David was tired of all the lies Rosalind had conjured up. It was time to stop playing along with her and pull her ho card. He knew that Rosalind would stoop low, but he didn't think she could stoop so low as to tell a lie about having a life-threatening disease. David was hurt, and not because Rosalind had lied to him, but because she had played on his emotions, having him feeling sorry for her, catering to her every need, and most of all, for pushing Alexis out of his life.

Rosalind stood in the kitchen questioning herself while she poured David a glass of freshly squeezed O.J. *Why did he ask me about my next appointment? He probably was just making general conversation. I really don't know what to expect when I get back into the living room.* Rosalind thought about going back into the living room and hollering out "April Fool's" or better yet, escaping out the kitchen window so she wouldn't have to face David ever again, but she just accepted the strong possibility that she had been busted, and walked out of the kitchen. As she walked over to David, he had a huge grin on his face instead of a frown, so she began to think she was being paranoid.

David took the glass of orange juice from Rosalind's hand and drank it straight down.

"So when was you gon' tell me?" he asked after he finished his drink.

"Tell you what?" Rosalind asked, dumbfounded, as if she didn't already know. She had been busted.

"Rosalind, stop fuckin' playin' with me!" he said in a raised tone. "Now when was you gon' tell me yo' ass don't have cancer for real?" Tears shot into Rosalind's eyes. "Man, save them mutha-fuckin' tears."

"What are you talkin' about, David? I do have cancer," she lied as the tears flowed.

"So you gon' continue to lie to me about being sick? I don't understand you." Looking at Rosalind made David sick to his stomach. "I knew you were devious and conniving, but to say that you're dying, Rosalind, come on."

David knew the truth so there was no need for her to keep lying. "David, I'm sorry," she cried.

"I don't know what to say, Rosalind." David's eyes became watery as he spoke. "I can't believe you would do this to me, you know that I watched my own father die from cancer." David could not hold back the tears any longer as they flowed down his cheeks. "You know it's still hard for me to handle the loss of my father."

"I'm so sorry, baby."

"I watched my mother do all she could just to make my dad's last days on this earth his best, and I tried to do the same for you. You wrong, Rosalind, you dead wrong."

"I'm sorry, David." Rosalind really was sorry for playing on David's emotions, but at the time she thought that was the only way to get him back. She knew if she made up a lie about that and had him feeling sorry for her, he would feel obligated to keep her in his life.

"I am too." Rosalind's pain slightly lifted. "I shoulda left you out on my doorstep like the mutt you are. I can't believe I let a real woman like Alexis slip away from me."

David's words were like a slap in the face to Rosalind. *How dare he call me a mutt and Alexis a real woman.*

"Bitch, get outta' my damn house, now!"

"David, wait, let me explain," Rosalind begged.

"There's no need for explanation, just get your shit and go." David turned and walked toward his bedroom, slamming the door behind him.

Rosalind walked toward his bedroom and stood by the door, contemplating knocking. David picked up his phone, dialed Alexis's phone number, and waited for her to answer.

"Hello, Alexis?"

"Yes?" Alexis said with a smile.

"I'm sorry, baby."

Rosalind's heart sank when she heard David call Alexis baby. She wanted to bust in his room and go off, but she was the one in the wrong, she had no one to blame but herself. If she would have just been a woman about the situation and tried to get David back without lying, maybe things would have turned out better; now she would never know. It was over for good this time and Rosalind knew it. She had pushed David away with all the lies, bickering, insecurities, and everything else that could ruin a relationship. Rosalind had pushed David for the last time . . . right into the arms of another woman.

Chapter Fifty-two

Hammer stayed by Keaundra's side. He made sure everything was intact. He cooked, cleaned, laid out her clothes, and did everything else he thought she needed done. Hammer had gone back to the hospital with Keaundra to take one final look at her brother. That was one of the hardest things for him because it made him think about his last moment with Kelly. Hammer even went with Keaundra to pick out an urn for Kenneth. India and Alexis had tagged along for added support.

The rest of the family wanted to have Kenneth buried in a casket, but Keaundra had the final say-so. She decided to have her brother cremated because she didn't want him laying in front of the church for people to walk by and look at him as if he were an exhibit at an art show. The family was enraged, but Keaundra didn't care. Gran's children had not spoken to her or Kenneth since they broke the news that Gran hadn't left them anything in her will.

Keaundra was home resting on the sofa as Hammer washed a load of laundry. Something told her to pick up the phone and check on Beverly's mother. Keaundra reached over, grabbed the phone off the coffee table, and dialed the number.

"Hello?" Mrs. Norton answered.

Keaundra hesitated.

"Hello?" Mrs. Norton said again.

"Hello, Mrs. Norton?" Keaundra asked quickly.

"Yes, this is she."

"This is Keaundra . . . Kenneth's sister. I was callin' to see if you needed anything."

Mrs. Norton broke down into tears. "I don't want anything from you. Don't you think you've done enough?" she shouted.

"But I didn't do anything," Keaundra protested. Keaundra stood up from the sofa and paced the floor.

Mrs. Norton became angry. "Your fuckin' brother killed my daughter and grandbaby!"

"What?" Keaundra asked, confused. Keaundra knew very little about her brother's murder-suicide because she knew she wouldn't be able to handle any gory details. Finding out that Beverly was pregnant came as a shock to her. She began crying as Beverly's mother continued talking.

"Yes, Beverly was pregnant and your psychotic-ass brother shot my baby twice in the stomach." Mrs. Norton's words were malevolent as they rolled off her tongue. "Shooting her in the head wasn't good enough?" she asked as if Keaundra had the answer.

"I'm sorry, I didn't know," Keaundra cried.

"Sorry is not gon' bring my daughter or grandbaby back. I'm sorry about your loss, but for your safety, do not show up at the funeral and don't ever call my house again!" With that said, Mrs. Norton hung up the phone leaving Keaundra devastated.

Keaundra fell to her knees and began screaming. "Nooooo, why, God, why?"

Hammer dashed from the laundry room to check on Keaundra. He ran over and wrapped his arms around her.

Keaundra rocked back and forth as she continued crying and questioning God.

"Baby, what's wrong?" Hammer asked.

Keaundra was too through to even speak. All she could do was cry as the tears rushed like raging waters.

"Baby, what's the matter?" Hammer asked again and again. Hammer panicked and ran over and grabbed the phone. He called India and asked her if she could come over quick.

India dropped what she was doing, no questions asked, and rushed to her friend's side. By the time she made it to Keaundra's, Hammer had her in the bed, rubbing her back while she cried.

"Is she okay?" India asked when she walked into the bedroom.

Hammer stood up from the bed and motioned for India to follow him. India glanced over at Keaundra once more before leaving the room.

"Did you know that Beverly was pregnant?" Hammer asked once they made it to the living room.

"I've heard rumors, but you know how that is."

"You're right, but it's true, she was pregnant. Mrs. Norton told Keaundra."

"Damn, that's deep," India said, shaking her head in disbelief. "I don't know what Kenneth was thinkin' about."

"That ain't even the fucked-up part."

"It can't get no worse than that."

"Check this out then, Kenneth shot Beverly in the stomach, not once but twice."

Hearing that made India cringe. "Whoaaaa! Now that's fucked up."

"Ain't it?" Hammer agreed. Hammer got quiet for a few seconds. "You know it's gon' take a long time for Keaundra to heal. First she loses her grandmother and a few months later her twin brother."

"Yeah, I know. We gon' hafta help each other and be the strength that Keaundra needs," India said. She looked over at Hammer. "You in or what?"

"I don't have no choice but to be in, that's my woman and I love her."

"That's what's up?" India smiled as they walked back toward Keaundra's bedroom to check up on her.

The day of the memorial service turned out to be a typical rainy day. Hammer was in the bathroom getting ready while Keaundra lay in her bed, lifeless.

"Baby, you ain't up yet?" Hammer asked as he walked back into the room.

Keaundra didn't respond. She continued staring into space as Hammer continued to talk.

"The memorial starts in less than an hour and you haven't even picked out an outfit to wear." Hammer walked over to the the closet and opened it up.

Keaundra turned her head and watched Hammer as he began pulling clothes out.

"You can wear this," he said, holding up a plain black dress with no style to it at all. "I don't like this," he said, tossing it on the bed. Keaundra still didn't respond. Hammer began pulling out dresses and tossing them on the bed. "Baby, what you gon' wear?" he asked, sounding defeated.

Tears streamed down Keaundra's cheeks. "I can't go, Hammer."

Hammer walked over to the bed and sat down next to Keaundra. "You gotta go, Keaundra. Kenneth is your brother."

"Was," she said. "Kenneth was my brother, but he's gone now. Just like my mom, my dad, and my grandmother. They left me here all alone," she cried. "Everybody who loved me is gone."

"Baby, you're not alone. You have me, Alexis, and India," Hammer explained. "And we all love you."

"It's not the same though," Keaundra cried.

Hammer prayed that Keaundra wasn't having thoughts of suicide. He wanted to ask her, but he didn't want to put any ideas in her head.

"Baby, we gon' get through this together and I promise you that I will be here for you to help you get over the hump." Tears formed in Hammer's eyes as he spoke from his heart. "I know you will hurt for the rest of your life, but just let me be the Tylenol that eases your pain."

Hammer's sweet words gave Keaundra a sense of hope. She leaned over and kissed Hammer as passionately as she could to show her appreciation before getting up to get dressed for her brother's memorial.

Keaundra had to force herself to go inside the church. Her feet felt like there were cement blocks on the bottom of them as she walked. She looked around at the large crowd of people as she and Hammer walked in. Alexis and India sat in the front row next to Kenneth's best friend, Alex. Her aunts and uncles from both sides filled the pews. Kenneth's friends from the law firm he worked at were there to pay their respects, a few of his childhood friends, as well as a couple of Kenneth's ex-girlfriends. There was also family she hadn't seen since her mother's and father's funerals. Her branch manager, Angela, showed up with a few of the girls from the bank. Keaundra was grateful to have a boss like Angela. She had called her right after Kenneth's death and gave her a leave of absence until she was able to come back to work.

Keaundra began crying before she made it to her seat. Looking at all the eleven-by-fourteen pictures of her brother brought on the tears. One picture was of Keaundra and Kenneth when they were eight years old. Another one was of Gran kissing Kenneth on the cheek the day he passed the bar exam, and the other pictures were just of Kenneth being silly. Keaudra cried the entire time Reverend Powell gave the eulogy, along with the rest of the church. Family and friends were shocked beyond belief to find out that Kenneth murdered someone and then himself. Kenneth was always so kind, caring, and giving, making what happened so hard for everyone to believe.

After the funeral, Keaundra went down to the basement of the church with the rest of her family and friends. She talked to everyone she wanted to talk to, passed out her number to a few family members, and promised to call, even though she knew she wouldn't. Keaundra said her good-byes, grabbed her brother's urn, and took it home, placing it on top of the mantel right next to her mother's picture.

Chapter Fifty-three

Over the next couple of months, Keaundra began getting back to her regular routine. It took a lot of hard work, but Alexis, India, and Hammer were there as promised. Through the nightmares, the sudden breakdowns, and just listening to her reminisce about her childhood memories, they were there. Hammer had moved into Keaundra's place in order to be there with her twenty-four seven. Keaundra had subconsciously argued with Gran back and forth about letting Hammer move in without them being married. "Why plant the tree when you can get the fruit for free?" Keaundra could hear Gran saying over and over in her head.

After Keaundra's vacation and sick time ran out, the checks stopped coming. Hammer stepped up and began taking care of all the bills, including her car note and car insurance, along with paying his own. Keaundra was too independent to continue letting a man take care of her so she decided to go back to work.

Keaundra pretended like she was asleep as Hammer climbed out of bed. She waited with her eyes closed until she heard the bathroom door close before getting up, throwing on her robe, and walking over to the dresser. Opening up the drawer, she dug all the way in the back and pulled out an EPT pregnancy test and stuck it in her pocket. Keaundra was almost two weeks late. India and Alexis had convinced her to buy a pregnancy test. Keaundra heard Hammer come out of the bathroom. She waited until she heard pots and pans rattling in the kitchen before heading to the bathroom. She pulled the test from her pocket and followed the instructions.

Keaundra nervously waited. It took forever for the results to show up. She watched in terror as one blue line appeared and then another. She dropped the test on the floor and sat down on the toilet.

"I'll be damned! I'm pregnant," she said.

Keaundra picked the test up off the floor, put it back in her robe pocket, and turned the water on in the shower. The entire time, she stood in the water wondering how she would break the news to Hammer. As long as they had been together, they had never once talked about having children. Once Hammer mentioned the son

Kelly was pregnant with but that was as far as the conversation went.

"Are you gon' come eat or what?" Hammer knocked on the bathroom door and asked, making Keaundra jump.

"Yeah . . . yeah, I'll be out there in a minute," she stammered.

"You're paying the water bill this month." Hammer laughed as he made his way back to the kitchen.

Keaundra cut off the water, stepped out of the shower, and began drying off. She looked at her flat stomach in the mirror from every angle and imagined how she would look with a protruding belly. She put her robe on and headed to the kitchen.

"'Bout time, the food is cold," Hammer joked.

"I'm sorry, baby," she cooed before kissing him on the lips. Keaundra sat down and waited for Hammer to set her plate in front of her, just like he did every morning.

Hammer had piled Keaundra's plate with five pancakes, a mountain of eggs, and half a pack of bacon and sat it down in front of her.

"You tryin'a be funny?" She asked, pretending to have an attitude.

Hammer laughed. "What? You been throwin' down lately, so I thought I better feed you more."

Keaundra laughed too. "Forget you, nigga."

"Take two of them pancakes off and put them on this plate," Hammer said, placing an empty plate on the table. Keaundra took her fork and lifted the two pancakes from the stack.

"What's this?" she asked, dropping her fork and picking up a two-carat diamond ring that lay on top of her three pancakes.

"Oh, before I forget," Hammer said as he got down on one knee. "Will you marry me?"

"Hammer," Keaundra squealed with joy.

"I'll take that as a yes," he said, standing up.

Keaundra stood up as well and untied her robe, revealing her banging body. "No, that's a hell yes!" She smiled. Hammer began kissing Keaundra all over her neck. "Wait, I have somethin' to tell you," she said, pushing Hammer back.

"Can't it wait until after I have you for breakfast?" he asked and started kissing on her again.

"No, it can't wait. I need to tell you this while you're in a good mood." Keaundra shoved Hammer again and tied up her robe.

"What is it, baby?" he whined playfully while untying her robe again.

"Hammer, I'm pregnant," she blurted out. She didn't even wait for a response before she rambled on. "I know we've never talked about having children, but it's done and abortion is out of the question, I'm keepin' my baby. If you don't want no parts in this pregnancy I'm fine with that, I'll raise my baby by my damn self. Shit, women raise kids on their own every day."

"Oh my God, Keaundra. I don't know what to say." Tears came to Hammer's eyes. Keaundra didn't know if the tears were from joy or pain.

"Say somethin'," she demanded.

"I'm 'bout to be a daddy," he said happily before picking Keaundra up and swinging her around.

"You're happy?" she asked, confused.

"Happy? I'm fuckin' ecstatic," he yelled before putting her down.

"What a relief, 'cause I damn sho' didn't wanna hafta raise this baby on my own," she laughed.

Hammer kissed Keaundra on the lips. "Neva that! Like I told you before, Hammer got ya back. Now look, I need to eat something before I go to work."

Keaundra pushed the plates to the side, climbed on top of the table, and lay back with her legs spread. "Dig in," she said devilishly and Hammer happily obliged.

"Bitch, I'm so happy for you," Alexis screamed into the phone receiver as she, India, and Keaundra talked on three-way.

"Me too," India added. "My girl 'bout to be somebody's wifey and mommy."

"Imagine that," Alexis said. "Who woulda thought in a million years that Miss Prude would finally let a nigga sweep her off her feet and plant a seed up in her?" Alexis laughed.

Keaundra laughed as well. "What can I say, I've turned soft."

"You're not soft. You were just fortunate enough to find a good man," India added.

"You betta hold on to him," Alexis warned.

"You don't hafta tell me twice," Keaundra responded.

"That's what's up," India said. "Y'all know we all gon' hafta go out and celebrate this joyous occasion."

"That's what I'm talkin' about," Alexis agreed.

"Where we gon' go?" Keaundra asked.

"I think we should go to the place where you and Hammer first met," India suggested.

"The bowling alley?" Alexis asked rhetorically.

"I like that," Keaundra said.

"Me too," Alexis agreed.

"It's gon' be like déjà vu," India said.

"Yeah, except this time Martell's punk ass won't be there," Alexis laughed.

"Alexis," Keaundra spat.

"What?" Alexis asked innocently.

"It's okay, girl. I'm so over Martell. I'm ready to move on to bigger and better things," India said, stretching the truth a little. In fact, India missed the hell out of Martell, but she would rather miss him from long distance than have his lying, cheating ass in her life.

"I heard that," Keaundra said, happy for her.

"I feel you, girl," Alexis said.

"So, it's all set. Saturday we'll meet up at the bowling alley," India said. "Shit, I forgot I gotta put my truck in the shop on Friday."

"You can ride with me," Alexis offered.

"Okay, it's set then," India said.

"Look, hoes, I do got work to do," Keaundra said.

Alexis laughed. "Okay, love y'all."

"Love you too," India and Keaundra replied simultaneously before they all hung up.

Chapter Fifty-four

India was getting dressed to go out with her girls when her cell phone rang. She answered without checking her caller ID, thinking it was Alexis.

"Hello?"

"What's up, baby?" Martell sang into the phone.

"Martell, why do you continuously call me?" India huffed, irritated.

"'Cause I miss you and I want you back in my life."

"I already told you that's not gon' happen in this lifetime or the next."

"Can I come over tonight?"

"For what, Martell?" India grimaced.

"So we can talk."

"Martell, you crazy."

"No, I'm persistent."

"No, you're a stalker and there's laws against what you're doing to me." India said smartly.

"So what if it is? If lovin' you is wrong, I don't wanna be right."

"You so fuckin' corny! Stop callin' me, Martell."

"I'll be over tonight, I don't care what you say."

"Whatever," India said before hanging up. "You can come over if you want, I'm not gon' be here," she laughed to herself as she continued getting dressed. India knew there was a big chance that Martell would really pop up at her house. India knew she had to be strong, so instead of being there for him to talk his way in, she packed an overnight bag and waited for Alexis to come swoop her up.

"What's the bag for?" Alexis asked India when she got into the car.

"Are you stayin' over David's house tonight?" India asked Alexis as they drove to the bowling alley.

"I hadn't planned on it, why?"

"Because I wanted to stay at your house tonight if it's okay."

"You still having problems with Martell callin' and riding by?" Alexis asked concerned.

"Yeah, he called me tonight and told me he was coming over and didn't care what I said."

Alexis became angry. "That nigga got some serious problems."

India strongly agreed. "Who you tellin'."

"You can stay at my house tonight. At least you won't hafta worry about him coming over there to look for you."

"Thanks," India said gratefully.

"I know you don't wanna go through all the hassel with gettin' your numbers changed, but I really think you should. That's if you *really* want Martell to stop pestering you."

India cut her eyes over in Alexis's direction. "You ain't slick, hefah."

"What?" Alexis asked innocently.

"You gon' try to slide that snide-ass remark in. 'That's if you *really* want Martell to stop pestering you,'" India said, mocking Alexis' words. "I don't go backward like some people I know."

"Put some names to the people you're referring to," Alexis snapped, already knowing who India was talking about.

"Alexis," India snapped back. "Look how many times you took Ronald's punk ass back."

"That was then, what about now?"

India rolled her eyes. "Shit, ain't no tellin' with you. You probably still messing around with Ronald, you'll never tell."

"Yeah right. I tell you and Keaundra everything," Alexis lied, smacking her lips.

"Whatever, Alexis. I don't even wanna talk about it anymore."

Alexis and India rode without saying a word to one another. "I'm sorry if I made you mad," Alexis said, breaking the silence.

"I'm not mad."

"Yes, you are."

"Would you shut up and watch the road." India smiled.

"I'm watchin', I'm watchin'." Alexis smiled back. India's smile confirmed she was not mad. Alexis was relieved, because the last thing she wanted to do was hurt her best friend's feelings.

India and the rest of the crew sat around the bowling alley laughing, talking, and enjoying themselves as they sipped Coronas. Hammer asked Keaundra not to drink anything other than cranberry juice and she didn't refuse his request. After putting a whooping on the fellas, the girls were buzzed and ready to do something else.

"This is gettin' boring," Alexis said to her girls as they finished beating the men for the sixth time in a row.

"It sure is," India agreed. "Plus I'm tired."

"I got some good movies at the house. Y'all wanna come over and watch 'em?" Hammer asked.

"What you got?" David asked. Hammer rambled off the names of the movies and everybody agreed to go except for India.

"I think I'll pass. I had a long day in school."

"Well, here," Alexis said, handing India her car keys. "I'll just ride with David and you take my car."

"That's fine with me." India yawned while taking the keys from Alexis's hand. "You got some ice cream?"

"Don't eat all my cookies-and-cream," Alexis warned with a smile.

"Don't worry, I'll save you some."

They all walked out into the parking lot and stood talking to one another.

"Go home and put ya feet up so my godbaby, li'l India, can get some rest," India said, rubbing Keaundra's flat stomach.

"Godbaby? Li'l India? Please," Alexis contested.

"Ladies, please, don't start. I don't even know the sex of the baby yet and y'all fussin' over the name already," Keaundra intervened, before Alexis and India began arguing. "And believe me, both of you will be his or her godmothers."

Alexis and India were both pleased with the decision.

"I love y'all," India said, opening up Alexis's car door.

"We love you too," Alexis replied, speaking for Keaundra as well.

"Ahhh, ain't that sweet," Hammer joked.

"Whatever, nigga," India laughed.

Alexis, India, and Keaundra all gave one another a friendly hug before they got into different cars and parted ways.

Chapter Fifty-five

Ronald's eyes burned with tears as he sat tucked away in his car, which was parked underneath a burnt-out street light. He began talking to himself as he waited for Alexis to return home.

"I'ma kill that bitch," he cried as he turned up the fifth of gin he held tightly in his hand. Ronald had a 9 mm that he had stolen from his uncle's closet resting menacingly on his lap. "I can't believe this bitch is still fuckin' around wit' this nigga!"

Ronald had gone to Alexis's apartment earlier to ask her to give him another chance, but saw she was in the process of pulling out of the parking lot. Deciding to follow her, he trailed two cars behind as she stopped at India's house and picked her up. His heart broke as he followed her into the bowling alley's parking lot, where she had met up with David and some other guy he'd never seen before. Ronald became heated as he watched David embrace his woman.

"Oh, them bitches must be out on a double date," Ronald shouted angrily as he sped off. The only thing that kept going through his head as he drove was that Alexis had put him out just so she could get back with David. He conveniently overlooked the fact that Tyisha, his pregnant ex-girlfriend, had popped up at Alexis's apartment and told all his business.

India pulled into the assigned parking space in the half-lit parking lot of Alexis's apartment complex. She shut the engine off and looked around nervously to see if she could see anybody lurking in the dark. She almost backed out and went home because she didn't want to get out in the dark, but she was way too tired to drive. India grabbed her overnight bag, got out of the car, scoping out the scenery as she made it up the walkway. Once inside the apartment, her nerves were at ease. She double locked the front door and headed straight for the shower. India took a quick shower before going into the kitchen to fix herself a big bowl of ice cream.

"This gon' be that bitch's last time playin' me for a fool," Ronald vowed, punching violently on the steering wheel. Ronald fell asleep while he waited for Alexis to turn off her lights.

India called her mother to say goodnight, checked the locks, and turned out the lights in the living room before turning in. She walked into Alexis's room and climbed into the bed, pulling the comforter over her entire body. In a matter of minutes India was out like the lights.

Ronald jumped up out of his sleep and noticed all the lights were out in the front room. He then got out of the car, tucked the 9 mm on the side of his pants, and crept around to the back of the apartment. He checked R.J.'s bedroom window to see if it was unlocked; it came open with no problem. Ronald quietly climbed in and tiptoed his way down the dark hallway to Alexis's room. He stood in the doorway watching Alexis sleep with pure hatred in his eyes. She let out a few soft moans, which angered Ronald even more.

The bitch must be dreaming about David, he thought as he walked closer to the bed. "I told you I was gon' get you," he whispered as he pulled the gun from his side. Ronald aimed the gun at Alexis's body and fired one single shot. He didn't even stick around to see if he had hit her; he panicked, . . . and ran down the hallway and back out the way he came in.

"Man, let me hook it up, nigga," David said to Hammer as he struggled to get the cable cord into the back of the DVD player.

"Be my guest." Hammer stepped back and let David work his magic.

"This is Claudett, reporting live from WBAJ News Center 12. Police responded to a call at an east-side apartment complex," the anchor woman reported.

"Get out of the way, David, that looks like my apartment complex," Alexis said, shooing David from in front of the TV.

"Whatever," Hammer laughed.

"Neighbors reported hearing one single gun-shot. When Officer Tanelli and his partner arrived on the scene, they were told by witnesses that they heard the shot coming from the apartment behind me," the anchor reportersaid, pointing. "Police had to kick the door in because no one seemed to be at home, but upon entering, Officer Tanelli found the body of a woman with a single gunshot wound to the back of the head. Police do have a description of a possible suspect's car."

Alexis began screaming when the camera showed her neighbor, Carolyn, in the background. "Oh my God!" Alexis shouted. "That is my apartment complex." Alexis, Hammer, Keaundra, and David all watched in terror.

"Call India and see if she knows what's goin' on," Keaundra shouted.

Alexis dialed her home number and India's new cell phone number over and over again. "She's not answering." Alexis panicked.

Keaundra became nervous. "I hope she's okay."

"Calm down, baby, she might just be asleep," Hammer said, hoping to ease everyone's fear.

"Let's go check on her," Keaundra suggested as her heart beat with fear.

"Let's go," David said, grabbing his car keys. They piled in David's truck and drove over to Alexis's apartment like he had no speed limit to abide by.

When they tried to turn in the parking lot, the police had it blocked off with yellow tape. They all jumped from the truck.

"You can't come up here," an officer said to them.

"But I live here," Alexis protested. The officer lifted the tape and they walked toward Alexis's apartment. Their worst nightmare became reality as they watched two paramedics wheeling a body bag out of Alexis's front door.

"Noooooooo, oh my God, noooooooooo," Alexis screamed at the top of her lungs. David ran over and hugged her while she continued to scream.

"Not India too." Keaundra was calm as ever as she shook her head in disbelief. Hammer wrapped his arms around Keaundra's body and pulled her close, but she was so out of it, she never even recognized his existence.

Keaundra couldn't believe that this was her best friend's dead body being loaded into the back of the ambulance. How could this be happening? Keaundra was numb to tears. She couldn't cry, couldn't think straight, or show any other sign of emotion as she stood in the middle of the apartment complex staring. She stared into space as the thought of losing her mother, father, grandmother, brother, and now her best friend danced around in her mind. Once again, God had taken away someone she loved and actually loved her back. Of all the people in the world, why India? She didn't have the answer to the question and she didn't have the strength to find it.

Chapter Fifty-six

Alexis stuffed two plastic flutes and a bottle of Alizé into a duffle bag and headed out the door. She stopped, grabbing the mail out of the mailbox on her way to the car. She got in and sorted through all the bills. She ran across an envelope with no return address on it. At first she hesitated, fearing it was one of those chain letters, but took her chances and opened it anyway. She pulled the letter out and a picture fell onto her lap. She picked it up and studied the picture of the two little girls. Alexis smiled. The twins had a heavy resemblance to Ro'nisha. She laid the picture back onto her lap and began reading the letter.

> *I know I'm the last person you were expecting to hear from, but I thought I would send you a picture of R.J. and Ro'nisha's sisters, Taylor and Taelynn. Sorry to hear about the loss of your best friend. You know it's funny how life works.*

*Ronald was always good at taking things
and never giving anything back other than
grief or a black eye or two (smile). Let's see
if he can take doing the life sentence that
the judge gave him. He deserves it. You
take care, I'll be praying for you and the
children, do the same for me and mines.*

Tyisha

Alexis looked at the picture again, folded the
letter up, and placed it back in the envelope along
with the picture before pulling out of the parking
lot. She swung by Red Lobster and picked up two
carry-out meals. Different thoughts ran through
her head as she drove. She blamed herself for
India's death every day. If she hadn't made the
mistake of letting Ronald back into her life once
again, India would still be alive. She wanted to
confess to Keaundra so badly, but couldn't bring
herself to do it. That would be a secret she would
take to the grave.

At first, everyone had pointed the finger at
Martell, but once the lady across the street gave
the police Ronald's license plate number, everything fell into place. "Why would Ronald want to
kill India?" everyone questioned. Alexis knew it
was not India he was after; it was her. As fucked
up as it sounded, Alexis looked at India as a

lifesaver. Miss Jane, Ronald's mother, was mad at her again, because she refused to let her take R.J. and Ro'nisha to the prison to see Ronald. He was no good for them on the outside, so he damn sure couldn't be good for them on the inside.

Alexis pulled up into the cemetery and spotted Keaundra pulling weeds from around India's tombstone while the twins babbled back and forth to each other. Alexis grabbed the duffle bag and the food off the passenger's seat and headed over toward Keaundra.

"Hey, girl." Keaundra looked up and smiled.

"Hey," Alexis responded, while laying the food and the bag on top of the blanket that Keaundra had spread in front of the twin's carrier. "Hey, India and Ariel. How's Ti-Ti's babies," she asked in baby talk. The twins smiled widely as Alexis spoke to them.

"They bad, girl," Keaundra laughed.

Alexis stared at India's tombstone. Every time they came to visit India, Alexis couldn't stop admiring the smooth, jet-black marble tombstone with India's picture engraved in it. The words "Mommy's Li'l Angel" were engraved below her picture. She ran her hand across the marble before sitting down on top of the blanket.

"You know I've lost a lot of people in the last year or so," Keaundra said out of nowhere. "The average person would have lost their mind. Don't get me wrong, I thought I would," she chuckled as she continued pulling at the weeds. "The only thing that kept me sane. . . " she balked, but decided to continue. "Was when I heard India's voice whisper somethin' to me."

Alexis shot Keaundra a crazy look.

"I know you probably think I'm crazy, but I'm dead serious."

"What did she say?"

"She said if God brings you to it, he will bring you through it. And He did just that. He brought me through all my heartaches and pains. That's my testimony and I'm stickin' to it."

"Amen to that," Alexis agreed, while tickling the girls' feet.

"You know I was at a place where I started thinkin' of my life as a curse, because everybody that I love dies. I had gotten to the point where I didn't wanna love anyone ever again. I started resenting my husband, my babies, you, and everybody else who was around me. I was afraid if I loved y'all too hard, y'all would die too," Keaundra explained. "You understand where I'm coming from?"

Alexis was shocked to hear that. "Damn, that's deep."

"Tell me about it, I lived it. But I finally found the answer that I had been searchin' for, for so long."

Alexis shot Keaundra a look of confusion. "The answer to what?"

"The answer to the reason why certain things happen in people's lives."

Alexis waited for Keaundra to give her the answer because she too wanted to know the reason why certain things happened in life. "What's the answer?"

"It's only for God to know," Keaundra replied with a warm smile and left it at that.

Alexis wanted Keaundra to elaborate but decided to leave well enough alone. She grabbed a tray of food and opened it up while Keaundra pulled the flutes and the Alizé out of the duffle bag. Keaundra filled one of the flutes and handed it to Alexis. Alexis took the flute and waited on Keaundra to fill hers. They clicked the flutes together.

"Happy birthday, India," they both shouted simultaneously as tears ran down their cheeks.

Tears flowed as Keaundra spoke. "I love you, girl!"

"Me too," Alexis laughed through tears.

Keaundra knew no matter what she went through, she would always love and respect Alexis, India, and Hammer. Her grandmother had once told her that real people were hard to find. So Keaundra promised herself that if she was ever

blessed to find real friends, she would hold on to
them. Because true friends are a lot like fresh fruit:
in order to pick the right ones, you have to choose
them carefully.

ORDER FORM
URBAN BOOKS, LLC
78 E. Industry Ct
Deer Park, NY 11729

Name: (please print):_____

Address:_____

City/State:_____

Zip:_____

QTY	TITLES	PRICE

Shipping and handling-add $3.50 for 1st book, then $1.75 for each additional book.

Please send a check payable to:

Urban Books, LLC

Please allow 4-6 weeks for delivery